SEVEN NAMES
A Story of the Bale Family in Alta California, 1818-1849

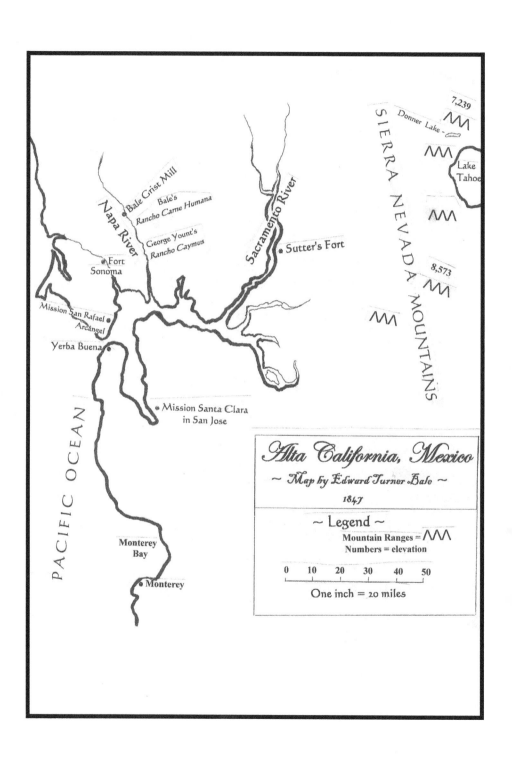

SEVEN NAMES
A Story of the Bale Family in Alta California, 1818-1849

A Historical Novel by

RC Marlen

All rights reserved.
Copyright © 2021 by RC Marlen

No part of this book may be used or reproduced by any means–graphic, electronic, or mechanical, including photocopying, recording, taping or by any information storage retrieval system–without the written permission of the publisher or author, except in brief quotations embodied in critical articles and reviews.

Books by RC Marlen
may be ordered
through booksellers
and
www.amazon.com

In this book, historic events, places, and people are presented, although the author did create the dialogue and some scenes. Thus, *Seven Names* is an historical novel. Readers with an interest in historical research are encouraged to consult the bibliography at the end. All the characters in this novel are authentic, except for those in the List of Characters marked Fictional and they were created to have a compelling storyline within the flow of history.

ISBN # 978-0-9906247-3-8
Sunbird Press
Salem, Oregon

Cover: Mrs. Bale, date unknown.

Back cover: Bale Mill, CA 128, St. Helena, CA 10-22-2011 Wikimedia Commons [This is an image of the building that is listed on the National Register of Historic Places in the United States of America. Its reference number is 72000240.]

Additional Books By RC Marlen

A Trilogy:

Inside the Hatboxes
The Drugstore
Tangled Threads

And The Prequel:

Drop of Fire

Historical Novels about Oregon:

GRIST: A Story of Life in Oregon Country, 1835-1854
Unbeknownst: People of Oregon, 1845-1881
POCKET in the Waistcoat: Scenes of Oregon Country, 1806-1839

Sci-Fi:

Unbeknownst II: Time Travel to Mid-Nineteenth Century Oregon

eBook in Spanish

Dentro de las Cajas

Note: All books are available as eBooks

Preface

One doesn't give much thought to threads; yet threads are important to our lives. Humans have searched for centuries, discovering and valuing material from which to make thread.

Twist and pull the soft, white, downy balls to make cotton threads.
Twist and twirl the fine, curly, fleece to create threads of wool.
Twist and twine the coarse threads of hemp to produce rope.

Threads exist everywhere. Beyond the comfortable cotton, warm wool, and strong rope, nature makes a plethora, as thread from worms spinning shimmering silk and gossamer thread for spider webs.

In whatever form, threads make a complicated path, weaving through and around, looping over and under, or winding back and forth to form rugs, nets, sweaters, and fabrics. Whether one has a piece of yarn, a strand of silk, wool, cotton, a filament of lamb intestine, a metal wire, or any thread-like material, the path can be lost as it twists and curves into a product with colors, textures, and sounds. Yes, sounds! Pull strands from the gut of a lamb and one has threads—twisted, braided, or wrapped—for strings of violins; pull hairs from the tail of a horse for the gliding violin bow. These special threads vibrate into notes, to blend into music, to fill the air and our minds. When the bow touches the strings, notes are connected, flowing out into a piece of music. Even when the sound vanishes, a thread of music can play in our heads.

Weaving threads.
Stitching threads.
Crocheted threads.
Musical threads.

Now take the idea of threads into another dimension. Threads can display stories. A well-known way is through tapestries; people have created tapestries for centuries to depict stories. The tapestry in Bijou near Normandy, whose threads were woven nine hundred years ago, depicts William the Conqueror's invasion of England. Scholars have looked deeply into this tapestry to follow the threads and learn the special stitch of the linen and wool, to learn the secret of the art, to gain all they can know. But few of us want to follow threads. Few of us want to delve into the secrets of the intricacies of how things were made.

Beyond these ideas, I find that lives are made of threads. Each life is a continuous thread of events; woven, stitched, and knitted, connecting the past to the present and made by some enigmatic weaver. Some call the weaver God, others destiny. Your weaver starts with one thread and, day by day, more threads are added and blended to create a story. Slowly and carefully the weaver works, adding colors, carefully connecting events, and developing your special tale. But every now and then, problems occur in a life; it's like a dropped stitch in a sweater. How does one mend the situation? With a sweater, one needs only to pull the yarn, return to the mistake, and start again. Life cannot be fixed as easily.

Once a mistake occurs in life, one can try to cover it with a patch, but it never disappears. To remake the threads of life or to unravel a problem is impossible.

In this story, we will follow the threads of Edward Bale and his wife, Maria Ignacia as they weave and wind in daily life, blending with family and friends, creating times of humor and happiness, as well as hate and horror, while holding onto their secrets. The threads of their lives will be difficult to understand as they twist and curve often disappearing behind or between events, as they mix with people and places. Knots form, nettles sting, and the threads of the Bales' life mangle and snarl into undesired events. Can they be rewoven or mended? Their lives are complicated, not only filled with love and kindness but also with disgust and repugnance that tears into the fabric of their story.

Have you ever turned a tapestry over to see the back? Have you ever turned a dress inside-out to see the stitches? Have you ever taken the effort to learn why a friend has lost her way? Behind the beautifully made dress, hidden on the other side of the tapestry, and deep in the mind of your friend are tangled threads. Knotted in places, unevenly cut, ragged, and snarled into ugliness. Behind each life are messy secrets that may or may not be found. And, if once found, who can untangle them?

Rewritten from RC Marlen's novel, Tangled Threads.

LIST OF CHARACTERS

MAIN HISTORICAL CHARACTERS: (Parenthesis indicates the name or nickname used in story.)

1816-1901	Maria Antonia Juana Ignacia Guadalupe Soberanes Vallejo (Maria Ignacia or Mari)
1792-1830	Her Mother: Maria Isidora Vallejo* (Mari) and
1794-1859	Her Father: Mariano de Jesus Soberanes
1807-1890	General Mariano Guadalupe Vallejo*
1776-1855	His Mother: Maria Antonia de Lugo, (Lita) [* marks her children]
ca. 1810-1849	Edward Turner Bale

OTHER HISTORICAL CHARACTERS IN STORY: (In order of appearance in story)

1761-1826	Pablo Vicente de Solá: Governor of Monterey when story begins.
1780-1837	Hipólito Bouchard: pirate who attacks Monterey in 1818.
1713-1784	Father Junipero Serra: Spanish Priest from Franciscan Order and founder of California missions.
1791-1872	John Bautista Rogers Cooper: businessman from America who settled in Monterey.
1809-1902	Wife: Maria Jerónima de la Encamación Vallejo* (Martha).
1802-1858	Thomas Oliver Larkin: Half-brother and business partner of Cooper and storeowner in Monterey.
1807-1873	Wife: Rachel M. Hobson Larkin.
1813-1876	Jose Manuel Salvador Vallejo (Salvador)*: Brother to Gen. M.G.Vallejo.
1809-1882	Juan Bautista Alvarado (Juan B): Political leader and nephew who helped General M.G. Vallejo to power; he was raised in the same home with the General, his uncle,

1798-1838	Estanislao: Native American, original name Cucunuchi, from Lakisamni Tribe of the Yokuts [the present-day Stanislaus River near Modesto, California is named for him],
1794-1865	George Yount: American fur trapper and first white settler in Alta California at *Rancho Caymus*.
1811-1886	Second Wife: Eliza Gashwiler Yount.
ca. 1829-1855	Mia (fictitious name): George Yount's adopted native daughter.
1798-1851	Chief Solano, a.k.a. Sam-Yeto, a.k.a. Francisco Solano: A 6'7" tall Native American friend of General Vallejo and George Yount.
1802-1849	Nathan Spear: Constructed small grist mill for the Bales.
1803-1880	John A. Sutter: Built fort in area that became Sacramento.
1813-1890	John C. Frémont: Main leader in Bear Flag Revolt

FICTIONAL:

Pepe: Ohlone man working as helper for Vallejo family.
Eduardo (Lalo): Childhood friend of Maria Ignacia.
Julia: Ohlone woman working as maid for Soberanes & Vallejo families.
Friar Mo: Priest at Mission Yerba Buena.
Lord Willington: English patient of Dr. Bale.

HISTORICAL PEOPLE WHO ARE MENTIONED BRIEFLY: (In order of appearance in story)

Francisca de Vallejo: Wife of General Mariano Vallejo.
Ewing Young: Trapper, explorer, mountain man, and trader who bought horses and cattle in Alta California, Mexico and herded them to Oregon settlers.
Raimunda Castillo: Mistress of Juan B Alvarado, later the second wife of Maria Ignacia's father.
Padre Viader: Priest at Mission Santa Clara.
Father Narciso Duran: Priest at Mission Santa Clara in San Jose.
Manuel Alva: Physician in pueblo of Monterey before Dr. Edward T. Bale.
Jose de Jesus Vallejo* (1798-1882): Older brother of General Mariano Vallejo.
Petronio: Native medicine man who worked in forts at Monterey and Yerba

Buena.

Chief Jota: Native American who was enemy of General Vallejo.

Reverend Clark: Man of the cloth who helped fight natives with George Yount.

Friar Gil: Franciscan friar from the Missions Purissima Concepción and San Rafael Arcángel.

Friar Juan Amoros: Beloved Franciscan friar at Mission San Rafael Arcángel.

Jose Maria Soberanes and Maria Josefa Castro: Paternal grandparents of main character, Maria Ignacia.

Jacob P. Leese: General Mariano Vallejo's brother-in-law who married Rosalia*,

Kelsey brothers-Granville P. Swift, and Ezekiel Merritt: Americans who were friends with Dr. Bale.

Cayetano Juárez: Spanish subject born in Monterey and friend of Salvador Vallejo.

Ralph L. Kilburn: Man contracted to construct Bale Grist Mill, but who never finished.

Thomas Kittleman: Man, who completed construction of Bale Grist Mill.

William Ide: Selected leader for a group in the Bear Flag rebellion.

Commodore Robert Field Stockton: Commander-in-chief of all land forces in California in July 1846.

Canulo: House servant of General Mariano G. Vallejo.

Grave children from Donner Party: Sarah, Mary Ann, William, Eleanor, Lovina, Nancy, and Elizabeth Grave.

Glossary of Spanish Terms

abuela (abuelita): grandmother or grandma (little grandmother; shortened to Lita)

aji: a red sauce to add to food for a hot spicy sensation; made from hot red peppers

armario: chifforobe, clothing closet with drawers and a rod to hang items

asado: an event where meat is cooked outdoors over fire—usually with fresh, vegetables and wine, beer, or an alcoholic beverage accompanying the meat

Asunción: refers to the Virgin Mary's assent into heaven with her whole body

bandera: a flag

bote: a container for liquids, usually made of leather

buenos dias: good day (a greeting)

buenas noches: good night or good evening

caballo: horse

Californios: a term for the people of Alta California, Mexico in 1800s

Casa Zemita: a name (with no meaning) for house in story

Dios mios, mi amor: exclamatory phrase of surprise (literally: My god, my love)

En el Nombre de Dios: informal expression of surprise, (literally: In the name of God)

encina del castigo: (literally: oak for punishment); it means a hanging tree,

Gente de razon: (literally: people of reason); the higher-class people with important jobs and pure Spanish blood; also, defined in terms of racism, those thought more intelligent and entitled

horno: an outdoor oven made from mud

hombre: man

Los Gigantes Tres: The Three Giants or The Three Powerful Ones

madre: mother

maldito: a curse word like shit or damn it all

mancha: mark, stain, spot

mamá: mama, mom, or mommy

mi amor: means *my love* and is a term of endearment often used for children

mi hermano: my brother

mi madre mio(a): an expression of endearment meaning *my mother mine*

mi Madre del Dio: an expression of surprise meaning *My Mother of God*

muchacha: maid

Navidad y El Año Nuevo: Christmas and the New Year
no importa: means *it is not important*
nos vamos: let's go
padre: father
papá: papa, dad, or daddy,
perdoname: excuse me
piraña: piranha—a small man-eating fish
pirata: pirate
poncho: outer covering made in a square, used as a coat with a cut for the head
por supuesto: means *of course*
Punto de Pinos: name of place in Monterey area (literally: Point of Pines)
rancheria: a settlement, often of Native Americans in Alta California
ranchero: a person who owns a *rancho*; also, a rancher or farmer
rancho: large farm or ranch in Alto California
Señor: the title for a man, equivalent to Mister
Señora: the title for a married woman, Mrs.
Señorita: the title for an unmarried woman, Miss
simpatico(a): character of a person with a friendly and likeable personality
tio/tia: uncle/aunt
vaquero: a male horse rider, usually Spanish or Mexican, with excellent equestrian skills and knowledge about the use of a lasso
Yerba Buena: (literally: good herb); name of a town that became the city of San Francisco

Presidio of Monterey in 1818 when the pirate, Hipólito Bouchard, attacked.

CHAPTER ONE

Pirates, Bulls, and Grizzlies

1818

Personalities are formed by heredity and nurturing, but in Maria Ignacia's case, she had one uncle who shaped her more deeply than anyone else. Obviously, she inherited her family's bone structure, dark eyes, and black hair; and possibly she had more brains than her brothers but, without a doubt, she had a temperament of her own making. Other influencing factors in her life—the culture she lived, the prejudices and idiosyncrasies she observed, and her family's mores—she decided to defy, more often than not. Maria Antonia Juana Ignacia Guadalupe Soberanes Vallejo would grow to be a strong woman who wondered if having a name with seven words added to her strength—or not. She was born a Spanish citizen on the eighteenth of December in the year 1816, in Monterey, Alta California, Mexico, which was often referred to as New Spain, and her story starts in 1818.

During early morning in a tower on the twentieth of November 1818, a watchman faced west at Punta de Pinos—located at the southern end of Monterey Bay—and peered into heavy and impenetrable fog along the Pacific Ocean. Shivering, he took a moment to adjust his *poncho* of coarse wool to keep the cold from his neck. He wore the uniform of the Spanish Army of Mexico, with pantaloons open down the sides below the knees, leaving nothing to keep the cold from his legs. As happened most mornings when the sun rose, the fog seemed to melt, leaving white wisps of clouds traveling toward the southern horizon. His eyes followed the clouds until they dissipated, and he gasped as those fading clouds exposed the unexpected.

That soldier reached for his spyglass. His heart jumped and mouth went dry upon seeing the two Argentine flags fly against the blue sky—one flag on a frigate, the other on a privateer. Without a doubt, he was witnessing an oncoming disaster.

He shouted, "*Atención, peligroso vista al sur!*" telling "Attention, there's danger in the view to the south!" and alerting the other on-duty soldiers. He rushed down the stairs, mounted a horse, and sped to inform his superiors.

Monterey, Mexico, the capital of Alta California, consisted of a small colony of soldiers with their families and native Ohlones. Fewer than one thousand people lived there, and those who held high offices, such as the governor, were of Spanish descent and had Ohlones working in their homes as servants.

At this time, the governor was Pablo Vicente de Solá, who had anticipated that ships might attack them. He paced among his men in a large meeting room and roared a curse upon hearing the report delivered from the tower, "*Maldito!* I read in the *Clarion* last month that two corsair vessels were possibly heading our way. Pirates! Pirates coming to plunder the California coast! I know who— that French-born pirate who sails for Argentina—Hipólito Bouchard!"

Fear filled the room. Many of his men muttered among themselves, "*Pirata Buchar.*" Everyone had heard how he killed, raped, and stole. "He has no conscience and will kill a child as easily as a man," someone said.

Another man shook his head and told what he had heard about the destruction that *Pirata Buchar* leaves in his wake, "What he cannot take he burns."

They sat in the main building in the Monterey Presidio—a fort without high walls—surrounded by lush lawns, a wooded area of scrub oaks, pines on the south, and a small river on the north side. Everywhere, among the dozens of whitewashed one-story adobe homes and buildings, horses roamed and were as abundant as the chickens and dogs. Monterey had no designated streets and no stables, so the horses were free to graze anywhere on the green grasses. Though the more valuable horses were branded for ownership purposes, few cared who used their horses. Any person grabbed the most convenient one, saddled it, and, after reaching their destination, attached the horse to a tree or post with a long leather rope. The horses dragged the lengthy rope behind them as they grazed because, after saddling a horse in the morning, a man rode the same animal throughout the day. Many of the governor's men sitting for the talk had a waiting horse saddled and tethered outside.

The men gazed outside, concerned about the coming attack, and heard children's voices drifting through the large open windows in the adobe building. They watched other soldiers on the green preparing for the daily noon parade and heard the discordant din of trumpets and drums playing a few notes in preparation. A flag bearer with his tri-colored, tattered *bandera* stood ready to march.

The governor shouted, "*Maldito*! I cannot think!" He turned and ordered, "Corporal, go out and stop that noise and cancel the damn parade." The other men remained in their seats and watched the people outside disperse in confusion. The governor resumed pacing and talking, "Without the daily parade, everyone will wonder what's brewing, so we must work fast.

"Before the pirates start any confrontation, all the women, children, and our elders must be far away." He raised his voice to emphasize his concern and the men felt his fear. "Immediately, we must send them away—in different directions, to different missions—send them hours away to hide." He lowered his voice and added, "Any of the missions will do. Send along Ohlone workers to help the women and children. No large groups should stay together because Bouchard will send men to find them. Tell the people to take their sacks of wheat, ground corn, other foodstuffs—enough for a month or so—and, of course, all their valuables. This pirate is brutal, and we must protect our families. I will send my men with rifles to guard against a surprise encounter with a grizzly, since I have received reports that the area is alive with bears this fall." He shook his head and ran his fingers through his hair.

Since the year had been dry, bears found fewer berries and fruit, and the grasses and clover had turned brown early. However, the oak trees produced more seeds when stressed in a drought, and acorns grew in abundance in this area. So, grizzlies were everywhere, sitting beneath the oaks, eating acorns.

"I worry," he continued, "I worry that the bears will smell the foodstuff our people must take." Many men nodded while others squirmed in their seats and the governor continued, "But let's talk about the problem that is sure to happen—Bouchard!

"In the newspapers sent to me weekly from Mexico City, I have read all about him. We must be prepared, so I am telling you what we will be fighting. First, I read he had two ships, but now Bouchard has three vessels. One is his frigate, but it has a deep draft that prevents it from coming close to shore. The second is his corvette *Santa Rosa*, which will come to attack us. However, Bouchard has a third ship, a privateer, he obtained in the Sandwich Islands. It's a warship!" He paced once again before continuing. "Since that damn pirate works for Argentina, King Kamehameha let Bouchard take the Argentine privateer that had been seized by mutineers."

Upon learning that Bouchard had a warship in his possession, a gasp escaped from the men. "Yes, you should gasp. That privateer is a powerful warship made to harass and kill all it encounters. We can give a good fight, but we cannot take any chances with our women, children, and elders. You know what the fate of your wives and daughters with Bouchard's men would be." He stood motionless for a moment with his brow furrowed. Finally, he blinked and growled, "Damn Bouchard. Get the word to everyone to begin packing. Attach every team of oxen to a cart and find a reliable bullock-driver for each one because the women and children must leave without us. The Ohlones manning the carts and a few soldiers will be the only able-bodied men with them."

Within the hour, Monterey was a scene of tumult: Frantic women shouted orders to their workers, distressed children cried upon seeing the fear in their mothers' faces, and nervous dogs barked at all the activity. While packing, people searched for space in their carts and argued about the importance of taking some items; carts were being shared among several families.

One young family, scrambling to gather their belongings, had two small children and an aging grandmother. The mother, Maria Isidora Vallejo de Soberanes, was arguing with her elderly mother-in-law, addressing her as *Abuelita*, hoping the children would call her by that name—little grandmother.

"*Abuelita*, you must ride a horse. I can offer you no other way to go. Look, there is no room in the cart."

"But you let your daughter go in the cart," said the grandmother, who turned to point at little dark-eyed Maria Antonia Juana Ignacia Guadalupe Soberanes Vallejo, who was called Maria Ignacia. The girl peered out from a space made in the middle of the cart. A large sack of flour had been placed for her to lean back on and she was surrounded by stacks of clothing on one side, a wooden cage with chickens on her other side, and cooking pots here and there. Two goats were tethered to the back of the cart and dogs ran about nipping at the goats' feet.

The girl called out to her preoccupied mother, "*Mamá*," and was not heard.

"*Abuelita*, my two-year-old takes no space. She is tiny and when we travel the bumping of the cart will not bother her. Your bones would break. Please, you have ridden horses all your life. You must do it now." Maria Isidora Vallejo took her mother-in-law's hand, placed the reins to the horse in it, and walked away. "I have much to think about. Oh, I just remembered, I forgot to take our family's candlesticks from Spain . . . oh, and my ivory giraffe. No more talking to you, *Abuelita*."

Again, during the chaos, the little girl called to her mother from the cart but was ignored.

A moment later, a worker named Julia came to the cart with a pair of foot-tall brass candlesticks and an ivory artwork carved in the shape of a giraffe. She had wrapped those beloved articles in an old *poncho*. The mother pushed items in the cart this way and that to make space, "Julia, they will fit here." They wedged them between a smoked leg of lamb and the water jar. The full water jar was in the back corner of the cart for easy access. As the mother leaned over to kiss the top of her little girl's head, her baby boy almost slipped from her dress. He had been nursing and would ride inside her dress.

Her busy mother could not take time for little Maria Ignacia, who stretched her pudgy arms out. The girl said something again but was ignored again, as the eleven-month-old boy was being tucked back against his mother's chest; she tightened the sash around her middle. "We don't want your brother falling out," she blurted as she rushed back inside the house.

Maria Ignacia screamed to her mother and started to cry but stopped at a distraction. Her father rode up. He was with an Ohlone man called Pepe. The little girl rubbed her dripping nose with the back of her hand, smearing dirt across her face, and shifted from crying to smiling. "*Papá, Papá!*"

Her father addressed his wife as *Madre* for the same reason that his wife called her mother-in-law *Abuelita*. "*Madre*, here is Pepe to be your bullock-driver." Irritation entered his voice when he saw an object poking out. "Why are you taking that ivory thing! I have never understood why you hold it to be important. Leave it for the pirates." He turned his horse and started to leave. "I must return to the meeting for more instructions from the governor." He saw her scowl and, as his horse pranced in place, he spoke his endearing name to her, "Mari, you will be fine." A tender smile replaced the scowl as he leaned from the saddle to touch her cheek. "You have two women workers to help you and Pepe. Now, I must go." He rode away dodging people scurrying here and there with articles to load into carts or in saddlebags on their horses.

The name Mari was not only the endearing name her husband used, but also the name she called herself in her thoughts. Not unlike her daughter, she smudged dirt across her face when brushing a tear with the back of her hand. Dust was everywhere from all the activity—horses, oxen, goats, dogs, and people shuffled across the dry ground. The last rain had been a month ago.

She turned toward her daughter and explained his irritation about the giraffe. "He thinks I had an affair with the sea captain who gave me the ivory giraffe. I didn't, yet there is no way I can convince him." She touched her little girl's nose and whispered, "This is our secret. I find it amusing and like to tease him. I pretend that the giraffe is something special to me." The child did not understand. Not that the little girl needed to understand, Mari just wanted to tell someone.

Her little girl pointed to her mother's face. "*Mamá* dirty," she said with a giggle.

Reaching for the end of the sash that tied the baby boy against her chest, Mari wiped her own face before cleaning her daughter's cheeks. "Everything is covered in dust, *mi amor*." Again, she kissed the little girl on top of her head, but before the child could tell her mother what she wanted to say, another horse and rider stopped beside their cart. Pleasure filled Mari's face upon seeing her younger brother. "Mariano Guadalupe, *mi hermano!*"

He slipped from the saddle and hugged his sister. Though he was only eleven to Mari's twenty-six years, they were the same height. With fondness, they pressed their cheeks against each other, and she asked, "Are our parents ready to go?"

Little Maria Ignacia was standing and jumping up and down at the sight of her beloved uncle. "Mari-oope," she called because the name Mariano Guadalupe was beyond her ability to pronounce.

He reached over and gave her hair a tousle, "*Hola, mi amor.*" Without hesitation, he lifted his niece into his arms while he told his sister that he needed help. "Our parents act as if they don't know what to take." He tickled the girl and she giggled. "Please come help. They need to get on the road."

"*Por supuesto,* (of course), she said, and went for a horse.

Mariano twirled the girl in circles at arm's length while she laughed with glee. Though usually he was a serious young man, acting older than his eleven years, the child in him laughed uncontrollably with his niece as they spun.

"More, Mari-oope!" she insisted over and over.

When her mother returned on a horse, "*Mariano, nos vamos.* Let's go get our parents packed for this trip."

"May my niece ride with me?" Upon seeing a nod of agreement, he said, "Maria Ignacia, wrap your arms around my neck," and he pulled her into the saddle by grabbing the pommel. After securing the girl in front of him, they rode with caution through the throngs of bustling people.

By the time Mari returned with her two children, few people were left as the afternoon sun began to sink into the horizon. November's days were short. When Little Maria Ignacia was placed back into her space in the cart, the girl realized she still had not told her mother that they had forgotten her favorite little blue blanket, made from soft merino wool. Her mother had sewn a satin ribbon around the edges, which little fingers caressed each night when going to sleep. All her life the child had slept with it. Again, she called to her mother to no avail, because Mari and the two women workers had mounted their horses and were riding ahead of the cart. Pepe, on foot, preceded the two oxen and held a long branch from a willow tree. He tapped the head of the lead animal to start the cart moving. It jerked forward and Little Maria Ignacia fell against the chicken cage. Pepe knew the art of using a willow branch to give directions to the lead bullock by touching different parts of its body.

The child struggled to her feet in the swaying cart. For a moment she peered ahead at the departing adults before deciding she could get her blanket without them. She climbed over the chicken cage and piles of clothing, slipped off the cart, and ran toward her house.

Once inside her house, Maria Ignacia realized she did not know where her little blue blanket was kept during the day. Every night her mother or one of the women who helped in the house had given the blanket to her. She had never noticed from where it had been taken. The blanket would just appear.

Such was the life in Monterey. The wives and children of all the soldiers, no matter what their rank in the army, had native people to wait on them hand and foot. No one used the word *slave* for the Ohlone people who worked for them; however, although they were called "workers," the Ohlones were not paid. The workers were taught how to cook by older workers—for meals they slaughtered animals, harvested vegetables, prepared, served, cleaned afterwards, and ate whatever was left. The same order of work occurred for clothing: After the workers washed, repaired, folded, and put away all apparel, what was to be discarded was given to the workers. Whenever the owners of the house wanted something—a glass of water, a fire or more firewood, a shawl while the lady of the house did embroidery, or anything else—a worker was called to accommodate them. All homes had Ohlones as workers. Little Maria Ignacia had had a personal maid since her birth.

Once in her bedroom, little Maria Ignacia turned in a circle to look for any possible location for her blanket. She opened the *armario* to search among the shelves and looked through the long garments that hung on one side. Not there. And the top of the tall *armario* was rounded so she knew her blanket was not up there. Moving across the room to a wooden trunk with leather hinges, she opened it and rummaged through, finding no blanket.

Stopping her desperate search for a moment, a thought came to her, "*I take too long.*" In a panic, she ran outside. No one was in sight. Everyone had left.

Of course, soldiers were down at the Presidio, yet too far away for her to see or hear them. All was calm and quiet. Many older horses had been left behind and still grazed; no one was in sight. Standing where the cart had been, she stared into the distance, trying to understand how they could have left without her.

Just then, an owl glided near her. She screamed and ran back into the house. She scurried to her room and climbed onto the bed. Letting her fears subside, she sat in the middle and sucked her thumb. Pulling her thumb out from her lips, she realized her mother would be upset with her. A moment later, she put it back, sucked, and felt comforted. "*Mamá,*" she said. "*Mamá,*" she called. At long last, she digested her dire situation and screeched in her loudest voice, "*Mamá!*" Spent with more anger than fear, she flopped onto her side and rolled into a ball, sobbing.

Presently, the sun dropped below the bay's waters and the room was in complete darkness. For the first time in her life no one was there to light candles before she fell asleep, and the atmosphere of her bedroom seemed strange without the flicker of candlelight. She heard a noise outside and peeked out the window. Windows in the adobe homes had no glass only wooden shutters that closed from the inside. The ones in Maria Ignacia's bedroom were not solid wood; instead, they were made with wooden slats to allow a view to the outside. With a bright moon sending light through the slats, shadows painted the walls with the movements from bushes and trees. The shadows came alive to dance across the room. The wind whispered soft sighing sounds. She blinked and was sure she saw the outline of a grizzly bear walk past. They were common and numerous. Terror! In her short life she had seen dozens of these bears, but only from a distance. Adding to her fear were the frequent conversations she had heard about the dangers of grizzlies. She scrambled up to the headboard, bumped her head, slipped under the covers to hide, and suddenly she smiled.

Her terror had turned to delight.

That was how she found her little blue blanket—folded neatly and tucked under the covers. She buried her face in her little blanket with a silky ribbon sewn around the edges and felt better. She dropped her clothes to the floor—not concerned with finding her nightdress—and scooted back under the bedcovers. Into her mouth went her thumb from one hand while the other hand rubbed the silky edges of her blue blanket. After several contented minutes, she peeked out from the covers to look again at the shuttered window. No more grizzlies for that moment; now the local coyotes began to bark in the distance. She shouted, "No! Go away." From her darkened room, she watched the shutters for many minutes until the sighing and murmuring of the wind lulled her into a deep sleep.

Meanwhile, at the Presidio, preparations were almost complete. The governor had ordered two-thirds of the barreled gunpowder to be sent away as well as a large amount of their food stock and all valuables—silver coins, jewelry, and any papers that would give the pirates information about the military. He sent men to move most of the army's cattle as far away as they could before morning, yet he was wise enough to leave enough animals for the Pirate Bouchard to have a bounty, in case they lost the battle. Every cannon was rolled along the coastline and the garrison was sent to man their battle stations throughout the night.

Late in the night after everything was ready, the governor called his officers to a meeting again. "I want all of you to know as much as I do about this pirate because it might give us an advantage. Hipólito Bouchard is the devil himself. As far as I know, he has been a corsair throughout his life. However, in Argentina he is not a pirate, he is a hero and patriot." He stopped his pacing, shook his head at his last comment, and looked directly at his men before continuing. "He has pirated for Argentina for years and attacked Chile, Peru, Manila, many other places, and," he hesitated again before finishing his sentence, "and Mexico. Yes, he has been here and is familiar with Monterey."

Murmurs filled the room.

Someone asked, "So does he know the lay of the land here?"

"Yes, he does." The governor continued, "Our man in the tower reported earlier that Bouchard's frigate *La Argentina* has been towed far from the range of our cannons. So, we know he will be sending men in his corvette, *Santa Rosa*, which holds about two hundred. I hope not all of them will have firearms."

A man rushed into the meeting and the governor huffed, "Speak up! What have you to report? I have no secrets from my officers."

"Sir, the corvette full of men has anchored here in the waters in front of our Presidio."

A few officers stood while others went to windows to see. Everyone began talking while dread rippled around the room.

"Sit down! We must plan." After they settled into their seats, the governor asked, "I want to hear from each of you. Who is first and tell me what you think these pirates will do?"

Someone volunteered, "They are anchored close to the shore. Why didn't they attack right away?"

An answer came. "I think they are waiting for the light of day."

Another interrupted, "No, they don't need light. They need sleep. They worked hard to row into our waters after towing the large frigate away from cannon range. They're tired. We should attack them now."

The governor agreed with the last explanation of why the pirates had not attacked, "But I don't think it wise for us to attack now. It's after midnight. I think just before dawn will be best."

The men talked until one in the morning. Half went to bed for the remainder of the night, planning to switch with the other half after a time. The governor took a stroll outside to see the situation for himself and was pleased. The corvette was anchored close enough to the shore for the Mexican soldiers to win the attack with their cannons.

Boom!

With the first explosion from the cannons in the morning, Maria Ignacia jerked upright in bed and shrieked. Confused, she peered around the room, not knowing what was happening; it took another loud blast for the situation to awaken her memory. She remembered she had been left behind. Upon hearing more salvos, fear crept through her body and released her bladder. She began to sob as she scooted away from the puddle in her bed and with a fast jerk pulled her blue blanket away from the mess. "*Mamá!*" she cried, even though she knew she was alone. After a few minutes with no more explosions, she heard her stomach growl with hunger. Little Maria Ignacia dressed in yesterday's clothes from the floor and went in search of food.

In the moment when Maria Ignacia had awakened, the governor in the Presidio had been standing watching the attack. The Spanish army of Mexico had opened fire with cannon balls falling closer and closer to the corvette. After fifteen minutes of explosions and before the cannon balls had been calibrated to hit their target, the pirates surrendered.

Aboard the frigate *La Argentina*, Bouchard had been watching as well. He stood with his spyglass and saw the defeat of his men. He marched back and forth on his deck, cursing and hollering in an angry tirade. Minutes passed. He lifted the spyglass again and puzzled over what he saw—the soldiers were not taking the corvette or any survivors. He stared and, at last, realized, "Aha! They don't have boats to go out there and get them." He smirked before laughing aloud.

Back on shore, the Mexican governor cursed for the same reasons. "We won the battle yet can't claim a victory. *Maldito!*"

The rest of the day was quiet except when Bouchard ordered his boats to weigh anchor and move toward the shore to pick up the corvette with his men. During that maneuver, one pirate slipped unseen into the water and swam to shore to act as a spy. He swam underwater for most of the distance, undetected by the soldiers, and made land north of the Presidio. When walking, he circled wide, hoping to find someone to take as a hostage. This was Bouchard's idea: If they lost, a hostage would provide them with bargaining power.

Once the other pirates were brought back onto the frigate, they planned the next attack.

All day Maria Ignacia had been busy. She was a resourceful little girl and had been independent all her short life. She had walked at nine months, talked in two-word sentences at fourteen months, dressed herself during that stage, and learned how to find any sweets no matter where they were hidden—even if in a high place—because she loved to climb.

Now, with the urging of her stomach, she went out to find food. Each home had a detached kitchen, and she went from one kitchen to the next in search of food. She found many bread scraps, a square of fresh cheese wrapped in cheesecloth on a windowsill, and a plate with a napkin covering a forgotten bean tortilla. She pocketed extra bread scraps and devoured the delicious bean tortilla. Though the vegetable gardens in November were almost empty, she had seen the maid pick lettuce, so she did the same. As she wandered, she carried her blanket and would spread it on the ground to eat when she found food. She had access to any home, for the custom was not to lock doors. In fact, doors were often left wide open unless the weather presented a reason to close them.

The spy never crossed paths with Maria Ignacia. Even when crouched on a hillside while watching the activity in the fort from a distance, he did not see her scurrying from one neighbor's home to another. However, he did see a young grizzly eating under an oak tree. He decided to avoid the bear.

Eventually the girl saw the same small grizzly. The animal sat under a spreading oak tree, calmly munching on acorns. In fact, she walked to within twenty feet of the bear before she noticed him and abruptly stopped.

Crouching on his haunches, the young bear leaned forward and ate acorns off the ground with his supple lips gathering them into his mouth until he nonchalantly turned his gaze to the little girl. He moved to an upright position, though still seated, while watching her and continuing to chew. Before bending to eat more acorns, he emitted a low, conversational sound, "hmm, hoof, woof."

At first, Maria Ignacia stood stiff until deciding that the bear posed no threat. Anything the adults had said about dangerous bears seemed false. When the animal muttered again with a casual and quiet, "woof, woof," she relaxed and puzzled about him. She decided to answer him with a greeting, "*Hola*."

The acorns were getting thin in the area where he sat, so he rose on all four legs and ambled a bit closer to her before breaking off a branch full of acorns and plopping back down on the ground. He began to paw the nuts into his mouth. Again, he looked at her and made a soft utterance.

"What?" She was sure he had spoken to her.

Any prior memory she had about any adults discussing grizzlies dissolved from her head. Her experience of the moment wiped away any dangerous story she had heard. When he turned his head, looked with gentle eyes into hers, and said, "mough-mough," she decided he had asked for her help by saying, "*mas, mas*." He wanted more acorns.

"I help." She began to gather acorns and drop the brown nuts into the skirt of her dress, which she held to form a collecting bowl. She talked as she worked. "*Mamá* say, 'No eat acorns. They bad.'" The animal seemed to answer with a soft guttural sound of contentment. She made a little laugh, "Hee-hee, no look sad. *Mamá* say, 'Acorns good for bears.'"

With her skirt full, she turned toward the bear and stopped. She had a moment of doubt, but the grizzly lifted his nose up toward the sky and made a soft childlike moan that sounded like delight, and her doubts disappeared.

"Oh, see I give you." She moved with care toward the bear, "My acorns for you," and released her cache of food to the ground for him.

Up he stood on all fours and moseyed toward her and the pile of acorns. If there had been apprehension, it dissolved because she saw no aggression. Soon the little bear was leaning into and munching on her pile, and she went off to pick more. "I think we friends," she told him.

When she brought the next batch of acorns, she noticed a white blotch above his left eye. "What on your eye?"

He mumbled one of his soft sounds and looked to her.

She could see the white spot was fur. "Oh, I like your white *mancha*. I name you Mancha. You like?" She detected no dissatisfaction from the bear, so she confirmed her decision on his name. "You my friend, Mancha."

They conversed more while he ate her second pile of acorns. When all were eaten, the grizzly stood. Each stared at the other, unmoving, before the grizzly turned and walked away.

"Goodbye," she called to him. The sun was dropping low, and she understood he had to go home.

Off and on throughout the day, she had returned to her home to take naps and to cry. Watching her new friend disappear in the distance, she said, "Bye, Mancha," and walked home.

At her house, she crawled up onto her parents' bed while the spy was walking around the deserted adobes to choose one for sleeping that night. He heard her whimpers as they drifted into the quiet evening.

Creeping closer and closer to her home without making a sound, he entered the open front door. Now he heard her sobbing more clearly and made his way by the light of the moon. Pulsations throbbed in his chest in hopes of finding a young maiden, however when he stepped in the bedroom doorway, disappointment flooded his whole body.

Maria Ignacia did not notice him until she smelled him. He exuded a mixture of body odors that even his swim in the ocean had not washed away. Startled, as if she were a cornered bird, her eyes bounced from him to the window and back again.

"No, no, my little dearie, ye is mine now."

Maria Ignacia grabbed her blue blanket and sprang from the bed. He lunged to encircle her pudgy middle. His freckled hand squeezed her arm, and his repulsive smell intensified around her. Her eyes flared with a fear she would remember for the rest of her life. She would always remember: His grin stretched a scar across his lip and exposed two missing upper teeth; his red cloth tied around his forehead, matching the red sash around his waist; his dirty open shirt, showing a medallion hanging from his neck and resting on a hairy chest; and his speech, full of sailor's slang and a slurring caused by his missing teeth yet she could follow the gist. As he pulled her against his body, she bumped his flintlock pistol tucked at his waist and saw a dagger on the other side.

She struggled and pulled to free herself. Screaming, she called for her mother and kicked. "Me go!"

"No, no, ye mine. I wish ye were a wee bit older but ye is my prize. Bouchard going to be happy I got a hostage."

For the next hour he taunted her. "Ye don't scream. Ye hear." He would let her run outside, catch her, and drag her back by her hair or an arm. After a while, he tired of molesting her in that way and pulled his dirk from his waistband. He began to scratch his lower arm until a drop of blood oozed from the cut. He was sitting on a downed tree trunk. She sat on the ground next to him, unable to stand with his foot on her legs. He held the knife in front of her face and claimed, "Now is ye turn."

Each time she had screamed, he had slapped her and told her he would keep hitting until she stopped screaming. After several slaps, she no longer screamed. "Now ye better not scream no more." He pulled out his dagger again and her fearful eyes widened. "Now I put my mark on ye," he said. Finally, she made no more screams. As she trembled with tears dribbling onto her clothes, he said with a cynical cackle, "Nah, no mark for ye."

At last, he had tired of tormenting her and rolled her into the blue blanket.

"Ye goin' ta sleep now cuz I want ta sleep. It's been a long day." He tossed her onto her parent's bed, wound his red sash around her cocooned body and tucked her under his arm before closing his eyes.

Her arms were held straight down at her sides. She yearned to suck her thumb and could not. When her fingers found the silky edging to her blanket, she found relief and slept.

Before dawn when the sky began to glow, he roused her, and they ate the remaining bread scraps she had collected the prior day. Afterwards he took her outside for more taunting. "I know they will attack today. We must be ready. Tell ye what, I going to let ye free." He pulled her blanket from her arms, rolled it into a ball, and threw it. She did not understand his sadistic game and ran for it. He would catch her, slap her for running away, and continue, over and over.

Presently he could hear the gunfire from hand-to-hand combat at the

Presidio and gloated, "Now, we go to the fort to show my prize."

Not too far away, Mariano, who had ridden through two nights to return to find his niece, heard the gunfire in the Presidio and dismounted with his rifle. Standing on the outskirts of Monterey, the boy tied his horse to a tree and took to the woods on foot at a fast pace. He headed to the house of his sister, thinking it to be the best place to start his search for her.

Looking to the distance with every step, Mariano began to hear voices and saw the pirate with Maria Ignacia. Feeling content to have found her, he was careful not to be seen. During many minutes, he calmly watched them, trying to plan his next move. He patiently waited to see if there were more pirates until he saw him slap her. Fueled with emotions, he clenched his teeth and clutched the rifle in his grip as he proceeded stealthily among the trees, closer and closer. Enough time had passed to give him confidence that there were no other pirates nearby. When he knew he was close enough for an accurate shot, he stopped and crouched to prepare the rifle. When ready, he sprawled prone on the ground and steadied his aim.

Again, the pirate began slapping her. Raising his arm to hit again, he exposed his complete body in the rifle sight, Mariano fired, and the pirate fell backwards.

Maria Ignacia screamed, "Eeeee!"

Hearing constant gunfire from the Presidio, Mariano was sure neither the pirates nor troops would notice the sound of his rifle.

While his shot still rang in his ears, Mariano jumped up and ran to his niece. Within seconds, he had her in his arms.

"*Tio, o, mi Tio.*"

"It's all over, *mi amor*," he said, squeezing her in his arms. "I have one more job to do before we can leave. Keep your face against me." He cradled her head to his shoulder as he walked to the supine pirate, who seemed to wear a smirk. Mariano noticed the scar on his mouth, which lifted one side to form a grin. Bending close enough to notice a hairy chest poking from the shirt, he took the dagger from the pirate's red sash and ran the blade along a crease of black muck on the neck. The blood gushed. "Now I can be sure you're dead."

In a whisper, he soothed her. "That dirty pirate can no longer hurt you." Mariano dropped the dagger by the body and pulled the flintlock pistol from the sash.

Peeking over her uncle's shoulder, her wide eyes stared at the dead pirate and the puddle of blood beneath his head.

Mariano's face glowed in pleasure. "Oh, I know this kind of pistol. It's a good one—not fancy, but it fires even after being in water. Now it's mine" He grinned while slipping the pistol into the waistband of his breeches. He saw the black powder bag and grabbed it, too. Satisfied, he turned to leave.

Starting in the direction of the horse, Mariano wanted to know everything. "Oh, Maria Ignacia, we were so afraid. No one knew where you were. What happened?"

"I want my blanket. See!" She pointed to where it had been thrown to the ground. He went and picked it up, wrapping it around her.

Boom!

The soldiers began the assault with the cannons.

Boom!

"Eeeee!" screamed Maria Ignacia, throwing her arms around her uncle's neck. With each explosion, she squeezed tighter.

"We must hurry, *mi amor*. The battle is progressing." Carrying his niece, Mariano rushed and found his frightened horse pulling at the reins to get free from the tree. The horse whinnied. "Settle down, *caballo*, we are going."

Boom!

"Maria Ignacia, you are choking me." Trying to appear calm, Mariano grasped her arms and pried them from his neck while saying, "Let's get on the horse."

Again, the cannon exploded.

Boom!

Maria Ignacia was frantic with fear and screeched, "Eeeee!" The horse pranced and pulled.

Reaching, the boy untied the reins. He continued to talk in a quiet manner. "Maria Ignacia, I am here. Be calm." Grabbing the pommel and slipping his foot into the wooden-boxed stirrup, he pulled himself and his two-year-old niece up to the saddle. Clutching her against his chest with one arm, the horse galloped away as the sun rose above the eastern hills. With his mouth to her ear, he whispered, "Do not be afraid. You are with me. Let's go find our family, *mi amor*." They left as the battle continued out of their sight on the other side of Monterey.

Bouchard had had his men make land about four miles south of the Presidio in a creek hidden from the guard tower's view. Two hundred men, bearing one hundred thirty rifles and seventy spears, walked the distance and began the battle.

They barely fought an hour in combat until the Argentine flag was hoisted up the flagpole in the Presidio. Gunpowder smoke lingered in the air above lifeless bodies. While the victors were corralling the soldiers into their own barracks, the fort's medical doctor was allowed to enter to attend the wounds. Weapons had been confiscated and laid stacked outside, while the pirates shoved and prodded with their spears and rifles until every soldier was pushed into the buildings. Only Governor Solá, with a pirate pointing a pistol at his back, remained out on the parade ground when Bouchard approached.

"Good afternoon, Governor Solá," Bouchard said with a grin and exaggerated bow, as he swept his wide-brimmed hat with an exotic red feather fluttering in a flourish across his chest. When he stood back up, the grin was more of a snarl, "As you may know, I am Hipólito Bouchard, otherwise known as *Pirata Buchar*. Am I not correct that your men have given a Spanish flair to my name? Or do your people call me *Piraña Buchar*, the man-eating fish?" He gave a hearty laugh at his little play on words.

The governor made no move to answer, standing proudly and dressed immaculately in a freshly pressed white shirt open at the neck and a short jacket of silk over a brocade waistcoat made with gold and red threads. His breeches were of blue velveteen, ending above his boots, and a wide red sash covered his waist. His black, broad-brimmed hat had gold gilt around the crown.

Bouchard tilted his head and raised one brow to show his indifference. "Well, it's neither here nor there what they call me. *No importante*." He stood erect, clicked his heels, and made a slight dip at the waist, not an exact bow. "Hmm, our first order of business is this. Why don't you see to ordering a fine feast to be prepared for us? A feast presented with mounds of your finest beef, for which you are well-known. Oh, and with all the trappings to make a memorable meal to commemorate our success in battle.

"Also, I would like to see a grizzly. I have heard much about these gigantic and fearless beasts. I understand they can fight and kill a large bull. After you have people working on our feast, you and I will talk about creating a bear-and-bull fight to entertain us." He signaled with an uplifted arm for another one of his men. "Here are your guards while you get to work on ordering the preparation of our feast." He turned to his men, "Tie his arms." With that said,

Bouchard turned to go into the main room of the Presidio to meet with his designated leaders and make new plans.

Within an hour after the brief battle ended, Bouchard learned that all the inhabitants of Monterey were gone. He ordered his men to bring Governor Solá to him again and insisted, "Damn it all! Governor, where have you sent your people?"

Feeling satisfaction upon seeing Bouchard's frustration, the governor answered, "I sent them nowhere in particular. I told them to go in all directions to keep you from finding them. So, I do not know where they are, and none of my men know either." Though his voice spoke with a sneer, his eyes showed delight.

In anger, Bouchard picked up a glass from the table and flung it across the room. This meeting was not going as planned. He turned to his still-seated men, shouting, "Learn who can ride a horse. I see plenty of horses outside, so have those men pick one and go search." Everyone knew that finding the people of Monterey was not as important as finding the women of Monterey.

The pirates scurried from the room.

Bouchard turned to face his adversary, "I don't care to be tricked. When we find your people, we will not be generous in our ways." He shouted to one of his men across the room, "Get me another drink," then stood and waved his arm at the men guarding the governor, "Get this man out of my sight."

To the chagrin of the pirates, they found no one. Had they been experienced horsemen instead of seamen, they might have been able to travel for more than a couple of hours. However, even then, they still would not have found everyone since the people of Monterey had scattered to different places away from the fort.

Returning empty handed left the pirates angry. Having a woman after winning a battle was an expected personal prize for each man; their feeling of victory was diminished.

The Argentine pirates held the Monterey Fort for six more days, and those were busy days.

During the first of those six days, Bouchard sent a group of ten pirates on foot to search all the adobes in Monterey to evaluate what valuables to confiscate, and those men came across a family of three grizzlies feasting under an oak tree next to the body of the spy who had abused Maria Ignacia.

After one pirate took a shot and hit the largest grizzly, the two smaller bears ran away. Without hesitation, the injured bear charged the shooter. The men, not accustomed to an animal retaliating, ran.

Grizzlies are fast, besides powerful. The bear leaped and, with her five-inch claws, opened the man's gut in one swipe.

He cried out to his shipmates, "Help me, you assholes!"

Many shots were fired at the bear. No one aimed at the head and that was their mistake. Shooting for the head is the only sure way to bring down a grizzly; the ball from a flintlock firearm lacks the power to penetrate through the bear's thick fur and fat layers. In preparation for winter, the new pelage of grizzlies grows long and coarse with an increased accumulation of fat beneath. Many a man who had skinned a grizzly would attest to finding bullets lodged in the fat layer.

The huge, unfazed grizzly growled loudly, jumped on a second man, sunk her teeth into his neck, and held on. He died quickly. Hanging from the bear's mouth, the limp man was the size of one limb of the beast.

Finally, a pirate who had not fired, aimed his flintlock at the bear's head, pulled the trigger, and everything went quiet. The bear fell. Stunned, the remaining men were not sure if the beast was dead, or not. Some had crumpled on the ground in fear, one on his knees tried to reload with shaking hands, another still hid behind a tree, and the two dead pirates remained prone among the acorns. No one spoke or stirred for the longest moment.

Spontaneously, the grizzly's leg started an after-death-twitch.

Someone fired a shot into the carcass, screaming, "Shit! It's still alive!"

"No, it's dead. I think, we don't need to keep shooting."

Another man admitted, "That scared me."

One pirate asked, "What were those three bears eating when we surprised them?"

At first, no one answered, and no one wanted to move closer to investigate. At last, step-by-step and one-by-one they walked toward the bloody mound.

"Holy Maria Mother of God! Can you see? It's a man."

The carcass of their shipmate was too maimed to detect the shot Mariano had made to the chest or the slash to the throat, but they recognized the remains. "That's our spy!"

As they stood over the bloody mess, someone said, "Guess the bears were hungry and killed him."

How wrong they were. The bears, sitting next to the corpse of the spy, had been feasting on acorns. The bears preferred acorns to the flesh of the spy. The pirates had arrived after the bears had scared away the vultures consuming the spy.

"Look, here's his dagger. Maybe he was fighting those beastly bears."

"Let's get out of here. If they're still hungry, they might come back and kill us." Unknown to these pirates, grizzlies do not kill humans for food. A grizzlies would kill humans when surprised or when protecting their young; nevertheless, they usually don't eat them. For food, the bears will kill and eat any small animal—moles, gophers, squirrels, ground-dwelling birds, waterfowl, and fish—and might eat dead carcasses even when putrid, like a beached whale, an old elk that died, or cattle slaughtered for their hides. The grizzly is an omnivore interested in many kinds of flora, such as bulbous plants, grasses, clover, and all the berries—huckleberry, elderberry, manzanita, and more. Humans were not a preferred part of their diet.

"But we can't leave those dead men here. We should take them back."

"Like hell! I ain't going ta haul 'em anywhere. In fact, I ain't going ta stay here till another bear comes. Not me!"

"If Bouchard wants to bury them, he can send someone with a cart."

As they hurried away, the sky darkened with huge shadows crossing their paths. One of the men looked up and screamed, "God help us. Run for your lives!" When fifty feet away and with nothing following them, they stopped and looked back. Two condors had returned to finish the meal they had started before the bears ran them off.

"Hell's fire, did you see the size of them birds?"

"Shit! Birds? How could that be? They's bigger than a man! What hell hole is this!"

"Let's get out of here," one said, as they scurried back to the fort.

During the second of the six days, preparations began for the bear-and-bull fight. Because of their Spanish heritage, the Mexican soldiers not only were familiar with these events but also were experts. At the Monterey Fort, they had celebrated with animal fights throughout the year. In fact, the men and women's temperaments craved fiery excitement to take them away from the humdrum life at the Presidio. They desired the dangerous spectacles. For centuries their ancestors in Spain attended bullfights and public shows with battles between bears and bulls. Therefore, to continue their Spanish heritage in California, they devised the grizzly-and-bull fights. Other festivities such as all-night dances, fiestas, and rodeos were enjoyed, however the bear-and-bull fight often was a Sunday-happening.

While a group of soldiers and their pirate guards went to choose a formidable bull to bring to the pens, another group used a tried-and-true technique to catch a grizzly. Grizzlies liked horsemeat so, they took an old horse to a designated place, shot it, slit its throat, and left it below a tree where a high platform had been built for men to wait until a grizzly arrived to feast on the horse.

In the mess hall with all his men, Bouchard ate his meals at a table with Governor Pablo Vicente de Solá, who was untied for the occasion, though well-guarded. After swallowing a bite of a most tender piece of beef, Bouchard commented, "My men have heard from yours that the first formal grizzly-and-bull fight was preformed here in your honor back in 1816 when you became the governor. Is this correct?"

Governor Solá nodded and continued to eat.

"Yesterday, I saw your arena that's made of stone and adobe. It's impressive. I must commend you on its construction. I saw I will be seated high above the fighting animals when I watch from the benches in the stands. Safe from the danger."

The governor nodded again.

"However, I believe I want to be at the tree when you capture the grizzly," Bouchard said with a wide grin, "because that will be the real excitement."

The governor frowned and no longer could be silent. "You would be in great danger and may cause more danger for my men. You are a seaman and a captain of many ships. Do you even know how to ride a horse? My *vaqueros* are among the best horsemen in the world. They must be! And their horses are like an extension of them. These special horses think the same thoughts as their riders. It is rare that riders need to use their spurs; the horse senses what the man needs before any indication is given. The horses and my *vaqueros* know their life depends on the skill of the other."

This time, Bouchard nodded.

"However skilled they are," the governor continued explaining, "often something goes wrong. Only the speed and endurance of the horse can save them because the grizzly can run as fast as a horse, though not as far. If you are not a natural horseman and not on a horse that you know, you could lose your life in an ugly and painful way."

Bouchard sat straighter and said, "I could sit on the platform high in the tree and watch the capture."

Solá burst with laughter and the room full of pirates went silent. "Yes, why don't you go." He made a quiet laugh before saying, "Ha! I have seen an angry grizzly shake a tree with a girth the size of you until all the fruit he wanted came tumbling down. A grizzly has even more strength when angry and if he gets away from the *vaqueros*, he will kill anyone he can find."

They finished their meal in silence.

Later that day, as the setting sun pulled darkness over the sky, word traveled like the wind around the Presidio that a grizzly was eating the old slain horse. Ten *vaqueros* were already there; they had headed out to the tree to hide and wait, long before the bear arrived. Each man had taken only his horse and lasso.

No one had told Bouchard when the ten *vaqueros* had left, and he was furious. He went to the room where Governor Solá was kept and pushed the door open with a bang. Bouchard seethed, "You deliberately did not tell me when I needed to leave," and he hit him across his face with a gloved backhand.

They stood in silence staring at the other's eyes. Beads of sweat formed on Solá's lip, and he told the pirate, "Go with the cart driver who will bring the grizzly back to the arena. You will see a lot of excitement." The governor resisted rubbing his cheek that had flared red. He clenched his jaws before saying, "You would have made the same decision as I. For the safety of my *vaqueros,* I did not want you there."

Unflinching, they stood facing the other. These two strong leaders knew they must maintain an unnatural relationship for survival, since each had a power the other lacked. The governor had the knowledge of survival for this place, and the *Pirate Buchar* held the weapons.

Solá blurted, "You should be thanking me for possibly saving your life. I heard about a grizzly killing three of your men. Living here in Monterey, we have learned never to walk around the area. Hundreds of grizzlies roam the land and can kill at any moment. That is why we ride horses everywhere. I told you earlier that a horse can outrun a grizzly." He shook his head, correcting himself, adding, "Well, the bear is as fast as the horse at first, but if the bear lashes out with its five-inch claws, it can maim the horse. Again, what saves us is that these bears cannot run for long distances, and we do not go out alone.

If the bear brings down your horse, you scramble onto the other man's horse."

Bouchard's stance relaxed. Though a treacherous pirate, he understood his role. Like his men, he could and often did fight and kill. Yet, when he must lead, he knew the importance of discussion, concessions, and compromise.

Solá saw that he had persuaded Bouchard. "Go now with the cart driver. Believe me, getting there now will not disappoint you. Take a few of your men." After a short hesitation, he added, "Of course, all of you on horseback."

They smirked at each other.

Even from a great distance, Bouchard could see the difficulty in overpowering a grizzly. The *vaqueros* were still working hard. The man in charge of the cart suggested, "We wait here. No reason to be closer. If the bear gets free, he is so angry he would kill us all."

Bouchard did not argue. He could see well enough. He saw a wounded horse on the ground and asked the cart driver, "What could have happened to that horse?"

"I don't know, *Señor*, however I can guess. The bear is a big one and that makes him strong. You see those six *vaqueros* have their lassos on the bear?" After Bouchard nodded, the man continued talking. "One front leg of the bear is free. The other three legs have been lassoed and are being held tight. I am guessing, when I say that I think they had the two front-paws secure, but the grizzly pulled one free. In the past, I have seen bears pull on a rope, paws over paw, despite the strength of the horse resisting. I have seen this many times. The grizzly pulls the horse and man to him until they are close enough, and then he uses his claws to injure the horse. The man jumps onto another horse."

Bouchard nodded and said, "I see two *vaqueros* on one horse. You must be correct."

Loud shouts were coming from the *vaqueros*.

One of Bouchard's men pointed and exclaimed, "Look, the bear has the tail of a horse."

The six lassos were not enough. The main problem was that they did not have both front paws secured. The scene looked like this: Around the bear's neck, two ropes pulled in opposite directions, not to strangle him, only to control him, and three lassos were around one of the hind legs to hold it taut at three angles. So, the main problem seemed to be that the one rope on the other hind leg did not suffice. They needed at least two ropes on each appendage and the men must pull in different directions to overpower the strength of the bear.

The grizzly pulled the horse's tail until he had that second horse down. The bear leaned onto the steed with two paws on the flanks. Just as a throaty growl carried across the distance to Bouchard's group, the bear tore into the horse with his teeth. Bouchard's mount began to dance nervously even from the great distance. The wounded horse screeched unlike anything Bouchard had ever heard. He turned to the cart driver, "Was that the cry of the horse?"

"*Sí, Señor.*" The driver frowned and shook his head. "If the *vaqueros* do not get that bear down soon, we should leave. The grizzly has three feet free and, as you saw, the two ropes on his neck do not stop him from moving. He a strong one."

Just as the cart driver started to turn back, the scene changed.

Lassos flew and caught the front legs while the animal was chomping on the horse. The *vaqueros* plied the spurs to their horses, giving them a signal to move back quickly and hold the ropes taut. That action pulled the bear off the horse and onto the ground with three legs splayed. The last back leg was roped, and each man yanked him simultaneously in opposite directions. The bear was down, fuming with rage and beating his feet on the ground. They pulled the ropes tighter.

Whoops and yells of victory rose from the *vaqueros*. The cart driver hurried to the scene. Bouchard decided to remain where he was with his men. He knew it could not be easy to lash that bear to the cart.

One *vaquero* rushed by Bouchard toward the fort to signal everyone to be ready for the coming of the bear. The fight in the arena was scheduled for that evening, in only a few hours. They wanted the bear as fresh as possible for a fight; therefore, he was to be held captive no longer than necessary.

The *vaqueros* hauled in the ropes until the bear's limbs were stretched to a painful position. Many more ropes were secured around the grizzly before the horses pulled him across the ground onto the two-wheel cart. The wooden bed of the cart tilted to the ground to assist the loading. Before they had tied the bear down in a secure spread-eagle position, he remained dangerous and could still flex his legs to pull a horse and rider to him. The bear was furious, still violent while frothing and struggling, until he could no longer move anything except his eyes. At last, he stopped fighting the ropes and assumed a sullen disposition. He was motionless on the ride to the arena.

Once back at the fort, Bouchard headed straight for Governor Solá. "I was not disappointed at being late to see the capture. You were correct. After what I saw, there's no doubt that the grizzly is the most formidable animal alive. I have never seen such power. I cannot imagine the bull winning tonight."

"Shall we make a wager?"

Bouchard laughed, "I know, if you win, I must leave."

"That would be much to my liking."

"No wagers between us," said Bouchard. "Just make the fight in the arena something I will remember for the rest of my life, and I will not let my men be cruel to you and yours."

"There is no worry on that score. These two animals seem to have an inherent antipathy to each other. No spectacle in the arena with them is ever boring."

"Just give me a worthy show, Governor."

Everyone—pirates and soldiers—filled the stands of the arena. The soldiers' hands remained tied behind their backs and pirates stood guard at the ends of their benches. Bouchard surmised it was safer to have the soldiers here to keep an eye on them. More importantly, if he had picked guards to stay back and miss the bull and grizzly fight, he would have caused animosities among his men.

Bouchard sat with Solá in special seats above where the bull would enter the ring.

The show began with a nod from the governor.

Two horsemen dressed in colorful and fancy attire entered to circle the arena. Strings of bells attached to their saddles jingled as they moved. After circling twice, they left and six more horsemen, the *vaqueros*, entered with the irate grizzly in the middle of them while they contained him with their taut lassos. The grizzly struggled, snapped, and lashed his paws in the air.

Bouchard turned to Solá and asked, "Apart from the ropes they hold him with, I see a wide strap attached to his hind leg."

"Yes, a leather strap that has something important at the other end. Watch it."

With a flip of their wrists, the *vaqueros* released their lassos from the grizzly and, in seconds, made their exit through separate gates, leaving the grizzly unencumbered in the center ring. Simultaneously, when a gate closed, another opened. Bouchard observed that the leather strap reached across the ground through that other gate. He turned to Solá, "Aha, now I can imagine."

The governor elaborated, "Yes, the bull and grizzly are tied together. This way, the grizzly cannot climb up here nor get away from the bull. Well, not more than ten yards. Not that he wants to get away. Well, sometimes we have a grizzly that wants that, but we must wait and see what this grizzly does."

Out rushed the bull, a big Spanish bull—thick-necked, sharp of horn, quick of foot, and wanting a fight. He stopped abruptly to take notice where he was and snorted. The leather strap circling the forefoot of the bull jostled as the bull pawed the ground. He had not noticed the grizzly who sat on his haunches against the rock wall. The bull, seeing men above, began to run along the base of the wall. He threw his head up to gore them, but they were too high. Furious and ready to fight, the bull continued his frantic efforts to reach the people.

Not the grizzly. He sat calmly watching and slowly crouched lower. Only his eyes moved with the bull.

At last, the bull reached the end of the strap, and his next step jerked the grizzly forward. Now they glared at each other. The grizzly rose on his hind legs and an inherent antipathy seemed to flow between them.

The bull stared, scrutinizing the bear, and began to paw the ground. Curving his neck down with horns at a level with the stomach of the bear, he charged. Fast and raging he went. They had been apart the full length of the strap, so the bull ran ten yards toward the grizzly, who remained motionless until the last moment. The bear leaped, just before impact, and landed on the back of the bull. He no sooner had landed than he sunk his teeth into the bull's neck and held on.

The crowd shrieked and shouted.

Governor Solá stood and cheered with flying arms. When he sat back down, he commented, "They chose a clever grizzly. This is going to be an exciting fight."

The grizzly, still on the bull's back, yet ready to fall, reached out and clawed the face of the bull with his five-inch claws before jumping down. Unlike the bovine, the bear moved almost human-like—flexible and agile.

The bull was bloodied, though with no life-threatening wounds. He dripped blood yet seemed oblivious to his injuries. He turned from the wall, snorted again, and did not wait to attack. The grizzly was standing close, and the bull turned his head while he dashed closer. Turning his head allowed him to dig a horn into the abdomen of the bear.

"Ooorrh," wailed the grizzly and, in an instant, bit into the nose of the bull and scratched at the eyes.

Now the bull bellowed with the intense pain on his tender nose. "Maoogh!" He thrashed his head back and forth while the grizzly dug his teeth deeper. The bull could not gore him from this position and ran, dragging the one-thousand-pound bear along. At last, the bear released.

Cheers filled the air. The soldiers, who saw a fight often, and the pirates, who were witnessing their first, all screamed with excitement and jumped in their seats. This audience, witnessing the fight of natural enemies from the wild, felt exuberant with their own wild feelings.

Trails of blood covered the ground in the ring. Blood dripped from the bull's mouth and neck; the grizzly's stomach made puddles, yet neither seemed to notice.

After several more attacks, more bites, more goring, and an endless flow of blood, the two animals stood at opposite ends of the arena, not moving, but staring at each other.

The crowd was wild, agitated, and aggressive, as they shouted orders:

"Just kill him now!"

"Grizzly, use your teeth, he's tired."

"Get him by the balls, that will do it!"

With slow movements, the bull stirred. The bear noticed and stood up to his full nine feet. After making a loud snort, the bull took off running; and, when they were only a foot apart, the bear stepped to the side and wrapped his goliath arms around the bull's neck, leaned into it, and twisted. With his paws pushing on the horns, he wrenched the bull's head to the side.

CRACK!

The loud crack silenced the audience.

"What was that crack!"

As the bull began to topple, he went down on his knees and ever so gently keeled over.

"What happened?"

"I think the bear severed the spinal column."

The grizzly collapsed onto the body of the bull and was still.

Now the people started murmuring with their neighbors. No one was sure if the fight was over or not. The arena was quiet. Two workers ventured out toward the animals. The men approached with caution though they saw no movement of the bull or grizzly.

Silence continued across the arena.

When they were almost within arm's reach of the grizzly, the bear rose and heaved a backhand swat to one worker. The other man pulled his gun and shot the grizzly between the eyes.

Now it was over.

The roar of the crowd continued for several minutes. Bouchard was on his feet cheering. When the people settled down, he said, "I did not think such entertainment possible. What thrills. This event has filled me with joy. Thank you. To show my satisfaction, I plan to kill no more of your men."

Apart from the bear-and-bull festivities, the length of time the pirates remained at the fort was determined by how long it took to gather and load the bounty onto their vessels. The cattle—finding, herding, and transporting them out to the ships—took many days, with the soldiers and natives doing the work. After all the guns and powder were confiscated from Monterey, every pirate had a gun of his own and an ample supply of gunpowder. All the food stock not eaten during the six days were loaded onto the ships. The most valuable trading commodity was the animal skins—bundles of cured, cleaned, stretched, and dried hides—from cattle and a few wild animals. They took many *botas* filled with tallow, which was a by-product from cattle fat used for candle making and soap—a desired trade item in South America.

Anything the pirates thought worth taking from the homes disappeared into the stores of the ships. Bouchard kept his word, killing no one else. When the last day arrived, only the buildings remained—the fort, the governor's residence, and most homes—but not for long. The pirates stacked any remaining furniture into the center of each structure and set all ablaze with torches.

Since adobes are bricks of baked mud and straw, they did not burn; so, the populace of Monterey would return to blackened adobe shells, still-smoldering, with debris and wreckage inside. All their material objects were destroyed.

But the intangible spirits of the little girl and her young uncle not only survived but blossomed. This horrible incident created trust and a lifelong bond between Maria Ignacia and her Uncle Mariano Guadalupe Vallejo. A bond never to be broken.

The Missions of California

		Present-day Cities
Mission Basilica San Diego de Alcalá	1769	San Diego
Mission San Carlos Borromeo de Carmelo	1770	Carmel
Mission San Antonio de Padua	1771	Monterey (moved south near Jolon)
Mission San Gabriel Arcángel	1771	San Gabriel
Mission San Luis Obispo de Tolosa	1772	San Luis Obispo
Mission San Juan Capistrano	1776	San Juan Capistrano
Mission San Francisco Asis (Dolores)	1776	Yerba Buena / San Francisco
Mission Santa Clara de Asis	1777	Santa Clara
Mission La Purisima Concepción	1787	SE of Lompoc
Mission San Fernando Rey de España	1797	Los Angeles
Mission San Miguel Arcángel	1797	San Miguel
Mission San Jose	1797	Fremont
Mission San Luis Rey de Francia	1798	Oceanside
Mission San Buenaventura	1782	Ventura
Mission Santa Barbara	1786	Santa Barbara
Mission Nuestra Señora de la Soledad	1791	So. of Soledad
Mission Santa Cruz	1791	Santa Cruz
Mission San Juan Bautista	1797	San Juan Bautista
Mission Santa Inés	1804	Solvang
Mission San Rafael Arcángel	1817	San Rafael
Mission San Francisco Solano	1823	Sonoma

When the 21 missions were being built, there were no cities in Alta California. Monterey became the first city and the capital.

Chapter Two

I Remember

1833

One evening, the western sky burst with colors—fuchsia, azure, and gold—above black silhouettes of two friendly ships in Monterey Bay. Stick-like masts poked into the sunset. The smell of wood smoke drifted up the hillside from distant adobe houses, and the sound of a whinny came with the wind. At the top of a hill, peering through a small nautical spyglass, a young lady watched men rolling barrels from the decks of one vessel until, hearing the approaching hoof beats, she turned to see a uniformed man approaching on horseback. She recognized him but could not recall his name.

He slipped from his mount and began to climb by leaning into the incline of the steep hill. She sat on a high rock outcropping. The young man placed his hands on his thighs to aid his ascent and sweat beaded on his forehead just below his black, gilt-banded, broad-brimmed hat. He called out, "Señorita Maria Ignacia, I had difficulty finding you." He stopped to take a deep breath. "Your grandmother sent me." Still panting, he took out a handkerchief to wipe his face before sucking in more air. "You are to return to your home. Your uncle, my commander, will arrive at your house soon." That said, he collapsed on the grass next to where she had left her horse with the reins untethered.

Dissatisfaction showed on her pretty face, but nevertheless she nodded and prepared to leave by slipping the spyglass into a cloth bag tied to her waist.

Now, viewing her silhouette against the sunset, he stared. Feminine curves and delicate movements held his attention until she closed her sketchpad and turned to walk downhill.

Saying, "Good evening to you," Maria Ignacia dropped her drawing pad and pencil into the saddlebag and bent to look at her legs, "Oh my, look at all the seeds stuck on my stockings." She started picking off sharp-pointed seedpods, round fuzzy burrs, and flat sticky ones while complaining. "Why aren't you covered in these?"

"My legs are bare from the knee down."

Impatient with her task, her lower lip pouted as she blurted, "Oh, I cannot remove all these seeds now." She leaned forward to grab the back edge of her ankle-length skirt and petticoats, before pulling them through her legs and tucking the many layers into the front of her waistband. "Now I'm ready to ride but we don't need to hurry, because I know my uncle will arrive much later." She raised her eyebrows and shook her head, "I think you, like everyone, know my grandmother is impatient at times. Today, she's worried I will embarrass her by being late." As she raised her hands to mount the saddle, she said, "I have forgotten. What is your name?"

The young man jumped to his feet and lunged toward Maria Ignacia. She fell to the ground onto her back as he landed on top of her while pulling his flintlock. A roar from a grizzly mixed with the blast from the gun.

Boom!

Surprised, fear surged through her, and she screamed, "YEEEEOW."

The horses were just as surprised. They had been nervously prancing, and the shot made them bolt.

With a thud, the falling bear landed an arm's length from the two, and the young man frantically grabbed her arm to pull her up and away.

Maria Ignacia shouted, "Stop!" She pulled her arm from his grasp and took a step back toward the downed animal. "I want to see the bear."

He grabbed her again, blurting, "What are you doing? It may only be wounded."

Sprawled in the grass, the grizzly twitched. A foul smell filled the air, and blood rolled from its eye socket where the bullet had entered. At last, the animal ceased its movement. The soldier made the sign of the cross; grateful that he had made a perfect shot, knowing there would have been no time to reload his single-shot firearm.

After she had jerked from the young man's grasp and glanced at the bear, she saw no white patch above the eye and relaxed.

The soldier stuck two fingers between his lips and produced a shrill whistle and walked farther down the hill. As soon as they had distanced themselves from the carcass, the horses trotted back, and they mounted. He asked, "Why did you want to see the bear?"

She decided to ride without speaking, not wanting to explain why she went to see the grizzly.

The sunset finished its performance as frogs and insects began their evening songs. Lost in her thoughts, Maria Ignacia saw memories from her past; the small bear saying "woof, woof," and the gathering of acorns came to mind. *Why was it important to me to know if that grizzly was Mancha or not? I still think* about that little bear with the white blotch of fur above its eye, after so many years, because I know how unusual that day was. Something wonderful and something horrible. That day gave me satisfaction in making a friend of a bear and filled me with terror of the pirate. I like thinking that Mancha is living somewhere near me, and I like knowing the pirate is dead. I remember how my uncle killed him.

She smiled with the memory of the bleeding pirate. *I have lived a life unlike everyone I know. I relish my memories of that day—the good and the bad. I want the rest of my life to be as special. I am not afraid of any ugliness I may have in my life if I have some thrilling days, like my feeding a little grizzly under an oak tree.*

She smiled again at seeing herself with the little bear under the oak tree. *That day was no accident. I left the cart to find my blanket and opened the possibilities. I can do that again. I do not want to marry a nice young man like this one next to me. I do not want to have a life like my mother and grandmother. I want more. I want something that I cannot imagine; something other than what I see in Monterey. I know it will happen if I do something special. I need to jump out of the cart that is taking me down a road to a place I do not want to go.*

He started to chat and confided, "We had luck on our side today with that grizzly."

She still was not inclined to talk.

After allowing time for her to reply, he broke the silence by saying, "We men in the military have orders to shoot the bears. You must know that." He continued talking without her responding.

Not listening, her face continued to display the joy she felt, thinking about her future. *Yes. after all these years, I keep hoping to see Mancha again. I think that bear today was the right size, but with no white patch above the eye. He wasn't Mancha. I wonder if Mancha would know me. They say dogs remember our smell; I think bears must also.* While remembering, a faraway look came into her eyes. With a quiet chuckle, she reflected, *"When small, I often wished Mancha could be my pet. I still wish it could have been, even knowing it to be impossible. I never told my parents about feeding a little grizzly that day when the pirates came. I'm glad I never told my mother before she died. I think she would have fainted. Now I need to find a way to have that kind of excitement again in my life.*

They approached her adobe, one of dozens of one-storied adobe homes dotting the landscape. Following the Spanish custom, families named their homes, and hers was called *Casa Zemita*.

He had seen that she had not listened to him, so he raised his voice to address her, "Maria Ignacia, we are almost to your home. I wanted to ask you if you know about the dance at the fort this Saturday?"

She anticipated the direction of his conversation and said, "I am not going. I have plans with my family on Saturday. I hope you enjoy yourself at the dance."

They stopped their horses in the flower-filled courtyard formed by the U-shaped adobe. She slipped off her horse and pulled her skirts from her waistband. "Oh," she said while looking up at the young man still in the saddle, "and thank you for coming for me." From experience, she knew not to linger, or he would think she was interested in him.

The short and stocky Pepe, wiping his hands against a leather apron, approached. All her life he had lived and worked with her family. Taking the reins from her, he said, "Hope you had a good ride."

"Thank you, Pepe. Would you take my things from the saddlebag and ask one of the maids to bring everything to my room?"

While walking she ran her hands down her skirt to smooth out the creases and worried, *my grandmother didn't know I wanted to go riding and will reprimand me about my unladylike appearance.*

As she turned towards the house, the young man in uniform rode away and another young man approached on foot. "Good evening, Lalo," she said, looking puzzled, "this is a surprise. Did I forget a lesson with you today?"

After her mother had died three years ago, Maria Ignacia had begun to think about her future. Her father had asked his mother-in-law to come live with them and run the household, though he still held the purse strings. Maria Ignacia decided she wanted more in her life than just running a household; she wanted to learn something useful. Two years ago, she had spoken confidentially to John Cooper, her prosperous uncle, about learning accounting and bookkeeping at his Trade and Custom business. Cooper had told his worker, Lalo, to teach her.

She and Lalo had formed a comfortable relationship in those two years, yet each, unknown to the other, saw their relationship in different ways. She looked at Lalo as a good teacher who was giving her lessons in accounting. Lalo saw her as someone who wanted to be with him, using the lessons as an excuse.

"No, we had nothing planned," he said, as they continued walking to her house, "but I was going to the office to work on records for a ship that is being loaded and thought you might come to learn about that."

"I cannot today," she said, but asked, "may we work on bookkeeping and other accounting on Sunday afternoon? I have no time today."

"Of course. Well, not in the evening. I'm eager to go to the cock-fight."

"Oh, Lalo, don't gamble too much. Remember, last time you lost. You became angry." She watched him nod in agreement though he said nothing, so she returned to the other subject. "I will come early for my lesson."

The two arrived at her front door and stopped on the veranda—a covered porch surrounding three sides of the house—where chairs and tables were scattered in a random fashion. Eight doorways opened from the veranda: Six doors went to bedrooms, one door led to the hall separating the living room and the dining room, and the last door led to a large indoor kitchen. Two dogs slept in a corner on the tiled floor of the veranda, and chickens walked everywhere. Wiping the perspiration from her brow with the edge of her skirt, she said, "I don't want my grandmother to ask why my clothing is wrinkled. Please help me smooth it." At sixteen, Maria Ignacia worried more about an encounter with her strict grandmother than with an approaching grizzly.

Lalo obliged, and the soft white cotton of his shirt billowed from his arms with every brush of his hand down the back of her skirt. He stood and straightened his shirt just before the thrill of passing his palm down her skirts began to show beneath his breeches and before the door burst open to show her grandmother.

"Maria Ignacia, there you are! I have been worried. No one knew where you went." She faced Lalo and said, "Eduardo, you should have brought my granddaughter home sooner. We are having a large family gathering, and I did not need more to think about." She ranted on. "I expect you to act like a man and be responsible. At your age, you should know that." She reached for her granddaughter's arm and pulled her through the doorway. Looking back at him and with a quizzical voice, she asked, "I have forgotten . . . what is your age, Eduardo?"

"Seventeen, *Señora*. I, I, I . . ." he stuttered, knowing that she made a mistake and not knowing how or if he could contradict her. "I did not bring her home. I, I, I . . ."

"Humph, you should have! I hope I did not just detect a lack of respect in your voice. I am not sure I should allow Maria Ignacia to be with you anymore, now that she is of marrying age; it is improper."

"Lita, please don't talk to Lalo like that."

"Good night, young man." Hesitating before closing the door, she added, "I think it best that Maria Ignacia does not go anywhere with you again unless a chaperone is present," and she turned from him with a look of disdain.

When the heavy wooden door closed, inches from his long and straight nose, he stumbled a step backwards. Nevertheless, he didn't leave; he heard them talking. Listening, without decerning every word, he heard Maria Ignacia's voice flowing through the shuttered and glassless windows into the still night air. He was pleased by what she said.

The grandmother's voice became louder, "Maria Antonia Juana Ignacia Guadalupe Soberanes Vallejo, do not contradict me ever again! You are my namesake. Please make me proud that you have my name. And, as the eldest, you should set an example for your brothers and sister."

"Lita, you cannot use all seven of my names to scare me anymore. Nor does calling Lalo by his formal name of Eduardo accomplish what you want. I am almost seventeen, almost an adult. What is more important is that he is a fine person. As you said, I am a grown woman now of marrying age, so I can decide my own life, if you please."

Still standing on the veranda, inadvertently Lalo stared down at the tiles covering it. Scattered here and there along the terra cotta floor were special decorative tiles with colorful flowers, with blue or yellow borders, and a shiny surface. He gazed and saw nothing, only heard Maria Ignacia defending him with vehemence. Between listening to her words and smelling a roasting pig, he was reluctant to leave. *Casa Zemita* was a large and well-kept adobe with maids and workers everywhere, all busy preparing for the evening meal. At last, he turned to walk back to work, only minutes away. He passed their *horno*, an outdoor oven made from mud, where he smelled squashes baking inside, and he saw maids making flour tortillas on a small stove with red-hot coals. Pepe approached, almost at a run, pushing a wooden cart full of small firewood for the *horno* and the stoves.

Eduardo—still filled with euphoria from touching the clothing of Maria Ignacia—reached higher ground and stopped. He slowly turned full circle, while wondering if her feelings for him were as strong as his for her. He gazed at the hills that surrounded Monterey. Every angle was picturesque and calm in the light of the rising moon. The trees and shrubs on the hills above the houses were dark green in the gathering darkness. Horses were everywhere—untied and free—because no streets nor fences existed in the grassy hills. "Without fences the houses are free like the horses," he whispered to himself. Around him were a hundred structures, most topped with red tiled roofs. Mixed here and there among the adobe homes, there were granaries, the Presidio, and a chapel, but no mission. Years ago, the mission had been moved farther to the south. When he finished rotating, Eduardo peered out at Monterey Bay, feeling content. He loved where he lived, and his mind continued his thoughts of Maria Ignacia. With glee, he mumbled to himself again, "I want to marry her and live here all my life." He worked as an accountant for many people; yet being young and having little experience, he was not paid well. He knew he was poor, her family rich. He sighed and wrapped his arms around himself and grinned, saying aloud to no one, "But I could hear that Maria Ignacia wants to choose her own husband." This gave him hope.

Meanwhile in *Casa Zemita*, Maria Ignacia flew in a huff from her grandmother's side through the living room and, as she turned in the hall toward her bedroom, she collided with her dear uncle, Salvador.

"Salvador!" All her disagreeableness with her grandmother vanished; she chuckled and wrapped him in a hug. Standing a head taller than she, he held her tight and kissed the top of her head. Being a twenty-year-old to her sixteen years, one would not think them to be uncle and niece; relatives, yes. Their features were similar, and he was as handsome as she was beautiful. "Oh, Salvador, I am glad you are here. Lita just upset me."

"As she does to many of us. We must love our Lita for who she is. Listen, I'm sorry but I must return to the fort. I'll be back later for the meal. Let's sit side by side tonight at the table so we can talk. Well, we cannot talk about your upset with her while she is there. We'll talk about other things."

"Yes, let's sit together, but don't be concerned; I don't need to talk about her. I'm angry and get over it. Lita is stern but I know she loves me." All through their childhood she and Salvador had been close. As a little girl, she had dreamed of marrying him before she knew that that never could be. Their fondness for each other followed them into adulthood. Nevertheless, it should be noted that the fondness and affection displayed among everyone in the Vallejo family was part of their culture, but Salvador and Maria Ignacia were even closer.

"*Hasta luego*," he said and headed down the hall to the veranda to get his horse.

She turned, stopped at her bedroom door, and quietly opened it. The room was empty. Leaning against the heavy wooden door, decorated in hand-carved swirls and circles, she sighed, relieved that her nine-year-old sister, who shared her room, was not there. Being alone, Maria Ignacia began to imagine her future. *My grandmother will never understand me because I am not like her. I want to marry a man who is different from anyone here. I want to marry a man I love, not someone my family wants. He must be as handsome as Salvador. But . . . I want to live somewhere else. When Uncle Mariano took me to the fort in Sonoma, I loved seeing new places. Sonoma is farther away from the ocean so, everything's different—the plants, the views, the birds. I am happy he has a job there. I hope he takes me there again soon.*

Fumbling with hooks and buttons, she removed her outer garments covered with burrs, awns, and barbed seeds, and dropped them to the floor. Flopping onto her bed, she pulled her blue blanket out from where it always stayed during the day—tucked under the edge of the other covers. Though she no longer sucked her thumb, she liked to cuddle with her blanket.

Tap, tap, tap.

Her door opened, and Julia, the older native woman who lived with them, entered with a tray and said, "You missed the afternoon meal."

"Oh, Julia, we are having a large meal with the family tonight. I saw no reason to eat in the afternoon."

Julia nodded, "Nevertheless, I have brought you a little something. We will not eat for hours. If you smell the cooking, surely you are a little hungry, like me. Well, aren't you? Oh, do you want me to take these clothes on the floor to wash?"

Maria Ignacia did not answer the questions because she knew Julia knew the answers.

After placing the tray on a small trunk at the end of her bed and pulling a chair close to the food, the older woman sat. Their gaze met and Julia's look was calming.

"Oh, thank you, Julia, you always think of me."

Julia picked up a tortilla and began to spread jam across it while she spoke, "I heard you and your grandmother. Those words were upsetting for her and you. Be kind." They locked eyes again. "You will find your way for happiness. Be patient and be kind. You are still young."

All of Maria Ignacia's life included Julia. Their bond was deep, like the roots of an oak, not only because she had suckled from Julia's breasts or had taken her first steps with Julia, but also because she loved the stories Julia told. Their relationship grew with the same naturalness as an acorn forming on an oak tree. Julia was her oak, and Maria Ignacia was ready to fall to the ground and sprout.

Maria Ignacia scooted to the foot of the bed and took one of the rolled tortillas. "Why don't we go walking on the beach anymore?"

"Oh, Maria Ignacia, we haven't gone because you have grown up and have other interests. You enjoy reading books, drawing, and learning bookkeeping."

Chewing on the tortilla, the young girl swallowed and replied, "I want to go walking with you on the beach again."

"You let me know when you want to go. With so many more people in the house, I must ask permission from your grandmother because there's more work than in the past when your mother ran the household." Many family members had come to live in their home in the last three years since her mother died.

"I remember you told me a story long ago about your father, you, and the sea otter. Please, Julia, tell me that story again before I take a nap."

"Of course, that is a story about me when I was a little girl. Now that you are older than the last time I told you, I will tell parts of the story I never mentioned before." Julia folded her hands in her lap and took a minute for her mind to find the memory. Finally, she began. "As you know, in your language people call my people the Ohlones. So, I am an Ohlone who was born and grew up here in Monterey.

"One of my favorite pastimes was to go to gather the shellfish along our beaches. That's when I would see the little animal you call a sea otter. My parents called them *nawamooks*. I saw many of them everywhere in the bay, and when we were ready to return to our village, my mother would ask me why my basket had only a few shellfish. I told her that I was watching the *nawamooks*. I loved to see them float on their backs with a baby on their belly. To watch them eat was what I liked best. Once I saw one dive underwater and stay for a long time. I was frightened that something had happened because sharks kill them, but it popped back up with a spiny sea urchin in its paws. The *nawamook* rolled onto its back, floating in the sea, and turned the urchin over to where the spines are shorter and took a bite, licking with its tongue to get the soft meat out."

Maria Ignacia interrupted the story. "I have never seen one eat a sea urchin. I know how they open shellfish by hitting them with a rock on their belly. I don't understand where they get the rock. They pop up after a dive with a clam in their paws, but they have a rock, too."

Julia grinned and nodded, "Yes. I know about the rock because one of the last memories of my father was him skinning a *nawamook*. When he pulled the hide off, a rock fell to the ground. My father showed me a pocket that *nawamooks* have across the chest. They keep their favorite pounding rock in that pocket."

"You know so much about everything, Julia."

Julia's eyes saddened as she said, "Now there are not many *nawamooks* to watch. The Russians came here and hunted them for the furs. Now, few *nawamooks* are left. The fur is valuable because it keeps people extra warm. The Russians live in a cold place, and I have been told that snow falls and stays on the ground for many months, so they need fur clothing to stay warm."

"Yes, I have heard that, too. Someday I want to go to touch snow. Uncle Mariano said he would take me."

Julia nodded and continued. "Now here is the part of the story I have never told you.

"At that moment when I told my mother why I had only a few shellfish, we heard excited voices of our friends and neighbors. In the distance we saw people sitting on strange animals the size of an antelope or elk. When they were closer, we could see that those people were without color on their skin and had eyes that looked like the color of the sky. Their bodies were covered except their heads, and their hair was of many different colors, not like ours. We were frightened. Our men ran for their weapons. Everyone was shouting, screaming, or crying.

"Of course, now I know these were Franciscan monks who were riding mules and wearing gray robes of cloth with leather vests.

"Back then, we did not understand what we saw. My mother began to cry and took me behind a bush to hide. In the following days, those monks remained with us, and we realized they did not want to hurt us. We thought they were an animal-God. We called them The Children of the Mules in the same way we believed the Ohlones are The Children of the Coyote. In the coming weeks, they showed us large lengths of colorful cloth, metal pots, tools, and much other magic. We were sure they had to be gods to possess such items.

"Most astounding to us was their cloth that could be folded and refolded. It was woven just like our baskets but made from something like thin threads of spider webs because it was as light as air.

"Never before had we seen Spaniards. We soon met the most important one called Father Junipero Serra. After a while, we learned he was different from the others; he beat himself with a chain and put the fire of many candles to his chest. We feared him and could not understand why he did this. Yet that strange behavior gave him a power. We could see that the other Franciscan monks looked up to him and followed his orders.

"They wanted all of the Ohlones to become Christians. At first, we did not know what that meant. They gave us gifts and promised to show us how to make things they had. We were curious about everything, so we helped them build their mission. They told us what to do to make these buildings and we found it interesting to learn new ways to use mud and stones. After a while there were Ohlones who made the choice to be Christians, and that decision changed their lives.

"Much time passed. You know the Ohlones did not have a way to count months or years, therefore I do not know how long we worked with the monks. They did not approve of our way of life and made us change. They did not think our beliefs were correct and would stop us from living as we had in the past. People died, little ones were born, and we began to forget our old ways. We forgot because no one was making baskets, building tule boats, and living in grass huts.

"All the young girls were put into one building, which had only one door and was well-guarded because the monks claimed they were the guardians of chastity. When I was older, every day we had to spin wool, weave cloth, prepare soap and tallow, or do other tasks they had taught us. What I disliked the most were the classes about Christianity. Like me, many did not want to learn. However, to avoid punishment, we did. We were only allowed to leave that building for mass. They marched us to the chapel and back at the end of the service. If we did not go fast enough, they hit us with a large stick while we went to and from the church."

Maria Ignacia gasped wide-eyed and wondered if her parents knew all this. She asked, "How did you get away?"

Julia sighed and explained, "I heard about the possibility to come work in a home. They would let me go if I agreed to be baptized and marry a man they chose. That is how I got away. I married and came to work for your family. However, I never went to bed with my husband, and he ran away. I am so sorry I did not accept him because they sent soldiers to find him. A friend told me that after he was captured, they beat him with whips. He later died because of his injuries."

"Did my parents know all this?"

"I do not know. I only told you so you can appreciate your life. Your family is my family now because I do not know what happened to my parents. I do not remember where we lived. No one was allowed to tell stories of our life before the monks. I do not even remember what name my mother called me before they took me from her. The monks named me Julia. Often, I think I remember the sound of my Ohlone name, but I am not sure."

Tears rolled down Maria Ignacia's cheeks. "I am ashamed. How could I not know all this." She wiped her face with her hands and frowned. "Why did I never ask you about your life. I am sorry, Julia." A devastating thought crossed her mind. "I know Lita is in charge of the household, but my father surely pays you, doesn't he?"

Julia gave no answer. Wiping her mouth with the back of her hand to remove the beads of sweat on her upper lip, she said in almost a whisper, "I should not have told you all of this."

"Or maybe you should have told me sooner." Maria Ignacia shook her head in disbelief. "Oh, Julia, I didn't know your story." She leaned over the end of the bed and wrapped her arms around Julia while her mind raced. *Why would no one from my family mention Julia's past? She is a slave, even though we call her* muchacha, *a maid. How naive I have been. Today she has made me aware of and grateful for all she has done for me. I have been thoughtless, only thinking about myself.*

Long after Julia had left the room, Maria Ignacia remained sprawled across her bed, immersed in thoughts of Julia's past until she drifted to sleep.

Meanwhile, throughout the house, workers were busy.

The preparations made the day appear to be an important holiday. However, the day was nothing more than a celebration of the coming of her Uncle Mariano, the important Commander Mariano Guadalupe Vallejo, who had been assigned to the Mission San Francisco Solano. His visits had become a special event since his new workplace was more than a day's ride away.

In the last year, and soon after Mariano's father had died, he had been assigned to this new post. He had realized, with his frequent absences from his home, that new living accommodations were needed for his wife-of-one-year, for their infant son, and for his widowed mother, who was called Lita by the family. Therefore, *Casa Zemita,* where his niece Maria Ignacia lived with her father, a recent widower, and her four younger siblings, was expanded to be the family home for multi-generations—a Spanish-Mexican custom. They added two extensions onto the main house, which made it U-shaped with a courtyard. A kitchen was built inside the house for more convenience, and a fireplace was built in the living room. Most adobes in Monterey had kitchens separate from the house and did not have fireplaces inside.

After her nap, Maria Ignacia arrived in the dining area of *Casa Zemita* and saw her grandmother fussing with the table details, rearranging cutlery, and placing the wine glasses in (what she considered) the right position. After smoothing her hair with her hands, Maria Ignacia greeted her grandmother with a kiss as they touched cheeks. "*Buenas noches, Lita.*"

The elderly Lita stood tall in her black crepe gown, which indicated she remained in mourning for her husband. Nevertheless, every aspect of her clothing looked as if she were going to see a king. She wore a shawl, made from a square of silk cloth in a floral pattern of vibrant colors, adorning her shoulders over the black mourning attire. Her shawl was an acceptable piece of colored clothing to be worn during the first years after death, as was the silver jewelry made with the cross of Christ hanging from her neck and ears. A four-inch-high comb stood atop her black and shining hair, arranged in loops and bundles on her head. While one small streak of white at her left temple belied her age of fifty-seven years, her flawless complexion gave her an ageless beauty. Her features reflected the pure Spanish heritage of her family, putting them in the upper class of the community. People referred to families who had never mixed with the natives as *gente de razon*.

The grandmother was not unusual in her dress. The women of Monterey who were *gente de razon* had a fondness for dressing in fine clothing. Their gowns were in styles equivalent to those of rich Europeans, made of silk, crepe, and satin, except with short sleeves and no corsets. With the coming of many ships to their bay, they often would spend a whole day onboard, examining and buying fine clothing, fabrics, and many notions—silk and satin ribbons, buttons, braiding and other trimming—as well as ornaments to be made into jewelry or sewn onto clothing.

With anger, Lita exclaimed to God in the usual manner, "*Dios mios, mi amor.*" She hoped for help with her granddaughter. "This is a special evening, and you did not put on any bracelets or even comb your hair. Go back and make yourself presentable. How could Julia let you come to a festive event looking as if you were going on a horse ride?"

Maria Ignacia was accustomed to exaggerations from her grandmother. She looked around the room at her girl cousins and aunts to see if they had arrived in their best clothing. They had. Many had even loosened the daily braids to let long black hair flow over their shoulders. Colorful silk dresses adorned the cousins and were tied at the waist with a complementary bright sash. Soft kid shoes in matching colors poked out from the full skirts.

Thoughts filled Maria Ignacia. *They have so many bangles and earrings. I just am not that interested in jewelry or what I wear. I know it upsets my Lita. Hmm, Julia made me a pair of blue shoes. I will go put them on and comb my hair.*

When Maria Ignacia returned with her hair fixed, she wore her blue shoes. From across the room, she heard her father greeting John and Martha Cooper, saying, "Welcome to *Casa Zemita*." She saw Lita walking to greet them. As Maria Ignacia approached the group, Lita commented to her son-in-law, John Cooper, "Oh, I thought you were coming with your brother Thomas Larkin and his wife, Rachel. I was hoping to have the opportunity to meet them."

John Cooper answered with a shake of his head and solemn face, "I am sure you heard that their little girl died not long ago. The child was only seven months old. They are in mourning and will not attend festivities." Heads nodded in understanding, and the subject was ended.

Maria Ignacia greeted the Coopers with hugs, the usual kisses while touching cheeks, and a comment to her aunt, "Oh, Martha, I am glad you could come."

Lita's back arched, and she spat her words to Maria Ignacia, "If her husband decided to rename my daughter, that was his decision. You, however, are to call your aunt *Tia Encarnación*." Everyone in the room overheard, and a deafening silence followed.

Maria Ignacia blushed and replied, "Lita, I was speaking English to them, so I used her English name. I thought that was the proper way, using English names with English words."

Cooper spread his handsome smile across his face and spread his muscular arms around his mother-in-law's shoulders. He had experience with her stern opinions, and said, "*Perdoname, Madre Antonia.* Excuse me, Mother Antonia. My tongue cannot always say the Spanish, so I gave my wife a name that is easy to use when I call my wife. When I want her to pour a glass of wine for me, I call to Martha, because her real name takes too long to say, and my thirst does not want to wait." As he laughed at his own words, everyone joined him.

Martha took another approach to assuage her mother by lifting the older woman's hands into hers and whispering cheek-to-cheek, "When he says

Martha, I always hear it as *Encarnación*."

Cooper added a few more words to calm her, "You know how difficult it was for me to speak Spanish. You saw me struggling with Spanish during the years when I lived with you. If it had not been for your family helping me speak Spanish, I could never have started my flour mill or opened my supply store."

Just the mention of his businesses calmed his mother-in-law. Having a mill and store in her family was a source of pride and prestige for her. She told him, "Well, I am sure I am saying this for everyone living in Monterey when I tell you how much we appreciate your store and the flour mill. We had neither until you came. And I understand, now that your brother has arrived from eastern United States, he is helping you in your enterprises."

Cooper nodded, "Why, yes, we are business partners." With the new conversation, the confrontation passed.

Small groups began to converse again in every corner of the room.

Later, when Cooper had meandered away from Lita, he approached Maria Ignacia to ask, "How are the lessons progressing at my office?"

They both glanced over their shoulders to make sure that Lita was across the room. "Oh, Uncle John, I have learned so much in these two years. Thank you for everything. My Lita would be so angry with you if she knew. But I am so grateful."

He gave her a hug. "Let me know if I can help with anything else."

John Rogers Cooper had lived with this family for over three years after arriving on his schooner *Rover* in 1823. Once he had established his businesses and saved enough money to support a family, he proposed to Maria Jerónima de la Encarnación Vallejo, Mariano's sister. Though it was easy to fall in love with her, it was difficult to marry her. The family insisted he fulfill many requirements. He had to become a Catholic, be baptized and given the new name of Juan Bautista Roger Cooper, and, if he wanted to live in Monterey, he had to be naturalized as a Mexican citizen. When he had completed those requirements and married her in August of 1827, he was considered family.

Lita came walking toward them; he turned, looked at the table, and, raising his voice, spoke in Spanish to please his mother-in-law. "*Mira!* Look! How is it possible to eat this much food? Even so, I will try my best." Again, people laughed.

The long table adorned with food looked as festive as the family, dressed in their best. Tantalizing aromas filled the house. Sprawled on a huge platter in the center of the table, a roasted pig—with head and hooves—dripped with succulent juices and smelled of garlic. Baked red apples surrounded the pig and the family's brass candlesticks from Spain were placed at each end of the platter. Pottery in colorful geometric designs of red, green, and gold were filled with baked casseroles of yellow corn dotted with dried grapes and topped with slices of hard-boiled eggs. Terra cotta bowls were heaped with rice and bean mixtures in special sauces. Plates held several kinds of squash sprinkled with sugars. Tiny bowls, one next to each person's plate, contained the fiery red *aji*—a sauce for those who desired a hot spicy sensation—to be added drop by drop. Tortillas of corn and others of flour were stacked high on the tablecloth at several places to be within reach of whoever wanted another. Possibly the most important items were the four bottles of wine placed on the table in a position, like the bread, only an arm's length away.

The younger family members were standing and yearning alongside the dessert table, where meringue, fruit filled crepes and egg puddings waited.

Minutes later, Mariano arrived from the fort, and Lita told everyone to be seated, saying, "Finally, let us be seated; the guest of honor is here." He walked around the table and greeted all, one by one, with kisses to the cheeks.

During the meal, Maria Ignacia was not herself; she refrained from joining most of the conversations. Her thoughts concentrated on what she had learned from Julia. *I can see that my grandmother thinks I am pouting because of the words we had earlier about Lalo or the other confrontation when I called my aunt by her English name. Humph, I told her I was an adult, but now I know I still behave like a child. What is worse is that I think like a child. How could I not know what Julia told me about her life? Why did I never ask?*

In the first hour, Salvador arrived and was greeted by cheers from everyone. He started walking towards Maria Ignacia to sit with her, but Mariano shouted, "Salvador, pull a chair next to me. I want to talk with you."

Salvador turned to glance at Maria Ignacia and shrugged. When an older brother, who also is the commander, requests something, one does it. Salvador reached across the table and grabbed a tortilla before taking the plate filled with hunks of pork from a maid who had rushed to him before he sat.

Soon Mariano and Salvador were having a serious conversation about the military while they ate. With so many people around the table, conversations buzzed like a hive of bees; the two brothers huddled, not only to hear each other, but also, and more importantly, to keep the conversation private.

Mariano told him, "Salvador, I want to have you working with me at the fort in Sonoma. If you are there, I can help you advance in your military career. I had to go to war against the scoundrel Estanislao, to impress my superiors and earn a promotion. I nearly lost my life."

Salvador looked surprised, "When was that war? I cannot remember."

Mariano shrugged, "About five years ago. You were young. However, tonight, I don't want to think or talk about that ugly story, but I will tell you about the details in private on another day." He finished the last morsels of meat on his plate, stretched his neck, and sighed. "Tonight, I wanted to speak with you about other matters. Maybe I should not mention this to you, because the assignment I'm planning for you must remain a secret for now." He frowned and rubbed his bare chin; he wore long sideburns but no beard. "You must not talk about it. I know I can trust you to keep this confidential." Mariano waited to see a nod before continuing. "I am to investigate the Russians at Fort Ross. We learned from the Pomo natives that the Russians buried metal plates with writing on them. We guess that the Russians want to mark the land to claim it as their possession. I need men I can trust to help me with this assignment. I want you working by my side."

The main meal was ending and two of Maria Ignacia's younger brothers pulled their chairs over near their uncles. Maids began circling the table, clearing plates and the leftovers. Mariano stopped his discussion with Salvador.

After ten minutes of answering questions from the younger men in the family, Mariano stood and said, "Enough of our man talk. I have something to show all of you." He walked to the tack room where he had dropped his saddlebag and removed a roll of paper. Mariano then signaled for a maid to clear a space at the table by removing the large platter on which the pig was served. As he unrolled the paper across the table, he spoke excitedly. "I enjoy the terrain surrounding this fort and mission where I now work. Sonoma is a beautiful place, and so different from Monterey. I decided it's a perfect location for a town." His eyes met those of his wife, and he said, as if directing the words to her, "Not only a town, but also the place for a home." Looking up again and letting his gaze travel to his family seated around the table, he continued to speak. "Here are my ideas on how the town could be developed. See, I sketched streets and locations of important buildings." He pointed to the paper and explained his ideas. "The town's name will be Sonoma, a word from the Pomo people. It means, Valley of the Moon. Isn't that beautiful?"

His mother nodded and asked, "How did you learn to make a town layout?"

With a twinkle in his eyes, he chuckled, "*Mi madre mio*, my mother mine, I learned in the same way I have learned anything I know. With study, as well as the help and direction of others." Now he looked into the eyes of Salvador and said, "I have had many mentors and people who have helped direct my military career." He let his eyes travel again around the table. "Maybe you do not realize what my job involves. I oversee land distribution and land planning. You know I was ordered to oversee the secularization of the mission." He paused and took a sip of wine. "I have completed the first part by officially giving land to the native workers from the mission. Now they are landowners and no longer committed to work for the mission."

However, many benefits of his work with secularization he did not mention; those were ones that benefited only him.

The sweets from the dessert table were being offered as maids came with the choices on a tray. Maria Ignacia took a crepe and asked her uncle, "Will you be out riding tomorrow?"

"Yes, I am going to the fort in Yerba Buena. Want to come along?"

She smiled, her first that evening, and said, "Yes, I was about to ask you if I may go with you."

For the lengthy trip to Yerba Buena, the travelers rose early to begin the journey. As Mariano pulled himself into the saddle, he explained, "I am looking forward to being with you." As was protocol, several soldiers rode with him at enough of a distance to allow the uncle and niece to speak in private.

Within the first hour of travel, they passed a large herd of elk grazing in the distance and small birds sang their morning songs. As the group rode inland and wove between the rolling hills, Maria Ignacia talked endlessly and told Mariano of her conversation with Julia. "There's much I don't understand so I have many questions. I know little about Junipero Serra and want to understand about him. Also, Julia told me how she came to work for us, but I think she gets no pay. That means in return for her work we only give her a little room for sleeping and food to eat. She talked about the monks at the mission and how they separated the Ohlones. She doesn't know if she even has any family left. How could I not know about her life?" Not waiting for an answer, she shook her head and said, "During the night, I realized I had given no thought to Julia's situation. For example, I have been told that Julia nursed me because my mother was sick. So, she must have had a baby if she had milk. I never saw her child. Where is her child now?"

"You must stop asking more and more questions. Let me answer before I forget them."

"Oh, *Tio* Mari-oope, do you know about Julia?"

He turned in the saddle and annoyance showed red on his face. "I have always enjoyed you calling me by your childhood name for me. Nevertheless, I would rather my men not hear you say it."

She dropped her head in embarrassment and said, "It just falls from my mouth sometimes. I'll try to remember to call you *Tio*."

Mariano settled back in his saddle, and they rode a few minutes in silence.

"Being about ten years older than you, I do know the answers to a few of your questions. Julia was living with another family when her husband ran away. He was found and brutally punished. Afterwards he died. She was pregnant."

"Oh, she told me she did not sleep with her husband."

Her uncle laughed before saying, "Are you so naive as not to know the maids are there for the taking of any man in the household." Embarrassed by blurting his last comment, he did not wait for a response. "So, I do not know who the father was; I only know Julia was soon to birth a child and my sister needed help because she was pregnant with you. That is the reason Julia came to live with your parents. She had her baby about a week before you were born, and that's why she could nurse you. Nevertheless, it was a sad situation because her child died in the first month of life."

"Oh, poor Julia."

They rode without words while passing an eight-foot-high manzanita with flowers. "Look how healthy these plants are. The red bark is beautiful, isn't it?" He continued looking at plants and talking. "Remember the drought we had a few years ago when thousands of horses and cattle died?"

She nodded her head, sensing the end of talk about Julia, and asked, "Why did this plant not die? The grass and clover did not grow. I was maybe twelve or thirteen, but everyone has to remember those two years without rain."

"Some plants do well with drought. Look, this one does. It's called Black Sage and is drought resistant." He reached out and broke off part of a branch with the leaves. "Smell it."

She took the branch. "Oh, I know this wonderful smell. The maids offer us many kinds of leaves for our tea, but I never pick the leaves. I guess they do."

"Keep that branch to learn how to pick your own leaves."

She put the branch into her saddlebag before saying, "You studied Latin, so

I imagine you know the scientific name."

"Yes, that one is *salvia mellifera*."

"Tio, you know so much and speak French and English, too. I wish I had gotten an education as you did. Our family only had tutors to teach reading and writing to the girls. That wasn't fair. Monterey needs to find someone to start a school for boys and girls. It is appalling that we have no school."

He nodded in agreement and said, "Do you know that Governor Solá established schools when he was in charge?"

She looked surprised and said, "No! But I knew he tutored you and Juan B."

"Yes, but after a while, the funds for schools were not approved by his superiors in Mexico City, and they were closed. I think you were four or five years old and never had a chance to go." With a quick movement, he pointed without comment at a herd of hundreds of antelope moving south in the distance.

She turned her head to look, acknowledging the sight, and continued her topic of conversation because the antelope were common, much like the herds of elk. "I asked Uncle John Cooper if he would help me learn how to work with bookkeeping for a business. He understood how I feel. He said he plans to send his children to schools on the Sandwich Islands so they will have a good education. He told one of his workers to teach me, and I am learning. I do not want to be like my mother and sit embroidering all day." With a frantic look in her eyes, she blurted, "You cannot tell anyone in the family that I am doing this. Grandmother would put a stop to it."

He nodded again.

Her face brightened with excitement as she shared her dreams. "I want to learn to speak another language. Because Uncle Cooper lived with us and spoke English, I know a lot of English. I have promised myself that I will someday be proficient. For now, I am learning numbers. Also, I would like to know the history of where we live. Julia told me a little about the arrival of the Franciscan monk called Junipero Serra when she was a young child. Can you tell me more? It was horrible for her. I do not understand why they treated her people in that way."

He leaned out of the saddle and broke another branch from a different plant—one with berries. "I am glad to hear you're becoming curious. I have books you can borrow; many are stored in your home. I took them there when my mother went to live with you, and we closed our home." He handed the branch to his niece. "I am curious about everything and that is why I have learned. I want you to know you cannot learn only from books, you must use your mind. And you can learn from what people tell you, besides what you see, so I am going to tell you about Junipero Serra. After I finish, you can ask questions."

She looked at the branch and asked, "Before you start, I want to know why you gave this to me."

"First of all, I wanted to share the beauty of that plant. Secondly, there is a book of mine in your house that will tell you about all the plants you see every day. Please look for the book and borrow it. I hope you will be curious enough to learn about plants and tell me on my next visit what you learned about this branch."

Amused, she tucked the branch into the saddlebag with the other one. "I will. Thank you."

Mariano watched her and thought. *What is it about my niece that makes me glow with happiness inside and out? I am content when I am with her. Even seeing her from a distance, I go on my way happier for the sight. She is rather like a field of spring flowers full of young life and color, taking us by surprise as they bud, bloom, and display their beauty from one day to the next.*

He cleared his throat to begin to answer her other questions. "Junipero Serra died years before I was born, yet he is still in people's conversations because what he did affects our lives even today. Everyone knows about Fray Serra." He chuckled and said, "Do you realize that it's my job to undo what he built. I'm dismantling all the missions."

"Yes, I know that. But why did Fray Serra build these missions? I think there are more than twenty."

"Yes, there are twenty-one. Spain had one reason to build missions and the Franciscan monks had another. The monks envisioned making the perfect Christian community with the natives becoming the beneficiaries, after being taught that nakedness and their animal beliefs were wrong. The idea was for the monks to give gentle guidance and teach them about proper prayer, table manners with forks and spoons, the importance of covering their bodies with garments and, most importantly, teach them about cattle and agriculture.

"Spain's objective was something different. They wanted to gain wealth from the land through work preformed by the natives. They built forts for protection. Well, they said they were for protection. However, the soldiers working under the Mexican flag accomplished Spain's goal with the power of the military. The natives had to learn farming, weaving, blacksmithing, cattle ranching, and masonry to sustain themselves and the monks. Spain agreed to send ships with supplies—food staples, wine for the sacrament, clothing for the natives, tools, and necessary supplies—until they were able to produce everything for themselves. The ships brought supplies the missions could not produce and returned to Spain with the goods obtained though native labor in payment for those supplies.

"The monks thought that after ten years a Christian Utopia would be functioning with natives married in the church, their children baptized and saved from the fires of Hell, and this new society producing cattle, furs, tallow, and more to repay the Spanish government for the costs that began with the first mission in 1769.

"Neither the dreams of the monks nor those of Spain materialized." Mariano lifted his water bag off the pommel and offered it to his niece before guzzling at length.

"They built the last mission in 1823, and I worked in that one. Today, ten years later, the goals still have not been achieved at any mission. Not one mission is surrounded by farms where Christian natives prosper and live in happiness." He looked at his niece and shook his head before saying, "Think about that. The first mission was built over fifty years ago. What a failure of the Franciscan fathers' dream."

For several minutes they rode without speaking. The ocean was no longer in view as they progressed up the *El Camino Real* that connected the twenty-one missions. Coastal cliffs forced the route inland. As far as the eye could see, yellow flowers covered the sides of the roadway and formed a golden ribbon that grew from mustard seeds the monks had thrown, decades ago, to mark *El Camino Real*.

Maria Ignacia broke the silence. "From what Julia told me, the Franciscan monks did not use gentle guidance. As you said, Julia's husband was whipped and died."

"Yes, I know, I know. What I told you is what I believe was the original plan. You are correct that no gentle guidance was used. Perhaps those in power in the church in Spain or the powerful leaders in Mexico City had more cynical plans from the beginning. I do not know. I must believe in my heart that Junipero Serra and the original monks pictured a future with the heathens prospering on their farms, feeling happiness in their life, and virtuously attending church. What those monks did not realize was that the Ohlones already had a fulfilling life with an abundance of food that was there for the taking, without plowing and processing it before they could eat."

She looked to her uncle with confusion. "Julia said they were not forced at first. Why did the Ohlones go to the missions when they already had such a good life?"

"I imagine curiosity. To the natives, the monks looked different, had unusual materials, and knew methods that the Ohlones wanted to learn. Therefore, they went voluntarily to the missions and were given little gifts like glass beads." He shook his head and reflected a moment. "What a wonder a little colorful glass bead must have been to them—an object not found in nature." Again, he stopped and thought. "You see, the Ohlones liked to trade, and I think they thought they could make good trades. The monks urged them to be baptized, though the natives had no idea what that meant. Many Ohlones were dubious and refused; yet there were others who agreed to be baptized. After baptizing the natives, the monks saw them as Christians who had to follow the laws of the religion, and the soldiers stepped in, forcing the baptized natives to stay at the missions and honor the ways of the church.

"Each mission had a mixture of different groups of natives who could not speak to others because they had different languages. So, they were forced to learn to speak Spanish. As the years passed, they began to forget their culture, their ways, their old life. In these sixty-five years, their past disappeared from memory because they no longer could talk about it."

"Oh, *Tio*, all this is so wrong to me. How can you abide by it?"

"Maria Ignacia, I do not agree with any of it." He huffed and said, "I never agreed. It was planned and executed fifty years ago. I had no say." He closed his eyes and shook his head to find his words. "We are strong, and we are independent from Spain now, so we are stopping what they practiced at every mission. I was assigned to oversee the secularization. Do you know the significance of my job?"

"Maybe not. Tell me."

"Secularization means that the affairs of the military and the church are to be separated. No longer can soldiers force the natives to stay at the missions and be Christians. The military men from every mission are working together for secularization. That's why we are traveling to Fort Yerba Buena. Today I will present a progress report about what I am doing at my mission."

She grimaced and said, "We are going to the Mission San Francisco de Asis in Yerba Buena, and your mission is called Mission San Francisco de Solano. How confusing to have almost the same name."

"I imagine that Junipero Serra wanted to honor Saint Francis of Assisi, the patron saint of his order, the Franciscan fathers, and . . . "

Before Mariano could finish his sentence, a soldier appeared at his side and pointed into the distance. "Commander Vallejo, there are two grizzlies not far from here. Shall we shoot them as we always do?"

Maria Ignacia jerked her head to the right and saw two bears under an oak tree about one hundred feet in the distance. She stood in her stirrups and strained to get a better look at the bears.

Mariano turned his horse and followed the soldier as they trotted off to get closer to the bears. Three other soldiers, with guns in ready position, fell in behind them.

Maria Ignacia rushed to follow the group.

The larger bear must have heard them coming and turned. Maria Ignacia saw a white flash of a spot. *It's Mancha!*

"No, *Tio*!" She screamed as the guns exploded. Without hesitation, she dug her heels into her horse, galloping toward the bears and passing her uncle.

He turned to his men and ordered, "Stop her!" He shouted, "Maria Ignacia, what are you doing!"

Four soldiers jerked forward—two men heading to her right side and the others to the left. Hoof beats pounded in the air creating a cadence that matched Mariano's heartbeats pounding in his ears. As he followed, he called out, "*Maldito*! Stop her!" Within seconds they had overtaken her horse and grabbed her reins, stopping thirty feet from the downed bears. The bears were motionless, but not dead.

In a smooth maneuver Maria Ignacia threw her leg over the saddle and slipped off her horse. The four horsemen surrounded her, yet she ducked under one horse's neck and shimmied past another while heading for Mancha.

"Holy Mary Mother of God. My niece has gone crazy." Mariano shouted, "Shoot those damn bears again. In the head."

Bam!

Bam!

One of the soldiers went after Maria Ignacia and jumped from his horse to tackle her to the ground. She and he went down in the dust, close to the smaller bear which was recovering from the initial shot which had only dazed him. He wiggled and rolled over, making an eerie wail. The sound of the cub alerted the mother, and she came out of her daze and stood. In anger and with a shake of her head, a deafening growl escaped from deep in her throat. The soldiers at the scene had used their shots. They had no time to prepare their flintlocks to fire again.

Mariano had never considered himself to be a marksman, though he had brought down a pirate with a rifle. He was a thinker and leader of men, yet his deep feelings and instinctive protection for this girl rose in him. It was the same feeling that he had felt when the pirate was slapping his niece. Without rage or fear, he pulled his pistol, took careful aim at Mancha's head, and hit her between the eyes.

Still sprawled on her stomach an arms length from the smaller bear, Maria Ignacia whimpered and moaned, "No!"

More soldiers had arrived, and Mariano ordered another shot to the head of the small bear. He bellowed, "Be careful not to hit my crazy niece."

Maria Ignacia struggled to her knees and gave the soldier, who had most likely saved her life, a shove before she crawled to Mancha. Sitting on the ground she began to stroke the bear. "Mancha, I always thought you were a male. Now I see you were a mother. Oh, I am so sad."

Mariano came to her side. She accepted her uncle's hand, and he pulled her to standing. His jaw was clenched in a frown that covered his face, overshadowing the usual kindness he displayed to her. "I cannot imagine how you are going to explain what you did, and please do not start now. Later you must tell me." He walked to his horse and mounted, while shouting orders to his men to continue the journey.

Once on her horse, she glanced into the puzzled eyes of her beloved uncle. She wondered what she would say to him. She could not explain to herself anything she had hoped to accomplish. *Again, I behave like a child. I didn't think. I reacted to a daydream I have nourished for years. When will I grow up and think before I act?*

Commander Mariano Vallejo called a meeting at Fort Yerba Buena the next afternoon for many different groups: The military men, the religious people from the Franciscan order, the Ohlone workers, and his niece. He had asked her to attend saying, "To educate you on the reality of our life in Alta California."

After preliminary reports and discussions, Commander Vallejo stood and took the floor. "To help you understand the job we have ahead of us to secularize all the missions, I have the results of the livestock census from all twenty-one missions. After I share it with you, I want to hear a discussion on the questions I have. Please participate, to help everyone have a complete picture of our situation.

"Alta California is the biggest pasture any of you will ever see in your lifetime, making it a haven for animals to flourish. In addition to being immense, there's a large variety of grasses and clover that sustain our cattle and horses, sheep and goats, and mules and burros." He took a moment to look around the room to evaluate his audience and their attention. Satisfied, he continued talking. "Now for the resulting counts from the past year. I have the 1832 census from all missions:

151,180 head of cattle,
137,969 sheep,
14,522 horses,
1,575 mules and burros,
1,711 goats, and
1,164 swine."

A flurry of muttering swirled through the room. Vallejo—glad to know the numbers impressed them—let them whisper among themselves for a minute.

He slammed a book against the table to regain their attention and continued speaking, "Since we declared our independence from Spain in 1821, Alta California has belonged to Mexico; nevertheless, we did nothing to claim it. Now we are. And Spain is taking notice. We will be working with the Franciscan holy men to distribute the land and animals among all of us who live here, including the native people who have worked for the missions."

Cheers rose in the room. Delight was on all faces, except those of the Catholic friars and monks. The military oversaw the secularization, yet, unknown to Mariano and in defiance, the Franciscans were planning to profit by slaughtering over one hundred thousand of their cattle for hides and tallow within the coming year.

Vallejo continued. "Only two factors have retarded the success of accumulating livestock. Droughts, like that devastating one that lasted from 1828 through 1830, and Grizzlies.

"I want to hear from you men about what has been tried to stop the bears. I need to have a better understanding of how we are going to protect our livestock. For example, I know that back in 1801, at the Monterey garrison, the Commandant had men select old mares to slaughter as bait, and he gave the order that one thousand precious cartridges could be used for shooting the grizzlies when they came to eat the horsemeat." Vallejo shook his head, " As you know, a bear does not always succumb with one shot. They killed only fifty grizzlies."

The room filled with laughter and confirmations as, "That's right," "Yeah, we know about that problem."

Banging the book against the table again, Vallejo said, "tell me of any other methods to control these grizzlies—both successful attempts and failures. We don't want to repeat those failures, so we need to know about them."

One man stood and was recognized by Vallejo, "You have the floor."

"I heard from my grandfather that they tried to poison them with tainted horsemeat. Though they saw a few bears eat it, they never found any sick or dead bears. The condors ate it, and they did die." The soldier sat back down.

Vallejo pointed to another military man who took the floor. "About ten years ago, my father served at Mission Santa Clara. They built platforms in trees about fifteen feet off the ground. Each could hold several men. About twenty paces from the tree, they dumped a horse, dead for several days and decaying. The bears seemed to enjoy putrid meat. Padre Viader told me that he himself killed about a hundred bears from the platform. That number seemed exaggerated to me so I asked myself if a holy man can lie."

The afternoon slipped into evening as many more examples were given. Someone said he had heard about digging a pit and putting a man in it, who would shoot up when the bear was on the boards that covered the hole. That was considered too time-consuming to build to kill only one bear at a time. Another idea: Sharpshooters were hired who had more powerful rifles than the military. Again, there were not enough bears killed to make a difference. No techniques or attempts that were described would kill enough of the grizzlies to diminish the population. In fact, Mariano concluded it was the easy access to cattle that allowed the grizzly to eat so well that the population was growing.

No satisfying solution to the grizzly problem was presented that evening.

Not until the meeting ended were Maria Ignacia and her uncle alone. They went walking outside the fort, below clouds that had crept over the coastal hills. He strolled with his hands clasped behind his back and his face set in a cold expression as he said, "Now you can explain your behavior with the grizzly yesterday. Start when you are ready."

The story she told took them back to pirates and silk ribbons on blankets, to acorns and a white spot on a bear, and a little girl's arms around Mari-oope.

At first, he doubted, "Maria Ignacia, you were young. How can you be sure that you remember everything correctly?" They stopped with the bay in view, and he turned to face her.

She insisted and went into a rant. "I remember and know my memories are correct. That day has been in my thoughts through the years because I loved that bear. I formed a bond that day under that oak tree. I wanted to keep my recollections inside where they could not be taken or criticized. And, if I had told you years ago about Mancha, would it have made any difference today? No, you still would have had your men kill the grizzlies. Besides, you would not have believed me. However, now you have seen the white patch above his, I mean, her eyes. Surely you believe me." She saw doubt or disappointment on his face. "Oh, long ago I told Julia about Mancha, though no one else. How could I have known about a white patch if I had not met this bear before?"

Mariano said nothing.

They stood searching each other's eyes.

An idea came to her, and she said, "I remember about that pirate, too." She began in a whisper. "You saw him. Remember?" She closed her eyes and frowned as she said, "He had a grin that stretched a scar across his lip and exposed two missing upper teeth. Did you see his scar when you went to slash his neck? He had a red cloth tied around his forehead and it matched the red sash around his waist. I know you remember that." She saw his surprise and added, "Under his dirty shirt a medallion hung from his neck onto his hairy chest. You must have seen that when you ran his knife across his neck and took his flintlock pistol from his waist."

Mariano's eyes widened while remembering the details she described. However, he nodded in silence, no longer doubting her memories. He had the same memories. For a long moment he stared at her before looking out at the bay again.

She took her uncle's hand in hers. "I know you had me sit in the meeting to better understand your job to stop the bears from killing cattle. I wonder if the grizzlies really kill so many. I heard you list the thousands and thousands of cattle, horses, and the other animals. I am sad to think everyone wants to kill the grizzlies. Unlike you, there is nothing I can do to stop it. Why can't we live with them? Am I being naive? I know my family is upset when a grizzly eats our pigs, but..."

Mariano interrupted her by wrapping his arms around her for a lengthy hug. The evening fog crept around them, and the view of the bay gradually faded. Enveloped in their silent world with his head against hers, he whispered, "I don't have answers for you. You must accept that the Ohlones and the grizzlies are from the past and another way of life. Time moves on. Their time has passed, and their way of life has disappeared."

One evening in the next week after all workers had gone home, Maria Ignacia sat with Lalo at a desk in her Uncle John Cooper's office and prepared to work on an accounting lesson. Because she began to talk about what she had learned about the secularization of the missions and about her Uncle Mariano's plans, they got no bookkeeping lessons done that time.

When she finished her discourse, Lalo sat straighter in his chair with a look of astonishment on his face and proclaimed, "Look, I understand the military is not forcing any natives to work or remain at the missions, yet we know those people have lost all their knowledge of how to live as they did in the past. The Ohlone no longer know how to weave their baskets for everyday life, how to make a boat for fishing, how to capture an animal without a gun, and how to tell their children about their ancestors. I find this horrible to think about. The monks have erased their culture and everything about their prior life." Lalo stood and slammed his palms on the table. With a raised voice he continued his rant. "We took **everything** from them. Now they are to leave the missions and go live their lives. How? Even the language their families spoke is gone. There never was a single language for the Ohlones; there were hundreds. Every little tribelet spoke a different tongue, and the friars took advantage of that; those people had to learn Spanish to be able to speak together. Why didn't your uncle tell you about that? There no longer is any need to force the natives to stay; they have nowhere else to go. We took their land. Those fanatic monks destroyed the natives' way of living and could not see that God had already given them a wonderful life."

"Lalo, be calm."

"I cannot. This topic heats my blood." He sat and quickly stood again, seemingly oblivious of knocking over his chair. With his hands on his hips, he began to pace. "Now our leaders feel vindicated. For what? The Ohlones are still our slaves, because we need them to help with our farms and the cattle. Now we pay them a peso, and it assuages any guilt even when we know we should pay much more. Do you think we should be proud that we no longer force them against their will, no longer shackle and whip them?" Lalo did not wait for her response. "And your Uncle Mariano was too kind in his description of the monks' and Junipero Serra's motives. They were over-zealous fanatics who did incalculable damage to many cultures by enslaving natives. No, not only enslaving them, but also killing them. Before the missions, the natives were plentiful here in Alta California. Now they are few."

She stood his chair back into place and sat back in hers. "Lalo, you know they died from measles and smallpox. You can't say we killed them if they died from diseases."

"Yes, I can. The Spanish people of Mexico and the men on ships that came brought the diseases here. Those ships came because of the products the natives were producing. Did the natives profit from their own work? NO! It was their demise." Lalo put his hands on his hips again and growled, "Men have killed for greed forever. Using disease is one way. When I studied about the Americans fighting the British, I read about a British general who was negotiating peace with the Indians, and he gave blankets to them as a gift. Those blankets he took from a smallpox hospital, knowing that the Indians would soon have the disease."

Maria Ignacia looked long and hard at her friend before saying, "I have never seen you act like this."

He stopped his pacing and faced her, "And I never knew you were this naive. I ask again, your uncle and parents never talked with you about all this?"

She shook her head. "Not until the trip last week with my *Tio*."

He pulled the chair under himself and sat again, facing her. In a hushed voice he continued. "Maria Ignacia, use your mind. Everything I teach you about numbers, you learn quickly. So, I know you are smart. You need to think about all this. Think! Do you think those Franciscan monks did not know why Spain said they could come and build missions in Alta California? They knew. Shouldn't it have been obvious something was amiss when they had permission if and only if a fort with soldiers was built next to their missions?"

"I don't know. They had to be protected, didn't they?"

Lalo pulled his hands from hers and stood again, "Think, Maria Ignacia. Protected against whom? The bears?"

"Well, yes, and the pirates, too. I remember those pirates."

"Oh, do you remember how well the soldiers protected the people and their homes when the *Pirata Bouchard* came?"

Not speaking at first, she sat with her hands folded together on the table. She refolded them this way and that. At last, she pulled them apart and laid the palms flat on the table. In a soft voice, she answered. "Yes, I remember that they didn't protect much of anything. They sent the people away, the soldiers lost the battle, and all our homes were burned." She raised her face to look at her friend, "I remember."

"There were many other happenings you cannot remember, Maria Ignacia, because you were not there and did not see what I saw. I am only a year older than you, but I saw and remember different details than you." He turned his chair to straddle it and sat. He leaned toward her and spoke with a soft voice to share a horrible secret. "I remember despicable happenings. I dislike telling you because I will find it difficult to make the images leave my mind later. But I want you to know what I saw.

"As a small boy, my mother and I would walk past the courtyard in front of the chapel. My mother had native blood that she gave to me, so we could not attend church together with the *gente de razon*. You are *gente de razon*. You are of a higher class. We went when the Ohlones went to the church. Rows of Ohlone men were on their knees and repeating Spanish words about the faith. A priest was telling them what to say. In my dreams, sometimes I still hear their voices and strange accents saying, *Dios, Jesu, Cristo, Espiritu Santo*. Every day, when we passed we heard the same forced lesson. I could see blood under their knees because they knelt on the stone pavement of the courtyard. Often, a line of shackled men shuffled by with a soldier in front and behind. Those guards held whips and were taking them to mass. I remember because my mother was taking me to mass. I would see the girls and women being led to the chapel with guards around them. They never smiled. Their heads hung from their shoulders, and they looked so sad."

A tear rolled down Maria Ignacia's cheek. She took her finger and brushed it away.

"Think! One would have to be stupid not to realize that this was happening at every mission. If, as a small boy, I saw this and could understand it was wrong and cruel, the monks knew what they were doing. If they did not have enough chains to shackle the natives, they used a log and ropes. I saw many women, not only men, dragging a heavy log as they struggled to walk to church to give thanks to our God."

"Lalo, you said 'if they did not have enough chains', but who is *they* in your sentence?"

"Does it matter if it was the soldiers or the holy monks who shackled the natives? Does it matter who did it? To me, it's obvious they had an agreement between them."

Maria Ignacia stood and headed to the door to go outside. "I need a breath of fresh air." Without conversation, they walked side by side until they came to a horse munching grass. She leaned against the animal and began petting the long neck. "So, tell me if I am thinking correctly. I have never seen what you described, because they stopped the shackling and whipping when independence from Spain happened in 1821."

"More or less. But it did not stop overnight. In these twelve years, much of the cruel abuse has stopped. With the secularization happening, life is better for the native people, but . . . "

She finished his sentence. "But, for the Ohlones and the other natives, their way of life and knowledge of their past is gone and will never return. They no longer remember."

Incorrectly, she had finished what she guessed he was going to say, but he was going to talk about her uncle's manipulations. On another day, she would hear his opinion of her uncle, not on this day. He was tired of all this remembering and, more importantly, feared that if he was the person to tell her about uncle's greed then she would dislike him.

As if on cue with the ending of their discussion, the night sky burst into brightness. Looking up, Maria Ignacia exclaimed, "Look! Oh my, there must be hundreds of stars showering down."

"LOOK!" He pointed. "They come from the same point up there and spread out like a fan as they fall."

People started coming out of their homes. Her Uncle John Cooper came out of his house and joined them.

She asked, "What does it mean?"

Her Uncle chuckled, "You sound frightened. I think you know there's nothing to fear. It's a meteor shower; that's all. Although, I think, the most spectacular one that I have ever seen."

"Are you sure there's nothing to fear? Meteors are rocks, aren't they? Can't they hit us?"

Cooper continued to reassure her. "I'm pleased that you know they are not real stars falling. Only falling rocks, that are burning up. My, they keep coming."

Maria Ignacia exclaimed, "I wonder if my family is watching. I must go tell them. Good night to you both." She ran off, and Lalo went back into the office to put things in order.

On the way she thought. *I wonder if my Uncle Mariano is watching. He's gone back over to his mission. Maybe he can't see it over there; it could be foggy or rainy. I will get my sketchpad when I get home and draw it for him.*

The meteor shower went on for hours. Maria Ignacia's whole family and most people in Monterey hurried outside to enjoy this once-in-a-lifetime event. Laughter abounded amid her family and the neighbors.

In the coming days, when newspapers arrived, they read the details:

> *December 3. 1833*
>
> *An annual meteor display, seen for centuries, appeared this year for a duration of more than nine hours. Because it seems to burst from the constellation of Leo, hence, the name Shower of Leonid's. However, the storm this November was one of the most prolific meteor showers ever seen. People in Mexico, Alta California, in the entire Southwest, and over most of North America made a record of it.*

Natives across Alta California watched as well. They had a different perspective and no laughter.

To most native people, such as Julia, this meteor shower was an ominous sight, happening at the culmination of a destructive year. Later, Julia told Maria Ignacia, "I fear that it means more destruction is coming. We have had so much sickness that kills us. I remember that the newspapers reported that in 1830, it was estimated that eighty percent of natives, like me, in the Northwest died from smallpox, measles, or malaria.

"Afterwards, we had horrible floods that left standing water for the mosquitoes. So many groups of natives, including the Miwoks and Wappos of the central valley in addition to my Ohlones in the missions along the coast, were exposed and died this year from the sicknesses." Frowning, Julia stopped talking.

Maria Ignacia nodded, knowing an estimated twenty thousand natives had died.

An estimate of twenty thousand natives died.

On Mariano's next trip to Monterey, Maria Ignacio gave the sketch to her uncle and said, "Turn it over. I wrote a few details on the back of the sketch." He read:

> *For my Uncle Mariano:*
> *On the night of November 13, 1833, thousands of meteors swept down from the western heavens above Alta California, displaying the unbelievable and creating a phenomenon only Mother Nature can produce.*

Holding the pencil drawing, Mariano started talking and could not stop. "I consider the Shower of Leonids to be the most unbelievable natural sight I have ever witnessed. However, I know it was a different experience for each person. Was it an omen to be feared, a sign from God, or a vision of beauty?" He chuckled and said, "I am sure there were quite a few who decided they had had too much to drink, as they looked at the sky from their bedrolls. I imagine that it gave them a reason to toss their flasks away."

Maria Ignacia nodded in agreement as he babbled on and on. She knew she had another memory about Monterey to tell her children and grandchildren in later years. She would begin by saying, "I remember . . ."

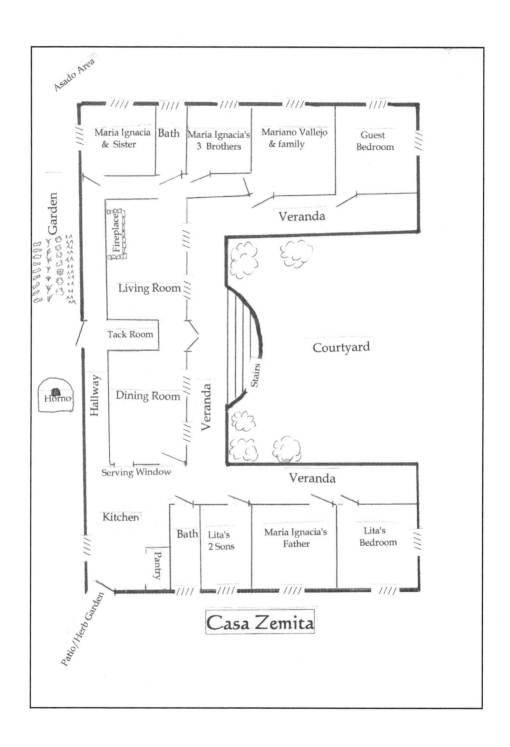

Chapter Three

Secrets from the Past

1837

Monterey was growing and changing. An approaching ship no longer saw only a fort without walls and white adobe houses scattered up a hillside. Now, the scene had a wharf, an official custom house, a flour mill, a warehouse, several stores, a school for children, and the first two-story wooden home. Most of those changes resulted from the business dealings of John Cooper and his half-brother, Thomas Larkin.

Being able to walk freely around Monterey was a big change because grizzlies were rare now. The cattle pastures and slaughter sites had been moved a greater distance from town, enticing bears to remain back in the hills, closer to those meals. After a walk toward the center of town on this warm and sunny winter afternoon after a cold night, Maria Ignacia saw Lalo heading to Cooper's office. She called to him, and they stood talking outside the door to the Larkin General Store.

Lalo said, "I shall be across the street, talking in the office with Mr. Cooper for a short time and making a few entries into the books. Can we meet later? I have some exciting news to share after my talk with Mr. Cooper."

"Of course, Lalo. I'm going in the store to visit with Rachel Larkin, since she works there on Thursday. Please come into the store to get me when you've finished with my Uncle Cooper. I'll be waiting to hear your exciting news."

They parted and Maria Ignacia turned the doorknob to the store, making the bell jingle. Barrels filled with door hinges, nails, and other metal items stood on the floor to her left. Across the back wall, bolts of fabric—cottons, linens, serge, and others—were stacked to the ceiling on rows and rows of shelves. Sacks of flour, both corn and wheat, were piled on the floor in a stack as tall as Maria Ignacia. Behind a wooden counter stood Rachel, wearing a tan work apron over her colorful blouse with tiny bright flowers. Their eyes met and they exchanged a pleasing nod while Rachel continued wrapping a customer's purchase in brown paper and tying it tightly with the string hanging from a spool hung from the ceiling. The string was thin, and she broke it easily after making a knot.

The customer departed with a nod for a greeting to Maria Ignacia as she walked past. At last, the two friends were alone in the store. Their friendship still was casual. Even though they had known each other for a few years, they had not shared deep feelings or problems. On this day, that would change.

"Oh, Rachel, where is little Thomas?"

Out peeked the three-year-old at the edge of the counter. "I here, Mia-naci," he said and scurried to hug her around her knees.

Rachel apologized, saying, "Thomas cannot say your Spanish name. For me, not only are many names too difficult to pronounce, but also, it's difficult to remember more than one name for one person, like yours. Maria Ignacia is impossible for him to say."

"I know, I know. I should take an English name as my Aunt Martha did. I love the name Martha and never liked her real name of Encamación. My grandmother chose such unusual names."

"No, no, don't change your name."

Because Rachel had lost two children—her first child, a girl before Thomas was born, and later, a baby boy who died last year at five months of age—Maria Ignacia was content that Rachel had a new, healthy baby boy and asked, "Oh, where is baby Frederick?"

"Sleeping upstairs like an angel."

The store was not busy; talk and laughter came easily while they jumped from one topic to another. Maria Ignacia and Rachel became friends after Rachel came to Monterey and married Thomas Larkin, in 1833. Back then, the two young women had decided to become more proficient in each other's language. If they met at *Casa Zemita*, they spoke Spanish; if they were at the Larkin's, which was a home with a store attached to it, they spoke English. Within these few years, they had grown comfortable speaking both languages.

Rachel commented, "Help me empty and stack this box of canned fish onto the shelves." While they unloaded cans, she continued talking about names. "Here is another aspect of Spanish I don't understand. When I asked you, what's the meaning of your aunt's name, you said that it doesn't mean anything. But in my dictionary *encamación* means to go in the right direction. So, why didn't you say that?"

Instead of replying, Maria Ignacia raised her black eyebrows and shrugged while holding cans in her uplifted hands. They laughed.

Rachel changed the subject to tortillas. "I followed the recipe you gave me, and I thought I made them well. But after John took one bite, he said he didn't like tortillas. Well, he said that, but when we go to dinner at your house, he eats many. I think I made them wrong."

"You should ask your maid to make them."

Rachel insisted, "No, I do the cooking. She does the cleaning and most other tasks. I want to cook. Well, I want to cook the chicken after she has killed and plucked it." They laughed again.

They continued to discuss trivialities until Lalo arrived to pick up Maria Ignacia.

Once outside and strolling toward *Casa Zemita*, Maria Ignacia noticed Lalo's face wore an extra-wide grin. For several minutes, they walked without conversation, until she could no longer restrain her curiosity. "Lalo, you were going to tell me something exciting after your meeting with my uncle. What is it?" The day was getting warmer, and she fluttered her skirts to make a little breeze to cool her legs.

He nodded, retaining his wide grin.

"Well?"

With his hands clasped behind his back, he stopped strolling and turned to face her. They were only a short distance from Larkin's Store and standing under a manzanita tree off to the side of the heavily traveled path. An oxcart rolled past until a wheel sank into a rut; the driver shouted profanities and flicked his tree branch at the head of the ox until the animal pulled the cart free.

Lalo watched.

A pod of pelicans in a V-formation flew over and turned, in perfect synchronization before heading the other way.

Lalo watched the birds and said nothing.

An old woman hustled past with a load enclosed in a faded cloth wrapped around her forehead and draped down her back.

Finally, Lalo turned to face Maria Ignacia, blurting, "They gave me a sizeable raise and an expansion of my duties!"

"Oh, Lalo, that is wonderful. How did it happen?"

"Yes, yes, I am so proud. You know that I work for both Mr. Larkin and Mr. Cooper. Well, you know they have many business dealings and are involved in shipping. They're always building something new, like the Larkin house. I imagine you've seen every room in Rachel's two-story house. Isn't it unusual? With so much happening, they need me for more bookkeeping and want me to write progress reports for their projects. You know, they want me to be more involved in everything and even to make trips."

"I only knew they owned the general store, a flour mill, and a lumber business. What else?"

He raised his fingers to count what he was to say. "Well, besides those three that you named, they are in control of Customs for all the ships, arriving and leaving. They buy and sell beaver and sea otter pelts. They have land and grow potatoes. They have too many enterprises to name, and they want me for all their dealings." He put his hands on his hips and made a little jump for joy. "I will have a healthy salary." His face glowed, and he bobbed his head as he, at last, said, "What I want to tell you is . . . " More pleasure spread across his face as he finished his sentence, "now I am able to have a wife and family."

Under the small manzanita, his bobbing head and the tree cast flickering shadows on the ground. Upon hearing his statement, she found herself transfixed by the intertwined and bobbing shadows, while trying to absorb his surprising declaration. Blinking, she slowly stood more erect and looked puzzled. She stuttered, not knowing what to ask. "Do you . . . I mean, do I . . . what I wonder is . . . " Stopping to gather her thoughts, she started again. "Lalo, do I know who she is? Have you kept your future wife a secret from me?"

Now it was he who was taken aback and looked puzzled. "Maria Ignacia, this is not the time to jest with me."

"I'm not . . . " With a look of shock, she guessed what he had meant; nevertheless, she hesitated to say it. *Surely, he is not thinking of me as his wife. No, he couldn't be.*

He stepped closer and took her hands in his. Looking embarrassed, he said, "I imagine that I am not doing this in the proper way. I should have chosen a special place and brought flowers to propose to you. I am so excited. I have wanted this day to come . . . "

She stepped back, yanking her hands from his. "Lalo, Lalo, no, stop talking. Let me get my breath."

They stood in silence staring at each other with wide eyes and furrowed brows.

She brushed away stray hairs from her cheek before speaking. "Lalo, how did this happen? I have never thought of you as my husband. I . . . "

His face shifted to anger.

She continued speaking. "Lalo, we are friends, but I never . . . "

Fury burned in his eyes as he interrupted, "Humph! Are you . . . " His voice changed in pitch. Reddish hives blossomed on his throat. "Are you saying that you never, ever wanted to marry me? Why did I think you did? I'll tell you!

Because you always let me touch your hands, and we always tell our deepest thoughts. Because you always spent time with me, pretending to want to learn bookkeeping. And because . . . " He began to lose his composure. He wiped the back of his hand across his dripping nose and turned from her to hide the tears. With his back to her, he could not conceal his crying; the movement of his shoulders betrayed him. Finally, he rubbed his eyes and inhaled deeply before he turned to face her; his face was full of wrath.

"Lalo, I . . . "

"Say no more. I understand. How could I be so blind! You and your family are *gente de razon*, unlike me. How could I have thought you would want to be my wife?" He backed away a couple of steps and gestured with his arm—a flourish at the length of her. "Look at you! Rich, and wanting for nothing." He jerked his head and pursed his lips with his last comment. "Ahem, I did not say that well. Not 'rich and wanting for nothing.' No, what I meant is that I am nothing and you are not wanting me." He ran a hand through his dark wavy hair. Beads of sweat had formed on his forehead, a scowl in his eyes.

He feigned a laugh. "Ha, why would I want to belong to your family! I wonder if you even know your family." He spit out his thoughts, "Of course you think you know your Uncle Mariano. Well, you do know that your uncle, Commandante General Mariano Guadalupe Vallejo, is the power over the free state of Alta California. He is our leader. A self-appointed leader, I should say. We are free from the tyranny of Spain now and have only the tyranny of your uncle. Do you know what he does? No, I think not. You do not know how he is overseeing the secularization of the missions. He gives a tidbit to the natives and takes large hunks of land for family, friends, and himself."

"Lalo, stop. You don't know what you are saying." A flush rose in her cheeks as she retorted, "Everyone respects my uncle. Maybe I should say they love him and know he's a good man. They . . . "

A cynical laugh escaped his frowning face. "Ho! Ha, ha, ha. You don't know. You really don't know your uncle. Why don't you ask him to tell you about leading the troops against the rebellion led by the native called Estanislao."

Maria Ignacia ears tingled. She had heard someone mention that name a few years ago, when the family had been celebrating at *Casa Zemita*. *I remember Salvador asking Mariano about Estanislao. Mariano put him off and said he would tell the story later.*

Lalo abruptly turned and walked away. His shoulders shook in such a manner that she knew he was crying.

She called out to him, "Lalo, we will always be friends."

He stopped without turning. "I think not," he shouted then continued walking toward his home. His words were correct. On this day their friendliness ended; no relationship would ever exist again, and her lessons on bookkeeping were over.

Three small children ran past, each shouting the greeting, "Hola."

She did not return the children's greeting and found that she could not move her feet to continue her way. Still staring at the retreating image of Lalo, her mind raced in confusion. She looked out at the bay where seagulls were flying—white movement against blue sky—and did not see them. A lump formed in the back of her throat, and her chest felt hollow. Salty saliva arose in her mouth; and, in a faraway manner, she heard her name being called.

There, a short distance away, stood Rachel outside the store with her child, calling, "Maria Ignacia! What's wrong? Maria Ignacia!"

Maria Ignacia was lightheaded. Taking a step backwards, she steadied herself with a hand on the manzanita tree; nevertheless, she slipped to the ground. Time seemed distorted because Rachel instantly was at her side.

Rachel lifted Maria Ignacia's arm around her shoulders and insisted, "We are going into my house. Help me get you there. Thomas, take her hand to help."

The child nodded, "I help Mia-naci."

A bed, sips of tea, and a nap did wonders. Upon waking, she could hear Rachel in the kitchen talking with her maid. Luscious smells from a roasting chicken drifted into the bedroom. She pushed back the covers and cautiously rose. As she entered the kitchen, she exclaimed, "I feel better. You have made me hungry with these delicious smells."

Rachel gushed, "Oh, you look much better. You have color in your cheeks again. Nevertheless, we should sit down." Locking elbows, she walked her friend to the doorway leading from the kitchen. "Now you are better, but I am suffering because you have not told me what happened." She grabbed two small dinner rolls from a serving tray and passed one to her friend. "Let's go to the parlor where we can talk in private." Briefly, she turned to the maid, "Anita, everything is ready for dinner. Let me know when Mr. Larkin arrives."

Between bites of the bread, Maria Ignacia told the details of her encounter with Lalo, and her spirits began to lift. "Thank you for listening. Sharing with you lessens my pain. Are you surprised about Lalo's proposal as much as I was?"

"Yes and no. You must admit it makes sense that Lalo wanted you for his wife." Rachel hesitated before saying, "Nevertheless, I think it rather strange that he never hinted about his feelings toward you."

Maria Ignacia stood and began to pace. "You are correct to say that he never hinted. I cannot think of any moment when he hinted that he wanted to marry me. Oh, Rachel, my grandmother has wanted me to marry for years. She's upset that I don't have a beau. For years and almost daily, Lita has talked about my need to marry. Just last week, she said, 'Our cousin has a young man visiting from Santa Barbara and he would be a wonderful husband.' Or she tells me about young people meeting for a party at the Presidio. She is always saying, 'I want you to go and meet new men.' But to marry now would mean I must throw my dreams into the ocean."

"What are your dreams?"

Beside a small table, standing between two large windows, she sat on the parlor chair. The parlor was a pleasant room with the late afternoon sun pouring in the windows before it dropped behind the Pacific Ocean. Lovely oil paintings with elaborate gilt frames hung opposite the windows. On the small table, a cut-glass vase held a variety of last summer's dried flowers.

Maria Ignacia scooted back in the parlor chair and began to share her innermost dreams. "I want to marry a man that is unlike anyone living here. I want to marry a man I love, not someone whom my grandmother or father thinks best. I want to live somewhere else. When my uncle takes me to the Mission San Francisco Solano, I love seeing a different place." She turned and took Rachel's hands in hers. "What is most important to me is, I want to marry for love. He must love me as much as I do him."

They sat quietly for a moment before Rachel said, "I understand. You described what I have. I love Thomas more than you can imagine. And he loves me."

"Oh, how delightful it is to hear you say that. I noticed how you and he look at each other when you think no one is watching. I also see what I might call respect for each other. Then again, I wonder, is that how love looks?"

Blushing, Rachel replied, "I don't know how we look to others, but I know respect is part of loving another. Oh, Maria Ignacia, I love him more than I can find words to say. And my love grows with each day, each month, each year."

A maid entered with a tray. Though they spoke in English and knew the maid did not understand, they sat in silence. Cups and saucers rattled, a sugar bowl and spoons were placed in front of them, and the tea was poured. After the maid disappeared, the tea was not touched. They had only a thirst for conversation.

Their friendship would grow deeper on this day. Maria Ignacia's upsetting experience opened a door toward trust. Rachel had a secret with ambivalent emotions attached to it, and, at this moment, Rachel would push that door wide as her secret tale unfolded.

"I have never told anyone about falling in love with Thomas. Because of my happiness, I would like to scream my story from the mountaintops, but I am going to find it difficult even to whisper it to you. When you hear, you will understand; you must keep it in confidence."

Maria Ignacia nodded.

Rachel inhaled deeply and scooted her chair closer to her friend. "Please say nothing until I finish.

"To start my story, I want you to know that my child who died back in 1833 was Thomas' child, not my husband's. I know I am starting in the middle of the story about our love, but I wanted to confess … No, I am not confessing. I am telling the facts." Rachel's hands trembled on the cloth near her teacup. She slipped them into her lap. "As you probably know, Thomas and I came on the same ship from the East, and we docked in the harbor of Yerba Buena. Oh, what a miserable place! I saw nothing much there among the sand hills, except a little trading post for the Hudson's Bay Company and a hut that was a tavern, offering meals yet, that day, they had no food, so we left. We knew before we arrived here that I carried his child. The whole voyage had taken seven months.

"Before I had started the voyage, my husband had written to me and said I was to meet him in Santa Barbara. He was going to be returning from a sailing trip and would meet me. I had not seen him in more than a year. So, if you are wondering if the child could have been his, it could not. Of course, you can surmise my dilemma. Thomas and I had discussed all possibilities before we arrived here and thought it best that I go immediately to Santa Barbara to have the child. We knew we could not be in the same place and not see each other because we were too much in love. The gossip, if people guessed the child was his, could destroy his business opportunities and, besides, we could not marry. I was already married.

"You may be thinking that it was cruel to leave me to face my husband alone about a child who was not his. That was part of the plan: I was never going to tell my husband who the father was. Also, I want to emphasize that you must not think whether I was willing or unwilling to go to Santa Barbara alone. We made a decision that I was to go because fewer people would be affected and hurt." Rachel put her hands over her face and cried.

Maria Ignacia patted her friend's knees, wanting to comfort, but did not speak. She had been asked not to speak.

Rachel reached for a napkin to dab her face. A moment passed before she looked up. "I know I am shocking you, and I suspect you think me a sinful woman."

When Maria Ignacia leaned closer and opened her mouth, Rachel put her finger to her lips and shook her head. "No, please say nothing until I finish."

Maria Ignacia nodded and placed her hand on the hands of her friend.

"My love for Thomas has changed everything, not only my life and its direction, but also my thinking. Before I met Thomas and fell in love, I did not think; I did not search for truth. I hope you will find love as I have, because only then will you understand what I am going to say."

Again, a quiet moment passed before she declared, "My love cannot be a sin. That is impossible. This love is what everyone should have in their life. A wonder beyond description. We care and trust, we are kind and thoughtful, and we fill each other with happiness and contentment. In turn, those around us seem to share in our love. I can't believe anything this wonderful can be wrong. This love made me realize that religions are wrong to condemn someone for exercising their love. The Ohlones have always known this, as I am sure all native peoples do. Love is to give freely. Who decided it was a sin? MEN. Men who claim they know what God wants and thinks. How egotistical. How can a man know what God sees as right? Men invented religions and decided the rules. Men made the rules and lied by saying that God told them."

Now, Rachel reached for her cold tea and took a drink. She dabbed her forehead with the napkin. "Well, I wanted to tell you my love story. You probably hate me now. I surely went . . . "

Maria Ignacia interrupted to say, "Let me speak and tell you that I do not think you are horrid nor sinful. I do not judge you. I love you as my friend and accept you. Hmm, I have never taken the time even to think about what you said about religion. I will later. We Catholics learn everything by rote and are taught not to think. Nevertheless, I am going to think about your words." She took a sip of tea, as well. "Sorry that I interrupted; please continue. I do want to know about you and Thomas."

Rachel bobbed her head. "Thank you for being my friend." Again, she reached for the napkin, "Forgive me, I do not have my handkerchief." She blew her nose, and they giggled.

"To end the first part of the story, which I think you may know, I learned that my husband had died at sea." She wrung her hands and shook her head. "However, I do not and did not take that as a sign of approval from God. No, I feel God puts us on earth and we are free to make our lives. What did I feel when learning he was dead? I was relieved; mainly because this avoided a confrontation. I admit that I did not love my first husband, yet I didn't want to cause him harm. During our whole marriage, I rarely saw him. I did not know him well. Now that I know what love is, I know he did not love me, nor I him. He lived his life and died. I am living my life."

Maria Ignacia stood and insisted, "I must relieve myself."

Rachel laughed, "I need to, as well."

Upon returning to the parlor, Maria Ignacia asked, "Where's Thomas? Wasn't he supposed to be here for dinner?"

"This is normal because he has many businesses. He will be here when he is here. I want to finish the ship story and falling in love before he comes home."

When the blackened logs crumbled in the fireplace and made a noise, Maria Ignacia noticed that new logs had been placed there in their brief absence. With night coming, the room was dimmer and lamps had been lit, too. It was a comfortable room for talking. She liked the wooden floors. *Casa Zemita* had tile floors in most rooms with a few small rugs. She found Rachel's house to be warmer and more relaxing.

"We should sit on the sofa, closer to the fireplace." Rachel picked up a lap blanket from an arm of the sofa and, once they were settled, she draped it across their knees. "If I remember correctly, I noticed Thomas immediately on the first evening in the ship's dining room. You might say, he is so handsome, how could I not notice him? It was more than that. In my mind's eye, I can still see what I saw that first evening. His personality showed in his movements; and, although I was several tables away from him and could not hear the conversation, I saw how people reacted to what he said. It appeared he was humorous, because the people at his table would laugh frequently as he spoke. Everyone was animated and seemed interested. He did not dominate the topic—whatever it was—because everyone talked, the women as well as the men. I was impressed from afar.

"Days passed before we were close enough to introduce ourselves to each other. Oh, what a day!" Rachel hugged herself and rocked with pleasure. "We were enjoying good weather—warm and sunny without wind—and experienced animal sightings in the water of new and different creatures who seemed to have no fear of us. Sweet animals, with a little snout and silky bodies, swam alongside the ship. I was watching them. I forget what they are called. I do remember that someone said they are mammals and suckle their young like us." Rachel scooted around on the sofa to face Maria Ignacia more directly. "Thomas came up to the railing next to me to watch them, and my hat flew from my head into his face. It was such an amusing situation. We both laughed and laughed.

"This is the important part. When he handed me my hat, our hands brushed. Oh my, Maria Ignacia, how can I find words to tell you what happened in that instance. I already felt I knew him, because for a week I had watched him during dinner. He seemed to be a marvelous person. I know the word in Spanish to describe him. He is *simpatico*. You know, special, likable, congenial, friendly, and—I was to learn—intelligent. After that day at the railing, he arranged to have me join his dinner table for the evening meals for the rest of the voyage. It changed the whole trip. I so enjoyed being among those people I had watched."

Rachel appeared to drift back into a pleasant memory before continuing her story. "Their conversations were sometimes trivial, but at other times, deep and educational. Thomas would often start the topics. We spoke about books, politics . . . Oh, he was knowledgeable about the countries we were passing. When I asked how it was that he knew so much, he nonchalantly told me that he studied a long time before leaving on this voyage. Well, I was impressed, yet that is not what made me love him. I loved him from first seeing him. His touch added to the love I felt. When he touched my hand, while returning my hat, I had the most profound desire for him. Desire gushed in my body. My feelings were sensuous and would not go away." She stopped talking again and put her hands to her chest. Her memory of the whole encounter was reflected in her face. "Not that I wanted my yen for him to disappear. For the rest of the voyage and upon waking every day, I lived to feel the pleasure of my desire."

A gust of night air flew into the parlor with the opening of the front door. Thomas called out, "I'm here and hungry." He appeared in the doorway and apologized, "Oh, hello, Maria Ignacia. Excuse my shouting." He came forward and kissed her cheeks before removing his coat. "What a wonderful surprise to find you here. I may be hungry for food, but I am also hungry for conversation with my wife's friend. I am glad you are here." He returned to a rack by the front door to hang his coat and scarf, never stopping his talking. "So, have the two of you had a good afternoon? I hope you had an enjoyable talk."

Rachel stood and kissed him with a slight brush to his lips, "We had the best conversation. Now let us eat. Maria Ignacia do not even try to decline. We will not let you."

In a few weeks, Lalo returned from his business trip in San Diego. He arrived with a bride.

Maria Ignacia learned of the marriage through Rachel, who said, "Lalo is married! He came home from his travels with a wife. Isn't that wonderful?"

"Oh, yes! I am truly pleased." Maria Ignacia added, "I imagine we do not know her. I'm guessing she's from San Diego."

Without a doubt she was happy for them and relieved for herself. Monterey was a small place, and sooner or later she and Lalo would have been in the same place at the same time. She sighed and said, "I worried that Lalo would propose again. Now, I know he can't."

When her bookkeeping lessons had stopped, she had extra time and started reading more books from her uncle's library. When he had suggested she do that years ago, she had only read a few of his books, but now she was reading constantly. She decided always to have a book to read. When she finished one, she perused his collection, found another, and started carrying one or two books with her in a book sack that fitted over her shoulder.

She also started walking regularly on the beach with Julia again, or alone when Julia's chores were too many. The weather was of no concern: Rainy, stormy, cold, warm, sunny, or whatever. If she had planned to go, she went. During a walk with Julia, she talked about Lalo's proposal.

Julia said, "I am not surprised that he asked, only surprised that you did not realize he would."

"Oh, Julia, I never, ever had that thought. Lalo and I are . . . I mean, we had a good relationship. He said he no longer is my friend. How can that change from one day to the next?" She sighed again. "I was fortunate that I am friends with Rachel. I felt sick after that horrible scene with him, and she helped me." Remembering that she was trying to think less about herself and more about others, Maria Ignacia asked, "Julia, do you have friends?"

"Only the other maids."

Maria Ignacia found that answer upsetting and could think of nothing to say. *We did this to Julia. She is not free to befriend just anyone.*

While walking on the beach, they were quite a distance from *Casa Zemita* and far from the family's scrutiny, as well as, away from the criticism of her Lita. So, they could speak more easily, nevertheless, Lita had presented Maria Ignacia with a new problem, a problem she could not discuss with Julia.

Maria Ignacia recalled the encounter with her grandmother when Lita had said, "I must emphasize that you should not have a close relationship with a maid. I know you became closer to Julia because your mother died, but now you must distance yourself from her." Lita threw up her hands in disgust. "SHE IS A MAID."

Maria Ignacia had listened with an expressionless face, not wanting to be disrespectful. That is, except in her thoughts. *Lita, you can't tell me what to do. I am twenty years old, and I want to make my own decisions.* And she knew that her actions might cause Lita to retaliate against Julia.

At the end of her walk on the beach, Maria Ignacia decided that she could never end her closeness with Julia.

Also, in her new activities, she often visited with her Aunt Martha, who was Mrs. Cooper to everyone in Monterey. Martha and Rachel each had a three-year-old child, and Maria Ignacia enjoyed being with the children.

On one warm day, while the three women were enjoying their conversation, the children played nearby. Being twenty years old, Maria Ignacia realized that, since she was an adult, the difference in ages did not matter, though her Aunt Martha and Rachel were about seven years older.

The three woman and the two children had finished an afternoon meal on a blanket in the grasses outside Rachel's house. Maria Ignacia asked, "My Uncle Mariano and Aunt Francisca had another child on January third; have you seen little Adelayda?"

"No, I haven't," Rachel said.

Martha hadn't either.

Maria Ignacia told them, "She is at *Casa Zemita* right now. Please come see the new baby. My Uncle Mariano and Francisca have built a two-story adobe in Sonoma that's well protected because of all the soldiers. Even so, living with the unsettled natives and grizzlies is dangerous, so she's happier to be here with family now.

Rachel asked, "Am I correct, this is her third child?"

"No, this is their fourth." Maria Ignacia hesitated to explain for it was a delicate fact but decided to keep talking. "Rachel, their first child died before he was a year old. It happened about the same time your child died. His name was Andronico Antonio; he was only ten months old."

Rachel gasped, "Oh, I didn't know. I was so distraught with the loss of my own... but wait. I know little Andronico. He plays with my child. How...?"

Maria Ignacia touched Rachel's forearm and said, "They gave their second child the same name. He was born only three months after the death of their first." She tipped her head to the side while her eyes began to puddle, before saying, "Everyone copes with life differently. I am sure my *Tio* and *Tia* wanted to feel as if they had their first son returned to them. And, unlike the first boy, he is healthy and should live to an old age."

One evening, Mariano, his youngest brother, and Maria Ignacia had not yet retired for the night and sat in the dining room in *Casa Zemita*.

"Maria Ignacia," said Mariano from his chair at the dining table, "do you have any idea how remarkable you have become?" He had arrived late, and the maids had prepared a plate for him.

"*Tio, en el nombre de Dios!* In the name of God why do you say that?" She sat curled in one of the bamboo chairs made in the Sandwich Islands which was full of pillows covered in bright fabrics with flower designs. "Please don't spoil me with flattery."

"Look and listen to her," Mariano said. "Not only do you appear more beautiful with each day, but also you are reading incessantly. When I was last here, I saw you with a different book, and I believe you said it was by an American woman and about the southern United States."

"Yes, it was entitled *Appeal to the Christian Women of the South*. Now I am reading essays by another American woman." She tilted the book to read the author's name on the spine and said, "Elizabeth Margaret Chandler."

Her younger uncle asked, "Why do you read American authors?"

She uncurled her legs and sat properly in the chair before answering. "These are books from your library," and she pointed with the book to Mariano. "Many years ago, you suggested I read more books, and now I do. And reading English helps me with my English. Oh, I wanted to ask why you have books written by Americans and especially why American woman?"

Mariano replied, "People arrive on ships with many books. And I meet most foreigners who come here. Because the voyage from the East takes months, they bring many books, read them, and discard them to me." He gave a chuckle, "I do usually read them, though in a quick manner if I do not find them of value. Why are you reading them, Maria Ignacia?"

"I told you, At first, I wanted to improve my English. Now the reason has evolved: Rachel Larkin is my friend, and I want to understand American women better. Also, Rachel cannot read Spanish too well, so I pick ones in English. In that way, she and I can read the same book and discuss it. I enjoy doing that." Looking at her younger uncle she said, "However, I do not read only the American authors. I have been reading other books. *Tio*, remember you suggested I read the books about plants? I did, and I keep them in my room."

The younger brother asked Mariano, "What books do you like?"

Mariano shifted his weight in the chair by turning to face the others; his thirty-year-old face displayed a double chin. "You would not remember, because it was fifteen years ago when your cousin Juan B. Alvarado and I went to be trained by Governor Pablo Vicente de Solá." He stood and picked up a burning candlestick and walked to light another over the adobe fireplace. Unlike in the Larkin home, there were no expensive glassware items displayed, no vases from Europe, no furniture made from fine wood, and no oil paintings. The tall brass candlesticks from Spain were one of the quality items in their home, the ivory giraffe another. *Casa Zemita* had what people referred to as gaudy furniture from the Sandwich Islands; and, because adobes were cold, with walls that never absorbed heat, colorful woolen rugs hung on the walls to make the room warmer.

He returned to his seat and leaned his forearms on the table. The other two waited patiently for him to continue.

"Do you know who Governor Pablo Vicente de Solá is?"

His younger brother shrugged and shook his head.

Maria Ignacia nodded and explained, "He was the man in charge of the Monterey Fort when the Pirate Bouchard came."

"I am impressed that you know that. Solá chose me to be trained in his household, because during that pirate attack, I returned to retrieve little Maria Ignacia, who had been left behind. He was impressed by that. My cousin, Juan B Alvarado, as you know, grew up in my house. We were like brothers and almost the same age. Solá was a mentor to us. During those years when Governor Solá gave us special instruction, he gave us access to his personal library, which had newspapers from Mexico City and government documents, besides hundreds of books. He arranged for teachers to train us in English, French, and Latin.

Solá referred to us as his Triumvirate and was proud of us. Three smart young men: Your cousin Juan Bautista Alvarado, Jose Castro, and me.

"Now, to answer your question about what I enjoy reading. Everything! Governor Solá's library had everything. However, my heart and mind were most impressed with Greek and Roman literature and history. History has allowed me to learn the highest form of reason, not only to possess truth but also to gain power. I often think just like the leaders from the past when I remember the phrase, 'Divide and Conquer.'" He reached for his wine glass and drained it. "You must excuse me; I smell beef cooking outside. It has reminded me that a few of my men are coming to have a small *asado*. They will arrive soon. I must leave and see if all is ready. *Buenas noches.*"

"Oh," Maria Ignacia blurted a request, "please save a piece of the *asado* meat for me for tomorrow."

Going their separate ways, the three left the room.

Maria Ignacia went to prepare for bed. Her younger sister was soundly asleep in their bedroom when she arrived. With the meat grilling outside, not far from her open window, the room smelled of cooking beef and goat. It smelled delicious. She hoped her *Tio* would remember to save a piece for her. After she washed from the basin, she blew out the candles on her dresser and gave her sister a loving glance. *She's just like me when I was young. My sister wants the candles glowing at bedtime. Julia always remembers to light them for her.*

Masculine voices began to drift through the shutters as she slipped into her bed and stretched under the cool sheets. Yet, she found she could not sleep because she strained to understand the conversations that were beginning outside. Her sister's bed was closer to the window, so Maria Ignacia slipped into that bed, being careful not to disturb the sleeping girl.

Men seem to love asados. I wonder what excites them about an asado? Of course, there's the abundance of cooked meat and lots of red wine, but I think men love asados for other reasons. Possibly the camaraderie! Or maybe the freedom away from women. Ha, no wives to contradict or criticize them. No, she pursed her lips and frowned while searching for the real reason. *It must be all the stories and bragging they do.*

She heard her uncle's voice clearly now.

"Of course, I like the Americans. They are what we need here. They are industrious. Look at Larkin. He has been here only for four years, and he is a rich man. He's involved with all kinds of businesses. Why don't we Californios do that?" When Mariano finished that sentence, a flurry of disagreements arose among the men. Not that she could discern the exact words with so many talking at once; it was in the tone of their voices that she heard complaining.

Mariano started talking again, "Hey, stab me a crisp piece of that beef, not goat. Pepe chose a tender cut especially for us tonight and cooked it to perfection. Thank you, Pepe."

My Tio must be the closest to my window. I hear him like he is in this room. She heard the clanking of many glasses while they toasted and thanked Pepe.

Her uncle started again. "No, we are not as industrious as these Americans. We have been here for decades and still have no agriculture of any size. Look at George Yount. We granted him land, and he turned it into a productive ranch." He burst with laughter and said, "Ha, ha! I should say that we granted land insisting on many conditions. This happened in February of thirty-six. Only last year! If he wanted to keep his two square leagues of *Rancho Caymus*, he was given a list to complete: To build a house and corral; stock his land with at least one hundred animals, both horses and cattle and . . . " Loud guffaws erupted from Mariano before he continued with his thoughts. "Ho, ho, ho! The last condition was the hardest for him. He's a Protestant, though a not-very-devout Protestant, and he had to convert to Catholicism to become a naturalized Mexican citizen. Well, he did it." Mariano laughed more. "Ha! He did all of it, even replaced his log cabin with a proper adobe home; and he had accumulated one hundred seventy animals by the time he became a Mexican."

Someone asked, "Did I hear correctly that he has a young daughter who is a native?"

Before responding, Mariano called out, "Pepe, pour us all more wine. Oh, and pass the plate of meat." He gulped the last bit of wine in his glass and cleared his throat. "What did you ask? Oh, yes, about Yount's daughter. She isn't his actual daughter. He found the girl alone in her native village and nearly dead from hunger, after all her people died in thirty-three from malaria. He couldn't find any natives who wanted her, so he adopted her. He figures she's seven or eight years old now." Mariano began to chew more meat and spoke with his mouth full. "I tell you. He is one tough *hombre*, but also, *simpatico*."

Someone commented, "But you are generalizing about Americans. You told only three examples: Cooper, Larkin, and Yount. Not all Americans are industrious and hard workers. As you must know, many are drunkards. In general, I find them brusque and rude."

Mariano was ready to defend his opinion. He drained another glass and said, "I believe I have met more Americans than you. I know their character.

Therefore, I can assure you that having Americans settle here will be a benefit to us. I sincerely don't want the Russians to take over our land and, if we befriend and make opportunities for Americans, they will help us keep the Russians away. We can entice them by awarding land to settle and raise a family."

Another man spoke up. "Ah, I see your ulterior motive. What about the foreigners from England?"

"No, no, no. They have all these titles and often are snobbish with their status. The Americans aren't that way. They're dedicated to making a better life through hard work."

Someone else suggested, "What proof have you of that?"

Mariano asked, "Anyone know the American Ewing Young?"

A few men affirmed with "yes," and others said, "of course."

Mariano explained, "He was here these past few months. I have been doing business with him. And this was not the first time. In 1835, he came here to buy horses from us and took them back overland to Oregon Country. He told me that the Americans are starting farms in Oregon without any natives to do the work. I liked the sound of that. On this trip, he came and bought eight hundred head of cattle to take back to Oregon. Before he took those cattle back, no settlers in Oregon owned a cow. They rented cows from the British to have milk and cheese. What a despicable situation!" He sat shaking his head and gulped the rest of his wine before continuing his line of thought. "This Ewing Young paid well for the horses and now the cattle. Just having the foresight to know he could herd that many animals from here to there showed me an industrious person. He had about ten other hard-working Americans to assist with the trip with horses and cattle."

Cheers interrupted the conversation and the men shouted, "Juan Bautista Alvarado is here!" After a lot of noisy chatter, she heard Juan B speaking.

He said, "I work hard! Did I hear you say otherwise, Mariano? Hey, I need a glass of wine before I take on Mariano. Stab me a piece of meat, too!"

Maria Ignacia heard a lot of the men shouting and teasing her uncle who laughed off all the comments. She turned in her bed, not disturbing her sister, and grinned. She was enjoying listening.

"Juan B, you are an exception to the rule. Yes, you do work hard." Then Mariano shouted, "Who knows my cousin's accomplishments?"

An outburst of answers filled the cooling night air: "Juan B is leader of men." "A fine horseman." "Good shot." And, after they made some references to women, Juan B raised his glass and drank.

A wind had come in from the bay and was swaying the bushes in the area. The men didn't seem to notice the cold, for no one commented. Maria Ignacia covered herself with the extra woolen blanket from the foot of the bed and saw a shadow of her Uncle Mariano appear on the bedroom wall through the slatted shutters; it wriggled from the candlelight.

Mariano had climbed onto a table, creating a clatter by overturning wine glasses. He raised his arm and began to praise his cousin. "Listen to me. Juan B was only twenty-seven years old when he accomplished the coup that gave Mexico our true independence from Spain. He has a courage that no other *Californio* has. Not even I could have done what he did. He is truly a hard worker."

"Yes, I remember! Last year in December," someone added in a loud voice.

Another man spoke up. "First we should talk about November of 1836. That's when you, our own Mariano Guadalupe Vallejo, were named Commandante General to the free state of Alta California."

The men cheered.

Mariano added, "Don't forget Juan B became governor."

More cheers and clinking of glasses.

Juan B added, "All of you make it sound easy. After I led that coup and had titles bestowed to us, I went south to negotiate with Mexico City to confirm our positions. It took me four months. It was hard work, Mariano. We *Californios* work hard."

"Hey, you are forgetting to mention me," Salvador explained, " I may only be Mariano's younger brother to you, but I was made Captain of Militia in Sonoma in 1836. Remember?"

Oh, Salvador is the same as when we were young. Maria Ignacia recalled how he was constantly trying to be as important as Mariano. *I have such fond memories of Salvador and me pretending in childhood games.* She shook her head as she listened to the commotion through the window slats. The men were well on the way to being drunk. Slurred words mixed with laughter; boisterous comments accompanied the sound of falling tables and chairs.

Mariano's voice boomed above all other chatter as he bragged, "Our family has been here since 1774, when my father, Ignacio Vicente Ferrer Vallejo, arrived in San Diego. He was friends with Junipero Serra." Mariano began to laugh, "He was friendly with a lot of native women, too. I have a lot of brothers I do not know."

One of the drunkards asked, "Are you saying your father was pro . . . I mean promis..."

Someone else finished the sentence, "Promiscuous with the natives!"

Juan B spoke up again, "Now, now. Let him who has not been promiscuous with the native ladies throw the first stone."

Mariano's laugh became a lengthy guffaw before he could speak again and tell of his escapades. "Ho, ho, ho! I know I have three others, at least."

"Three other... What?" One of the drunks asked.

"Children, Stupid. He means three illegitimate children." Laughter filled the air.

The gibbous moon appeared momentarily and disappeared as storm clouds rolled over, and the wind started to gust. Smoke from the fire in the grill filled the air, and the men began to cough. One could taste the coming rain. Large droplets began to fall, and Mariano insisted, "Let's go inside. Everyone, grab your wine glasses and plate! Pepe, bring the meat. This beef is too delicious to let it soak in rainwater."

Maria Ignacia's bedroom filled with smoke. She rose and opened her bedroom door to get a cross breeze. *This should clear the air. I hope I can clear my mind. Men can say disgusting things.* She decided to climb into her own bed. She fell asleep as the rain began.

Later, she awoke to the smell of petrichor and could hear the men in the dining room. *Hmm, they are making a whole night of this as they usually do. I wonder what they are discussing now.* In a surreptitious manner, she crept down the back hallway and slipped to the floor below the serving-window to the dining room. This back hallway was how the maids moved through *Casa Zemita* without bothering the *gente de razon*, and the open serving-window was used both to pass food from the kitchen into the dining room and to return the dirty dishes back to the kitchen. From her hiding place, she laid her blue blanket on the tiles, sat on it, and wrapped the edges around her legs to keep warm. She heard one of the men yawn loudly.

Juan B said, "None of that yawning. The night is still young for us *Californios*. How can we sleep when there's still wine? We work hard and play hard."

Salvador insisted, "Why return to that topic! I want to hear about the fight with Estanislao. Remember, I asked to hear it years ago, Mariano; you never told the story."

Mariano ignored Salvador's request and addressed Juan B by saying, "Work hard, play hard, and fight hard. Don't get me wrong, Juan B, I know we do that. Before you arrived, I was talking about how industrious the Americans are in business. Someone changed my point. I never said anything about us not working hard."

Juan B huffed, "Good to know that. I thought possibly your mind was growing weak in your old age."

Without a hesitation, Mariano whipped back his words, "Yes, never forget that I am the older . . . as well as your superior."

Not one to be intimidated, Juan B laughed and said, "Ha, you cannot cow me. You have lived four years more than I and that means nothing. Do you forget that I put you in the position of my superior after the coup." A lengthy lull allowed for a coyote howl to be heard before Juan B spoke again. "Pepe, I need my glass filled!"

Maria Ignacia could feel the tension coming from the room. She recognized the three voices she heard, though other men snoring made hearing difficult.

Mariano shouted, "NO! Pepe, you can leave for the night after removing all the wine. I'm not so drunk to know the morning is here. YOU, Juan B. Alvarado, are a drunkard and . . . "

As Pepe started to leave, a scuffle began. Juan B went for Mariano, and wooden chairs crashed to the floor. Maria Ignacia peeked through the serving window from the shadows to see Pepe and Salvador rush to grab Juan B's arms before he hit Mariano, who was sprawled on the floor. Juan B straddling him. She saw two other men sleeping slouched on the soft-pillowed chairs in the distant living room. They slept and snored through the fighting. Another man stood watching without expression.

Mariano spit accusing words at his attacker. "Look at you! A real man knows when to stop drinking. Not you! I heard that you proposed to Raimunda Castillo, your mistress, and she refused because you are drunk most of the time." Mariano rolled onto his side and struggled to stand. "You have two small daughters and show no responsibility."

Juan B pulled away. "Leave my little girls out of this," and kicked Mariano while taunting him. "Look at you! Old and fat! You eat too much. Don't tell ME how to live."

Salvador shouted, "Stop all this. Calm down!"

The other two grabbed Juan B again and pushed him onto the couch as he vomited on the floral fabric.

Salvador grimaced, "Call a maid to clean this."

Finally, Mariano stood. The scuffle had sobered him a bit. First, he agreed with Salvador and said, "Yes, we are ending this topic and going to the other room. I will tell the tale of Estanislao for Salvador." He assigned a task to everyone. "Oh, Pepe, find a maid to clean up this mess and make coffee for us." Pointing to another man, he commanded, "You, put more firewood in the fireplace. Juan B, let me lean on you," he said while doing the opposite. He grabbed Juan B's hand to pull him to standing while wrapping the arm around his shoulder. "You're a part of this story, and I can't tell it without you. Come, let's move over here."

When they moved closer to the fireplace in the living room, they disappeared from her sight. Maria Ignacia thought, *my Tio Mariano knows how to handle delicate situations, knows how to calm anger in others, and knows how to lead his men.* However, she had another thought. *Or did I witness just how close we are as a family? He would not have ignored Juan B's abusive language and kicking if he had not been a cousin who was raised with him.* She slipped through the back hallway again to be closer to the living room.

"Estanislao is tall—taller than Juan B or me—and his skin is light," Mariano began. "Did you notice I said the word 'is' ... because he still lives."

Juan B added slowly in slurred words, "Estaniss ... lao is smart and han ... sum, I mean handsome."

Mariano added, "Though born a native from one of the many tribes on the banks of a northern river once called the Laquisimas River, he learned to read and write."

Juan B quipped with slurred speech, "His mis ... mis ... take was ... he tried to be Robin Hood."

Mariano laughed at that last comment before he spoke again. "He and his family journeyed to the Mission in San Jose in search of a better life in 1821. He was in his early twenties at the time, and the Franciscans baptized him with the name, Estanislao, after St. Stanislaus. He learned everything quickly, seeming to absorb all knowledge. He speaks Spanish well and stood out as a leader among the other natives, whether Miwoks, Yokuts, or others. He stood out because of his skin color, height, and intelligence, as well as his strength. He has powerful muscles like a horse."

The coffee arrived. When they began talking again, Maria Ignacia was straining to stay awake to hear the story being told.

"Hmm, give me a moment to remember the years," he said, "ah, yes, it was between the years 1821 and 1827, at Mission Santa Clara in San Jose. Estanislao learned battle techniques—digging trenches, hand-to-hand combat, climbing palisades, combat on horses, and use of firearms—from the Mexican soldiers who trained him to be a part of the mission military.

Maria Ignacia's eyes closed, and she began to drift into sleep. The story became dreamlike with her uncle's voice:

> *Unknown to the military in charge, many native soldiers were becoming Estanislao's followers, and before long he had as many as four hundred. By 1827, Estanislao and his followers would secretly run surprise raids on the Mission Santa Clara, Mission Santa Cruz, and various ranchos. Estanislao had trained his men never to take a person's life, only possessions. He was taking from those who had and giving to those who had nothing. After a raid, sometimes he would leave his mark by carving an S with his sword on a door of the raided home.*
>
> *Other tribes joined him: The Chumash Natives, the Miwoks, and the Yokuts. We estimated that he had four thousand followers at the height of his pillaging. Finally, the Franciscan friars and the Mexican settlers pleaded for the Mexican army to help them.*
>
> *The first three expeditions by the military failed to capture or stop Estanislao. Those attempts seemed to be a game to Estanislao, who would overpower and insult the Mexican troops. They robbed and destroyed structures but did not kill. Estanislao's plans for attacks often made the military look foolish, because he created schemes to surprise and ridicule the troops.*
>
> *After the first three attempts by the military to stop Estanislao, in the spring of 1828, a second lieutenant was assigned the job and given a larger group of soldiers with whom to fight. It would no longer be a game. That second lieutenant was me, Mariano Guadalupe Vallejo, and my orders were to administer a total defeat to Estanislao and his army. I was to leave them completely crushed. I knew I could only accomplish that with brutality and deaths.*

Another man began to speak and interrupted Maria Ignacia's dreamlike state. She opened her eyes.

The man interjected the comment. "Because our Mariano Vallejo," and he extended his hand toward Mariano, "is such a superior soldier and studied the military tactics of the Romans, he used the technique of Divide and Conquer, for which he is known. Estanislao's men were from many tribes, so Vallejo worked to separate the tribes. He used any method necessary to turn one tribe at a time away from their support of Estanislao."

Vallejo said, "Yes, you are correct. By going directly to the village of one tribe and working with the leaders, often I could entice them with a promise of land. Ha! I was offering them their own land. At other times I offered cattle and other material goods. If my verbal negotiations did not *divide* that group, I had no other choice and would return with full force and *conquer* by destroying everyone in the village—every man, woman, and child. It became a bloody mess."

Maria Ignacia's eyes went wide with surprise. She was awake! She heard no shame or remorse in the brutality he described.

With the first light of day entering the windows of *Casa Zemita*, Mariano ended the story, saying, "In less than a year, I outmaneuvered Estanislao in bloody battles that were meant to crush the natives. By early 1829 it was over.

"Estanislao returned to his Mission in San Jose to ask the priests for forgiveness for his men and himself. Father Narciso Duran granted forgiveness in the name of the Catholic Church and petitioned for an official pardon from the Mexican government. It was granted.

"Here is the real end to the story. Even after Estanislao returned to the Mission Santa Clara in San Jose, a few native groups continued to raid and steal until they met an enemy so powerful, they could not win." Mariano stopped talking only long enough to add drama, and said, "Malaria! In 1833, malaria came to the valley and killed more than 20,000 natives."

One of the other men asked, "Did Estanislao die from malaria?"

"Oh, no, you must still be drunk. I already told you that he still lives. Not wanting the culture of the Yokut people to be forgotten, he teaches at the Mission in San Jose. He has been teaching the language, history, and ways of his people for over three years at the mission. I imagine he will live there until he dies." Mariano pushed back his chair and stood as a maid came in with a stack of firewood. "Come in, come in. We are going to bed."

Juan B was sleeping with his head on his arms, leaning on a side table.

Pointing to Juan B, Salvador asked, "What about him? Should we help him to bed?"

Mariano grunted and said as he walked from the room, "Humph, Salvador, *mi hermano*, you have much to learn. And to think that I actually made you

Captain of Militia in Sonoma last year." Mariano bumped against a door frame with his shoulder. "Oh, *maldito*!" He straightened his shirt and started walking again as he said, "We are not responsible for those who are snoring. Let's go to bed," looking over his shoulder at Salvador as he left the room. He retorted in a flippant manner, "We will leave Juan B as a problem for the maids to resolve."

Maria Ignacia thought, *He means a problem for our slaves, the maids, to resolve.* Not wanting to dwell on that line of thinking, she decided to dress and take a walk on the beach. *One can find many interesting items strewn on the beach after a storm.* After dressing, she walked down the back hall again to the kitchen to find Julia. *She may want to go with me.* Instead, she found Salvador nibbling on food from the *asado*.

"Maria Ignacia, good morning! Hmm, I find last night's meat even better the next day," he said with a handsome grin.

She greeted Salvador in a long hug and kisses to his cheeks before reaching for a piece of meat with crisp blackened edges and replying, "I agree." With a mouth full of beef, she invited him to the beach. "Why don't you come walk with me. If you are not too drunk, that is." She glanced to him with a teasing face. "You and I never have time together anymore. Well, not like when we were young." She hugged him again. "I know you are three years older than me, but we played together like we were the same age. My twenty-first birthday is at the end of the year. Only weeks away."

Taking a napkin, he piled more meat into it. "Let's go. I especially like the idea of a walk after a storm with a supply of delicious beef in hand. By the way, I am not drunk. I never allow myself to be a drunkard like them."

Teasing, she replied, "I like the idea of a walk with you whether there's a storm or not. And I would want to walk with you even without the meat. Mostly, I am glad you are not a drunkard."

Knowing the morning was windy and cold, they took extra clothing and left from the front door while making casual banter. In the courtyard, she stopped and blurted, "I thought you were drunk! I heard Mariano say so."

"How do you know what Mariano said?" An instant later, he surmised how she knew. "Oh, you were spying on us. Where were you hiding while you spied?"

"I was in the back hallway below the serving window to the dining room for most of the time." As they walked to the bay, she explained in detail. "Even when I was young, I always liked to overhear the adults' conversations while I hid. I admit that I could hear everything you men said last night before you came into the house, because you had your *asado* outside my bedroom window."

"No!" Salvador exaggerated his concern and said, "I should give you a spanking. Being the older, I need to teach you manners."

They were almost to the bay; she ran, while shouting, "Only if you can catch me!" The ends of her multicolored wool scarf came loose from around her neck and whirled into the air as her long legs loped down the beach.

He grabbed her scarf and quickly followed. Waves lapped gently on the shore. Sandpipers scurried back and forth, following the waves, and pecking in the sand. As Salvador chased, they saw a whimbrel, with its long-curved bill, fly up and away, before circling to land farther down the beach.

Maria Ignacia thought of herself as a bird in flight and held out her arms winglike while glancing over her shoulder to see how close her uncle was. When she turned back, she watched the wind whip a whirl of sand. As it came closer, she closed her eyes too late. Making an abrupt stop, she wailed, "Oh, Salvador, help me. I have sand in my eyes. It stings!"

In an instant, he was at her side and raised his poncho over his head while grabbing her at the waist and pulling her into the tented space. "I have a kerchief and will carefully wipe around your eye lids. Relax and let me do the work."

She giggled. "Salvador, my savior!"

She felt the wind stop blasting sand against her bare arms and said, "My eyes feel better. Thank you." Ducking out from the poncho, she opened her eyes, blinking over and over.

He flipped his poncho back onto his shoulders and asked, "Did I get all the grit out?"

"Yes, you did." She wound her scarf around her neck again as she gazed down the beach and saw something unusual. "Salvador, what is that? Look down the beach." Pointing, she grabbed his hand and pulled. They walked faster. "It's a strange bump!"

"Maybe it's a dead whale or . . . " he jumped at her and shouted, "a shark!"

Laughing, she pushed him away. "You can't scare me. If a shark is on the beach, why would I be frightened? It's dead. Oh, I know sometimes a dead whale comes to the beach, but that bump in the distance is too small."

They were getting closer to the mound. It moved. Legs stretched out from the bump. "Oh, look! Salvador, I see a person. Hurry!"

They found a man—a bloodied man, naked to the waist and shoeless. A thick wooden plank lay in the sand not far from him. With each beat of his heart, they could see more blood trickle from an open wound at his shoulder where a flap of skin had been ripped open.

The man coughed, forcing more blood to flow from the wound. Maria Ignacia dropped to her knees and tucked the flap of skin back into place. She removed her scarf and pressed it against the wound. He coughed again.

Salvador looked out at the bay searching for a ship. "Where did he come from?"

"What does it matter? We must help him!"

Salvador leaned down and gently turned the man onto his side. Water flowed from his mouth. "I must turn him more and push on his back. He must have a lot of water inside. Keep pressing to stop the bleeding." After water flowed from his mouth, they rolled him back again.

"Salvador, you can run faster than I can. Please go to the Presidio for help. We need a gurney to get him to the doctor at the fort. I'll continue to stop the bleeding. Oh, before you leave, please cover him with your poncho."

"Yes, of course. But I hate to leave you alone."

"Salvador, I walk here by myself all the time. Please go get help!"

Once alone, she took her handkerchief to wipe sand and little pieces of seaweed from his face. Small greenish plants were stuck in the stubble on his chin so, she bent closer and picked them out. The hair on his head, though wet, appeared brown and, unlike her straight black hair, had soft waves. She ran her fingers through it, pushing it back from his forehead, and saw a freckle on his left eyelid. Cautiously she touched it to make sure it was not more debris from the sea. The freckle pleased her. *He may not know he has that freckle. I am going to guess he never closed the left eye and looked at a mirror.* While making guesses, she guessed he was in his late twenties.

Unexpectedly, his eyelids opened, presenting eyes as blue as the sea! She jumped and softly gasped. His eyes closed as fast as they had opened. Her face flushed, and she wiped her blouse sleeve against her damp face. With her heart pounding, she began to talk to him in her thoughts. *My knees are aching from this rough sand. I think I will sit down. Oh, you're so cold. I should pull you onto my lap to warm you.*

She changed her mind about her lap and stretched long next to him, rolling under the poncho against the length of his body. *You are freezing.* She placed her head on his shoulder against the wound to continue the pressure while she rubbed his arms and chest with her hands. *This should warm you.*

Again, his eyes opened. This time she was inches from his face. This time his eyes did not close. *You may not know you have a freckle; however, I imagine that you know your eyes shine like the waters of the sea.* Looking at the blueness and feeling his heartbeat beneath her hands, she wondered, *did you hear my thoughts?*

Coughing, he struggled to mumble, "Are you real?" His voice was raspy but had the accent of an Englishman.

She didn't know what to say and only blinked.

A long moment passed with them staring into each other's eyes, until he spoke again, "A kiss will tell me." And he touched his mouth to hers.

Though the kiss was only a soft brush against her lips before he lost consciousness again, she tingled throughout her body. *What is happening to me?* With her fingertips, she touched her own lips. She could still feel his soft mouth on hers. Desire purled through her—a flush of fever and a gush of passion. *How can I feel this way about someone I do not know?*

Maria Antonia Juana Ignacia Guadalupe Soberanes Vallejo

Chapter Four

Life is Full of Surprises

End of 1837 through summer of 1838

During the following days, nothing was the same for Maria Ignacia. Thoughts of the man on the beach took her breath away; and she feared those thoughts were sinful. In her quandary, she went to confession and told the priest, "I think about him off and on all day. Is this a sin?"

"Tell me your thoughts, my child."

"I think about the softness of his brown hair and, unlike like my family's straight hair, his is wavy. I fret about his shoulder and hope it heals soon. I want to see his blues eyes again and the little freckle on his eyelid. I want to touch him to know he lives."

The priest almost chuckled at her innocence and assigned twenty Holy Marys for her to perform every day for a week.

Once home and after performing the first day of Holy Marys, she pulled her notebook from her dresser and sat at her small bedroom desk, which had a glass inkwell sunk into a small hole at the top. Reaching for her quill, she wondered if she was going to commit another sin. Not able to resist, she began a poem about his freckle:

> *Just a dot,*
> *A little spot,*
> *But, where and whose is what*
> *Makes that brownish fleck upon his eye,*
> *A mark upon my heart.*

On most days, since rescuing the man from the beach, she had gone to Rachel's home and shared her thoughts. Rachel felt amusement at what she heard and told her friend not to worry. "Maybe he is having similar thoughts and feelings about you."

"Oh, Rachel, how can he think about me? He saw me for only a few moments before he fainted again. He probably has no memory of me. Oh, I want to see his blue eyes again."

Rachel was dressing her little boy who said, "Mia-naci, no be sad. You see my blue eyes. See!" Pointing his little pudgy fingers to his eyes, he widened them.

Upon returning to *Casa Zemita,* Maria Ignacia entered the courtyard to find most of her family on the veranda, waiting for the meal to be served. She greeted everyone in the typical manner, with cheek brushes and kisses, before wandering into the kitchen to look for Julia. Of everyone in the house, only Julia knew about her infatuation. Everyone else only knew that she and Salvador had found a near-drowned man who was recovering at the infirmary in the Presidio.

Though the afternoon meal was about to be served, Julia was not in the kitchen. Two maids were carrying platters to the dining room, and another maid, who was mopping the floor, told her, "Julia is in your bedroom with your sister."

Walking down the back hallway from the kitchen to her room, she wondered why Julia was in her room at this time of day. No sooner was the bedroom door opened than Maria Ignacia learned her sister had become a woman. She saw Julia rinsing blood from a cotton undergarment. Without a mother, the two sisters still turned to Julia for motherly interactions. Within minutes, the three were involved in talk of menstruation.

The thirteen-year-old commented, "Yes, of course, I knew about this curse, but I never thought about all these bloody rags. Ugh, Julia, I would not like washing them. How do you do it?"

Julia chuckled and felt no reason to reply.

"Maria Ignacia, do you ever have an accident and bleed on your clothing?"

"Of course, that can happen. However, I am careful about folding the rags and placing them correctly. I have avoided any accident."

The girl buried her face into her pillow and screamed, "Eeeee!" Rolling over and pulling the pillow from her face, she said, "Oh, I am going to stay in bed all day when I have this curse."

The other two passed an amusing glance between them.

Julia finished, dried her hands, and said, "I must go help with the meal." As she headed to the door, she tousled the hair on the younger sister.

Maria Ignacia slipped onto the bed, rolled toward her sister, and gave her a long hug. "Let me braid your hair again before we eat. Look in the mirror. At this time of the month, your cheeks are rosier and lips redder. Enjoy that aspect of what you call a curse. With your hair fixed, you will look wonderful."

They stood at the mirror, talking while braiding, until they were called for the meal.

Later that evening, Julia and Maria Ignacia went to the vegetable garden to speak privately. With a basket hanging from the arms of each, they searched for ripe vegetables, gathering beans in long seedpods and squash, as they chatted.

Walking over to a bench next to the outdoor oven made of mud. Julia suggested, "Shall we sit for a while? I want to talk more." Raising her hands near the outdoor oven, she commented, "I guess the *horno* wasn't used today. There's no warmth coming from it." The days were getting cooler. "Any news about the health of the man you found on the beach? Oh, and did you speak to him today?"

Maria Ignacia answered, "Before my uncles left, they said he is mending well. Mariano and Salvador returned to the fort in Sonoma so, I can no longer ask them to tell me about him. They like him and say that he tells interesting stories. They find him to have a good sense of humor but could not give me any example of it."

"When you went to the Presidio, did he see you?"

Maria Ignacia shook her head. "I stood where I could see him, but he never looked my way." She sighed, "You know that I cannot speak with him until we are properly introduced. And I don't know how that will ever happen."

Julia agreed that was a problem. They sat without words for a while until Julia said, "I want to tell you something that happened to me last week. I have been waiting for the right moment to tell you."

Maria Ignacia nodded and, after setting her basket on the ground, turned to face Julia. "Oh, please tell me."

Swallowing and taking a deep breath, Julia put her basket down, too, and clasped her hands in her lap. "You and I have been walking on the beach more often; however, when you could not go last week, I went alone and walked to the north." Her eyes were shining with the next words. "I met an older woman whom I have never seen before."

Clouds rolled over them, and it was getting darker by the minute in the short winter day though a little light from a candle came from a bedroom window. On this back side of *Casa Zemita* and in the late afternoon, it was noiseless. Bats started darting in the air and the smell of smoke from the living room fireplace drifted past.

"Do I know her?"

Shaking her head, Julia, explained, "You could not. She is an Ohlone. She even had tattoos on her chin. Seeing her reminded me of my mother, who had those same tattoos on her chin—short lines down from the lower lip." Julia ran a finger down her chin to emphasize where.

With wide eyes, Maria Ignacia gasped with surprise and said, "Oh, I don't understand. Where did she come from?"

"At first I could not understand either. My heart was beating so fast." Again, Julia took a deep breath and the excitement in her voice spilled out, "Maria Ignacia, I could speak with her in my native tongue. I was amazed! Words came to me, though I could not speak well."

"How wonderful! I didn't know you could speak Ohlone. Tell me about the woman. How old do you think she was?"

"She looked about my age, hmm, maybe older." Julia's eyes took a dubious look as she sat thinking, while insects began their nightly songs to fill the air with soothing sounds. "I am over sixty years old and have not been with my people for most my life. How can I say words I did not know I knew? More importantly, how can the Ohlones still exist with villages?"

Maria Ignacia responded. "There must be an explanation. What is important now is that you met an Ohlone and spoke with her. Tell me more. Start at the beginning when you were walking on the beach. Tell me what happened." While Maria Ignacia turned on the bench until their knees touched, she made herself ready for a long conversation by pulling her shawl tighter around her shoulders and tucking it around her neck.

Julia began. "I was walking toward the north and did not see her until I was close. She had her back to me, while kneeling in the sand and digging for shellfish with a stick. Somehow, I startled her. Her shoulders made a jerk and she stood. That's when I saw she wore only a grass skirt. Her graying hair hung loose, and her feet were bare. We remained facing each other and did not move for a long moment. I think she could see I am an Ohlone.

"She greeted me in my native tongue, and without even thinking I responded. I was amazed that I knew what she said. I was excited! I still am." Julia brushed loose hairs from her face before continuing. "She looked over her shoulder, and I could see two other women digging. They had not seen me yet and could not hear us, with the surf hiding our voices.

"She asked where I live, and I pointed to the adobes in the distance. I asked her the same. She pointed to the wooded area in the northeast. We talked. I did not understand everything she said, nevertheless, I know she invited me to go with her, although I am confused as to why she asked me."

Maria Ignacia put her hand to her mouth. "Oh! What did you tell her?"

"We decided to meet during the next full moon at the same place. Oh, I forgot to tell you that she asked my name. I stuttered a bit when I said 'Ju . . . Ju . . . lia' to her. And, you know that the two letters, J and U, in Spanish sound like the hoot of an owl, she said, 'Oh, you are Hoo-hoo like the owl' and she called me Hoo-Hoo."

"How humorous. What is her name?"

Frowning, Julia explained, "She did not tell me. She said that we could talk about her name when we meet again."

"Do you want to go off with her?"

Bobbing her head, Julia explained without hesitation that she has not been able to stop thinking about that possibility. "Am I free to go if I want? I don't know. I have been living with your family for many years and never thought about being able to leave and live somewhere else. Now I wonder if I can go. Also, I am not sure I could manage. Could I feed myself? I could not buy things I need because I have no money and nothing to trade. I . . . "

Maria Ignacia interrupted by putting her arms around Julia and whispering into her ear, "I will find the answers to all those questions for you. Don't worry."

Julia thanked her.

Before they left the garden area, they agreed on a plan. Before the next full moon, Maria Ignacia would find answers about Julia's right to leave, and Julia would learn more about the Ohlones. When saying good night, Maria Ignacia said, "Isn't life full of exciting surprises?"

It was the end of 1837; a time for holiday celebrations—*Navidad y El Año Nuevo*. Every year the Presidio in Monterey held a celebration for Christmas and the New Year that included all the men in the military and their families. It was a grand event. If there were foreign visitors, they were invited, as well as the prestigious old families in Monterey. Of course, the wealthy Coopers and Larkins were also included.

As soon as the sun went down, the sounds and smells announced when people were about to arrive. Music could be heard all over Monterey; the military band played in the Presidio where the event was taking place; and, more enticing than the music, was the aroma of the tender beef drifting everywhere.

People paraded toward the party in their finest: Brightly colored taffeta skirts rustled; silver jewelry jangled; women's hair held elaborate combs of scrimshaw or tortoise shell; black uniforms shone stiff from pressing; and children bounced with laughter, as everyone entered the main hall.

The Vallejo family had a table in the most honored position, though they had not yet sat down. They were milling about, greeting everyone before the food was served. Juan B and Mariano, that is, Governor Juan Bautista Alvarado and General Mariano Guadalupe Vallejo, would give speeches later in the evening before the dancing.

Maria Ignacia, Lita, and others in their family had been talking with the Larkins when Maria Ignacia noticed the arrival of the Coopers. "Oh, I am going to greet them. Lita, I will not be long," she said and walked across the room.

A few moments after Maria Ignacia had walked away, Mariano approached his family with a good-looking man in uniform and announced, "Merry Christmas and Happy New Year to all! I am honored to present Dr. Edward Turner Bale. As most know, he is our new army medical examiner here in Monterey." Mariano was full of mirth this evening and chortled, "Ha! Dr. Bale washed up on shore just when I needed him." Mariano laughed heartily at his own words, "Ho, ho, ho! As many of you must know, I recently eliminated the prior doctor, Manuel Alva, because he attempted to overthrow Governor Juan B Alvarado in a coup. That traitor is not here tonight, though not far, " Now a louder guffaw burst from him, "Ho, ho, ho!" Mariano turned to Dr. Bale and said, as he pointed, "The jail is a stone's throw from here."

Many in the group politely smiled at Mariano's humor.

Mariano continued, "I believe most of my family knows that you are the man who arrived half-dead on the beach. Now I will say all my family's names to introduce you. Humph, I want to emphasize that we do not expect you to remember all our Spanish names. Well, not tonight," he laughed again before he began naming his brothers, nieces, and nephews, as well as the Larkins, and others standing around the table. Finally, he turned to his mother and said, "I have left the most important person until last. Mother, may I present Dr. Edward Turner Bale. Dr. Bale, this is my mother, Doña Maria Antonia de Lugo."

In this room full of dark-eyed Californios dressed in uniform, everyone knew who Dr. Bale was by his blue eyes and accent. He took her extended hand, covered in a lace glove, and kissed it while saying, "What an honor to meet you and to sit with your family for this event. In advance, I want to ask that you please forgive me for any inappropriate actions. I am not accustomed to your culture. although I do speak Spanish."

Lita commented, "You are British. Am I correct?"

"Yes, from London. May I take this moment to comment on the precise English you and your family speak. What a pleasant surprise to hear it. As I mentioned, I do speak Spanish, yet I appreciate the gesture to make me more comfortable by speaking my language. How is it that English is spoken so well by your family?"

Lita responded, "I appreciate your compliment, although I know I speak English with a Spanish accent and many errors. Nevertheless, I thank you."

Mariano said, "In my position, I must know how to speak English well. We have many important visitors with whom I must converse."

Lita put her hand on her son's arm to interrupt, and said, " Dr. Bale, I think you are asking, how we came to speak so well? Not why we speak so well as my son answered?"

"Yes, I was."

She continued, "Probably the main factor was Mr. John Cooper. Have you met him?" Seeing a puzzled look on Bale's face, did not stop her from speaking. "You will meet him. He is a prominent member of our community. Mariano, you should be sure to introduce Dr. Bale to him. When he first came to Monterey, Mr. Cooper lived more than a year in our home, and he helped the family to speak English. By the way, you have another name to remember, besides all the people in our family. Our home has a name. It is called *Casa Zemita*, and I invite you to come and visit."

The conversation between Dr. Bale and her family continued as Maria Ignacia was approaching. She had other thoughts on her mind and did not wonder about the man who was speaking to her family. She saw only his back and the uniform.

Even if she had had a moment to be curious about who he was, little Thomas distracted her. The boy ran to her, calling "Mia-naci," took her hand, and began babbling something about the band. They walked together toward her family. To the delight of Maria Ignacia, the boy did not walk, he bobbed and hopped and bounced along, as many children do. She loved being with children. When they stopped, they were standing behind Dr. Bale.

With the room full of people conversing and the band playing, the noise was loud, and she could not hear little Thomas, so she squatted to be at the same height as the boy.

A collision was to happen and the three involved were oblivious because of their distractions.

Mariano had seen Maria Ignacia coming and waited for Lita to finish her discourse before he could introduce his niece to Dr. Bale. He was concentrating on his mother's words, leaning closer to be able to hear when she would reach an end to her topic.

Dr. Bale was intently watching Lita's lips, since the din had made hearing difficult. He was trying to read her lips to capture her words.

Maria Ignacia was explaining to little Thomas why he could not go sit with the band.

At last, Lita's conversation ended. Mariano pointed to Maria Ignacia with an outstretched arm and exclaimed in a loud voice, "Dr. Bale, I want to introduce my niece, Maria Ignacia, to you."

Upon hearing her name, Maria Ignacia rose to stand at the same moment that Dr. Bale turned in the direction where Mariano pointed.

Bam!

Dr. Bale's elbow swiped the side of her nose and landed on her cheekbone. Because she had been in the process of standing from a squat, Maria Ignacia was knocked off balance and fell backwards to the floor. Her nose began to bleed.

Before Bale realized whom he had hit, and while her family clamored over her, he saw only a glimpse of Maria Ignacia's beautiful face before she disappeared behind Mariano's shoulder and Lita's handkerchief. Then pleasure flooded his face as he said quietly to himself, "She IS real!"

By the time that Bale bent down, more family members were huddled around her. In a commanding voice, he said, "I am the doctor. Please make space so I can examine her."

Layers of people peeled away from Maria Ignacia. He removed the bloodied handkerchief, slipped a napkin from the table, and held it to her nose. Though he directed his words to Mariano, his eyes apologized to her, as he asked, "General, please introduce us, and then help me get her to the infirmary, where I can attend to her injuries."

Early the next morning, Maria Ignacia was floating in happiness, oblivious to her red nose and bruised cheek. She and Julia went walking in the hills behind *Casa Zemita*. However, on this day, she not only walked but danced and twirled like little Thomas had done at the celebration when he felt as exuberant as she did this day.

Hundreds of droplets of dew in the grasses twinkled in the sunlight. Grasshoppers clamored around their feet as she told Julia about meeting Dr. Bale. "Oh, Julia, he is more handsome than I remembered! Of course, back when I found him, he was battered and bleeding on the beach." They came to a rock outcropping, and she sat only for a moment; the pleasure of her thoughts could be seen in her face. Impetuously she jumped up and clasped Julia's hands in hers, circling in a dance-like fashion. "Julia, I am full of life today! This end-of-the-year party is one I will remember forever." She dropped hands and stood still. "Well, I did not attend much of the event. We stayed in the infirmary for most of the evening, and a worker brought plates of food to Dr. Bale and me." As she went on speaking, her voice became serious. "Lita did not complain about us being together. It was proper because a medical assistant acted as our chaperone at all times." Her voice changed back to delight, and she giggled while admitting, "But I felt alone with him. Oh, Julia, we talked and talked."

"What could you possibly talk about? You had met him only moments before."

Maria Ignacia sat back on the outcropping next to Julia.

"I told him a lot about my family history and the history of Monterey. Oh, I told him about you." She sat down on the rock again.

"Me?"

"Yes, about you and the Ohlones. Knowing this was going to be his home, I felt it was important for him to know the history of all the missions, and how the Catholics tried to change the lives of the people who first lived here." She tittered and explained, "When he asked why many of the missions had the name of San Francisco, I told how the Franciscan Order took their name from Saint Francis of Assisi who wanted to be stretched on the ground naked when dying, to leave the world as humbly as he had arrived. To my way of thinking, the Franciscan Order was lacking in many ways; nevertheless, I emphasized to Dr. Bale that they embraced poverty and hardship, vowing to live a life of simplicity." Maria Ignacia hesitated a moment in thought and smiled.

"What are you smiling about?"

"Oh, Dr. Bale and I think alike about much of life. We had such an intelligent discussion. When I explained that the Franciscan monks practiced penance with pain, we agreed there's no purpose in that, especially Junipero Serra's methods; he took penance to the extreme with flagellation. Dr. Bale and I spoke with each other easily." Again, she went quiet, her face displaying blissful thoughts.

Julia interrupted the quiet to say, "tell me more about him. I know a few details. He is a doctor who is now working for the military here. He is from London, England. I also know that he came on a ship that was wrecked. Anything else?"

"Dr. Bale said he has no family because his parents have died. Oh, he is twenty-seven years old. He was the surgeon on a ship that crashed near our shores. I remember he said it was named *Harriet*. There did not seem to be any other survivors."

"When will you see him again?"

"When I told Lita that I would consider Dr. Bale as a beau, she accepted my choice and asked Mariano to invite him for the evening meal tonight." Maria Ignacia jumped up again and proclaimed to the world with uplifted arms and a loud voice, "I will be with him tonight!"

Julia stood and held her in a one-arm hug. "Good! I will see him tonight, too."

"I have always felt that my grandmother wanted me to marry more than I did. Now I may want marriage as much as she. Since seeing him on the beach, I think of him all the time." And she went quiet, smiling.

Pushing through dry grasses and stalks with seedpods that brushed their legs, they turned and started for the house. Gulls soared high above them by the dozens, screeching. Pelicans flying over the distant bay were diving for fish. A goldfinch flitted past a manzanita tree not far from them, landed in a bush, and made a tinkling warble that another answered with a high, clear *tleee, tseeeew* sound. The single, short, shrill whistle of an osprey came from behind them, where the bird fished in the river to the north.

Maria Ignacia started to speak, but a whale breached in the bay. Her mouth formed a silent "OH." and her face beamed. Whales were common, but always a thrilling sight. Nothing was said between the two, who turned their heads to look at each other with sparkling eyes and grins.

After the delight of seeing the whale, they started another serious conversation. "Julia, I spoke to my father about you. I asked if he considers you to be my maid. He said that there were no papers of ownership or anything of the sort. He told me that you, Julia, always were my mother's maid and because my mother is no longer here . . ." Maria Ignacia stopped and frowned. "That is how he said it because he cannot bring himself to use words as *died* or *dead* in the same breath as her name. He is still so sad. Finally, he told me that I could consider you to be my maid."

Julia acknowledged with a bobbing nod of her head.

"Anyway, I asked him more questions." Maria Ignacia took her handkerchief from her sleeve and dabbed her bruised cheek, saying, "My perspiration is stinging the cut I got at the party when I fell. It hasn't healed yet." She tucked the handkerchief back and continued, "So, I asked if I could take you with me when I marry, and he said, 'Yes, of course' and then I asked if I could give you to another family, like the Larkins, as an example. My father said that I could. I asked if I could let you go free, and he wanted to know why I would want to do that. I said I only wanted to know. Again, he said I could, yet explained that it was best to write a document about freeing a maid from her duties."

Julia stopped walking and turned to Maria Ignacia to say, "Remember when you told me that I was not a maid. You said I was a slave. At the time, I did not agree with you but, after hearing what you just said, I think you were correct."

"I am going to write that document and have my father sign it. Though we may not need it now, I want to be prepared. Julia, are you still planning to go with the Ohlones on the full moon?"

"Oh, yes. I may be as excited about my future journey as you are about Dr. Bale. However, I am too old to dance and jump." She let her kind eyes stare lovingly at this girl who was like a daughter. "I am glad I will meet your Dr. Bale tonight because the moon is full in three days."

That evening, Maria Ignacia was delighted that the English doctor made a good impression on her family. After he had talked a while with the adults, he excused himself and went toward the children. It was before the meal, and everyone waited out on the veranda for Lita to announce when they could be seated in the dining room. Dr. Bale took out his pocket watch and asked Maria Ignacia's twelve-year-old brother, "May I take your pulse?"

She wandered over to see what he was doing.

As the doctor held the boy's wrist, with fingers pressing on the artery, he peered attentively at his watch, saying nothing. Other children came close to see what was happening and circled around the doctor.

After a minute had passed, Dr. Bale said to the boy, "Your heart was beating seventy-two times a minute. Now, stand up and run around the courtyard three times and hurry back to me. I want to take your pulse again."

The boy returned and held out his arm. The group of children waited while the doctor repeated his measurement, saying, "Now your heart is beating at ninety-five beats. And they are strong heartbeats." He turned to the others,

"Want me to show you how to do this?"

Bobbing heads and eager eyes were the answers. He paired off the children and pulled out his pocket watch again, "Can all of you feel a throb in your partner's wrist? Okay, when I say 'go,' close your eyes and count the beats until I say to stop. Ready? GO!"

Dr. Bale pulled out a small notebook to record names and heartbeats. The children switched partners and repeated. They ran around the area and took their pulse again. When Lita came out to call everyone to the table, all the children wanted to sit with Dr. Bale, but Lita sent them to their regular seats.

Maria Ignacia's chest had filled with joy when he was teaching the children.

During the meal, Dr. Bale was attentive to Lita and her father, who asked him many questions. She thought, *He is as good with adults as he is with children.*

After the meal was finished and Dr. Bale departed, another idea for a freckle poem came to Maria Ignacia. Lita had sat them opposite each other, not wanting them to touch. It was a perfect position for conversation with him and to observe him coyly. She had noticed the freckle on his eyelid off and on, throughout the meal.

She went to her desk and notebook:

> ### That Dot Within Your Eye
>
> *It winks and peeks,*
> *And stares and cares,*
> *Then hides within your eye.*
> *I so want to touch that little speckle,*
> *To know,*
> *Yes, it's just a freckle*

She sat back in the chair and reread her poem. Satisfaction spread across her face, only to vanish a moment later. She blurted aloud, "Oh, no, I should be writing the document for Julia." Glancing at her sister's bed, where the girl slept soundly, she sighed in relief. *At least I didn't wake my sister with my outburst.*

Soon the paper for Julia was ready, and she went to speak with her grandmother—not about the document, but about an excursion with Dr. Bale. She knew she would find her Lita knitting before going to bed so, after getting permission from Lita to have Julia as her chaperone, she went to find Pepe to arrange a horse ride for the three of them on the beach tomorrow afternoon.

"Just remember," Lita had insisted, "you are not to touch him. No touching! Is that clear?"

"Yes, I understand."

Early the next morning, Maria Ignacia wrote an invitation to Dr. Bale about going riding. She designated herself and Julia as the people to introduce him to the creatures of Monterey.

Invitation

*You are invited to go horse riding this afternoon with
Maria Antonia Juana Ignacia Guadalupe Soberanes Vallejo
and
Julia
On the beach to see the creatures of Monterey.
We should see whales and nawamooks
(Also known as sea otters),
Many birds such as pelicans, gulls, sandpipers and maybe an eagle.
If we are lucky (or unlucky, as some might say)
We may see a shark.*

During that afternoon, it was neither high tide nor low tide, but somewhere in-between. The air was as hospitable as the tides; it was neither too hot nor too cold. The sun peeked down on them from time to time and warmed them before disappearing behind fluffy clouds.

They rode through the surf at full speed, with water splashing their legs and laughter lost in the wind. When they reached the end of the beach, they turned and walked the horses back.

Finally, Julia said, "I think I will spread a blanket now and put out the food. These sand dunes are covered in grasses that should protect us from sand blowing into our food and eyes." She dismounted. "You are to return in five minutes, never leaving my sight. We all know that your grandmother will ask me if you were in my view at all times, and I will not lie."

"Good idea, Julia. Oh, your mention of blowing sand reminded me that I never told either of you that I had sand in my eyes on the day I found Dr. Bale.

My Uncle Salvador helped me and got the sand out with his handkerchief. If he had not helped, I may not have seen the bump on the beach that was you." Maria Ignacia started to give him a little tap on his shoulder but pulled her hand back.

"I don't remember that name. Have I met your Uncle Salvador?"

Their horses trotted away from Julia. "No, he is in the military in Sonoma. Oh, do not worry; I will always help you with the names. I have so many people in my family. I will whisper people's names to you when you need to know."

Julia was amused at their chatter. She imagined that lovers were content to talk about anything.

The hours passed. The written invitation's suggested views of wildlife were fulfilled. They saw several sea otters, floating on their backs, and banging on their bellies with a rock to open seashells; two whales swimming in the distance and spouting; no eagles, though a condor circled high in the sky; and many shore birds—a whimbrel, two wandering tattlers, a ruddy turnstone in breeding finery; and a wide variety of little sandpipers, running in the sand.

Back in her bedroom, when sitting at her desk, she thought, *I don't think I could ever give Dr. Bale my simple poems about his freckle. However, this one I am going to fold to form an envelope and have Julia deliver it to him in the medical office.* Maria Ignacia had written:

> ### Thoughts Upon the Sand
>
> *I touched textures, time, and sand:*
> *For the smoothness of a pebble*
> *And the strongness of a man,*
> *Had me feel life flowing in my hand.*
>
> *But the more I think upon this day, I wonder:*
> *Am I telling what my touch did feel?*
> *or*
> *How I feel even untouched in the sand.*

On the next evening, the full moon crested in the east, while the three stood on the beach, waiting where the river flowed through a wooded area and into the sea. The light of day diminished quickly.

"I hope they come tonight." Maria Ignacia searched the distance before turning to Julia to say, "Are you nervous?"

Julia swallowed and took a deep breath. "Yes, though I am excited, too."

Dr. Bale commented, "Even I am excited. Thank you for including me in this adventure."

Maria Ignacia wrapped her arms around Julia. She rested her head against Julia's forehead. "I keep telling myself that you are not leaving me forever. Please come back and tell me everything. Please."

"You know I will if I can. Remember that I do not know where they will go, or how far away I may be. You and I agreed we would meet here during the next full moon, though we know it may not be possible." Julia flung her arms tightly around her. "I know where you live and can come to you. Remember that I will come when I can."

Maria Ignacia nodded and pulled a handkerchief from her sleeve to dab her eyes and blow her nose. All three stood quietly and stared into the distance. Clouds passed over the bright moon just as they saw the native people approaching—three Ohlone women and a man. The group stopped, made nods, but no one spoke. One woman handed Julia a bunch of tule reeds.

Julia took them and, spreading the reeds, saw it was a skirt. She turned to undress. Seconds slipped away with the splashing surf as Julia passed her clothing, piece by piece, to Maria Ignacia who draped them over her arm.

Another woman came forward and placed a rabbit fur cape over Julia's shoulders and tied it securely at the neck.

When Julia bent forward to remove her shoes, Dr. Bale said, "Keep your shoes. The others have feet hardened from walking barefoot everyday. You should expose your feet little by little. Walk without shoes only a few hours each day until they are calloused."

The Ohlone man said, "We are ready," and the four Ohlones turned and walked away.

Maria Ignacia face contorted, and she whispered, "Be safe," as they disappeared into the woods.

While walking back toward *Casa Zemita*, Dr. Bale asked, "How is it that the man spoke in Spanish?"

"I told you about the secularization that is underway. Remember, it's the separation of the church and the military. I will assume that he was let go from one of the missions where he spoke Spanish. I should say freed from a mission, and he must have found this group of Ohlones. Julia will tell us when we see her."

"I thought the native people were given land as their own."

"No, not all of them. I am not sure how they decide who gets land. We need to speak with my Uncle Mariano. Well, General Vallejo to you. He will explain more precisely to us."

"I am interested to learn more."

"By the way, my Lita does not know I am alone with you. Please let me walk the rest of the way alone." They faced each other. "Oh, I almost forgot to tell you that we have been invited to the Larkin's home for dinner at eight on Sunday. Do you know they live in the two-story wooden house near the bay?"

"Yes, I know. Before I leave, I want to give you a note like the one you gave to me." He held out a folded paper, which she took carefully without making any contact. He beamed, exposing straight white teeth, and jested, "I refer to our kiss on the beach. What would your Lita do if she knew?" That said, he made an abrupt turn and disappeared into the early fog.

When undressed for bed in her room she read:

> *Maria Ignacia,*
> *Too few are the times in the passing of life that one meets another and blends instantly. An elusive quality develops into a bond between the two and closeness grows, making each an extension of the other.*
> *Tender teasing looks can tell all thoughts, yet our words flow with such ease that our talk is as natural and stimulating to me as our kiss was.*
> *Love, Edward*

Maria Ignacia held the letter to her chest, collapsed onto her bed, and wondered when or if she would see Julia again. *Will life with Edward make up for my loss of Julia?*

When Sunday arrived, Maria Ignacia told Lita that she was leaving early in the afternoon for the Larkins' house to help Rachel with the dinner. Though she had the intention of helping, her main reason was to talk to her friend about Dr. Bale. She wanted to say a particular sentence. It was a sentence she could say to no one else, and she was bursting with eagerness to say it.

Upon arrival, Rachel led her up the stairs to the bedrooms. "As you can see, the stairs are now difficult. This birth should happen in May, but already I am so big."

"Are you wanting a little girl?"

"Oh, I want a baby that's healthy. Boy or girl does not matter. After losing two children and going through the horrible months after their deaths, I pray for a healthy baby."

"Yes, of course."

At the top of the stairs, little Thomas burst from his bedroom and hugged Maria Ignacia around the legs. "Mia-naci, come see my soldiers."

The whole afternoon passed without an opportunity for her to tell Rachel the one sentence she wanted to hear herself say, "I love him." As important as the sentence was to her, Maria Ignacia never found an appropriate moment to say it, with the two children there. The needs of the little ones distracted Rachel from any kind of private talk between friends.

Downstairs, a door opened and closed. A man's voice called out, "We men have arrived!" Thomas Larkin and Dr. Bale removed their coats and scarves to hang on hooks next to the door.

At the top of the stairs, Rachel went to the banister and responded, "We will be down in a moment. Please send one of the maids up to get the children ready for bed."

"Fine. We will be in the parlor having an aperitif before the meal."

As the men walked away, Bale said, "Forgive me; I must pass on the drink. I took my medication and should not mix spirits with it."

From the parlor, the voices of the men drifted up the stairs while the women descended them. They were speaking about the Larkins' house.

"I'm from New England, and I wanted to build a similar style here."

Dr. Bale commented, "You have an impressive home. The porch across the whole front, both upstairs and down, is something I have never seen. One would not find this in England."

While the men talked, they stood looking out the windows at the bay.

How elegant their posture, thought Maria Ignacia as she entered the room. *They are both quite handsome and both have blue eyes.*

After greeting the women, the men's conversation continued with Thomas saying, "I had built a sawmill in Santa Cruz that gave me access to all the lumber I needed for this house. I didn't want to make an adobe, like the other houses in Monterey."

Dr. Bale disagreed, "I want an adobe. Of course, I had never seen one before arriving here. At dinner in *Casa Zemita*, I was enchanted with the adobe. I probably embarrassed myself with too many compliments to the Vallejos about their home. I want to build a two-story adobe. Do you know if that is possible?"

Larkin chuckled, "Of course, I do. You are standing in such a house. My house is a mixture of wood and adobe, but it gives the appearance of a New England home."

Rachel turned to Maria Ignacia, "Which do you consider better for a home? A house like ours or a traditional adobe?"

She responded, "I am not about to make an enemy of any one of you. My choice is a secret at this moment."

"A wise strategy." Thomas grinned at Maria Ignacia, turned, and asked, "Dr. Bale, we heard you say that you prefer Monterey's adobes but want two stories. If the first floor were built with wider walls, I would think it possible to build."

The two women sat, and the men took a seat near Bale's cup of tea and Larkin's aperitif. They took a sip before Larkin asked, "Has anything else about life here impressed you?"

"Everyone speaks proper Spanish, whether a soldier, maid, general, or oxen driver. And, more amazing, I am impressed that people speak English so well."

"Yes, yes, I noticed the proper Spanish as well when I arrived. Concerning the English, probably you have only heard the people in the Vallejo household speaking English. Am I correct?"

Dr. Bale thought for a moment and nodded. "I do believe you are correct. I seem to recall only speaking English with them."

Thomas chuckled, "They learned English from my brother, John Cooper, who lived years with them." That conversation ended upon hearing a child's voice.

Little Thomas could be heard coming down the stairs, "My daddy say so." A moment later, a maid appeared with the two children. Little Thomas, in his night dressing-gown, had a toy soldier in his fist and declared, "Daddy, this one best, isn't he? He like Mia-naci's uncle."

Rachel took one-year-old Frederick into her arms.

Her husband lifted Little Thomas and studied the toy. "Yes, yes." He turned to Maria Ignacia for confirmation. "Doesn't this look like your uncle, General

Vallejo?"

"Yes, there is no doubt."

The boy turned to the maid and declared, "See. I telled you." The adults held back their amusement.

"Dr. Bale, these are my two boys, Little Thomas and Frederick." Running his hand over the baby's head, full of soft, thick hair, Larkin said, "Say hello to Dr. Bale."

Dr. Bale asked little Thomas, "Do you have other soldiers?"

"Lots!" and he tried to hold up all his fingers to show how many. "They lots."

"Do you have a toy that is a medical man like me? You know when soldiers are injured, they need a doctor there to help them."

Little Thomas, still in his father's arms, turned nose to nose with his father. He frowned and asked, "Do I, Daddy?"

"I don't know. We will have to look at all of your soldiers tomorrow to see if one is a doctor."

Rachel said, "Time for bed. Please say goodnight to everyone," and handed the baby back to the maid who disappeared up the stairs with Little Thomas talking the whole way about his soldiers.

During the meal, topics of discussion continually returned to business prospects. Since Larkin and his brother Cooper had had their hands in an assortment of enterprises, Dr. Bale asked questions about the different businesses as a maid offered baked vegetables from a tray.

"Yes, my brother John has been living here in Monterey since 1823. Unlike me, he is the seafaring part of the family. He came here on his own ship, called *Rover*, and sold it to the Mexican government. However, he cannot seem to get the sea out of his veins. He still makes trips for Mexico down the coast to Mexico City and the lengthy journey to the Sandwich Islands."

Reaching for a tortilla, Dr. Bales inquired, "What is the cargo?"

"Mostly, he transports important members of the Mexican government from Monterey to Mexico City and back. Always on the official ship of Mexico, the *Californian*. The cargo on those trips is mail and, at other times, prisoners." Thomas let out a guffaw, "Ho, ho, ho! Like I said, I am not like my brother in that respect. The sea flows in his blood and calls to him. Why else would he make those kinds of trips?"

"Hmm," said Bale. "I went into your store the other day. I found it well-stocked and bought everything I needed. Is it a profitable business?"

While cutting the chicken on his plate, Thomas said, "Well, I make more money from the sawmill, flour mill, and trading pelts from beaver and sea otters. However, my wife enjoys being part of our enterprises, and the store gives her an opportunity."

"Yes, I work there and help with choosing the products to purchase from the East. Thomas is correct that I enjoy being involved."

A maid came and poured more water into the glasses, as Maria Ignacia said, "Their stores have helped Monterey grow. I don't know how we existed without them. Oh, yes, I do. I remember my mother and grandmother going onto docked ships to make purchases where my grandmother complained that the prices were too high."

Later, Larkin asked, "Dr. Bale, what are you planning for your future?"

The group was sitting in the parlor having an after-dinner drink. Bale had tea again because of his medication. He took a sip and said, "As you must know, I cannot plan much of a future or even consider having a family on the salary that I have now. I am thinking of expanding my medical practice to include people in the community, not only the military." He stirred the tea in his cup and leaned forward, eager to talk. "Even before I expand my medical practice, I want to see and learn more about this part of the world. General Vallejo has invited me to see the valley of Sonoma. When I know more about where I am living, I can think about other enterprises I could try. I know nothing about raising cattle, preparing hides and tallow," he stopped talking and laughed. "I want to see the whole area—especially, all the wildlife that will be new to me. I have not yet observed a grizzly bear. As you can surmise, I have much to learn."

Larkin offered to asssist. "Come to me with any questions you have and let me help you learn if it relates to my world." He shook his head, before saying, "However, I could not help you learn to skin a cow or shoot a grizzly." With that light comment and laughter, the four of them ended the evening by walking Maria Ignacia home to *Casa Zemita*.

Within the next two months, Maria Ignacia's world began to deteriorate. Julia had not come to the beach for the last two full moons, so Maria Ignacia worried. Also, Lita had been furious that Maria Ignacia had let Julia go. When

Lita learned Julia was gone, she said, "How could you not have had the courtesy to talk with me first? You don't even know where she is. Well, if I knew, I would bring her back here. How can you accept that she will never lift a hand for us again when we have cared for her all your life?"

If those two situations were not enough, another problem emerged. Maria Ignacia had overheard a conversation between her father, Lita, and Mariano discussing doubts about Dr. Bale.

That conversation had happened in the dining room late at night, allowing Maria Ignacia to hide again in the back hallway under the serving window. She heard a few positive comments made about Dr. Bale, though not too many, because most remarks had been dubious.

The meeting had gone like this:

"We know nothing about this man's past. He appeared on the beach from nowhere. Of course, I know he did not swim here from London; nevertheless, we have only his word about what happened to that ship; he has said little." Lita had stopped her rant to take a breath before saying, "Did this ship, what did he call it? Oh yes, the *Harriet*. Did it go aground, or did he jump ship?" She stood and started pacing as she continued, "and he said he has no family alive. That cannot be. He must have someone. Even though I know the English do not have as many children as we do, he must have a relative. It seems he is hiding something." Lita took a drink of water and blurted, "What proof do we have that he is an educated surgeon? I tell you . . ."

Mariano interrupted, "Mother, he could not do what he does without proper education in medicine. He appears to be an excellent doctor. I had a visitor who is a physician from the Hudson's Bay Company in Canada who worked together with him on a man brutally maimed by a bear. This other doctor was impressed with Dr. Bale's techniques and ability." He gave other examples of medical achievements Dr. Bale had made at the missions.

After a lull in the talk, Maria Ignacia's father said, "Since he washed ashore, my daughter's character has changed. What compelled her to let Julia go! She seems to be under his spell. I wonder if he suggested, letting Julia go, for a reason that I cannot imagine. We are the most prestigious family in Monterey because of you, Mariano, and your brothers. He could be wanting to marry into our family for his personal gain."

Mariano spoke, "Surely, both of you can see that Dr. Bale and Maria Ignacia are in love. In fact, Maria Ignacia told me about her feelings for him. Mother, you have wanted her to marry for years, and no man interested her.

This man has lit a fire in her, and I know both of you know how that feels because both of you lost the loves of your lives." He hesitated in his discussion of the dead. "Though your loves are gone, I know you remember what you had." Again, Mariano allowed time for them to ponder his last comment. When he began again, his voice was raised and assertive. "Of course, she's changed! She's in love. She's happy. I think he truly loves her as much as she loves him."

Lita had more to say. "Humph, in love. He is poor, so how do we know if his intentions are honorable? He is courteous and thoughtful when among us, yet he has such an ironic smile. I worry about what is in his thoughts."

"Mother, I have an idea. We can test him. Let's have him prove himself. We need to let him know that he must be a Mexican citizen and a Catholic to marry her." He hesitated for an instant and remembered more requirements. "He must own land, as well. He must prove to us he can support a family by having a better job than the one I gave him. He is sleeping at the Presidio in the quarters designated for the doctor, and we need him to show he can provide a suitable home. We can speak with him about all this." Mariano hesitated again before saying, "We will not be asking too much because the law requires this, so he will understand." Mariano stopped again and, after a lengthy moment, nodded. "This is a good idea. After speaking with him, we can watch and see what he accomplishes."

Still sitting on her blue blanket on the floor under the serving window, Maria Ignacia felt her eyes fill with tears. *I love you, Mari-oope. Thank you for clarifying all those points. You are always there for me.*

Everything began to shake! Earthquake!

A loud crack split the wall beside where Maria Ignacia sat.

CRACK!

The floor rippled beneath her. Items were falling in the house—especially in the kitchen, behind her. The brass candlesticks from Spain crashed to the table and knocked Lita's water glass to the floor. Maria Ignacia heard Lita scream and bit her own lip not to let them know she was there. The earthquake continued for less than a minute, rumbling loudly, and stopped as abruptly as it had started.

Maria Ignacia scurried down the hall into her bedroom.

At the end of summer in the year of 1838, Dr. Bale officially requested Maria

Ignacia's hand in marriage. He often was invited to dine at *Casa Zemita*, and, during an evening when General Vallejo dined with them, Bale presented the proposal of marriage to *Los Gigantes Tres*. The title of *Los Gigantes Tres* or, in English, The Big Three, was the name Maria Ignacia and Bale had devised to call Mariano, her father, and Lita.

Los Gigantes Tres accepted his proposal but laid out the conditions that Bale must fulfill; there were no surprises, since Maria Ignacia and Larkin had forewarned him. Maria Ignacia had said, "Our culture and the laws require me to marry a man who is a Mexican citizen and a Catholic. However, I promise I will not make you attend mass every Sunday."

The two couples, the Larkins and Maria Ignacia with Dr. Bale, were together frequently. One such day, Larkin told him, "My brother John Cooper became a Mexican citizen, converted to Catholicism, and had to change his name to a Spanish version of John. At least they did not tell you to do that." Smirking with raised eyebrows, Larkin added, "However, it may still happen. Be prepared." Everyone nodded and, as an afterthought and glance at his wife, Larkin proclaimed, "I wisely married an American."

Bale retorted, "The demands could have been worse. They did not demand that I needed an income of thousands of pesos a year." Nevertheless, he worried about his finances. He had already rented a bedroom in an adobe in Monterey, to have his own place. In his mind, he knew he needed to earn more to deserve Maria Ignacia, and he had said that to her.

And the months passed.

On the evenings when Dr. Bale arrived to dine with the family, the younger children gathered around him. He often had something to amuse them. This time, he pulled silver coins from his pockets. "Do you know how to make them twirl?"

Maria Ignacia heard laughter and the excitement of children's voices, drifting into the house, and knew Edward had arrived. She wandered out to the veranda and found Dr. Bale kneeling on the tiles with the group. She asked, "What are you doing?"

Her youngest brother exclaimed, "Dr. Bale will give us a silver coin if we can make it spin for ten seconds." The boy bent and held his coin on the end and gave it a flip with his index finger. "It's hard to do."

Edward sat on his haunches and looked up to her. "Want to try?" The children encouraged her to try, and her coin toppled after a couple of seconds. "Keep practicing while I time someone else."

Finally, a cheer rose when one brother had a success. "See, all of you just need to practice."

After the meal, a walk behind *Casa Zemita* allowed privacy for the young couple. While he and Maria Ignacia strolled in the garden behind the kitchen, Edward lamented, "I am not progressing as I thought I would. I am beginning to feel embarrassed around your family. They asked what I have been doing, and I told them that I have several private patients in Monterey now, in addition to my military responsibilities. But what I didn't tell them is that I earn little with the military job and even less with my private practice. It's my own fault. I will not charge someone who needs medical help and cannot pay, and almost all the patients I have are poor people." He sighed. "I am trying to save money to have our own home when we marry, and . . . "

"Edward, Edward, please stop. You have not been here long. I know opportunities will happen. We will be fine." She shook her finger at him and chuckled, "Maybe you should not give silver coins to the children again."

"No, I want to be able to give the children enjoyment."

She nodded, "I should not have said that. I want you to do things with the children. If we do not enough money, we can live in the guest room at *Casa Zemita* at first and . . . "

"Maria Ignacia, no! Handouts from your family! I must prove I am worthy of you. Oh, I love you so and want you to be proud that you married me."

"I wish I could hold you and make you feel better." She tilted her head in the direction of the window where Lita stood watching them. "I imagine I should be grateful that we can walk and talk in privacy, even though we still cannot embrace." Her voice became stern, "I am upset that my family still has not set a date for our wedding."

"I have submitted all the paperwork for a Mexican citizenship. Your uncle said it might take months for Mexico City to process my application. Larkin said it takes forever for the bureaucrats to process everything."

"When my Uncle Mariano comes to Monterey, I will ask him to allow us to set a wedding date."

They stopped walking and sat on the bench next to the vegetable garden. With elbows on his knees, Edward dropped his head into his hands, and said,

"I am attending classes from the priest to become a Catholic. Please ask your uncle if he could arrange a wedding date to coincide with the completion of my Catholic conversion."

"I will."

Maria Ignacia sat straighter and said, "Because I have been sneaking out to be with you sometimes, I feel better. Don't you? It feels natural to hug and touch and kiss."

"No, I don't feel better." He turned to face her with a serious expression. "If we are discovered, your family might prevent our wedding. I don't want to jeopardize our future. I love you and want to spend the rest of my life with you."

They sat peering into each other's eyes, looking quiet and composed while their bodies surged with emotion. Maria Ignacia wondered if Lita had ever felt what she was feeling. *Probably not, or she would march out here and scold me.*

Dr. Bale broke the spell. "Oh, Maria Ignacia, as much as I want to be with you, I should return to the Presidio. This smallpox outbreak has everyone working long hours. I need to return to prepare medications. The sick keep arriving, and all the beds in the infirmary are occupied. In my opinion, there should be a hospital here in Monterey. This is the capital and should have an official medical facility. No official agrees with me."

"I don't understand. Who doesn't agree with you about a hospital? And what can you do tonight to help the sick?"

He sat back on the bench. "Most of the sick are natives, and it appears that the men in power do not think a hospital is needed for them." He stood again. "Why don't you come with me and see what I will be doing tonight?"

Her eyes widened. "I could do that?"

"I will just be working in the laboratory, away from the sick. Yes, come."

One of Maria Ignacia's brothers was curious about Dr. Bale's work, too, so he agreed to be their chaperone, and the three left for the Presidio. Once inside the laboratory, Dr. Bale lit candles and pulled two stools up to the counter for them. Bottles of unknown contents lined shelves, scientific apparatus was scattered on the counter, books and notebooks lay everywhere, and charts of the human skeleton and organs hung on the walls. "I will return after I talk to my assistant about the variolation preparations. Please wait. I will only be a few minutes."

Upon his return, she saw more weariness in his eyes, yet she wanted to understand about his work. "Can you explain what you meant by that word ver . . . varia? Oh, I can't say it. I know you are tired and rushed, but please tell me."

"The word I used is variolation. Variolation is a method to vaccinate healthy people and prevent the spread of smallpox. Please let me show you what it means in a minute. I am going across the hall for supplies."

This time, Dr. Bale appeared with two glass jars full of an unrecognizable material and placed them on the counter next to a mortar and pestle. "I'm glad both of you are interested." He removed an apron from a hook, slipped it over his head, and tied it behind his back.

Maria Ignacia stood and reached for one of the glass jars, and Dr. Bale stopped her hand by saying, "Please touch nothing. You are here to see and listen. You do not know if something can harm you or not. Do you understand?"

She nodded.

He shook some of the contents of one jar into the mortar and began to speak. "Variolation is a method in which we collect scabs from the smallpox victims. These are those collected scabs I shook from the jar."

The eyes of Maria Ignacia and her brother widened. "Oh my," she said.

Her brother asked, "These are scabs from the sick men in the infirmary?"

"We took scabs from dead men, and those alive in the infirmary."

Maria Ignacia scooted back onto her stool and placed her hands in her lap.

"After the scabs dry for several days, they can be ground into a powder," Dr. Bale said while mashing the scabs with the pestle, "or I could have taken the pus from a pustule, but that is harder to save." He added more scabs and continued mashing.

The room was quiet except for the scraping sound of the pestle against the mortar. An open window let in a soft breeze, and the candles on the counter flickered.

Dr. Bale stopped to walk to a cabinet and removed vials for storing the powder from the mortar. "Once I have this powder, I can rub it onto scratches that I make on the skin of a healthy person." He looked up at the two. "After I scratch the skin, it bleeds a little, and the applied powder can enter the body from that wound. This whole procedure is called variolation."

Maria Ignacia nodded.

"Then that person is vaccinated and might develop a less severe, but nonfatal, case of smallpox that can last for two to four weeks. But they do not die. Many of the vaccinated people never get anything except a slight fever.

When the scratches heal and other symptoms subside, they are left with a scar where I scratched them," he pointed to his upper arm, "and immunity for life. They never will get smallpox."

"Edward, a scar! I have one. Look," she pulled up her sleeve, "I have one because, when I was young, a doctor did that to me. I did not understand at the time, of course. You explained that so well." She beamed, proud of him.

Her brother showed his scarred arm and asked, "How do you decide who gets that procedure?"

"We want to go to every home here in Monterey and vaccinate anyone who has no scar. And I want to ask your uncle if I may go to Fort Yerba Buena and Fort Sonoma to administer the variolation to anyone in need there. I realize that the Americans may have been vaccinated years ago. But not the natives! I want to help the Wappos, Miwoks, Ohlones, and other tribes. I want to scratch them to stop the deaths of native people. Julia lost her family and culture. Knowing that has made me think more about the native people. I want to help the natives. So, I have my assistants collecting as many scabs as possible so I can vaccinate many people."

The two watched Dr. Bale for an hour or so before they stood. "We should get back home."

Dr. Bale walked them to the door.

She slipped her arm into her brothers to start down the steps, but turned to say, "Oh, I need to remind you that the moon will be full again in two days. Pepe is going with me to see if Julia comes to meet me. Please try to come, too. I pray Julia will be there this time."

Dr. Bale, Pepe, and Maria Ignacia found Julia next to the same stream as before. She and a small group of women were laboring with dip nets. This night was exceptionally bright, making the water sparkle as salmon reflected the moonlight. Though Maria Ignacia was excited to see her, no hugging occurred with Julia standing among salmon in water up to her knees.

Dr. Bale was amazed, "How can there be this many fish here in this one small stream?"

"The spawning season is now, and they have returned from the sea to their home waters. They go back to where they were born." Julia grinned, "Like me."

"Oh, what a wonderful analogy, Julia. Here, let me help." Dr. Bale started pulling the flopping fish away from the edge of the stream where the women tossed them. A few fish made their way back into the water. "In Europe we have the Atlantic salmon; however, I have never seen one."

Maria Ignacia interrupted, "Julia, I want to hear about what has happened since we saw you last?"

Once Julia started talking, she overflowed. "After I left you, we walked a couple of miles to a small temporary village. It had only four huts." Like her words, her dip net never stopped filling. "Oh, Maria Ignacia, I felt strange without clothes for only a few minutes. With all the women bare-breasted and in straw skirts, I was reliving my childhood. What a wonderful experience to feel at home after all these years. I worried that I would feel cold, but it didn't happen. The rabbit skin cape keeps me warmer than I thought possible. After a week, I learned this group of four huts was a temporary village. Only a few people had come to collect shellfish for everyone in a larger village where we went later. I counted thirty people living there."

Maria Ignacia and Pepe started helping with the fish.

"Oh, I learned much about my people—new details about daily life. For example, I did not remember that the Ohlone people swaddle their newborn child tightly with rabbit furs. After I arrived at the larger village, I met a young mother with a new baby. We have become friends. It didn't matter that I'm old, and she's young."

Julia flashed a look at Maria Ignacia. A subtle meaning passed between them.

Just as quickly, Julia returned to the topic and said, "Once swaddled, the Ohlone mother straps the wrapped baby to a cradleboard for their first two years." Seeing the surprised look on her listeners' faces, Julia emphasized, "Yes, two years. The children cannot walk or use their hands or move around until after those two years. Everything learned must be seen, heard, smelled, tasted, or felt through touch from another. At least twice a day, this mother unwraps her child for cleaning. They bath together in a nearby stream and recline on a tule mat in the sun, when possible, to air dry while she massages the child. Afterwards, cattail fluff is replaced to the child's bottom before being swaddled again."

Dr. Bale commented, "Julia, thank you. Oh, if only I had paper and pen to make notes of all this. I will make time later to write down what you have told us. Details like these should be recorded for historical purposes."

Maria Ignacia asked, "What was the baby's name?"

"Oh, they don't name the child until later. For now, we call him *Baby*. Isn't that sweet?" Julia went down on her knees and exclaimed, "I must hurry." She began to pack her baskets with the salmon piled on the side of the stream.

Dr. Bale squatted and helped. "All of this is interesting to me. Am I correct that you are speaking your childhood language?"

"Yes, and I did not know I could."

Maria Ignacia informed him that Julia had said she could not remember much, except the tattoos on the face of her mother, a few stories of her father, and walks on the beach.

He asked, "Julia, you said you lived with your mother and father about five years. I would think you were talking at that age."

"Yes, I'm sure I was." Julia explained, "but only my particular dialect of the Ohlone language. There are people now in our village I cannot understand. That's when we speak Spanish."

Maria Ignacia said, "What do you mean? Oh, I keep interrupting, but I have many questions."

"Most of the people were from the missions. With secularization happening, they were told that they could leave and came to this village. That is why I can speak Spanish with them."

"Why didn't you come on the other full moons?"

"Oh, Maria Ignacia, we go where the food is. We came tonight because the salmon are here. In fact," she gestured to the others who were waiting, "we have been here since the afternoon and have collected enough for today. I must go now. Come again tomorrow afternoon. We'll be dipping for more. We work as the fishermen; others back in the village dry the fish to save enough for winter." Julia turned, hoisted one basket heavy with fish. Tails hung over the edges. Dr. Bale grabbed her second basket—just as full—and slipped it on her other shoulder. Julia thanked him and rushed away as fast as the weight allowed.

"Look," Dr. Bale said pointed to Julia's feet, "she still wears her shoes but, if she continues to go in the water with them, they'll not last."

"Tomorrow, I will bring her another pair."

They watched until the group vanished into the woods by blending with the terrain. Dr. Bale commented, "The natural colors they wear make them invisible from one moment to the next." As they turned to walk back to Monterey, he chided himself with a burst of thoughts, "Oh, no, I did not even think about bringing anything to scratch them against smallpox."

"We didn't know if she would come. So, that's why you didn't think of it."

"Tomorrow I will bring my medical bag."

The next day they went with the shoes, vials with serum, and three horses. Lita had insisted that Pepe be their chaperone. The horses would make travel to Julia's village easier, and they could carry more fish for them, as well.

While more salmon were collected, Julia continued talking about the tribelet. "I asked if there were other groups of Ohlones we could visit. They told me that in the past they only would visit others to trade and to find a marriage partner. Nowadays they do not know of any other tribelets."

Maria Ignacia remembered. "You were going to tell me the name of the woman you met on the beach when you first saw the Ohlones."

"Oh, it was a bit strange. She was born and worked in the missions all her life until she came here with this tribelet and learned that the Ohlones never say the name of a person after they die. So, she decided to let her old name die. Therefore, no one used her mission-name. Like the baby who was not named during the first year, she waited to be named. That time passed, and we call her *Conejita* now."

"Oh, you call her Little Rabbit, what a fine name. I want to meet her."

Dr. Bale was helping with the fish after finishing the variolation and said, "Will you tell me about the last three months? What other food do you gather?"

"This is the time the salmon have come to feed us." She turned to face her three Monterey friends, "That is how we say it: *The salmon come to feed us*. We went to other harvests. We go to beaches when shellfish are ready, to the marsh when the ducks and geese come, to the oak trees when acorns ripen, and when the sun is low in the sky, we harvest seeds and roots from hills and meadows. I am learning all of that and how to weave baskets. We spend much of the day gathering materials—hemp, tule reeds, fibers—for our boats, huts, and baskets."

"Later, when we get to your village, will you show us the inside of a hut?"

"Yes, of course, Dr. Bale. However, you must wait until I speak to our leader about all this. I'm not sure he will accept the horses coming to our village or if he will allow you to scratch our peoples' arms against sickness. I must ask."

The leader was wise. He realized that, though they were trying to live like their ancestors, their life was not the same as in the past. He had lived in the missions, so spoke Spanish with the visitors. "Please, just refer to me as the leader as everyone in my village does. You would honor me to call me by my title." He bobbed his head to acknowledge people as they passed. "I know I do not live in the same way as my ancestors, yet I know I am as content as they were."

They walked within the village among the huts, passing people doing all forms of work: Women dried slivers of salmon over hot coals; men repaired fishing nets; others were grinding acorns to be a powder for making a dough; and children carried firewood.

In the leader's hut, they found a man repairing a section of the roof with new tule rushes. He took tightly bound bundles of the tule rushes and attached them to a framework of willow poles arcing over the roof. They saw blankets of deer skins scattered on the floor, and in corners, small stacks of rabbit skins strewn here and there. Hamper baskets filled with seeds, roots, dried meat, and smoked fish lined the outer walls. A variety of empty baskets, in many sizes and shapes, hung from the ceiling's willow branches, waiting to be used.

"This is our home. We have all we need to occupy us on a cold rainy winter day." The leader reached into a leather pouch hanging from a post, "See, these are our awls, bone scrapers, obsidian knives, and twisting drills for putting holes in leather and making beads. Oh, look I was given a gift of these abalone shells from a sailor when I was on the Monterey beach last year. People can be kind. We try to be kind. Kindness is most important to us."

The three visitors were invited to a meal with the leader. Sitting outside on tule mats on the ground, forming a large circle, they enjoyed the meal with the people telling of their day's accomplishments and misfortunes. One crooked-backed old man had caught no fish that day and everyone teased him in good humor. Kindness was being practiced when many people promised to give a part of their catch to him.

Bowls, woven tightly to contain liquids, held the acorn gruel with chunks of smoked salmon, sprinkled with flavorful seeds. It was the custom to use two fingers to put the food into their mouths with loud slurps.

Maria Ignacia made a sideways glance to Edward before dipping her fingers for the first time into the bowl.

Julia saw them exchange looks and was amused. She loudly stated, "Doesn't this food taste better using your fingers?" Laughter followed her comment; slurping accompanied the laughter; and pleasure filled their mouths with every bite.

Dr. Bale thought to himself how meals were important not only for eating, but also for pleasure and camaraderie.

Later, a basket filled with warm seedcakes was passed around the circle. Roasted hazelnuts filled the cakes. With this final treat, the slurps were replaced with soft guttural sounds of pleasure, "ummm" and "ahhh."

During this moment at the end of the meal, Julia and an elderly man stood. He said, "We have an announcement to make."

All went quiet as the chatter ended; everyone looked to the two who stood. Julia asked, "May I please translate everything said from our language to Spanish for my friends?" The leader agreed to the request.

While nods continued to ripple around the circle, the elderly man standing with Julia made a comment that produced cheers from all. Conversations and laughter began again.

Pepe, Maria Ignacia, and Dr. Bale waited—curious and puzzled. Maria Ignacia whispered to them, "I cannot guess what would bring such cheers and happiness."

The leader held up his hands, "Now, Julia must tell her friends what was said. Please, let us quiet our joy."

Julia clasped her hands tightly together, pulled them to her chest, and rested them over her heart. Her words burst forth like a seedpod popping open, scattering her joy to her friends. "We are to be married during the next full moon."

With that announcement of marriage, Maria Ignacia thought, *how wonderful! Marriage never happens too late in life. The euphoria of being in love never is too late.*

Mariano Guadalupe Vallejo
In Fall/Winter 1838

CHAPTER FIVE

MEETING THE MEN OF ALTA CALIFORNIA

FALL AND WINTER OF 1838

Like a child who is given a tantalizing treat, Maria Ignacia took the sweet taste of love and not only began to savor it, but also prepared herself to fight for it. Months had vanished without a wedding date. After bowing to her elders, plowing through all the rules and conditions, and allowing *Los Gigantes Tres* to control her life, she decided to face her uncle and fight for Edward Turner Bale.

Her Tio Mariano was in town, and she made it known that she needed to talk privately with him.

"No," she told him, "I will not sit in the living room or any room and talk. I said it must be private. The only way to accomplish a talk, without the eyes and ears of others learning everything, is for us to go walking. I know from experience." She looked at him, held his gaze, and clarified, "you will hear how I know this to be true once we begin to speak together. Please, let's walk outside."

"As you wish."

"Before it gets too dark, I want to walk to the oak tree where I met Mancha so long ago. I still enjoy the memory of him . . . I mean, memory of her. Of course, if you would like to walk elsewhere, tell me."

He shook his head and put his arm around her shoulders, "You are so serious. I hope you are not going to tell me anything upsetting."

Turning and kissing his cheek—they stood the same height—she assuaged his concerns by saying, "My intention is not to cause any upset. I think we can come to an agreement." She touched his arm and blurted, "I have four things to discuss. The first is to tell you that I overheard the conversation you, Lita, and my father had. I was hiding under the serving window when you sat at the dining room table that night."

Mariano commented, "You, a descrier. That is interesting." He hesitated in his stride to give her a devilish look before continuing to stroll up the incline.

"Therefore, I know the doubts the three of you have about Dr. Bale. I had concerns, as well. How could one not wonder about his story, rather, his lack of a story. He said no one else survived the *Harriet's* shipwreck. In a shipwreck, debris comes to the beach in the following days. None ever washed up."

With a jerk of his head, Mariano blurted, "How do you know that?"

"I went each day after finding him and covered the whole beach for two weeks. I believe you sent men to do the same, didn't you?" She did not wait for his answer and said, "I saw your men in the distance frequently. I found nothing. How does a ship go aground, break apart, and nothing floats to the beach? Oh, except that one broken wooden plank. Edward said he floated to the shore on it. He said that is how he made it."

"You have talked with Dr. Bale about our concerns?"

"Of course." She reached and took his hand. "Tio, I love him. I have deep feelings for him and, possibly more important, I trust him." They arrived at the oak tree. She stopped and turned to face him. "I am not the foolish young girl that wanted to save my Mancha. I know I still lack much experience about life; nevertheless, I have no doubts about his love for me and mine for him."

"My sweet niece, we know nothing about him."

Standing tall in her convictions, though eye-to-eye with her uncle, she blurted. "I know everything. He responded to every question I asked, and I believed every answer he gave me."

"His claim to having no family, what do you make of that?"

"My sweet uncle, who has always been here to protect me, you must trust me. I promised Edward that I would keep his secrets. Once he told me, I understood his reasons for wanting not to tell." She wrapped her arms around her uncle's ample middle and rested her head on his shoulder. "I am the one who will live my life with him. If I accept without problems all his secrets, please trust my judgment."

Mariano stroked her hair and put his other arm around her. They stood huddled for many minutes with him passing his hand over her hair. "So, you spied on the three of us. Hmm, I should know you are too clever not to muse about the same kinds of concerns that I have about Dr. Bale."

"Oh, I have another confession. Edward and I have chosen a special name for the three of you. We call you *Los Gigantes Tres*. I hope this does not offend you."

Still holding her, he shook his head. "That sounds just like something lovers might decide in their childish fashion."

She pulled back from his chest, "Oh, maybe I should not have told you. We are not childish—carefree and happy, playful and spontaneous, not childish."

"Now, now. I did not mean to insult you." He pulled her back into the hug. "en you said you wanted to talk with me, I surmised you wanted to beg me to set the wedding date. You have impressed me that you still have not asked that. I can see you are not acting like a child begging an adult. I apologize for calling you childish." He began to caress her hair again. "You understand our concern." He made a small laugh, "Ha, *Los Gigantes Tres* have concerns for you."

"I know. Which brings me to the next topic. No, not the wedding date. More important than that is how Edward will provide for a family. Oh, Tio, he worries about being able to earn enough for a family."

"That worry of his is worrisome to me, as well."

They started their return to home and, after walking in silence for a distance, Maria Ignacia offered an idea. "I think you could help Edward by assigning him to other places and introducing him to interesting people. If he could meet men who live in or near the forts in Yerba Buena and Sonoma, he might discover new ways to support a family. Also, you would get to know him better."

"Your idea is a good one. I will make it happen. Now, to your fourth topic."

"Oh, I am excited to say this." She made a little hop before saying, "Julia is getting married."

"What! She is so old. She could be my mother."

Maria Ignacia came to an abrupt stop and placed her hands on her hips. "I believe there's no age requirement for being in love."

"You are correct, though I am surprised. When one's hair is streaked with white, marriage surprises me."

"Yes, Julia's hair has much white and her face many wrinkles, but you have watched her work. She is strong and full of energy."

Before they arrived at *Casa Zemita,* he had heard everything she could remember about Julia's new life among the Ohlones. "I need your approval for my last idea. I want to give Julia and her husband two horses as a wedding gift from our family."

"Aha, this is a fifth topic. You must count more carefully." Quickly he held up his hands before she could protest and replied, "I approve the gift."

One by one, as the military men assembled outside the Presidio, General Vallejo's horse pranced in place. "Dr. Bale, you will ride to my left. We will talk on the way to Sonoma. When I invited you, I said that I wanted to introduce you to the valley where I work. However, I also wanted you to meet the American George Yount and to know his *Rancho Caymus*. I will tell you about him on our ride. Now, excuse me while I get these men organized. We must leave."

As the General gave instructions to his lieutenant, he watched Dr. Bale who was peering into the distance. He knew that the doctor was looking for his niece because he had covertly overheard their conversation after the meal the prior night. He remembered the scene:

Maria Ignacia presented Dr. Bale with her handkerchief, telling him, "Carry this close to your heart and think of me. I shall miss you so."

Bale responded, "This separation will be good for us. As we each yearn for the other, our love will grow. It will become something greater than we ever thought possible because we will realize how much we want to be together."

"Oh, Edward, I hope you are correct. Already I feel a pain in my chest. You have always been only a short distance from me. Now, we will be many days apart. I will be so sad."

"No, no, you must think how wonderful we will feel when we meet again. It will be like the first moment I gazed into your eyes on the beach. On that day, you put life into me. We will have that thrill again."

Maria Ignacia closed her eyes and spoke, "Oh, I remember that moment when you kissed me on the sand and the whole world changed." Opening her eyes to gaze at him, she nodded. "You are correct that I should think about that memory and know we will have a deeper love by falling in love again when we meet again." A tear rolled down her cheek. "Please give me your handkerchief. I want something of yours to touch while you are gone."

"Oh, I soiled it."

The corners of her mouth curved up. "Mine is soiled, too. I wiped my brow and pressed it to my mouth when I put a kiss inside it. Give it back. I want to wipe my tear." She briefly took it, wiped her cheek, and handed it back. "Look, I have tears and smiles at the same time."

As Dr. Bale passed his, their hands lingered, briefly touching.

She told him, "I will put an 'E' on it in blue thread while you are gone. Look for me tomorrow. I will wave goodbye to you from a distance."

Vallejo shook his head and let the romantic memory blow away along with the dust from the horses' hooves. He had no time to waste on those thoughts; he needed to get his men to the Napa Valley.

Not a mile down the road, General Vallejo began to tell Dr. Bale about George

Yount. "As I said, I plan to introduce you to him. What a man he is. Unlike any other I have met. Oh, often I call him by the Spanish form of his name, *Jorge*, because each day he becomes more Mexican. Ha! When he first arrived, he was still an American through and through. He built a log cabin. He cut down the trees himself and made a different design than what I understand to be usual. The natives who lived there became his friends while helping to build it." The General laughed, "Ha, ha, Jorge quickly learned he was sharing the land with many grizzlies and unfriendly natives—Yount calls them Indians—so he had to make the cabin with a special design. You will see. He is an outstanding marksman with his long-range rifle and kills many a grizzly. Mostly, he is known for his stories, being quite a *raconteur*. In my opinion, most are often tall tales."

Dr. Bale still had a forlorn look about him when he nodded. "I look forward to hearing Mr. Yount's stories."

Minutes ago, when the doctor had waved to Maria Ignacia, the General saw Bale's eyes fill with tears and decided his niece was correct that this man really loved her. He continued talking about Yount. "I'm not sure when Yount first arrived in Alta California. Nevertheless, before long he was trapping sea otters all over the area. He found them in the waters off Santa Barbara, in the bay of Yerba Buena, and when he went to the delta of Sacramento. He also found a daughter."

Dr. Bale turned in his saddle. "I don't understand. What are you saying?"

"I wanted to make sure you were listening." The General gave out a hearty guffaw, "Ha, ha, ha! However, what I said is true. While on the delta, he came across an abandoned native settlement. No people were left alive, except this little girl. He guessed her to be a three-year-old. That was in 1833, the year malaria swept through the native populations and wiped them out. He never could find any native people to adopt her, so he decided to raise her as his own. She's about nine now. We will see her at Yount's ranch.

"Now to return to my prior topic. I was telling about his log cabin. Once Yount realized he would have continuous trouble with bears and belligerent natives, he built what he called a Kentucky-style blockhouse—a two-story log house with the upper floor overhanging the lower—to allow men to fire down on attackers through loopholes. You know what a loophole is?"

"Yes, I do. Many castles in England have these long, narrow windows for warfare. Sir, I have a question."

"Ask it."

"You said 'belligerent natives,' but I thought Yount was friends with the natives."

"Yount became friends with the Caymus tribe. He even named his place *Rancho Caymus* in their honor. There are dozens of different groups in his area, and many are not too friendly. The Caymus grew to accept him because he killed many grizzlies and gave the carcasses to them. If he killed an elk, it was too much for him to eat, and he knew he would need to smoke the meat to keep it for winter unless he gave it to the Wappos, Miwoks, or the Caymus. Their women did the work. Of course, they always returned pieces of the smoked meat to him.

"I've been talking about Yount's log cabin and should explain that in the past months he finished constructing a proper Californian adobe. His ranch is to the east of the fort, and you need to understand when the Mexican government granted land to him, we made conditions of ownership. This happened in 'thirty-six, making him the first foreigner to settle lawfully here. However, if he wanted to keep his two leagues of *Rancho Caymus*, he had to build a proper adobe house with a corral, had to stock his land with at least one hundred horses and cattle and, like you, had to convert to Catholicism and become a naturalized Mexican citizen. Same requirements that you must do. Well, he did it all."

Bale asked, "Can you tell me how much land is in two leagues?"

"Two Spanish leagues are about twelve thousand acres."

"Why did he get so much?"

Vallejo explained, "To make a living for a family, raising cattle and crops, you need about that much. Yount planted wheat, put in a fruit orchard, berry patches, and a vineyard. Now, he's a farmer. Ha, ha, ha."

"If he lives at *Rancho Caymus*, wouldn't that make him a rancher, not a farmer?"

"Yes, but in jest, I tell him he's a farmer. He never gets angry, only retaliates with a joke about my life. Yount and I have a lengthy history together—good times drinking and a lot of bloody battles."

Bale's eyes widened in surprise, "I didn't realize you had fought in battles. I had not known."

"Dr. Bale, I'm in the military. One does not become a general without fighting battles. I've had to fight battles with guns against the natives and words against my Mexican opponents." He chuckled as he pulled his horse around. "Bale, you stay here. I need to look over my regiment."

Later in the day, as their travels were coming to an end, the fort in Yerba Buena appeared out of the fog that crept over the coastal hills. When closer, General Vallejo saw a ship docked in the water of the bay. His face beamed, and he said, "How fortunate, the *Californian* is here."

Dr. Bale asked, "We will go by ship to Sonoma?"

With his usual authority and a smirk, he answered, "That is my plan."

The next morning, they sailed north from San Francisco Bay to San Pedro Bay. Dr. Bale enjoyed the wind in his hair, the water spray in his face, and the sun warming his back while he stood on the deck.

Unlike on the prior day, General Vallejo's mood was serious, his comments brief and succinct. "To the west of us is Mission San Rafael Arcángel, it's our medical mission. You should visit it," he said before making an abrupt turn and striding across the deck.

Bale stared long and hard while he watched Vallejo crossing the stern and stopping to speak to two of his men. Bale was sure that something was amiss. *They must have told him something last night at the Yerba Buena Presidio. In his every move and gesture, I can see he is preoccupied. Something appears to be troubling him.*

The sprawling land north of San Pedro Bay came into view but, when the ship headed east, Bale was confused. He approached General Vallejo who stood gazing into the distance in deep thought.

Bale asked, "I understood that Fort Sonoma is to the north. Why . . . "

He barked, "My orders have changed, Dr. Bale. I will discuss them with you when I think you need to know."

Bale chastised himself. *I must stop asking questions. Obviously, I must wait to see what happens.*

Vallejo's stern expression changed to a look of concern, and he asked, "By the way, did you have enough time to finish administering the smallpox variolation to the troops in Yerba Buena?"

"Yes, I did, and I have nothing unusual to report. I still have sufficient vials for the troops in Sonoma."

Vallejo nodded and plodded away with his hands clasped behind his back.

Heading east, the ship entered the Napa River and sailed north. Thousands of waterfowl darkened the sky as they rose in flight, making a squawking din. One of the sailors shouted over the noise to say, "Geese!"

Bale nodded and peered over the side at the wetlands they passed.

Hundreds of birds, and many different from others, swam and pecked and dove in the shallow waters of the marshes. He knew none of the birds' names and had little interest beyond his amazement at their numbers. He was worried and not about birds. He did not know the destination of this ship, nor what was in store for him.

In what appeared to be the middle of nowhere, they stopped near the shore to disembark. There were no buildings, only a dock. With speed and efficiency, men herded the horses down ramps, mounted again, and rode away. General Vallejo said nothing. Bale ask nothing.

Soon, coming towards Vallejo's regiment, Dr. Bale saw a large group of riders, cresting a hill. He turned and looked at Vallejo. The General seemed to have no concern. Like wasps disturbed and pouring from their hive, the horsemen grew in number in an endless flow and, minute by minute, they drew closer.

Bale could not contain his surprise and trepidation. "They're natives on those horses! There're scores of them. "

"Yes."

"Who are they? Shouldn't we be fearful?"

Again, General Vallejo had to shout at him. "Dr. Bale, no questions! Dismount, follow me, and say nothing."

A few of the natives slipped from their horses. One was exceedingly tall, possibly the tallest man Bale had ever seen. This giant of a man, with his horse in tow, approached the General. Standing ten feet apart, they saluted each other.

"Chief Solano, I greet you."

"Thank you, General Vallejo," said the tall native. He was dressed in leather pants and moccasins, both trimmed with fringe. Weapons protruded from his waistband—a huge hunting knife, and two pistols. Hanging from his saddle was a quiver of arrows, a saber, and a long rifle. His chest was bare except for the string of his bow which lay across his muscular body. All the other natives were dressed the same with their weapons, military pants, and moccasins. Many had heavy war clubs as well as their bows with quivers of arrows, but no guns. The towering man spoke in perfect Spanish, without an accent and said, "You know that the Tuolumnes and Moquelumnes, as well as other hostiles, have been raiding settlements. But there are new developments. They're not only raiding and leaving with the plunder, but also committing cruel acts and murders. And, by observing where they have been, I think they are making their way to your fort in Sonoma. We'll have a difficult battle to stop them."

Vallejo responded, "What are your numbers? My regiment has only one hundred, though they are all armed with short-range rifles, bayonets, and sabers."

"Chief Solano smiled, "What you see are only my select warriors. I have over one hundred Suisuns out of sight and another hundred Patwin warriors watching the enemy's movements for us."

The two leaders turned and began to walk together as Chief Solano continued to give details about the enemy. Vallejo clasped his hands behind his back as they strolled away; that was a pose Bale would see often in the coming days. When Vallejo walked with his hands clasped behind him, Bale had learned that the general was concentrating and not to be interrupted.

Dr. Bale stood where they had left him, not knowing what to do. A militiaman dismounted and approached Dr. Bale saying, "You should follow them."

Vallejo turned to wait for Bale, "Chief Solano, may I present Dr. Edward Bale. I have brought a surgeon to sew all our wounded back together." No one laughed because it was not said in jest.

The tall Suisun Chief leaned down with an extended hand and greeted Bale. "Good to meet you, Dr. Bale; you have a big job ahead of you."

Bale cringed upon hearing those words but hid his fears. *This is a job I had not expected. I have never wanted to be in a war.* He was aware he had begun to perspire, and his knees quivered. This journey to see the Napa Valley in all its beauty was not turning out as he had envisioned. He managed to mutter, "Glad to meet you as well."

General Vallejo turned to Solano. "You said you learned that they are a thousand in number?"

"In my opinion, that must be an exaggeration, though it's possible. I think it best to plan as if we were up against one thousand."

The General squatted and took out a knife. Chief Solano went down on his knees next to him, and Bale belatedly lowered himself. Vallejo began to draw in the dirt and said, "If you are sure they are descending into the Napa Valley by way of the lower ford of the Napa River, this is my idea." They discussed possible maneuvers by drawing in the dirt and shared tactics for several minutes. The battle was planned for tomorrow.

On the ride north, General Vallejo seemed unconcerned about the pending battle. In fact, his demeanor showed enthusiasm. He seemed energized as he continued Bale's education. "Chief Solano's real name is Sam-Yeto of the Suisun

People. They are part of the Patwin; however, I suggest that you do not try to remember all the tribal names you hear. There are too many." The General turned and nodded at Bale. "We are heading to *Rancho Caymus* and are almost there. You will meet George Yount soon."

Surprised, Bale grew wide-eyed in confusion. "I will?"

Vallejo seemed not to notice Bale's bewilderment. "As I was saying, when Sam-Yeto was about ten years old, the same men who had raided his Suisun settlement and killed his parents took him to the mission in Yerba Buena. They brought about twelve other children from his tribe. Over the years, as Sam-Yeto grew and learned much from the friars, the natives at the mission came to honor him as a leader. Not only the Suisun People looked up to him, but also people from other tribes.

"In 1823, when the mission and fort in what is now Sonoma was being built. Sam-Yeto and many other natives from Yerba Buena moved there to construct and populate the mission. Those people have been happier there because it's closer to their Suisun homelands."

Hearing the word 'happier' made Bale reflect on the mood of the General Vallejo; he seemed happier now. *Without a doubt, he is eager to go into battle. That amazes me, for I am terrified!*

Vallejo kept talking. "I didn't get assigned to Fort Sonoma until 1835, when we began to secularize. On my first trip there, I went by land on the *El Camino Real*. It ends at the fort in Sonoma. I stopped frequently and met many groups of natives. My objective was to explain what secularization meant for them."

Bale listened unable to control his fear of the upcoming battle. *How can he think about all this history? I am finding it difficult to listen. I can't stop thinking about going to war with natives, against other natives. How will I even distinguish between who is friend and who is foe?*

The General talked endlessly. "I worked with the coastal Miwok tribe while at Mission San Rafael. After a few days, I proceeded on to Novato where, under the direction of Sam-Yeto, about three thousand curious natives had amassed to meet me. My men and I pitched tents and began our work to persuade the natives to sign treaties with us. This was the first step in secularization. We went from one group to the next. It seemed to be an impossible task. There were many natives, and only about one-third of them seemed friendly toward us.

"That's when Sam-Yeto stepped up to help. He became the interpreter and urged the natives to listen. Later, he began to persuade people to sign by explaining that the military would protect them and punish their enemies. He knew there were many tribes battling others, and he convinced a large number that we could help. He has been my friend ever since."

Bale knew he might be offending the General with his question. He asked anyway. "Has the military protected those natives who signed?"

Vallejo gave off a lengthy belly laugh. "Ha, ha, ha! Yes, Dr. Bale, glad you asked. We have been protecting them and are going to be doing that tomorrow." He laughed more and added more details. "We have been fighting for months and months. We are slowly seeing the results with these enemy tribes.

"Enough talk. Oh, I should explain that these enemy tribes are the ones that never went to the missions, and they dislike sharing the land with the natives who are now leaving the missions to come live on the land."

The light of day was fading upon their arrival at *Rancho Caymus*. Chief Solano, Bale, Vallejo, and his officers were welcomed into Yount's adobe; the other soldiers put up tents.

Within the first hour, Bale was under the impression that Yount seemed as unconcerned as Vallejo about the upcoming battle. *Younts talks as much as the General. No, Yount talks more.*

They sat at a table spread with food, and Yount was saying, "When ya met Sam-Yeto, ya wondered how tall he is, didn't ya? Well, wit' the American way of measuring, he's six feet and seven inches tall. I know cuz the span of my hand is a foot wide, and I measured him. Ain't that right, Chief?"

Chief Solano had a bone, thick with meat, in his fist and it held his interest more than the question asked. Nevertheless, he responded, "If you say so, George."

Turning to Bale, Yount insisted, "Eat your bear meat. Ya gonna need your strength tomorrow." He called to his daughter, "Mia, bring the doctor more meat."

Bale finished a piece of the meat as a young girl approached him with a platter. She held a finger on her left hand raised, and Bale noticed an infection in her middle finger. He commented, "George, may I tend to your daughter's hand? It looks infected."

"Why, sure. Did you hear that, Mia? This man's a doctor and might be able ta fix yar hand."

The girl dipped her head in a shy manner as Bale took the platter from her. "Leave this meat here. Please get a bowl for hot water and bring it to the hearth." Bale grabbed his medical bag and sat on the floor near the fire, where a kettle hung. When the girl arrived with a wooden bowl, Bale patted the floor next to him to indicate she should sit. He noticed that she had not yet matured, and he guessed she was not even ten years old. "How did you get that cut on your finger?"

Yount had been watching and shouted, "Mia, he ain't goin' ta bite. His name is Doctor Bale. Talk ta him."

Without looking at Bale she whispered, "I skinned a rabbit and cut myself. Um, two days ago, I think."

Bale grimaced at Mia and said quietly, "It must hurt a lot with all the swelling and pus. I think we can fix it. Yes, I said **we** can fix it because I am going to tell you what you need to do." He poured hot water from the kettle to the bowl and reached into his bag for a bar of soap. "Tonight, we are going to soak your hand in this bowl of hot soapy water. I want you to soak it again before you go to bed, and tomorrow soak it three times. By then, it will begin to look and feel a lot better. That's easy, isn't it?"

She still would not look at him but bobbed her head in understanding.

When Bale felt that the water was not too hot to touch, he lathered the bar of soap in the water and reached for her hand. Gently, he immersed it. "I want the water as hot as possible without burning you. Understand?"

"Yes," she whispered.

"I want you to soak it for a long time. You need to see soap bubbles to know it's soapy enough to help fight the infection." He put the bar back into the water and agitated it until there were more bubbles. "See? Now, you do that."

She relaxed, made more bubbles, and finally looked at him.

Bale continued talking, "Anytime you cut yourself, get a splinter, or bleed for any reason, you should soak the wound in hot soapy water, so it won't get infected. Will you do that?"

She nodded.

"I imagine that your hand is starting to feel better." He lifted it and saw that the crusty dried pus was softening and melting away. "It's looking good. What can we do while you soak? Oh, I have an idea,"

He reached for a lantern on the table and placed it where he could make shadows on the wall. He formed hand shadows of a wolf, a rabbit, and a hawk. Mia's eyes widened, and she laughed as he made an eagle that landed on the shadow of her head.

Yount was talking again. "Yeah, Mia shot a rabbit ta eat. It made us a good meal. I haven't shot a bear in a week. Usually, thar's lots of Americans passing through, and I need a bear to feed 'em all, but no one's here right now." Yount claimed. "The critters are keeping away, too. When I came here it were a howling wilderness. Everywhere I looked, young beasts frolicked like spring lambs around my ranch. You know, the deer and elks, the wolves, and coyotes. Especially those grizzlies! They weren't ready to share this place with me. Well, I had ta teach 'em who I was. They thought I would run when I seed 'em. Ya know, run like most humans do. So, I had to take care of his one huge grizzly who claimed my place was his home. He were the biggest brute I ever seed. He liked to recline under my favorite wide-spreading oak. One day, I was coming his way when he seed me, and I seed him. That beast got on his feet, well, not fast, cuz he were fat and clumsy. Moved more like a boar than a bear. He expected me to make a fast retreat, like an Injun would. Not me! That thar bear knew the Wappo warriors feared grizzlies. He didn't know 'bout me! The brute opened his jaws an' roared a warning, and I opened my mouth an' roared right back! I never go anywhere without my rifle—even take it with me to shit. Well, I pulled my gun up and didn't need to look through the sights cuz he were so close. Then I squeezed the trigger and shot 'im between his eyes. That monster never knew what hit 'im."

Vallejo had a thought, and commented, "Young Mia knows how to shoot and kill game for the table. Dr. Bale, do you have a gun?"

"I do not."

The General pulled a pocket pistol from his jacket. "Here, take my pepper-box. I have other pocket pistols I can use."

With apprehension, Bale stood, walked over to Vallejo, and held out his open palm, saying, "I've never fired a gun." His hand dropped to the table when the small gun was placed in it. "Oh, it's heavy!"

Vallejo turned to one of his officers, "Show him how to load and fire it before tomorrow." Turning back to take another bite of his meal, he said while chewing, "See, it has three barrels. You can take three shots without reloading. That should do for you. If you are working on an injured man and a native comes close to attack you, you only need to pull the pepper-box from your waist, point it, and pull the trigger. It has no sights for making a precise aim."

The gun still laid in Bale's palm. He stared at it.

Chief Solano commented, "Maybe you should teach him right now. He seems to fear putting it into his waistband. Dr. Bale, it appears you know nothing about firearms. Am I correct?"

"You are correct."

Yount took a long swallow of his drink and wiped his mouth with his sleeve before saying, "After ya learn how ta shoot that little pistol, I'll show ya how to shoot a rifle. Or, I'll have Mia show ya."

Mia looked up and agreed to it with a nod.

Bale turned to the girl and said, "Thanks. Oh, that's probably a long enough soak. Dry your hand with a clean cloth now and don't forget to soak it again before you sleep."

Mia took a step towards Bale and said, "Thanks."

Bale placed a hand on top her head and patted.

General Vallejo volunteered a story about Yount and his rifle, "Speaking of shooting, Yount is quite the marksman. John Cooper is another one. Once Yount and Cooper came to help against the Russian River Sotoyomes. Those natives had no rifles, only bows, clubs, and spears. The militia had muskets, and our vaqueros came with their lassos, which are deadly in combat. Those two riflemen—Yount and Cooper—rarely missed a shot. After the battle, the Reverend Clark who was watching from a distance claimed that every one of Yount's shots, except two, brought down an enemy. Of course, the story may have been exaggerated in a bit of bravado."

Bale turned to George Yount and said, "I imagine the General is grateful that he can rely on you for assistance."

"Why, it works both ways," Yount explained. "When the Wappos swept down from the mountains to attack my ranch, I sent runners to Sonoma for help. This was back when I was in my log blockhouse. The General came and helped me out." He stopped for the moment to drink.

Everyone seemed to be finished eating, yet Yount wasn't finished talking. "Another time, this Indian called Chief Jota, who were the devil himself, came and stampeded half my longhorns. You remember this, Sam-Yeto, don't ya? We had ta swim the rain-swollen Napa River to keep on the trail of Chief Jota and those cattle thieves. Course, Jota couldn't hide all the hoof prints in the mud. When we got ta their camp, Vallejo's forces attacked with us. It were a long battle. In the end we burned their camp and kilt a lot of those thieves. We thought it were over, but it weren't.

"On our return march to Napa Valley, two hours before daylight, about four hundred savages attacked us. And . . .

General Vallejo stood and declared, "Jorge, my boy, we have a battle to fight tomorrow. No more stories tonight."

Bale left with the officer for his pepper-box lesson.

Standing to go to his tent, Vallejo noticed that Bale had not touched his drink. They had been drinking homemade hard liquor. The General drained Bale's mug without comment.

In the dark before dawn, the General, Chief Solano, and their men assembled to head south and, at prior agreed upon locations, separated into smaller groups. The terrain of the area needed no light of day for the two leaders to know where they were. They knew every hill and knoll, wooded area and meadow, every hiding place and area to avoid.

A runner returned to report that the invading enemy had been seen on the east side of the Napa River. "They'll soon cross the water," he said.

As Yount approached the river, he directed his native mercenaries into a secluded hollow on his right flank with orders not to show themselves until he signaled. "Bale, ya ought ta go with 'em."

Yount went with his mounted natives to the left flank, and Vallejo ordered most of his military platoon to circle wide and position themselves to be behind the enemy as they left the river. Chief Solano and his men were strategically positioned in various areas where the enemy might retreat.

All was ready, and Mother Nature was doing her part with the tide coming in. In a short time, the river would be impassable, making an escape unfeasible.

Minutes before the sun rose above the horizon, General Vallejo and his men rode up to a knoll in conspicuous view of the enemy. They were the bait. In their position, the enemy must circle to the left and right to surround them before attacking.

Bale hid in the ravine wondering about the quiet. He felt his blood throbbing at his temple. When the birds began to sing their morning songs, the native's war cries erupted and silenced the birds. With the war whoops of the enemy flooding the air, Bale dropped from his horse to the ground and squatted. Others in his group watched and waited for Vallejo's signal.

Storming toward General Vallejo and his men were enemy natives with hideous designs colorfully painted on their faces and bodies. All were naked, except for feathered headdresses held on with a band wrapped around their forehead and their weapons draped on their bodies. They had no guns—only war clubs, bow and arrows, knives, clubs, and their bloodcurdling cries.

Waiting until the enemy created enough space to allow the regiment to surround them, Vallejo gave the signal by raising his saber high above his head and shouting, "Charge!" That command was lost in the din, but his blade flashed in the sunlight for all to see.

As the dew started to rise in the air, blood began to fall from the battle. Unable to reload with the arrows flying at them, each military man fired his one shot before resorting to a bayonet, knife, sword, or the stock of his rifle to batter. Soon, heavy war clubs knocked many from their horses. Hand-to-hand combat began on the field: Swords slipped into and out of the natives, clubs bashed faces of the soldiers, and arrows made punctures wherever they landed. Men collapsed without life yet bled.

General Vallejo was mounted and under the protection of his bodyguards, who blocked any natives coming at him. He saw within the horde two special men—obviously chiefs—with eagle feathers decorating their headbands and grizzly claws dangling from their necks. The two were maneuvering toward him. He shouted a battle cry and dared them to fight him. "Aaeeee! Come closer, *Maldito*. You want my life? Come try!" A bodyguard saw and fired his musket; one chief fell—though only wounded. General Vallejo raised his rifle. It misfired, exploding in his hand and burning his arm. Without hesitation, Vallejo turned the gun around and grabbed the barrel in his gloved hands, using it as a battering ram against natives who had managed to get closer around his horse. He looked up to see the remaining chief coming fast. That momentary glance distracted Vallejo, and he was pulled from his horse by a native whom Vallejo slashed with his knife across the neck. Now, he stood on the ground next to one of his dead bodyguards, whose pistol was still tucked at his waist. Vallejo grabbed it and shot a warrior, who fell dead against him and knocked him over. As Vallejo pushed the body away and scrambled to his feet, he saw the enemy chief close with an arrow poised to leave the bowstring. Vallejo fired his pistol again, but missed, as Solano rode up and leaped off his horse with his knife ready. He landed hard against the enemy chief, who screamed when the knife was buried into his back. Vallejo and Solano's eyes met, ever so briefly, before they pivoted and attacked more of the oncoming enemy.

By now, Bale was standing and watching at a distance away from the main foray. All the men with whom he had been hiding were out fighting. He was alone, clutching his medical bag. He felt such a coward, yet he knew he was a doctor, not a soldier. As soon as he saw a wounded soldier not far away, he hurried to the man, crouched down, and began to work on the bleeding, slashed cheek. He slipped the skin back where it belonged and took the soldier's hand, saying,

"Push on it to stop the bleeding while I pull off your sash to wrap your wound." Within minutes, he was working on the next soldier, then another, and another.

General Vallejo and Chief Solano managed to pull themselves back onto their horses and tore through the enemy with their sabers. Solano was exceptionally powerful and decapitated one.

All of Vallejo's men were fighting, when Chief Solano's Patwin warriors arrived, whooping and yelling. The enemy began to retreat, dragging their wounded away. The arrows of the Patwin warriors sang in the air before hitting their marks, and their knives soon dripped with blood.

The war cries of the enemy turned to cries of pain, and the aggressive fighting switched to solitary death throes. Watching the enemy run, Vallejo surveyed the mess of bodies and saw movement. The wounded chief was crawling toward Solano. Vallejo called out, "One coming behind you!"

Solano pivoted with his saber drawn, kicked down the chief who still wore his eagle feathers, and slashed his belly open.

Though the battle was ending, it was not over for Dr. Bale who continued to tend to the wounded soldiers in the field for many hours.

Chief Solano and his men gathered the enemy's dead into a pile, added wood, and set them afire. They executed an enemy chief and forced his remaining warriors to watch. Finally, Chief Solano told them, "Return to your settlements and live in peace or we will come again. We are too strong; you will never win."

Vallejo added, "Go back and tell your people to stop raiding and stealing. If we hear of killing, we will go to battle with you again."

On the return ride back to Yount's *Rancho Caymus*, Bale saw a quiet countryside in the light of day. Endless expanses of land covered in tall bunch grass that spread up gentle hills. Bale rode closer to a tree, "Look at this tree. It has acorns, so surely, it's an oak, but who has seen an oak this immense? If I hollowed it out, I could live inside. It's as wide as a house. How could an oak grow to this size?"

They were valley oaks, possibly centuries old, that would soon disappear just as the natives disappeared with the coming of white people.

They rode close to the Napa River and passed familiar willow, cottonwood, and sycamore trees which Bale recognized, but he noticed berry bushes he had never seen before. "Look at all the tiny berries on this bush," he said, as he plucked off the wild grapes. Earlier, he had passed and tasted huckleberries for the first time in his life. Finally, he commented, "This is the most beautiful place I have ever seen."

Yount agreed, "I said that when I first seed this valley. Hell, and tarnation! After today, I don't want to leave *Rancho Caymus* ever again. I'm sick of battles."

Dr. Bale said, "I want to live here. Look at this river! With this river running through your land and what will be mine, we can do so much."

Yount had another thought and asked, "Mariano, . . . I mean, General, sir, I was thinkin' and wonderin' if ya could help me get cattle to replace the ones that the Injuns stole."

Vallejo needed no time to think before replying, "Yes, of course. The missions have thousands of cattle and horses that I am dispersing. I should be able to work something out for you."

Before Bale went to bed that night, he pulled his bottle of ink and a quill from his medical bag. He unrolled a paper he had brought, knowing that he would want to write to his love:

My Thoughts on Pain

Today I witnessed a battle and saw bodies covering the field where it was fought. I could not help everyone, and I saw so many injuries. This experience has made me think about pain.

Pain is an important part of life. Even in our daily lives pain warns us that something has happened or is happening that needs attention.

The parts of the body that can sense pain are the nerve endings within tissue (such as our skin). The pain warns us to care for a cut or to bandage the broken bone or to cut off the gangrened foot.

However, tonight I am feeling pain within my heart and more pain in my mind. I am missing you. Being away from you causes pain within me—a special pain, not the pain needing medical attention. Even so, this special pain I am feeling for you needs my attention, and so I write to you.

Without pain, life would be dangerous. What would warn us that we are hurt? How would we know that something is wrong? How would I know how much I love you and want to be with you if I did not feel this pain?

All my love,
Edward

p.s. Besides the horrible battle, I saw beauty, too. I found the place where I want to live with you. I will tell you more when I see you.

Back in Monterey, Maria Ignacia was with her Uncle Salvador in *Casa Zemita*. He had come on military business from Fort Sonoma. They were walking into the dining room to join the family for a meal. She locked her elbow with his and leaned against his arm as they walked. "Salvador, I am so glad to see you. You should come more often."

"My duties don't allow me. I came today because Mariano was not there to bring these reports. He is off somewhere fighting a battle."

She came to an abrupt stop, slipped her arm from his to be able to face him, and said, "No, you must be mistaken. He took Edward . . . I mean, Dr. Bale, with him. He cannot be fighting."

They reached the table, where many of the family were beginning to eat. Everyone had heard their conversation; all eyes were on them.

Salvador took both her hands in his and coaxed her to a chair. "Hello everyone." He proceeded to walk around the table and greet the eight members of his family with cheek kisses before he returned to sit beside Maria Ignacia. He started filling his plate and plopping food on her plate since she seemed in a daze. At last, he turned to her and said, "Please do not be concerned. You know Mariano always returns unscathed. I am sure he will protect Dr. Bale to the utmost."

Maria Ignacia gasped.

Amidst the odor of cilantro and baked chicken filling the room, people waited to hear Salvador's next words. In the quiet, some ate but most stared at Maria Ignacia and Salvador. While watching and waiting, many felt the same fear for Dr. Bale's life.

Salvador decided to make people laugh and said, "From what I understand, the hostile natives Mariano is fighting number over one thousand. The powerful General Vallejo can destroy them in minutes with his regiment of one hundred men."

Some chuckles and chortles came from the family, but not from Maria Ignacia who jumped up. "Oh, no! One thousand of them to one hundred of our men!"

Salvador stood and wrapped her in his arms. He rocked her. "Maria Ignacia, I was jesting. George Yount is there with his Caymus warriors, and Chief Solano went with hundreds. Please, don't be upset." He took her chin with his hand and kissed her forehead. "Where is my niece who is strong and lighthearted?"

"Oh, Salvador, you frightened me with your jest." Though he had misled her for only seconds before she knew the truth, she needed to calm herself. She took a sip of water, smiled half-heartedly, and waited to regain ease and her appetite.

Everyone began to speak around the table.

She cut her chicken, stabbed a chunk with her fork, but did not eat it. Finally, she turned to Salvador to say, "Will they go to Fort Sonoma as they had planned?"

"I'm sure they will."

"I had hoped you would be there to meet Edward."

With a wide grin, Salvador said, "I met him on the beach with you. Don't you remember?"

"Oh, Salvador, you know what I meant. I want you to get to know him before we wed."

"Oh, has the date been set? I want to be there and enjoy all the celebrating."

She shook her head. Feeling calmer, a twinkle came to her eyes, and she told him, "No date yet. *Los Gigantes Tres* still are waiting for his conversion to Catholicism and the papers for his Mexican citizenship." She giggled, knowing he was curious about who *Los Gigantes Tres* were.

"Hmm, *Los Gigantes Tres*. Maybe our General, my mother, and who?"

She punched his arm. "My father, of course."

The two of them spent time that afternoon together on the beach. He asked, "Tell me about this man who has taken your heart."

"Oh, Salvador, I love him so much. I am glad you are here. With you I can bare my soul." She danced in a circle leaving bare footprints in the sand. She was holding her shoes by the shoestrings. The day was warm. "Looking at you, I realized that he looks a bit like you. Slim and tall, handsome with dark hair, and a wonderful smile like you." She poked him in the ribs, "Let me see that smile of yours."

He made an exaggerated grimace and grabbed her around the waist, swinging her around and around.

"Oh, Salvador, more." She laughed uncontrollably. "I remember when you would do this many years ago. We always had the best times together."

After leaving the beach, they stood on the plank sidewalk, not far from the Custom House, until Salvador had to return to the Presidio. They embraced with hugs and cheek kisses before stepping apart. Without any more words, only a slight nod, he turned and left.

She watched his retreat. The thump of his boot heels on the wooden walk gradually disappeared among the sounds of gulls screeching, the military band practicing, and many passersby conversing.

She blinked with a pouting lip and went home.

Leaving Yount to enjoy his *Rancho Caymus*, General Vallejo, Dr. Bale, and the troops headed to Fort Sonoma. Bale absorbed the beauty of the terrain, drinking in every detail. However, nothing impressed him more than the land north of *Rancho Caymus*. Without a doubt, Dr. Bale desired to live there and said so.

Vallejo had similar thoughts about his choice of land. "I, too, know where I want to live. It's just a stone's throw from the fort in Sonoma. It has a natural spring bubbling from the earth and flat land leading up to the foot of the hills. I plan to build my house there. Unlike you, Dr. Bale, I want a wood house like the one Larkin built. Do you still want an adobe?"

They had been riding quietly for a while and Bale responded, "I do." He asked, "Have lands been legally given to the natives already?"

"Oh, of course. For example, when we started secularization back in 1835, the neophytes of the San Rafael Mission were even given a choice."

"Neophytes? What does that mean?"

"Those natives at the missions who were baptized and became Christians are called neophytes. They chose land west of the mission on a peninsula across from Yerba Buena. The area is called Nicasio. The Governor of California ordered me to notify those Christianized natives that the land of Nicasio was granted to them. They were given full ownership."

More than a year had passed since Dr. Edward Turner Bale had been found on the beach of Monterey. Since then, a plethora of information about the customs of the area, the history, the social structures of the people, and the layout of the land had been presented to him. Now he found himself questioning much of the knowledge that he had acquired. Even his perspective of the Vallejo family confused him because he could not comprehend the affectionate mannerisms among uncles, aunts, nephews, nieces, and distant cousins. Foreign to him were deep family relations, which are part of Spanish customs.

When he returned after what turned out to be a month-long journey to the eastern valley with General Vallejo, he was anxious to finalize his citizenship and Catholic training. The trip had shown him where he wanted to live in the valley, and he was excited to share all that had happened so, his words tumbled out. "Maria Ignacia, it's beyond beautiful. You know the area around Fort Sonoma, but I want us to live farther east in a place north of George Yount's *Rancho Caymus*. I know you will love it."

It seemed to her that he had grown with the trip; he had more enthusiasm and confidence, and a direction for their future.

They exchanged the writings each had made for the other. Maria Ignacia was especially taken with the following:

> *Maria Ignacia,*
> *Within me is a definite need to share. Of course, sharing means a communication in both directions. Expressing my experiences becomes more meaningful as your experiences begin to unfold, showing the similarities, coincidences, contradictions, et cetera.*
> *For a true sharing to occur, there must be interest.*
> *I have that with you.*
> *And I felt in your absence the need to share.*
> *Love from Edward*
> *p.s. Before I returned to Monterey, I wanted to let you know how wonderful you make me feel by fulfilling my need to share.*

She wrote a little poem in response:

> *To share,*
> *A pair.*
> *Where?*
> *Don't care*
> *Just . . .*
> *Together*
> *Two share.*

Their separation had increased the yearning they had for each other. The separation had made their being together more difficult, as well, because they still were not allowed to embrace or kiss, though they did in secret. Their desires were growing harder to deny.

Edward lamented, "I had hoped that I would return and find my citizenship papers waiting here for me. Please speak with your family. Surely, they can get word to Mexico City to finalize them." He took a deep breath and sighed. "I had an idea. To expedite the religious requirement, I am going to Yerba Buena. I can perform my medical duties there and go to religious training at the same time. The friar in charge told me that he could help me complete everything by the end of this year. So, I will plan to come home for the holidays with my religious training completed."

Neither of them had to say aloud how much the separation would create a daily sadness, though the distance would control the frustrations of their desires. They parted again, knowing they were only a day's ride apart.

Getting to know the Franciscan friar at Yerba Buena opened Bale's eyes and mind to more than the Catholic religion. Bale learned the truth about what had happened in Nicasio. He realized that General Vallejo distorted parts of the story and twisted the truth by not sharing the latest decisions about the Nicasio lands for the natives.

Friar Mo was a small and frail man who opened his heart to Bale. "I am grateful to teach you and prepare you. In fact, I thank you for coming. I am overburdened with this life I have here. I'm so weary. Little of my day is spent, as I would wish, in prayer and devotion. Instead, I sow grain, raise cows and sheep, direct carts hauling stone, lime, and dirt, as well as oversee the burial of the dead, and care for the sick. After doing all that, where is my time to be tranquil and pray? To teach you will help fulfill my religious needs and the health of both my body and soul."

Bale asked, "Why did you come here? Surely you had a choice."

"Yes, I did have a choice; however, this place was made to sound wonderful. I was told about the hundreds of natives here to do our bidding and help with the thousands of acres of fertile land, with well-tilled fields of wheat and other grains, and of orchards and gardens. All of that was true for a while. No one could predict the coming of diseases and the deaths of so many natives."

"How long have you been here?"

"Decades. I have seen monstrosities preformed in the name of our Lord. By 1800, syphilis was in all the missions, and we were living in hell. The women had stopped giving birth to live babies."

Dr. Bale's eyes frowned, awaiting a clarification of that statement.

"The babies were born dead because they had syphilis. One of us, Friar Gil, learned how to perform caesarian sections. He rarely could save the mother; however, a baby could be taken out and baptized before dying. We did caesarian sections to save their little souls from eternal damnation."

Bale was horrified. "My god!"

"Oh, there is more. In 1808, I saw almost every native child less than ten years old die from the measles. Usually, their parents died as well. The neophytes ran away to save themselves from the measles. They didn't know, of course, that they could not run from it; they took the disease wherever they went."

"Have you no pleasant memories from your stay at the missions?"

Friar Mo apologized, "Yes, I do. I am sorry to burden you with sadness. One mission worked. It was a medical mission called San Rafael Arcángel."

Bale brightened, "Yes, I have been told to visit it, across the bay from here."

The little friar shared uplifting facts. "I do the paperwork for that mission as well as Yerba Buena. Between 1820 and 1830, syphilis was under control and the other epidemics passed over it. They were prospering by producing wheat, and I have the numbers right here." He opened a ledger and pointed to a list:

2,450 bushels of grain, half wheat,
1,533 head of beef,
188 sheep, and
450 horses.

"Why do you think they did so well?"

Friar Mo shrugged and shook his head, before saying, "Well, I cannot say exactly." Then his face changed, as he thought about the question. "However, I know that they did everything differently, and that may be why. For example, the runaways, if they returned, were not given lashings nor put in the stocks. Oh, and they never shackled the natives. I am sure that the honorable leaders in charge are one of the reasons. When Friar Gil became sickly and left, they replaced him with Friar Juan Amoros, whom everyone loved. He was the best at teaching children and instructing adults. He was delightful, and even was friendly with the military men assigned to San Rafael." He laughed for a moment and wiped his mouth with his sleeve. "Just now, I was thinking about a water clock that he built. He was mechanically inclined. Such goodness flowed from him; like the waters in his clock, his time with us was good."

Wanting to share his newfound knowledge about the Nicasio lands given to the natives, Bale said, "Yes, I understand other fulfilling events happened there at San Rafael Arcángel. General Vallejo told me how, in 1835, the lands of Nicasio were given to the Christianized neophytes of that mission. That was wonderful."

Friar Mo blinked and frowned before saying, "Yes, that was true. However, they no longer have claim to that land. Two years after giving ownership of the

Nicasio land to the natives, General Vallejo declared that they were not making wise use of the land, so he took it back. He took the ownership away from them, claiming he would return it to them when circumstances were favorable."

Bales eyes grew wide, "No, how could he do that?" Trying to grasp the truth of the story, trying to understand why Mariano did not mention this, and trying to remain calm, he asked, "Has he returned the land to them?"

The little friar, standing in his long white garment, shuffled his feet and shook his head. "No. Well, not yet."

Bale went to bed that night pondering what he had learned that day about the esteemed General Mariano Guadalupe Vallejo. He realized, if he wanted to learn what had happened to the Nicasio land, he could never ask a direct question of Vallejo, who soon would be his in-law. Also, Bale understood he was in a difficult position with Vallejo being so powerful. Bale's mind swirled with images from his personal experiences that demonstrated the power General Vallejo had among the military, on the battlefield, and with the family. *I must step carefully and speak little. I have much to lose because of what I want—a life with Maria Ignacia. Everything depends on this man.*

Bale swore to himself to work harder toward accomplishing his goals of becoming a Catholic and obtaining a Mexican citizenship. He was determined to maintain his focus and not confront Vallejo.

Yet, the following morning the urgency changed.

Walking from his bedroom in the fort at Yerba Buena, Bale turned a corner to go to the dining hall and bumped into Vallejo.

"Oh, excuse me," Bale exclaimed.

With a smile reaching from ear to ear, the General said, "I was coming to find you, Dr. Bale. You must come outside to the edge of the bay. Yount is here and building something extraordinary. I know you haven't eaten breakfast, but your hunger can wait."

They walked outside, hearing hammers hitting nails, wood being sawed, and men laughing.

"Remember when Yount asked me if I could get cattle for him to replace the animals stolen from him? Well, they will be here tomorrow, and we needed a way to get them across the bay to his ranch. Yount devised a method. At first, I thought him a mad man. His idea seemed insane and simply impossible."

They were walking toward a flurry of activity around a wooden structure that lay on the ground next to the water of the bay. Vallejo continued talking. "Yount is building a floating corral with the help of all these men. Of course, he is supervising because no one understands his plan. He alone knows how he wants to make this."

Yount saw them coming and came to meet them. "Ah, it's the General and the good doctor. Top of the mornin' to ya both. Come see the Noah's Ark I is buildin'. But my boat is only fer cattle, no birds or elephants." That said, Yount produced a long, hearty laugh. "Ho, ho, ho!"

Vallejo looked to Bale and explained, "I don't think I told you that George is an expert carpenter. That's how I met him. He was hired to repair the Sonoma Mission. Instead of using clay tiles for the roof, he made wooden shakes to repair the roof. I was impressed and have been using his skills for many buildings.

"Now he has invented a way to carry cattle across the bay. Well," Vallejo said, slapping Yount on the back in a friendly gesture. "We still don't know if it will work."

Bale pointed to men measuring the length of an oil cask. "What are those barrels?"

Yount explained, "When people ship whale oil, it goes in them casks. See, there's a lot of 'em stacked around here and there, waitin' to be sent back on a ship to a whaling company. That's where I got this idea ta put 'em under the corral an' make it float."

"That's ingenious. Well, if it works. How many animals will the casks hold up and still float?"

Vallejo said, "I asked George the same question, and he doesn't know. But he is building corrals for fifty head." He pointed and said, "See all the compartments. The fencing makes rows of tight enclosures, the perfect size for one cow, so she can't turn around and unbalance the floating corral."

Yount stated, "We ain't takin' no bulls. Too much trouble if they get riled."

The three watched the progress of the construction before returning to the fort for breakfast. While they ate, the topic of floating cattle never changed. Soon, it became apparent that Vallejo wanted to move cattle onto his own land in the future.

Yount laughed, "Now I know why ya got money fer me to build this. What the General needs, he gets. Ho, ho, ho!"

Bale didn't say much but laughed as hard as the other two while they celebrated the possibility of a floating corral. When they returned to the water's edge, it was almost finished.

Yount explained, "Look at it. Ain't it somethin'! See there's a wide pathway around all the corrals for the crew to work. They still have ta put on a rudder after we get the casks attached in the right places to make it float. Then we'll slip it in the water. Hell, I's so excited."

By evening, the floating corral was waiting in the bay for the arrival of the cows the next day. It bobbed in the water while men worked to finish details before getting it moored for the night. The six long oars, called sweeps, were fastened in place on the deck. It was ready to row when loaded.

Vallejo, Bale, and Yount were standing on board in the crew's walkway as excited as children. They leaned on the railing and bobbed with the water's movement. The tide was coming in, and, as the craft was lifted higher and higher, their spirits were lifted, as well, in anticipation of the coming event.

Vallejo asked, "Bale, you are going to float across the bay with us? Wait! Allow me to rephrase that. I want to make you a deal. If you come across on one of the cattle runs, I will set the date for your wedding."

Bale jerked to standing and turned to face the General. "But, but, I mean, I have not finished the conversion to be a Cath . . . "

Vallejo bellowed, "Now, don't complicate my gift to you. Are you going to ride the floating corral or not?"

Bale was grateful for the early darkness of the short December day, because he did not want Vallejo to see the puzzlement in his eyes or the confusion in his furrowed brow. "Yes, of course. I'll even man an oar, herd the cattle on board, or clean the shit off the decks."

As they walked at a fast pace back to the Presidio, Bale was thinking, *I hope my voice did not deceive me and let him hear my confusion. I feel he is playing with me. Why did he tell me he is ready to set a wedding date at this moment? Oh, I want to tell Maria Ignacia right now. I wish I could.*

Like the power of the tide when it gives or takes water, Vallejo filled Bale's hopes more by presenting another surprise; he said, "This morning I became distracted with all the excitement of Yount's floating corral. I was coming to tell you that we have appointed you to the post of Surgeon General of the Mexican California Army. It becomes official with the coming new year. I want to mention that there has never been an Anglo to hold this post. Besides more salary for you, you are being honored as the first Anglo."

After thanking the general profusely, Bale knew to ask no questions and to accept the changes, though the reasons were never made clear. He knew Vallejo could make the tides in his and Maria Ignacia's life rise or recede.

Larkin House in Monterey

Side view of Larkin house showing expansion on house for Dr. Bale's Pharmacy. (Rachel put a CLOSED sign in the window and blocked the door with a bench.)

CHAPTER SIX

DRINKING IN THE TRUTH

1839-1841

Just before their marriage, Bale was appointed officially to the post of Surgeon General of the Mexican California Army. Dr. Edward Bale was a dedicated medical doctor, a proficient surgeon, intelligent, amicable, and suited to the position. Nevertheless, there had never been an Anglo to hold this post and that fact made the appointment unpopular among the Californios. Yet the power of the Vallejos prevailed in many ways.

To quell any disagreements and to end all discussions among the military men, General Vallejo's older brother, Jose de Jesus Vallejo issued this statement:

> OFFICIAL ANNOUNCEMENT
>
> *With reference to the appointment of Doctor Edward Bale to the position of Chief Surgeon of the California Army, I will say that those who criticize it show poor taste, for it is known that the Northern part of new California is continually exposed to the attacks of Indians, and we have no other physician of ability in this area. Our only other healer is the Indian man, Petronio, who always seems to cure his friends and kill his enemies.*

In general, people knew they were wise to heed the official announcement as if it had been an order from General Vallejo himself. Among most, wisdom prevailed.

Friends, not wanting to offend the Vallejo family, discussed with joy the upcoming Bale wedding planned for springtime in 1839. The priest in the Presidio's Chapel of Monterey set the date as March 21, 1839, though Dr. Bale was not yet a citizen or a Catholic. He knew better than to comment or question the powerful Vallejo family.

Edward Bale would not get his citizenship in Mexico for two more years, and he never understood why those requirements no longer mattered for his wedding. He, the priest, and all others were wise enough not to ask.

And wise enough not to complain when he was baptized with a religious name added. He became Edward *Asunción* Turner Bale.

His friend Thomas Larkin had a hearty laugh when he learned of his new name. "Didn't I warn you that these Mexicans would give you another name? I told you earlier that my brother was given a couple of Spanish names. You must accept your new name, as a condition to be part of the family."

"I know, I know," Bale told Larkin, "Yet I find the translation of *Asunción* to be an uncomfortable name to have to explain to my American friends. It refers to the Virgin Mary's ascent into heaven with her whole body. I would have preferred a more masculine and simpler concept like your brother's name of John the Baptist. If George Yount asks me what it means, I am going to pretend I don't know, so he won't laugh at me."

Larkin had become Bale's closest friend. They talked at length about possible business ideas when the two couples were together for dinner at the Larkins. Sometimes, the two men socialized by themselves, but it was the closeness of Maria Ignacia and Rachel that knitted the men's friendship into a warm relationship. By 1839, the Larkin's had four children—all boys and the oldest only five years old—so, Rachel found few opportunities to socialize with Maria Ignacia.

Rachel lamented, "Not that I am wanting to be pregnant now, though I would love to have a sweet little girl. I have no time for myself even with two women to help with the children. My days exhaust me, and I think it's because boys are always into mischief."

Bale had made another friend while working at the Presidio in Yerba Buena an American named Nathan Spear, who had recently moved from Monterey, where he owned a warehouse. Spear went to live in the village of Yerba Buena, which was located between the mission, where Bale was getting his Catholic studies, and the Presidio, where Bale conducted his medical duties for the military.

They came to know one another when a ship arrived at Yerba Buena and the two men went to the docks to pick up the supplies they had ordered. Nathan Spear was expecting materials to build a grist mill, with equipment manufactured on the East Coast. Bale had ordered medicines and medical supplies.

Meeting someone with the knowledge of how to build a mill was of interest to Bale. He saw it as an opportunity to learn and plan for a mill on his future land. "Why would you want to build a grist mill here in Yerba Buena?" Bale asked. "There are only a few buildings and almost no one living here. There are definitely no wheat fields."

Spear disagreed, "Every month, another structure is built. I see this place as a growing community. Besides, both the Presidio here in Yerba Buena and the San Rafael Mission across the bay have large wheat fields planted and will use my mill. I imagine you have seen that other people are settling the area. I know of many who will come to me to process their wheat."

Bale asked, "But what puzzles me most is there are not any streams running here to power it."

Spear agreed, "Yes, on that point you are correct. I will power it with mules."

"Oh, I understand now." Bale shared his dream, "I have a wedding soon and I want to make our home near the mission in Sonoma. But first, I want to build a grist mill on the land. Maybe you would help me."

"Why, of course, I can after I have my mill up and running. Am I correct that you are not in any rush because you want to get married before you start your project?"

"Yes, first things first. I'll begin the mill after the wedding."

They became serious friends. When on duty in the Presidio in Yerba Buena, Bale often went to the site of Spear's mill to observe the progress. What he saw gave him confidence that he could have a grist mill one day.

To the chagrin of Lita, the wedding was a small affair only for family and a few friends. A small wedding satisfied Edward Bale, since he was not proud of all he lacked. He had hoped to have a prosperous business before he married, and he did not. Also, he had planned to have a house ready to start a family, and again, he did not. At least, with all his medical work, he had hoped to be a prominent member of the community when he married; however, he could not surpass the prestige of the Vallejos. Even with the position as Chief Surgeon of the California Army, he knew many people were resentful that an Anglo held the job.

After the wedding ceremony in the Presidio's chapel, the family gathering at

Casa Zemita was small. It was similar to the size of their Sunday meal, not a special celebration of a wedding. This did not bother Bale either. However, Maria Ignacia found it to be a disappointment. The only part of the wedding day that Edward Bale regretted was the end. At the end of the day, he and Maria Ignacia would be sleeping in the guest room in *Casa Zemita*. Not that he regretted finally being able to sleep with her, he only regretted the Vallejos controlling even that detail in his life.

To consummate the marriage without the whole family being aware of the moment, Edward had planned that the two of them would discreetly disappear, upon a signal from him. He would go out to the garden and circle around the house to enter the guest room, while she would go to change to more comfortable shoes that were in her old bedroom. After a few moments, they would meet in the guest bedroom, make love, and return to the party.

The possibility of discovery made the moment more tantalizing; also, knowing he could accomplish his lovemaking without the Vallejo's knowledge, hardened his desire. Openly, he walked from the dining room, through the back hallway to the outside, standing for a casual moment at the doorway not to look as if he were in a rush.

A moment later, Maria Ignacia left the living room and went to her childhood bedroom. When no one was in sight, she quickly slipped past the other bedrooms, went along the veranda to the guest room, and rushed inside. Her mother's lace nightgown which she had saved for years laid draped across the bed. She unfastened her bridal dress to don the diaphanous nightdress.

Meanwhile, Edward was in the garden, slipping past the rows of dried pea plants tied to lattices from last summer's harvest. The wooden structure and vines brushed against his legs and private parts. The touch aroused him and took his breath away. In the darkness, he thought he saw a shadow move as he turned the corner of the house. He stopped and pressed his back to the wall of the house. He stood motionless and waited to see the shadow again. No one was there. All was silent except the distant howl of a coyote. His desire was so hard it hurt, and he pushed it to relieve himself before rushing to the next corner of the house.

Now he was sweating with anticipation, and he gave a small whistle to Maria Ignacia as he passed the guest room's back window. Ten feet left to go. Edward grabbed the railing to the veranda and pulled himself up and over. He was only five feet from the doorway when the living room door opened. Light spilling out onto the veranda, and two figures appeared as blackened silhouettes. They stood talking and laughing, unaware of him. Edward could see wine glasses glittering in their hands.

He took an educated guess that their eyes had not adjusted to the darkness, and he rushed unseen to the door of the guest bedroom and slipped inside.

Maria Ignacia turned toward the door as he entered. They fell into each other's arms in giddiness, like children. She giggled. He could feel the heat from her flushed cheeks when he wrapped his hands around her face and pulled her mouth to his.

"Edward," she whispered while placing her hand behind his head in his soft wavy hair. "Edward, I love you so."

He stepped away to unbuckle his pants and let them drop around his ankles.

She pulled him onto the bed and onto her. Like a hummingbird's tongue needs no practice to find the sweet nectar, he slipped into her. She marveled at the ease and fit and thrill and heat. They rolled together over the bedspread, still locked, experiencing ecstasy until the whole world seemed to explode and send thrills from their toes to their lips.

Although they had not made much noise, they noticed the silence as they collapsed with exhaustion, unmoving for several minutes. Finally, unwrapping from the embrace, she giggled with delight and gave him a quick kiss. He chuckled.

Maria Ignacia whispered, "Get dressed and go back, so we can do this again in an hour."

He agreed and pulled up his pants.

Usually, Vallejo was aware of all events around him, but he had not noticed their disappearance. He was preoccupied with another plan, an idea he wanted to prove, if only to himself.

He wanted to test an assumption he had formed since meeting Bale. General Vallejo had concluded that Dr. Bale never drank any alcoholic beverages, because a few times he had seen Bale leave a glass without drinking the wine, and there was that time he walked away from an untouched cup of hard spirits.

Vallejo shouted, "Attention, everyone! Fill your glasses. I want to toast the bride and groom."

Maria Ignacia heard and entered the room arm and arm with her sister, whom she met in the hallway. Edward entered through the opposite door.

Vallejo walked around, filling every glass. Lita helped, doing the same. Finally, he raised his glass and announced, "To my lovely niece, Maria Ignacia and her husband, Edward. I drink to their having a long and loving life, and I drink to many little feet filling their home."

Other people chimed in with "Prosperity!" "Health!" and cheers for the couple. While everyone tipped their glass and drank, Vallejo watched Bale, and saw that he touched the liquid to his lips and did not drink. Deep in thought at that moment, Vallejo was sure he had learned one of the secrets that Bale had told Maria Ignacia. However, months would pass before he knew the dire significance of his discovery.

Maria Ignacia approached her uncle. "*Tio*, the hour is late, and I still do not see Salvador anywhere. I have been waiting for him all evening. Do you know why he's not here?"

"We needed him back at Fort Sonoma."

Her face filled with a pained expression, "Oh, he was supposed to meet Edward. They have never met. He promised me that he would come to our wedding."

"That's surprising that he has not met Dr. Bale." Vallejo shook his head. "Only one of us could come, because of problems at the fort. I made the decision that he remain behind."

"I am so disappointed." She hesitated to say her next concern. "As long as I am mentioning disappointments, I will tell you that when you made the congratulatory toasts, I had hoped you would name my dowry. I have heard nothing about it."

"Now, now, my dear," he said and, to make light of the subject, he used their title, "*Los Gigantes Tres* have not had the opportunity to discuss this. As I mentioned a moment ago, I have many problems at the fort in Sonoma." He reached out to hug her, but she stepped back. "Maria Ignacia, this is not the time nor place to discuss your dowry. Please know you will have an adequate one; however, I don't know when we can present it to you and Dr. Bale." He picked up his wine glass. With a strained look, he attempted to placate her by saying, "This is your wedding day. You should be joyful and not contemplating problems. Where is your glass? Let's drink to your future."

A pouting lower lip trembled with her answer, "Of course." She reached for her glass and sipped with a tilt of her head before walking away and going straight to Edward. She stepped close and slipped her arm into the crook of his arm, whispering, "No more playful games; let's just go to bed."

"I do not object." They turned and left the living room for their bedroom.

"I am tired and only want to be with you, Edward." She saw no reason nor benefit in telling Edward about her conversation with her uncle. The newlyweds went to bed.

Months of blissful union followed.

By fall, the October nights in the guest room of *Casa Zemita* were chilly, until they had made love and heated the bed with their activity. On moonlit nights, when the rays of light poured in the window, Edward would often awaken and watch her sleep. He marveled at her face—the long dark lashes, wisps of curly hair around her forehead, and a perfectly shaped nose. He was amazed that she always awoke pink-cheeked and pleasant—never with puffy eyes or mussed hair. He relished looking at his beautiful wife.

"You look beautiful even when you rise in the morning, Maria Ig . . . " He interrupted himself and declared. "May I shorten your name and call you Mari?"

"Oh, that was the name my father used for my mother. Oh, I would love you to call me Mari. But I must warn you that Lita will frown on you changing my given name. Were you there when she complained about Cooper calling his wife Martha? Oh, of course you were not. I had not found you on the beach yet." She muffled her laugh and reconsidered her agreement. "Please only call me Mari when we are alone."

He was standing and stretching next to the bed. "I can try," he said. Simultaneously, as he walked around the bed to where the chamber pot sat, she slipped from under the covers.

It was the moment for their first argument.

She complained, "If I get out of bed and you are not using the pot, you cannot start to use it. Once I touch the cold floor with my toes, I must relieve myself immediately or I will drench myself."

He was filling the pot at a slow rate, while she danced in place awaiting her turn.

Defending his position, he stated, "I was out of bed first. You should have waited. If you had stayed in bed, your urge would not have demanded immediate attention, and I could have finished." He put a hand on her shoulder as she danced around. "Stop that. Your dancing makes it hard for me to finish."

"Hurry, hurry, I cannot hold it much longer. Edward, please."

But their love prevailed and their desire for each other was never-ending.

Often, one or the other awoke in the middle of the night. If one inadvertently rolled over in bed and touched the other, they would soon be making love.

One warmer night after such an encounter, Edward said, "I am hungry. Let's go to the kitchen."

They rushed in their bare feet across the veranda to the doorway to the kitchen. "Shush," he said, "you are giggling too loudly. You will awaken someone."

"I cannot stop," she whispered, "I am happy."

Once in the kitchen, they found slices of the pork roast from last night's dinner. Mari pulled green linen napkins from a cabinet and dropped a stack of pork slices into one. "Now I want bread and salt to go with it. Oh dear! They are in the pantry and the pantry door squeaks."

Chewing on the meat, they leaned into each other's shoulders and made muffled laughter. He said, "Why worry? The pantry is on the other side of the house from all the bedrooms. Why are we concerned about the squeak?"

The pantry was a large space with shelves on all sides and baskets on the floor with onions in one and squash in another. Tortillas were stacked under a bowl, and they took a few before reaching for one tiny, shallow dish of salt that sat among dozens of other stacked salt dishes that the maids would set next to every plate to be used by taking a pinch with the fingers.

Although they had come with a candle, it did not light every corner of the pantry; carelessly, Edward kicked a large basket.

The contents tinkled.

"Oh," he declared, "that sounds like glass. What's in this basket?"

She explained, "My mother collected small bottles. She especially wanted the tiny ones, and though she died when I was fourteen, we still have all her bottles." Squatting to the floor, Maria Ignacia reached for the basket to retrieve a few and held them close to the candle for Edward to see. "Reading the label, this one was a powdered spice called coriander. Here is a bottle that contained vanilla. I like the fancy designs on the labels. Oh, this one had medicine in it because I recognize my doctor's handwriting. I remember how he wrote on a bottle of horrible-tasting medicine I once had to take."

Edward was amazed, "But look! There must be hundreds of these little bottles and lots of cork stoppers thrown in, too. I cannot believe it. Why did your mother save them?" He slipped to the floor next to her.

"I don't know. When I was small, we would sit and look at the artistic designs on the paper labels and talk about what once was in the bottle. She often told a story from her imagination about a bottle." The candle flickered and shadows moved on the walls. Mari remained quiet a moment, pondering thoughts of her past. "I never heard my mother mention any plan to use them."

Edward's voice showed excitement, "Mari, could I have these bottles?"

"Shush, did I hear someone?" For a moment, they did not move while listening. After a minute, Mari decided no one was there and said, "Let's talk back in our bedroom." They stood to leave, and Edward gathered a few of the glass bottles into another napkin.

With napkins holding their nighttime nibbles, they scurried back across the veranda. When they were passing General Vallejo's bedroom which was next to theirs, a baby started to cry.

Mari stopped and made a silent, "Oh, no." with her mouth. Edward grabbed her arm and pulled her the few remaining steps to their room.

"Why did you stop? We did not wake the baby. She is only a year old and still wants to have a nightly suckle. Listen, the crying has stopped, because Francisca already has the baby in her arms. All is quiet now."

"I know. I know. Before we were married, I helped Francisca with baby Natalia. She has four little ones in that room and the other night that baby just would not stop crying. Before the other three woke, I hurried outside to walk with her until she fell back asleep.

Edward said, "That was thoughtful of you, and it was possible for you to do that before we were married. But you know you cannot do that anymore." They crawled to the middle of the bed, spread the napkins open on the covers, and began eating their slices of pork nestled in tortillas and sprinkled with salt. With a mouth full, Edward continued sharing his thoughts. "I can understand why your uncle, the General, rarely sleeps here when he is in Monterey. These rooms are large, yet I cannot see him sleeping with all those children in the same room. I will not sleep here when we have a child. We must have our own place. Oh, Mari, I am concerned about that. For us to have a home I must earn more money."

"We will," Mari assured him. "Now, with the twenty-six pesos you earn with the Chief Surgeon position, we can save money for the future."

Edward jolted upright from the bed and went to the dresser, where he had left the napkin with bottles. "I have an idea." Bouncing back onto bed next to her, he unwrapped the napkin and four little bottles tumbled onto the covers. "I have an idea how I could use these bottles, if I owned them."

Without being able to distinguish his expression in the flickering light, Mari knew he was jubilant. His voice was filled with joy. She explained, "I think no one wants the old bottles. They were my mother's; I think I can take them without asking anyone. Tell me why you want them."

"In my office in the barracks here in Monterey, I came across a book on the back of a shelf—a dusty book, in English, called *Pharmacopoeia*. Well, the whole name is *The United States Pharmacopoeia: A compendium of drug information, therapy and diagnosis, and recipes of drug preparation*. I had a copy in England; therefore, I am familiar with the book."

"Edward, what do you mean? Please explain."

He took her hands and said, "Don't you see that, with those bottles and that book full of recipes to make medicine for the sick, I could have a business and make money for us. The only other detail is, I will need a storefront . . . " For a moment he stopped talking while his mind dreamed of the possibilities. He finished saying, "I am saying that I would need a room to make and sell the medicine." Doubts came to mind, "Of course, I hope this to be a profitable business, but I realize that it may not be. I cannot know until I try it. Oh, Mari, I am excited thinking about it." Embracing, they kissed and rolled over the napkins, bread scraps, and little bottles to make love once more. That night, they conceived their first child. It was October 1839.

One cold, calm January night, someone pounded on the guest room door at *Casa Zemita* and woke the Bales.

Bam, bam, bam!

Edward slipped from the warmth of their bed and opened the door to see Mari's sister with Julia. Julia said, "I went to Maria Ignacia's old bedroom and was told you were married and in the guest room. I am grateful you are here, Dr. Bale. My husband is sick. Please, can you come help him?"

Hearing Julia's voice, Maria Ignacia grabbed a robe and rushed to hug her. "Don't stand in the cold," she said, pulling the three inside the open doorway and closing the door.

Wasting no time, Dr. Bale began dressing and asking questions, "Julia, tell me what's wrong with your husband. Describe his symptoms."

"He has extreme pain in his lower stomach. He cannot stand because of the intense pain. It started two days ago."

"Is the pain on one particular side?"

"Yes, on his right side. Oh, and he vomited more than once. Also, he has not wanted to eat for a couple of days."

Now, Maria Ignacia was dressing and said to her sister, "Go tell Pepe to prepare horses for me and Edward. In the morning, tell the family that we have gone with Julia." She turned to Julia, "You rode here on one of the horses we gave you, didn't you?"

"I did."

Stars shared the night sky with a thin crescent moon. After they stopped at the medical office in the Presidio to get additional supplies, they were on their way. Maria Ignacia had wrapped a woolen scarf around her head and across her nose and mouth. Her trapped breath warmed her face, but even with leather gloves and boots, the cold chilled her fingers and toes. They traveled quickly, without conversation, hoping speed could make a difference.

Going west and traveling along a stream, they rode in open sandy expanses along the water's edge, into wooded areas, along embankments of rock walls where the horses had to enter the water, and through meadows of high grass.

Dr. Bale began to recollect his last patient in London and hoped that Julia's husband was not suffering from the same problem. His mind transported him back to England. Remembering, he saw:

> *The operating room white and bright, almost blinding, as he swayed over the man on the table. Nitrous oxide hissed into the patient's mask through a long white tube. Bale blinked, trying to focus on the black silhouette of the nurse holding the mask.*
>
> *Another dark silhouette—an assisting physician—stood next to him, speaking in an agitating tone. "Be careful. Your hand is shaking. Shall I take over?"*
>
> *White, everything white, except the blood.*
>
> *The white sheet, covering the man who was of the Royal family, and a favorite one at that, exposed only the lower abdomen and the incision that Dr. Bale had made.*
>
> *White, glaring lights beamed down like a heavy weight on Bale's*

shoulders, as he leaned over the body.

Bobbing along on the horse, he shook his head, trying not to remember his disgraceful experience. The irate physician kept shouting commands:

"You must be quick. I'll open it wider. There! There is the appendix! Look at its size! It is quite infected. You must stop your hands from shaking."

The nurse turned to the two doctors and said, "What's that I smell?"

The three riders slowed as they entered the Ohlone village, and Dr. Bale's mind returned to the present, as he noticed the morning light beginning to flow over the tops of the hills.

Though in a different location than on their last visit, the village was arranged in the same layout as months ago. They stopped at a dozen round huts scattered along a small stream. Julia dismounted and led them to her tule dwelling. She lifted a deerskin hide serving as a door, and they ducked into the darkened interior. Inside, the leader of the village and a woman, who was said to be the shaman, met them. Julia's husband groaned on a bed of furs; he rocked with pain and flailed his arms.

As his greeting, Dr. Bale dipped his head to the leader before unbuttoning his coat and dropping to his knees next to the suffering man. He pulled back the fur coverings, exposing the man's naked body. Herbs filled the hut with a pleasant smell though Dr. Bale detected a lingering odor of vomit. He noted the sweat beading on the patient's face. With a light touch, he placed his fingers on the distended abdomen. It was hot.

Dr. Bale looked up at Julia and said, "I need light. Open the doorway." Cautiously, his experienced fingers probed the abdomen.

The patient screamed, "Aghhhh!"

Julia slipped to her knees next to the doctor and leaned towards her husband with soft words as she placed a kiss on his cheek, her tears dropped onto his hair. She sat up and whispered, "Please help him."

Without commenting, Dr. Bale sat back on his heels and pulled his medical bag closer. He reached into a side pocket, grasped a bottle labeled Tincture of Laudanum, and removed the cork. "I want you to drink this to help your pain." Then he slipped his hand under the man's head to raise it and put the bottle to his lips. After allowing two long swigs, Dr. Bale lowered the man's head and stood, saying, "You will feel better in a little while."

The leader and the shaman were speaking quietly beside a wall. Julia went back on her knees next to her husband as Dr. Bale said, "I am going outside for a moment. Mari, please come with me."

They circled around to the back of the hut toward the stream. They walked, while buttoning their coats again and donning their gloves. At last, he stopped and faced his wife to say, "Mari, remember when I told you why I left London? I told you about that horrible operation on an important man. Do you remember? I told you that I botched it, and that the operation cost me my reputation as a doctor; it also caused my parents to be disgraced."

Birds were singing their cheerful morning songs and the stream rippled past with a pleasant sound that contradicted his sullen words. Mari nodded. "Yes, I remember."

"When Julia described her husband's symptoms, I feared that he had the same infected appendix as that lord in London. I was tormented by that memory as we rode here this morning." He swallowed and frowned. "Mari, I am positive of my diagnosis of Julia's husband. He has the same illness. I can do nothing."

"Can you operate as you did in London? You may not have the same problems as you did back then."

He made a cynical laugh, "Ha! You're correct; the same problems do not exist—neither the poor circumstances nor the good ones. This is not a surgical arena with adequate lights and equipment. I have no way to subdue the patient with gas, to make him sleep and feel no pain while I operate." He shook his head and rubbed his hands over his face. "Oh, Mari, I did all I can do. I can do nothing more. Julia's husband is going to die."

"Oh no! Are you sure, Edward?"

He leaned against a tree and pulled her close. With his face against her hair he whispered, "Yes, I know he will die soon. This is the most difficult part of being a doctor. I must tell Julia that there's no hope. I ran away from London because I operated and failed. Here, I cannot operate because I do not have the proper equipment. Yet, I still feel as if I have failed."

They stood locked in each other's arms with the songs of the birds and the sounds of the stream offering no solace.

After returning to the hut, Dr. Bale reported his prognosis, and Maria Ignacia opened her arms to Julia. For a while, Maria Ignacia and Julia clung to each other, saying nothing. When they slowly pulled apart, they went outside and walked with the wind. Their hair flew into their faces and off again. Soon they arrived at a clearing near several live oaks where they sat in the grass and rested against the trees.

"Julia, I have a couple of things I want to say to you. This is not the best time, but we've no other time to talk." She stopped to touch Julia's forearm, before finishing. "First, I want to say that I am so sorry that you are losing your husband and losing the love you found." They touched forehead to forehead and let minutes slip away. "My other comment is . . . I want you to know that I have told no one else. I wanted you to be the first to know . . . I am with child."

Julia's gaze hovered just as a curious hummingbird's does when close to a human face; puzzled at what it sees. She blinked and managed to say, "Thank you for sharing your joy with me about your coming child."

Maria Ignacia entwined her fingers with Julia's and whispered, "You are losing your husband. I don't want you to be alone. Would you come and live with us? You could help raise my child like you raised me."

Their faces still were inches from each other, and they stared. Eyes searched into the depths of the other's eyes, not able to understand each other's thoughts because they lived different realities.

Maria Ignacia saw joy in her memories of their time together; she saw the Julia as family. *With a child to raise, Julia will have a reason to live after losing her husband.*

Julia knew the *gente de razon* were oblivious to whom the Ohlones were—people equal to them. *They look down on us but depend on us. I love this girl, yet I had hoped she could realize the truth about how I love my life with my people. She is still young; maybe someday she will.*

Maria Ignacia interrupted the quiet to say, "Don't answer now. Just consider what I asked. You know how I love you and, raising my child might . . . "

Julia placed a finger to Maria Ignacia's lips to stop her words and said, "I will think about this and let you know."

Meanwhile, when Dr. Bale went to pick up his medical bag, the leader invited them to stay for the meal.

During the meal, Dr. Bale digested more than food.

While chewing a bite of tender rabbit, the leader turned to Dr. Bale and said, "You know that I lived in a mission for years. So, you know that I know the ways of the Spanish and Mexicans. We are different from them and find it difficult to understand how they think. They value possessions—objects and things. We Ohlones think such things not to be important.

"Of course, if we had too many items, we could not travel easily from one place to another to gather food. We must travel light, so we make baskets that have no weight and houses from tule plants that dry and blow away when we leave to go from gathering acorns to somewhere else to harvest salmon. We cut more tule and build our huts again." The leader stopped to take another bite and chewed awhile before adding another thought. "Oh, we weave beautiful designs in our baskets and make beads from seeds for lovely necklaces to wear; however, more pleasure is felt when we give them away. To give is more important than to own."

Dr. Bale held a woven bowl with chunks of rabbit in it and stopped eating. He saw the wisdom in what he heard. That was how he felt: Pleasure comes when one gives to someone else. The Ohlones' ways were wise. He glanced to his host and nodded. "Yes, I agree. Generosity is important to me as well."

The leader looked wide-eyed and said, "You are truly different from the others at the missions. Oh, we have our own form of wealth. Someone, who finds a shell of an abalone or the antler of a deer, will keep it. We can see they have more wealth than others, but usually they give it to another, to attain happiness and prestige."

Dr. Bale had a question and asked, "When I was here with you months ago, you took me into your hut. I saw pride in your eyes when you showed me awls, bone scrapers, obsidian knives, and twisting drills for making holes in beads and leather. Are you not a wealthy man to have those tools?"

A twinkle came to the leader's eyes although he did not smile. "It seems you question if I practice the ways of the Spaniards or my Ohlones."

"No, I . . . I mean . . . forgive me, I want to understand."

The leader burst out with a hearty laugh and turned to another man next to him to share what had happened. Now the two laughed, and they told the others, until the story had flowed around the circle where all were eating. "Forgive me. I am not laughing at you, Dr. Bale. You chose an example of my wealth, and you were correct. However, since I last saw you, I have given all my tools to others. Therefore, we laughed. We are content to give and explain about our ways."

Dr. Bale peered across the circle to where his wife sat. They exchanged long loving looks. Turning to the leader, Dr. Bale confided, "You are teaching me how I want to be. Thank you. I plan to be more generous in the rest of my life."

"Oh," the leader said, "we are generous all our lives, and even generous in death. We give many possessions away before we die; whatever is left, our friends will break and burn in our funeral byre. Today, Julia's husband gave me a carving he had made."

"He knows he is dying?"

"He does."

Later, Dr. Bale went to Julia's hut.

"I will leave this bottle of laudanum with you, Julia. Give drinks to your husband to lessen his suffering. As you can see," Dr. Bale turned to look at the resting man, "this medicine will calm him and reduce his pain."

"Thank you, Dr. Bale."

"But, Julia, it will not make him better or save his life. You do understand; I hope."

She nodded.

On the ride back, they talked. "Knowing Julia and her people has made an impression on me," he said. "Lately, I often think about the Ohlones and other native people in the Americas. The European explorers came to find gold, silver, and other riches. The Aztecs and Incas did not disappoint them, but the natives in California did. I was raised to want to be rich; therefore, it made sense to me when I learned the history of explorers and conquerors." He stopped and rode in silence for a while. "But I have changed my mind and think the Ohlones have it right."

Maria Ignacia agreed, "All my life, I have heard the men in Monterey speak of the natives in California as poor and backward people because they never learned agriculture and they never built cities. I think those white men are the ones who are ignorant. The Ohlones had everything they needed for a fulfilled life—an abundance of materials to make what they needed, and all kinds of food ready to harvest. They succeeded in many ways."

He added, "They even developed a philosophy for life: Be generous to be happy."

They rode without words for several miles. Finally, he began to speak again. "Mari, I must make enough money to care for you and our coming family. I do not need to be rich; however, I don't want to live with your family for the rest of our lives. I must find a way to provide for you and our family."

"Edward, I understand and agree with you. I will support you in every way."

Delight spread across his face. "I am glad to hear you say that because I took a bit of our savings to have a grist mill built on the land where I want us to live." Not hesitating long enough to let her respond, in his excitement, he continued. "There are settlers planting wheat fields, out where George Yount is, and there's no way to grind the grain. We should make money with our grist mill." He sucked in a long breath and glanced over to her.

Her eyes had a twinkle and her face delight.

"Also . . ." He sat taller in the saddle and encouraged the horse to go a bit faster. They were almost to *Casa Zemita*. "Also, I talked with Thomas Larkin about renting a room in his store so I can make a pharmacy. I noticed he has a storage room with its own entrance, and it is almost empty. You may not know about that room because it's located at the back of their house."

Maria Ignacia watched him as he spoke. His enthusiasm was apparent. She was glad he had talked with Larkin. She was glad he had a friend in Larkin. She listened and enjoyed his every word.

"You do remember my idea to make medicines for my patients, with the book called *Pharmacopoeia* and the little bottles your mother collected, don't you?"

"Of course, I do."

"Well, Thomas agreed to rent the room to me."

The closer to home they were, the more excited they became. Excitement about their future and their coming family deepened their love.

In a few months, Dr. Bale opened the storefront called Bale Pharmacy. He put a sign in the window—Open for Business from 4:00 to 6:00.

During the first week, he stood at the open door in anticipation of customers. He had spoken with many of his patients and hoped they would stop in to make purchases. Men hustled past on the wooden sidewalk with their boot heels marking their retreat as the sound disappeared in the distance. Women bustled down the pathways in twos and threes then turned and went into Larkin's Store, a few feet away from Bale's door. Before long, Dr. Bale stepped outside and started conversations with passing people to encourage them. "Good afternoon, recently I opened my pharmacy with medicines and elixirs for your health and well-being. Please stop in, and we could talk about what is best for you."

He made few sales that first week. Maria Ignacia encouraged him to give the endeavor more time. "People do not know about your business. It cannot grow overnight."

He lamented, "If you could help, we could have more hours. I have my position as surgeon-in-chief, occupying most of my day. I think I need to be open for more hours."

She retorted, "But, Edward, I know nothing about medicine, so I cannot help, and you told me to stay off my swelling legs."

He agreed with a nod. "You are correct. Only I can prescribe for each person and mix the medicine, so I must work any additional hours."

A month passed, then another, showing little improvement in business. Yet, time was not Edward's problem.

One evening, Larkin wandered over to the pharmacy and they talked. Edward said, "I think I will add hours later in the evening to my schedule. If I had more hours, I could sell more medicine. I will put the new hours on my sign."

Larkin wondered if Edward had deluded himself that a pharmacy could be successful and asked, "Tell me how many patients you have, so we can analyze this on paper." Together, they sat in the quiet room with bottles and medicines lining a couple of shelves above their heads and with no customers among the passing people. They calculated that each of his patients would need to buy fifteen bottles a month to pay the rent.

Edward blinked and shifted in his seat, seeing on paper the mistake of this adventure. The realization, of his oversight and of how Larkin quickly and simply pointing out a realistic method to calculate what he could earn, irritated him. He defended his venture by saying, "I expected people other than my patients to come and talk with me. I expected to sell elixirs to strangers and improve people's health."

Larkin suggested, "Edward, those words you just said might help. Put those words on another sign in the window. Have the sign say: *Elixirs to improve one's health*."

In June of 1840, the Bales welcomed a daughter into their lives and named her Maria Isadora Bale but called her Lolita.

Rachel Larkin had had another boy in January, her fifth boy. She went to *Casa Zemita* with her baby boy to see the newborn little girl. "Oh, how sweet! May I hold her?"

"Of course, Rachel. Let me hold Francis while you hold Lolita."

Passing her little boy into the arms of Maria Ignacia, Rachel lifted Lolita from her cradle.

"Oh, he smiled at me. Isn't that early for a six-month-old?"

Rachel sat in a chair near the bed, cooing and cuddling the little girl, seeming not to hear.

When the baby boy fell asleep, Maria Ignacia placed him on the bed, since Rachel was still enjoying Lolita.

After a while, the topic of the pharmacy was discussed. Rachel said, "Thomas told me that sales have not been going well at the pharmacy. I guess you knew that."

"Yes, Edward talks with me. I want to help him, though I cannot think of how."

Clearing her throat, Rachel said, "Do you know that the rent is due today? And Edward has not paid last month's rent either?" She stood and placed Lolita back in her cradle. She shook her head. "From the look on your face, you did not know. Am I correct?"

"Yes, you are. I guess Edward and I have not been talking as much as we should. He travels to Yerba Buena for his medical work at the fort, and he is working evenings in the pharmacy. He mentioned that the grist mill in the valley is costing more to build than he thought. And he did say he must finish the mill before the harvest of the wheat." Maria Ignacia let her words trail off into silence as she stopped to ponder. "I imagine our money went to the mill construction. When we start getting paid for processing the wheat, we will have more money and . . . "

Rachel interrupted, "I should not have mentioned this to you." She sighed. "Because I imagine you can do nothing about this problem." She walked to the window, not wanting to face her friend, "I am sure you do not know that Thomas has me collecting the rent from Edward every month. I wanted to be involved in our affairs, so he made the collection my responsibility." She stopped talking for a moment and sat down again. "This is embarrassing me to tell you about the rent being late. Oh, Maria Ignacia, I have another problem, in that I never told Thomas that last month's rent was not paid."

"Oh, my!"

They locked eyes in strained silence. Moments later, Maria Ignacia reached into a drawer next to her bed. She pulled out a drawstring leather bag and said, "tell me how much the rent is for a month. Maybe I have enough to pay for last month."

Money was exchanged, and a promise to secrecy, as well.

With secrets, deception begins.

Maria Ignacia could have told Edward, but she didn't. Because he had not told her about the rent being late, she did not know how to begin. She was searching for the right time and the right words.

Unknown to her, he was keeping another secret from her, but his deception would not become apparent for months. Even with their secrets and the guilt that comes with keeping secrets, their love never waned. When they were in bed, the joy of lovemaking continued.

Soon their oxen-powered grist mill was running, and the tensions weighing on Dr. Bale were alleviated for the months through the fall when wheat was being ground and payments were being made. Even the overdue bills were paid. So, Rachel returned Maria Ignacia's payment without Edward knowing about it.

Maria Ignacia was so relieved not to have to reveal her secret payment. To add to their happiness, Julia arrived to live with them.

Edward suggested, "Lolita is big enough for a journey. Let's take a trip to visit the place where I want to build our ranch. Julia can go with us and see it, too."

Squinting against the setting sun, Edward's eyes had the same crinkles in the corners as when he laughed. But he did not need the sun or laughter for his whole world to shine brightly; he only needed his little girl, wife, and Julia. He felt euphoric. He had taken them to see the grist mill first and now was going to what he had called a "surprise."

In the distance, Maria Ignacia saw the surprise and knew it was hers. "Look! Our home! Edward, you have started building our home. Oh, I cannot believe my eyes! I remember you designing a two-story adobe. This must be ours because no one else has a two-story adobe." Trotting ahead with Lolita, who slept tied against her chest with a long cloth, Maria Ignacia clutched her child to dismount. Once off the horse, she rushed inside.

Edward and Julia joined her.

"Oh, Edward, I love it! I can see this is to be a kitchen. Where is our bedroom?"

He laughed, pulling his two girls into a hug. "Come, I'll show you our bedroom. I had hoped it would be ready to use tonight. But it isn't. We'll spend the night with George Yount. His place is so close."

Beyond the unfinished house, dozens of naked natives worked in a wheat field, cutting and gathering stalks. Maria Ignacia asked, "Who are all those people outside?"

"Our Wappos. I am so excited to tell you about everything. Over a hundred natives were living on this land when I chose it to be our *rancheria*. And I must admit that I cannot distinguish between the tribes; they may be Miwoks or Wappos. They are wonderful and help with everything."

Maria Ignacia stood silent with puzzled eyes. "You have told me that you abhor how the Spanish and Mexicans used the natives as slaves. Isn't this the same?"

They walked outside.

"No, no, they are workers. Many are neophytes from the missions, although not all of them. Many of them knew how to plant wheat, cultivate, and harvest—unlike me. I bought the supplies—plows and seeds—and told them that what they plant is theirs, if they give us a small part for our family. I asked for help to build our adobe, since they knew how to make the adobe bricks, as well. But they are not our slaves. Their lives are free. I paid for the seed and bought tools for farming because they had none. We work together. As I said, I asked them to share with me, and I share with them. I told them they could have the wheat ground at my grist mill without charge. At first, the two large grindstones were driven with the manpower of those Miwoks and Wappos. I am so indebted to them; they did all the work until I got the oxen.

"You know that I do not own this land. Officially, I have no claim to this land any more than they do. We are using the land to survive, just as they did for centuries before the Spanish came. Well, they did not grow wheat years ago..."

With her back to her husband, Maria Ignacia frowned. Her Uncle Mariano controlled the distribution of the land, and only he could give papers of ownership. She still had no dowry from her family. She said nothing, knowing this problem could be resolved only by talking with *Los Gigante Tres*.

Edward squatted and scooped up some dirt. Standing, he opened his hand, "Look how rich this soil is. I think we could grow anything." Looking out at the distant field, filled with people working, he took a deep breath and said, "We're going to have a wonderful life here, and I hope to be living here by next year."

When his hand reached out to her, what she saw in his face and heard in his voice made the frown slip from her face. Oh, how she loved him. He took her hand and poured dirt into her palm. Everything about their life and future looked hopeful.

He asked, "Will you enjoy living here?"

With her head tilting down to peer at the soil in her hand, they stood quietly a moment until Maria Ignacia responded, "I will."

Edward's face beamed.

Lifting her dirt-filled hand toward Julia, Maria Ignacia said, "Look at this beautiful soil. Oh, Julia, I am so pleased you are coming to live with us." After seeing a nod in agreement from Julia, Maria Ignacia smelled the dirt. "Our future is going to be wonderful; the smell of this soil tells me."

They wandered around their future land, seeing the river, hills, fields, and a location for a sawmill and, finally, headed over to George Yount's place.

That evening before dinner, sitting outside at *Rancho Caymus*, George entertained them with his stories. "I heard you say that you saw a grizzly near my cattle when you arrived. Well, since I brought these heifers over on my floating corral, that grizzly has been eatin' them. She's not an idiot but knows how to act like a halfwit, and my cows are curious. Every week the grizzly does tricks and gits a cow for her meal. I gotta kill that grizzly!"

Maria Ignacia was intrigued. "I don't understand. What are you saying, George?"

"Why, you lived in Monterey all your life, surely you heard 'bout how grizzlies trick the cattle."

She shook her head.

"Well, I saw it many times with my own eyes. Once, I was ridin' past a meadow with the wild clover knee-high. Cattle were grazin' there. And I mean the clover was knee-high to me on my horse. I could pluck the heads off without bendin' down. Then I see'd somethin' move in the corner of my eye. A huge she-grizzly rolled on her back in the clover with her paws in the air, like a young playful dog. All the cattle watched while they chewed their cud. They were curious." George shook his head and spit. "Well, so was I. This was the first time I saw a grizzly actin' so strange. That bear kept rollin' with her feet up in the air, an' then she jumped up to do half-somersaults. Why, she even ran in a circle chasin' her tail. Those stupid cows kept gettin' closer and closer with their curiosity. One of 'em started bawlin' and soon more bawled. At last, a young heifer lowered her head, with her horns ready to butt, and ran up to the bear. That's what the grizzly was waitin' fer. Why, the bear rose-up on her hind legs, leaped and pounced on the heifer's back an' neck while fixin' her jaws deep in the cow's nose. What a ruckus. All the cattle went crazy, makin' more noise than you can imagine."

Maria Ignacia sat on the edge of her chair, wide-eyed and exclaimed, "George, are you making up this story?"

"Why, no ma'm, I ain't. This is true."

His daughter Mia came out and said, "Food's ready to eat."

George said, "Let me finish my story before we eat."

Mia joined them and sat next to Dr. Bale. She said in a soft voice, "I seed that bear act crazy, too."

Julia nodded and said, "I have seen something like that happen. Grizzly bears know how to lure cattle closer by making strange behavior. They are smart. Well, the cattle must be stupid."

Yount turned to Mia, pointed with a bob of his head, and said, "Mrs. Bale, this here is my daughter Mia. I don't think you an' Julia know her."

Maria Ignacia said, "Hello, Mia. We will be your neighbors someday. Have you seen our adobe house that Dr. Bale is having built?"

Mia nodded and looked at Dr. Bale with affectionate eyes.

Bale reached for her hand. "Mia, I can see you took care of your hand. It has healed well. When we move here, I could use a nurse. Would you help me?"

She bobbed her head enthusiastically, though with a shy expression.

George continued, "Where was I in my story? Oh, yeah. When the she-grizzly let go of the nose, she sunk her teeth into the neck and tore it open. Blood gushed and the heifer fell to her knees. That's when all of 'em in the herd took off for the hills and left behind all the delicious clover. Much of it was covered in blood anyway. I took off, too, and never looked back."

Dr. Bale shook his head and said, "I've never heard of such a thing. Now, I do believe you are telling us what you saw, but I can't picture a bear being able to kill so easily."

George turned to Maria Ignacia, "I guess, he ain't seen a bull and grizzly fight in the arena."

"No, he has not," she said, "but I saw a poster that said a fight is scheduled for Easter next year."

George slapped his knee, "Damn, I want to go to that. Hmm, Easter of forty-two. I'll remember."

The doctor disagreed and said, "I would rather not see such a horrid spectacle. Mari, do not even think about taking me."

After George roared with laughter at the doctor's reluctance, everyone decided it was time to eat.

Like the bulb that hides beneath the soil, secrets can remain hidden only so long. When the slender leaves emerge and the flower blooms, all can see where the bulb had been under the soil.

One of Edward's secrets emerged with the sprouting spring flowers of 1841. Like the first slender, green blade that pokes through the soil into the light, people saw. At first, only a few people noticed that Dr. Bale was different. Dr. Bale who was intelligent, dedicated to medicine, and thoughtful became impetuous, rash, and insulting. After the spring flowers had budded and later bloomed, everyone knew that Dr. Bale was drinking most days. They saw he was a drunk.

Why? Why did he succumb to drink? Simply put, he had little money and began drinking because he had three problems: His pharmacy was failing; the grist mill had only seasonal customers; and his debts were growing.

However, the real reason was all the poor decisions he had made. The last idea he implemented was the worst: He decided to sell his medicines mixed with large amounts of wine. Once he started filling larger bottles with those concoctions, his clientele became sailors from the ships, men on hard times, and other drunks. Most nights, they loitered not far from his storefront, and Bale began to invite them inside to buy and consume the drinks. Soon, he joined them.

Maria Ignacia was one of the last to learn of the problem. Edward was smart enough not to go home while drunk, excusing his absences with lies of having to stay overnight for work in Yerba Buena or remain in San Rafael with a patient. She knew he should not drink because that was one of the secrets that he had told her. She also knew that he had been drinking in London when he bungled that operation, which had haunted him and caused him to leave England. When he had told her, he had sworn he would never touch spirits again.

That Edward had started drinking was tragic, but what he did next created a disaster.

When the police arrived to arrest Edward Bale at *Casa Zemita*, Maria Ignacia first learned of Edward's drinking in Monterey. She asked, "Are you sure that he had been drinking?"

The policeman admitted, "We did not see him. The word *drunkard* is written on the Order for Arrest filed by Thomas Larkin."

Maria Ignacia gasped upon hearing the name of Thomas Larkin. Of course, she did not know where her husband was and said as much. After the police searched *Casa Zemita*, she donned a shawl and walked to the Larkins' house.

Meeting her outside his front door, Thomas shared the whole story with her, saying, "Apparently, Rachel went to collect the rent and found Edward inebriated in the storefront with other drunken men. He refused to pay and made insulting comments to her. Edward told her that he knew about our love affair on the ship coming to Alta California. I think that you, Maria Ignacia, must have told him." He held up his hands to stop her reply. "I just want to finish this story.

"Edward shouted to Rachel, 'Don't you call me a drunk! You are nothing more than a whore. No, you were a married woman having an affair, so I think that makes you a strumpet.'" Thomas stopped to take a deep breath. He furrowed his brow and started again, "Edward roared with laughter, woke one of his drunken buddies on the floor by tripping over him, and continued insulting Rachel. He said, 'I can think of other names. Give me a minute; I am a bit under the weather right now. Ah yes, slut is another name.'

"Embarrassed, Rachel turned from him and stumbled back into our home. She was sobbing uncontrollably from the minute it took her to walk around the corner to our door. A maid ran to get me.

"I was on business at the wharf. When I arrived, she was hysterical. I put her to bed with the maid to watch over her and went down to Bale's Pharmacy.

"I stormed into the storefront, found Bale, and bellowed, 'It appears you are running a saloon, not a medical pharmacy. How did you dare to insult my wife! I can never forgive you for what you said to her. If you weren't so drunk and could stand on your feet without falling, I would sock you. Bale, you are a disgrace and I want you out of this storefront by morning.' Then I turned and left.

"I heard Bale follow me out the door. He must have stood and watched me walk along the side of the house because a minute passed before he aimed his pepper-box pistol and fired. Hearing the shots, I turned to see him swaying and pointing his gun at me. He had fired two shots.

"Both missed. The pepper-box has three shots, but he didn't shoot again, thank heavens. But I was not going to miss my chance to get retribution. I went to the police. Evidently, while they were issuing the order for Dr. Bale's arrest, he fled."

Maria Ignacia stood staring before she begged in a soft voice. "Thomas, please can you withdraw the Order for Arrest?"

Thomas was adamant, "I cannot. Rachel would never speak to me again. She was more than offended by what Edward said, she was devastated, and will never forgive him. He was brutal."

"Oh, Thomas, you know that is not his character. He told me before we married that drink changed him to a devil. He had been avoiding drinking since he came to Monterey, and I did not know that he had started. If we keep him away from the spirits, then . . . "

Interrupting, Thomas said, "No, this arrest will encourage him not to touch any drink again. Please, I must attend to Rachel. I am sorry." He stepped inside his home and said, "Good night."

The next day, the police found Bale in Yerba Buena in one of Nathan Spear's rented rooms. Edward was jailed for eight days, but he would have been in jail longer if it were not for Maria Ignacia involving her family to have him acquitted. It took eight days because her Uncle Mariano was not working in Monterey, so she sent letters by horseback to Sonoma, pleading for help.

While she waited for the help from her family, she visited Edward on the third day of his incarceration. Standing outside the bars of his cell, she was appalled at the stench and filth of the jail. She told him, "I didn't come sooner because I wanted you to be sober. Edward, how could you do this?"

They stared at each other until he found his voice, "Mari, I am so sorry this happened. I have no excuses. I know the devil in me emerged and has destroyed much of our life. Can you ever forgive me?"

"Edward, I cannot answer your question. I need time to pass. I hope my uncles can help us. But, if they do not or cannot, you will go on trial for attempted murder." She dabbed her eyes with the handkerchief clutched in her fist and turned away from him. "Oh, what you have done!" After blowing her nose, she faced him again and stood tall. "While you are here, think about the future of your family. Think about what we had and how you have ruined our lives and the Larkins'. Oh, how could you have done this? I have nothing more to say and am leaving this wretched place."

He pleaded, "Please wait. Don't go just yet."

She stopped and looked intently at him. She thought about their wedding vows. She thought how Edward had no one except her. She thought: *All of us have our weak moments and make poor decisions. Even in this situation, I feel love for him. I want to wrap my arms around him and hold him. He had told me this could happen. He had told me about the devil that lives within him and emerges with drink. I should forgive him and help him.* She sat down on an old wooden bench outside his cell. When her skirt caught on a splinter and tore, she pursed her lips and frowned. "Look at where you have put yourself." Sitting on the bench put her closer to another prisoner who had collapsed to the floor in the next cell and emptied his bowels. The smell was overwhelming.

With her handkerchief to her nose, she complained, "The place reeks."

"Maria Ignacia, I am so sorry I did this to you. I know that you need to distance yourself from me. I will ruin your life if people see you standing beside me." He took a step back and sat on the cot in his cell with his head in his hands. "There's no hope for me."

"Edward, stop. My uncles will help you."

He returned to stand at the bars and grasped the cold steel until his knuckles went white. He shook his head and tears welled in his eyes. "No, I doubt that they will or can help. I tried to shoot Larkin. Besides, I have never spoken with you about how I feel about your Uncle Mariano. I do not trust him. He has told me lies."

She stood and blurted, "Edward, what do you mean?"

"He told me about giving land to the neophytes in the Nicasio area. Later, Friar Mo said that your uncle, the *good* General Vallejo, took it back from them. A couple of years later, when the leaders of those native people appealed to other authorities, your uncle gave the natives back only small portion of what they deserved. Oh, he also gave three cows and a horse to each native to quiet them. For an unknown reason, the inspector who oversees the distribution of land to the neophytes quit his job. That's so suspicious." Bale stopped. "I never meant to tell you all this. I am sure it makes no difference to you. You seem to give undeserving love to him."

"Edward, my Uncle Mariano is a good man. Look at his position. He is admired by many and I . . . " Her eyes grew wide as she remembered her uncle talking about the battles against the native Estanislao and how he slaughtered men, women, and children. Doubts about his character seeped into her mind at that moment.

"Mari, I do not trust him. I know other examples of how he is deceitful in his work."

"No, stop; this is not the time nor place to discuss this." She backed away from him while shaking her head. When she reached the outer door, she looked away and said, "I have faith that my uncles will rescue you. I must go. I am finding it too painful to be here. Goodbye for now."

As she had thought, her uncles found a way to have all the charges absolved, and Dr. Bale was set free after eight days in jail. However, Maria Ignacia did not know of his release until someone knocked on her door in the guest room at *Casa Zemita* late at night.

She wrapped a blanket around herself and asked through the closed door, "Who is there?"

"I have come to tell you where your husband is staying."

When she opened the door, she faced a stranger, "Who are you?"

"Please do not be frightened. Your husband sent me to tell you that he has been released and is staying with me in Yerba Buena. I am Nathan Spear."

"Oh, *Señor* Spear, Edward spoke of you. You are the man who built a grist mill that's run by mules."

After a short discussion, Nathan Spear assured her that Edward was safe and sound. "If you go to the General Store in Yerba Buena, they will point you to the boarding house where I have rooms." He stood to leave. "It's late, I know. I should go. Edward will be waiting. Shall I give him a message?"

Shaking her head, she bit her lip and said, "No, I don't know what to say to him."

Everyone soon learned about the terrible incident. One of the drunks, who had been present during Edward's fit of madness, spread the specifics to the community.

No longer was Edward Bale seen as a respected doctor.

No longer was Rachel Larkin seen as a good woman.

Bale had caused his disgrace through his own actions.

But Rachel was wronged through no fault of her own.

Wherever Rachel walked in Monterey, people whispered and gossiped of her affair with Thomas on the ship and of their child who died. Rachel's disgrace resulted from Edward's words and from Maria Ignacia sharing the Larkins' secrets with him.

Maria Ignacia lost her dearest friend, Rachel, who would never speak to her again.

General Vallejo Reviewing his Troops In Front of *Casa Grande* and Fort Sonoma in 1846

Chapter Seven

Storms: Natural, Foreign, and Familial

End of 1841 through 1844

As 1841 ended, storms formed in the Pacific and hit the coast of Alta California with unprecedented wind and rain. The creeks overflowed in Monterey, winds uprooted trees which then crashed against buildings, and the pelting rain tore the clay tiles from most roofs. During nature's display, Maria Ignacia unleashed her wrath as well, by storming into her Uncle Mariano's office in the Monterey Presidio.

Dropping her dripping wool poncho to the floor, she leaned over his desk. "Why? Why did you not tell Edward that you had received his naturalization papers for his Mexican citizenship?"

The pleasure that had started to form on his face, when she came through the door, dissolved. He defended his position with words that did not convince her, saying, "Maria Ignacia, I only arrived from Sonoma yesterday and learned about those papers."

"I have difficulty believing that no one sent a message to you about those papers. You knew how Edward was struggling to make a living, to be independent from our family. He could not get paperwork approved for his grist mill and other endeavors without Mexican citizenship. His frustration and feelings of failure made him start drinking, and . . . "

He interrupted, "Now, now, Maria Ignacia, you know I do everything I can to help you and Edward. The arrest order for his attempted murder of Larkin is gone because of me. However, I have no idea where he is. He disappeared and hid after leaving the jail. I could not deliver the paperwork to him."

She collapsed on a chair facing his desk and retorted, "Please do not insult my intelligence. You knew where I was, and I knew where my husband was." She stared at him. "While we are speaking about what you and the family withhold from Edward and me, help me understand why no dowry has been presented. I have been so humiliated by this that I have not even spoken with my husband about the lack of a dowry from my family. In a few months we will have been married for two years. We have one child and another on the way, yet my family has given us nothing."

"I didn't know you were with child again." He stood and came around the desk to sit next to her. He reached for her hands and said, "I am a busy man. Your grandmother and father should have . . ."

She pulled her hands away and rebuffed his words. "Oh, please. You are the power and decision-maker of everything."

Finally, he relented, "You are correct. I am sorry. I have been negligent in my family role. I will see to your dowry as soon as possible." He stood and walked back behind his desk as loud knocking thundered against his door.

He shouted, "Enter."

A young soldier entered—wet and out of breath—and blurted, "General Vallejo, I have ridden from the Yerba Buena fort with this urgent message." He extended a wet envelope to him.

The three were quiet as the General read the soggy paper. At last, he turned to the soldier and said, "Go get something to eat in the fort kitchen while I write a reply. You'll need to return to Yerba Buena as soon as possible when I finish."

When they were alone again, Vallejo avoided the subject of Maria Ignacia's dowry by talking about the message. "With these horrible storms in the Pacific, a ship has sought refuge in our bay in Yerba Buena. An important man is on board, and I must attend to him."

"Do I know him?"

"Possibly you do. He is an Englishman, Sir George Simpson, the governor general of the Hudson's Bay Company, usually referred to as HBC."

She nodded, "I do know of him. He holds a high position. HBC is the most powerful and established company in North America." She sat straighter and nodded again. "Hasn't HBC been on this continent for more than a hundred years?"

"It depends how you measure the ownership of HBC. The French and English took turns claiming the fur trade in North America, specifically in Canada, in the seventeen-hundreds and before. It wasn't until 1713, when France signed the Treaty of Utrecht, that England could claim ownership of HBC." Vallejo stopped talking. Then, without warning, he burst into hearty laughter, "Ho, ho, ho; another way to look at how long HBC has been here is in the initials." In his amusement he chuckled at his forthcoming words, "I have heard HBC stands for Here Before Christ."

She could no longer focus on anger for this beloved uncle. She admired his knowledge, capabilities, and humor. She laughed, too.

They parted after he invited her to go to Fort Sonoma, by saying, "I am going to write Sir George and suggest he come to Sonoma for a grand celebration for him in my home. Maria, Ignacia, I named my house *Casa Grande*, and it **is** grand. You must come see it. There could not be a better time. I want all of the Vallejo family to be there to impress him."

Two days into the new year of 1842, Sir George Simpson walked with his men from his ship, still docked in the bay; they headed on horseback toward Sonoma. He and his traveling party saw little of the terrain in the dense fog and were drenched from the rain upon their arrival. Some of the Mexican military accompanied the group, and, when they were close, two soldiers rode ahead to alert Vallejo and the military of their arrival.

The brass cannon exploded in an official salute, as they entered Sonoma. The fort was in the center of the plaza, surrounded by a boulevard one hundred ten feet wide. The grand scale of the town was the product of General Mariano Vallejo's design, and he proudly shared that fact, during celebrations the following day.

Even with General Vallejo having health problems and needing to rest in his bedroom, off and on that evening, the festivities were impressive. The table overflowed with food and lacked for nothing—roasted pigs, baked chickens, many choice cuts of beef, and bear meat were served. The colors of peppers, squashes, beans, and all kinds of other vegetables blended beautifully across the table, and smells of garlic, cilantro, cinnamon, and an assortment of spices filled the air. The serving dishes and pottery looked like works of art, and wine never stopped flowing.

At one time, when General Vallejo was absent from the table and resting, Sir George Simpson commented to his fellow Englishmen about their host. "He has risen in the world of Mexico by his own talent and energy. I understand he is an exceptional swordsman and a renowned leader of the military." He took a sip of his wine and continued talking. "I have heard that his courage and inventiveness is unsurpassed here." He stopped to clear his throat and lowered his voice before making his next observation. "You would think, with his education and influence, that he would know more about decor and a palatable cuisine. I feel I have been poisoned with so much pepper and garlic!"

The other Englishman cheerfully agreed, knowing that the gaudy furniture from the Sandwich Islands did not compare with furniture made in England, and he added, "They have no carpets on their floors. I am sure that ships with rugs from the Orient must pass here."

A minute later, General Vallejo returned from his bed, wrapped in a cloak, and sat next to Sir George again. "Please forgive me for my absence and appearance."

"Oh, please, forgive us for imposing on you while you are ill."

Sir George, being an experienced spokesman for the British Crown, began making a persuasive argument for England. "If California were to become a protectorate of England, we would provide for more and better benefits than any other country. Without a doubt, we are powerful and prestigious, being the leading maritime nation."

When topics arose, that Mariano did not want to discuss, his illness became a benefit. Before he could respond or think of a way to change the subject, he made the excuse that he needed to use the bathroom. "Again, I must be excused. Please forgive me." He signaled his brother. "Salvador, please sit in my place, while I am gone and converse with our guests."

Mariano, though not wanting to say it, preferred to have closer ties to the United States of America than to England. To him, it made more sense because the Mexicans and Americans shared the same land mass together. Besides, as he had often said to friends, he disliked all the titles of nobility and preferred the idea of a republic; however, he refrained from discussing that. The main reason he avoided the discussion was the matter of fifty million pesos that Mexico owed Britain. So, all through the evening, Vallejo reminded himself to avoid the topic of that debt, too.

Mariano had a troublesome hip, that made walking difficult and created a lot of pain. Dr. Bale had sent medicine for him, and Maria Ignacia had brought it, since her husband did not want to go to the celebration. The medicine was a blister of cantharides, to be taken orally.

But it was the wrong medicine!

Vallejo had ingested medicine that did not help his hip pain and instead caused him to make many trips to relieve himself. Exhausted from his incessant pain and constant need to urinate, he took to his bed again.

In her son's absence, Vallejo's mother talked with Sir George, who commented to her, "Doña Antonia Lugo de Vallejo, how I envy your life surrounded with your family. For me, that is a luxury. We are twenty people here at this table and half of them are your family, who have distinguished themselves in this country. How proud you must be."

She politely bowed her head, "Thank you. I do feel privileged." She offered, "Sir George, if you have finished your dinner, you might want to stroll outside with the other men, while we women retire to the living room. I see that the rain has abated, and there is sun. We should enjoy the warmth before the rain comes again. And it will. 'Tis the season."

General Vallejo rose from his bed to join the men. Once outside, Salvador and Mariano walked with Sir George who asked, "Did I hear you say your niece married a Dr. Edward Turner Bale?"

"Yes, that is so. Why? Since he's an Englishman, do you know the doctor? He did not come tonight; nevertheless, we could have you meet with him."

Sir George shook his head, "No, no, I do not know him personally. However, when I heard the name, it sounded familiar. At first, I could not place how I knew the name. Now I have remembered. So, though I have not met him, I know of him."

As they sat on benches and sipped small glasses of an after-dinner drink, a surprising story unfolded.

Sir George told them, "Please stop me if you know these facts. Hmm, I cannot remember how many years ago it was." He stopped speaking for a moment to ponder. "Oh, the year is not important. I read in the daily paper about a Doctor Edward Turner Bale. It was four or maybe five years ago." Chuckling, he admitted, "With age, my memory is often slow. So, the incident could have been more than five years ago." He frowned and pursed his lips before saying, "Let me collect my thoughts. Oh, yes, this is how it went. A fellow nobleman, whose name escapes me—a lord, he was. Hmm, I cannot remember his surname. Anyway, a Dr. Edward Turner Bale operated on him, with another physician, in London. They were at a well-equipped facility with modern equipment for a new procedure on one of his organs. I believe they called it an appendix, or something or other.

"It seems that, after they had opened the abdomen, the nurse, who was giving the gas to the lord, accused Dr. Bale of being drunk. It was a critical moment in the operation. It was when the infected appendix was to be removed. The other physician pushed Dr. Bale away, while shouting that he would sew the wound closed before the lord bled to death. Bale fled the surgical room, ran from the hospital, and was never seen there again."

Salvador and Mariano exchanged a brief glance.

Sir George said, "Do you know the story?"

"No, no, we do not. Please continue."

"Well, the other physician thought the lord..." Sir George raised his finger to comment, "I do believe his name was Lord Willington. Though I may be wrong." He shook his head and said, "Excuse me for interrupting myself at such a critical point in the story. The other physician thought Lord Willington was going to die and said as much to the nurse, to the other staff at the hospital, and to the family of this ill man. It came to pass that all those facts about his possible death were printed in the daily papers. However, as the days passed, the lord kept getting better and better. It wasn't until several days later, and after an investigation, that it became apparent that Dr. Bale had completed the operation successfully. Before he had been pushed aside, Dr. Bale had removed the infected appendix, unknown to the nurse and that other physician. The worker who cleaned the operating theatre told everyone that he found a small piece of flesh on the floor, so he dropped it into a bottle and stored it on a shelf. After Lord Willington recovered, the worker retrieved the bottle and showed everyone. It was the infected appendix.

"Dr. Bale had completed a difficult operation and saved the lord's life before he disappeared. Lord Willington wanted to meet him and show his gratitude face-to-face but, of course, that never happened."

Mariano commented, "What a surprising story. So, it seems you are telling us that Dr. Bale may not know the ending either."

Sir George said, "Well, I have no idea if he does or does not. I would ask him if he were here."

Mariano looked to Salvador again before saying, "You can rest assured that we will let him know."

And they would, after a few years had passed.

On that day, when everyone was in Sonoma celebrating with Sir George Simpson, Dr. Bale spent the day at his adobe. The house was still under construction but, since his arrest, he had decided to not live at *Casa Zemita* any longer. It was an advantage that his job as Surgeon General of the Mexican California Army allowed him to work in any of three locations: The forts in Sonoma, Yerba Buena, or Monterey. He had moved all the paraphernalia from his infamous pharmacy out of Larkin's rented room and now was mixing medications in his home. He stood working at a tabletop, mixing a healing plaster with a concoction of herbs for General Vallejo's hip.

He was humming a pleasant tune as he reached for his mortar and pestle to grind seeds to powder. When finished, he planned to ride to Fort Sonoma to deliver the soothing plaster to Mariano and to work with anyone who needed medical attention.

He loved being in his adobe, especially since Mari had joined him after the celebration dinner. She had decided to stay at their adobe with him for a while. However, this was not necessarily why he was happily humming. Also, he had been ecstatic when she had let him know that she was with child again. Nevertheless, neither, of those facts, was that the reason for his humming.

The reason was *The United States Pharmacopoeia* book laying open on his desk. It displayed a page with the recipe: Blister of cantharides, also known as Spanish Fly, a preparation of powdered green beetles mixed with herbs, to use as a diuretic and aphrodisiac.

When he had first arrived at the Monterey medical office in the fort and took an inventory of all the medications, he noticed one of the many vials had the label *Mosca de España* which was a green powder. He did not know what he had until much later when he was searching for a diuretic for a soldier and came across a recipe needing Spanish Fly. At that moment, he remembered that *Mosca de España* meant Spanish Fly, so he made the medicine for the soldier.

On this day, he was smiling and humming because he was thinking of what Vallejo had gone through the night before. He was content that he had decided to mix the wrong medication for Vallejo. Talking quietly to himself, he was sure that, "No one knows of the discomfort I caused my lying and deceiving in-law, General Vallejo."

Soon he finished making the plaster he should have sent last night.

Once outside, he saw his wife, standing with Julia and Lolita, and he went to say goodbye. They were gazing out at the fertile field behind their house where the crags of Mount St. Helena—part of a volcanic belt that had erupted centuries ago—appeared to the north. The mountain stood more than four thousand feet above sea level.

Julia was talking while looking at the mountain. She turned to him as he approached. "One of the Miwoks told me that they have an ancient tale about this mountain that overlooks your land, Dr. Bale. They said it exploded with fire and stones long ago. They say it spit all this fertile soil out all over the valley for their food to grow. The berries are better here, the roots they dig are bigger, they say the oak trees make tastier acorns, and the grasses are taller."

He nodded, "Ancient tales often have some truth in them. It is true that volcanic soil is more fertile."

"I enjoy these people. I want to hear more of their tales," Maria Ignacia said, "and I like to watch them work. They are the best workers." Dozens of native men, many naked, toiled in the winter wheat pulling unwanted plants. "When will it be time to harvest?"

With a sheepish look he replied, "I don't know. But I am going to learn all those facts. For now, I don't know. Thank heavens the natives do. Although I abhor the thought of what they endured all those years at the missions, I am grateful they know how to farm. And I hope they are more satisfied growing food for themselves."

Maria Ignacia added, "and for us." This was the second day of sunshine after many days of rain; the workers hurried to finish before more rain began. "Julia and I were wondering where all the women are."

Pointing to a hill in the distance, he said, "On the other side of the hillock they have built a village, in a wooded area."

Julia turned to Maria Ignacia and said, "Let's walk over there and meet the women later."

After Bale rode away that day, Maria Ignacia wandered back to his room, saw his open book of pharmaceutical recipes, and a glimmer of understanding occurred as she read the recipe. After recalling all the trips her uncle had taken to the bathroom, she knew what her husband had done. At that moment, she learned her husband was capable of dark humor—a part of his character she had not known.

She sat on a stool and thought, *my dear Uncle Mariano, Edward found a way to pay you back for the suffering you have caused us when you withheld the paperwork on his citizenship and my dowry.*

When the storms abated, Sir George Simpson sailed north to return to the fort of the Hudson's Bay Company, located on the Columbia River in Oregon. Before leaving, he wrote to General Vallejo to thank him for his hospitality:

> *Sunday, 30 January 1842*
> *Monterey, Alta California, Mexico*
> *To the Esteemed General Mariano Guadalupe Vallejo:*
> *You have my thanks and gratitude for the relaxing time I spent with you and your family in this pleasant place. I felt I could have been in the north of my Scotland observing Auld Yule. Please let your gracious mother, Doña Maria Antonia de Lugo, know how much I appreciated her conversation and hospitality.*
>
> *I must tell you, who may not be aware of the characteristics of the English, that I was quite impressed with how your compatriots seemed far happier than one would find Englishmen in the same situations. Also, I was amazed to see how people of all social strata mingled in harmony, including both sexes. Such social democracy is unknown in England. I found it refreshing.*
>
> *I look forward to a joint relationship between our countries in the future and I remain indebted to you for your hospitality. I extend an invitation for you to visit in Oregon to allow me to repay you.*
> *Sir George Simpson*
> *Governor General of Hudson's Bay Company*
> *Oregon Country*

One day, a few weeks later, Edward and Mari noticed riders approaching their home. She had been planting flowers and bushes around the front of the house and talking to Edward of her plans to plant pear trees and an orchard farther away, between the stream and hill. Edward was playing with their daughter, Lolita, who was still not too steady on her feet.

Soon, Maria Ignacia recognized the head rider and shouted, "Juan Bautista Alvarado is coming!" She turned to Edward, "Do you remember my cousin Juan B from the holiday party where you and I formally met? Remember, you knocked me on the floor with your elbow."

Edward picked up Lolita and walked with his wife toward the riders. He shook his head. "That was a long ago, and I met so many people."

"Of course, I understand. Oh, please pretend you remember for my sake. He has an important position and could be offended. That's his personality." As they got closer to the dismounting riders, she lowered her voice and finished, saying, "He is the governor and honors us by coming to our home."

She threw her arms around Juan B and held fast for a lengthy hug. Upon releasing him, she turned her head up with a coy teasing look, as she said, "I hope I am not embarrassing you, Juan B Alvarado, in front of your men."

"Embarrassing me! How could any man be embarrassed to have a beautiful woman rush to embrace him?" With one arm, he grabbed her around her waist and pulled her close for a kiss on both cheeks.

Edward glared at the scene. He wondered if it was anger or jealousy rising within him. He did not enjoy these displays of affection by her male family members. Nevertheless, to honor his wife's request, he approached Alvarado while holding his daughter in his left arm and extending his right hand. "Good to have you come visit, Governor."

Maria Ignacia gestured toward the house, "You must be tired and thirsty. Please come inside to sit and have a cool refreshing drink. Possibly you are hungry, as well."

"No, no, we had a hearty meal at the fort, and we are here on business."

Looking puzzled, she asked, "Oh, what type of business?" A cold chill ran down her back, in fear that Edward had committed another crime unbeknownst to her.

Standing stiff and straight in his uniform, with coils of braiding running across his chest and brass buttons shining down his coat, Juan B gestured to one of his men who hastily handed Edward a rolled document.

Juan B, said, "In honor of your marriage, our family has deeded four square leagues to the name of Edward Turner Bale. This is 17,962 acres; the amount that is granted for a single family.

"I am here to measure and stake the perimeters according to what Edward shows me today. We'll ride everywhere, so my men can mark and measure. For instance, I need to know the site of your grist mill, and where you want to make the sawmill that I heard you were planning to construct. I must know of any other structures you plan to build, and those that exist. In this way, my men and I can designate the boundaries of your property."

"Oh, my," escaped the lips of Maria Ignacia.

Edward stood speechless and said, "I had no idea and do not know what to say." He unrolled the document and showed Mari the paper making him a landowner.

Juan B made a lighthearted laugh, "No need to say anything. We are late in acknowledging our gift to your marriage. I am the Constitutional Governor of the Department of Alta California; therefore, I am honored to sign this deed. However, I need Edward to show me the land to be designated as yours for the making of a Plat Map. Oh, there are a couple of other details, in addition to the gift of land, we will be sending cattle: A dozen cows, a few goats, and a pregnant pig. Oh, also, you must tell me the official name you are giving your ranch."

It took the whole day to complete the survey because they had to stake each boundary. The Plat became an unusual shape as it followed the Napa River. When completed, the plat map looked like stair-steps on the eastern border, followed many hillocks on the western side, and formed a straight line on the south where the Bales' land met with George Yount's *Rancho Caymus*.

That night while nestled in bed, giddy with excitement and full of joy, they talked about what to name their ranch. Before deciding, their lovemaking interrupted, and they fell asleep.

Morning brought an idea. While sipping their tea, they peered from the kitchen window at all the naked Miwoks and Wappos working the field. Edward turned to her with an idea. "I want to honor all those natives who are living on the land. Look, they stand in the flesh, naked, sweating and making the land better. I do not do well at translating Spanish, yet I know I want to call our land *Rancho Carne Humana*."

"Oh, Edward, that translates to *human flesh* and people will not understand."

"Ho, ho, ho." He roared in laughter. "All the better. Look at the human flesh out there working." He laughed again and turned to her. "Please tell no one how the name of our ranch honors the natives. Let people try to guess my meaning."

Still looking dubious, she said, "Some may think it means to eat human flesh because *carne* is the word for meat."

Now Edward was bent over in laughter. His display of mirth continued for too long, and he choked on his own dark humor. He began to cough excessively.

Concerned, Mari rushed to pour a glass of water for him.

After he drank and sat at the kitchen table, the laughing and coughing subsided. He looked up at his wife and cleared his throat, "Yes, yes, I insist on the name, *Rancho Carne Humana*. No one will know what we mean, and it will stir assumptions and conversation. Oh, my side is aching from laughing so much."

Again, she noted the dark humor her husband enjoyed and could no longer not show delight. She joined with him, liking their clever and misleading name. They spent the day looking at each other with love in their eyes and laughter in their voices because of their little secret.

They felt so carefree, and, on and off throughout the day, she thought, *if only this could last forever.*

While Edward and Mari were at their *Rancho Carne Humana*, life was blissful. They made sure no wine or spirits were available to tempt him. They planted fruit trees around the adobe and along the stream. Together, they walked the terrain to become acquainted with the land they owned. They mingled with the Wappos and Miwoks who shared their land, making friends of many. They spent months on their land, with the child growing inside her, until the time came to return to Monterey for the birth.

Maria Ignacia birthed another daughter whom they named Carolina.

Coincidently, the same year, the Larkins finally had a daughter. However, much to Maria Ignacia's surprise and possibly to the chagrin of Rachel, the Larkins' girl was named Carolina, too.

Edward suggested, "Let's ease the tension by using the English version of our daughter's name and call her Caroline."

Maria Ignacia agreed. "Isn't it amazing that we chose the same name, although we haven't spoken in years? I so miss Rachel. I hope someday we can be friends again."

Edward shook his head. "I'm sorry you lost your friend because of me."

"I know," she said, "You must never drink again. You told me before we married that with drink you became another person—a devil. Now I know that is so true. You must never let that devil out again."

While she and their two children were at *Casa Zemita*, every other month Edward would go to Monterey to attend to his medical duties at the Presidio, and he swallowed his pride to stay with his wife at his in-laws' adobe. During his visits, they made plans to live permanently at their ranch in the next year, and, during the nights of his visits, they conceived another child.

Soon, Bale resigned his post as surgeon-in-chief, stating his ranch needed all his time. Without work in Monterey, he was relieved to no longer need to sleep at his in-laws' adobe.

One day, when her pregnancy was reaching its term, Maria Ignacia told her father and grandmother over breakfast, "Lita and father, please plan to come stay with us at our ranch when we move, after the baby is born. You will enjoy the beauty there," she said. "Oh, though you have the letter I wrote to thank you, while I am sitting with both of you, I want to thank you again for your gift of land and animals for my family. You were generous to us." Mari wrapped her arms around her grandmother and whispered into her ear, "*Te amo,*" walked around the table and hugged her father, too. "I love you both so much".

Lita responded by telling of another gift. She said, "I want you to take the family candlesticks. You know that your mother prized them because her grandparents had brought them here to Mexico from Spain. Well, this place was called New Spain back then. Do you remember the names of your grandparents, your father's parents?"

Her father, across the table from Maria Ignacia, said, "Jose Maria Soberanes is my father's name and Maria Josefa Castro was my mother. Remember their names to tell your children."

"I remembered their names."

He continued, "You are taking the family candlesticks, and I want you to take that other item your mother so greatly prized—that ivory animal."

"Oh, the giraffe! I'd love to have it."

"Humph," he complained, "I will be glad to never have to see it again. I never understood why your mother prized it so. A ship captain gave it to her. Humph. I had to endure my wife loving an object given to her by another man."

Maria Ignacia offered a reason, by saying, "she told me that she wanted to travel to where that animal lived and see a live one. She wanted to see a giraffe and the animal that has the ivory tusks. Oh, what is it called?" A second later she remembered. "Yes, an elephant. She wanted to see those two animals from Africa."

"Humph."

Lita said, "Oh, and take Pepe with you when you move. He asked me if he could go, and I want to honor his request. Would you like that?"

"Oh my, yes, yes, of course." Maria Ignacia reached for Lita's hand and kissed it. "Oh, thank you. I am happy to know Pepe will be with me. He has been in my life always. I want my children to know him."

Lita had another thought. "Oh! Please take one of our dogs to guard against grizzlies coming into your yard. No, take two, a male and a female."

Though nothing can last forever, the Bale's life during this period was filled with contentment.

Elsewhere, discontentment was building. As if on a giant chessboard, players were arriving in California and positioning themselves for a game to take Alta California from Mexico. Although Mexico City was the Capital, those in power had assigned General Mariano G. Vallejo and his nephew, Governor Juan B. Alvarado to oversee Alta California. To win this game of chess, the Vallejo family must be subdued, and one player, the Swiss immigrant John A. Sutter, planned to influence the outcome.

Sutter, soon after his arrival by ship, obtained permission from Juan B. Alvarado, Mexico's Constitutional Governor, to establish a colony in the valley east of Sonoma. Juan B liked Sutter's character and envisioned this new settler's plans to build a fortress as a buttress to guard the frontier against encroachment by the Russians, Americans, or the British. Also, Juan B had heard that Sutter was not always on the honest side of dealings: He fled Europe to avoid debtor's prison, was pursued by people he had swindled from New York to Missouri and was known for selling a herd of stolen horses. Juan B calculated there was a future opportunity by helping a man of his character; so, Sutter obtained his Mexican citizenship in 1840, finished his settlement within the next year, and was granted 48,827 acres on the Sacramento River.

To grant such a large amount of land demonstrated the confidence and support that Juan B had for Sutter's fort and settlement.

Other men, adding to the players in the chess maneuvers, had been arriving in California off and on during the several years while the Bales were building up *Rancho Carne Humana*. Most were Americans. Although Edward did not befriend Sutter, Edward's friendship with George Yount grew substantially.

Yount was friends with any American who ventured into Alta California, and many of them camped and socialized at *Rancho Caymus*. Like Yount, Edward found the Americans to his liking, but those friendships put him among men who drank liquor. Before long, his resistance waned, and he was frequently drunk.

Maria Ignacia would remain unaware of Edward's drinking until she moved permanently to live at *Rancho Carne Humana*. Also, she was unaware of the growing number of Americans who were friends of her husband. Though he frequently went to Yount's ranch, more often than not he would return home the next day, after he had sobered. She was busy with her children. Their third child was a son named Edward Guadalupe Bale.

Maria Ignacia had no reason to venture over to her neighbor's place, but Yount's daughter, Mia, had reason to come to *Rancho Carne Humana*. She liked being with the Bale's three children.

Mia was holding little Edward and cuddling him when she said, "Oh, he is so tiny next to your little girls. I love holding him."

Julia told the young girl, "Little Edward seems to like you. He is quiet and looking at your face. I think you have made a friend."

Mia looked content.

Maria Ignacia turned to Julia and commented, "Back at *Casa Zemita*, I never made tortillas because of all the kitchen help. These that I make here taste better. Do you think it's my imagination?" They were outside making tortillas with the flour that had been grown on *Rancho Carne Humana* and ground at their grist mill. The stack on the table next to the outdoor fire pit where they worked was growing taller.

Julia shook her head. "You are using wheat you harvested and ground at your mill. It's fresher. I think that's the reason. The flour used at *Casa Zemita* is older because it was stored for a long time."

Mia was seated under the wooden trellis covered with new grape leaves on the vines outside the kitchen doorway. They had been planted two years ago and, already this spring, had a few clumps of small grapes forming. At Mia's feet, Lolita and Caroline were playing on the ground with a pile of rocks. Mia walked over to the older women and stood until they finished their conversation. Finally, she said, "I think the baby and Caroline need to be cleaned. Both stink worse than a skunk."

Julia wiped her hands on her apron and grabbed a couple of cloth squares from inside the house. "I'll take Caroline. Mia, you bring baby Edward. Let's go to the stream and clean them. You need to learn how to do this."

Maria Ignacia reached for the baby. "Oh, Mia, you don't need to . . ."

Mia held on to him and said, "No, I want to learn. Someday, I will have babies." Off she walked, a few steps behind Julia.

A browning tortilla on the fire pit started to burn. The edges blackened and a spiral of smoke rose; Lolita pointed and shouted, "Mamá, it burn!"

Maria Ignacia pulled the tortilla off as a rider approached. Turning, she held up her hand to shade her eyes from the sun. When the horse reached the large oak in their front yard, the rider entered the shade and became visible. Maria Ignacia saw a military uniform, then recognized who he was, and ran toward him, shouting, "Salvador, Salvador!"

With a smooth movement, he slipped from the roan, flipped the reins over the horse's head, and ran to meet her. They opened their arms and fell into each other. Soon, he tightened his hug and twirled her around.

She giggled, "Oh, Salvador, more, more. Twirl me like when I was small. More, more."

When he came to a rest, she could not contain the excitement she felt and began to cover his face with kisses. "I miss you," she said between kisses. "I love you so much."

She did not know that someone watched.

Neither Julia and Mia at the stream, nor Salvador and Maria Ignacia outside the adobe, had seen anyone else arrive. Nevertheless, Edward had come home from Yount's. He had been putting away his riding gear in the shed next to the house and was looking out the window of the shed when he witnessed Salvador's arrival and the affectionate welcome that Mari gave him.

Edward had spent the night at Yount's ranch, drinking with his American friends, and he was not completely sober. Therefore, the devil who lurked within him witnessed his wife's interaction with Salvador; the rash and impetuous side of Edward grew with each passing moment. His chest tightened and his anger intensified until jealousy exploded. He rushed out from the shed and grabbed his wife, while shouting, "You bastard! Who do you think you are! Get away from my wife." He pulled her roughly from Salvador's embrace.

Maria Ignacia screamed as she fell to the ground, "Aeeeee! No, Edward, no!"

Edward took a swing at Salvador who stepped away from the oncoming fist. As a military man, Salvador was known to be adroit in all his actions. Edward swung again and missed again.

Maria Ignacia scrambled back to her feet and pulled at Edward, "No, Edward, this is my uncle!"

Edward pivoted and intentionally smacked her with the back of his hand. She fell again. He screamed, "Is this what you do when I am not here? How many men are you seeing?" He grabbed her forearm and pulled her up with his hand cocked to administer a blow.

Salvador jumped and grabbed his arm. "Leave her alone. You are a madman!"

Now Julia and Mia appeared. Julia cried, "What is happening here?"

The two men were ready to fight when Maria Ignacia pulled one of Salvador's hands away from Edward and stepped between them. She shouted to her husband, "Stop this! Stop! This is my uncle Jose Manual Salvador Vallejo, the brother of Mariano."

"I don't care who he is," Edward said and wrenched his arm free from Salvador's grasp, hitting him across the face with the back of his hand, "No man can hold and kiss my wife as you did. I want to kill you." He put his face closer to Salvador and seethed, "I challenge you to a duel. I will kill you!"

"I accept. You challenged me; therefore, I have the right to choose the weapons. I pick swords, for tomorrow at dawn, in the marching grounds." Salvador straightened his jacket, bowed to Maria Ignacia, "Forgive me, Maria Ignacia. I will leave only if you can assure me that you are safe with this wretched husband of yours."

She nodded.

Once mounted, Salvador directed his horse close to Edward who had to jump from the path to avoid being sideswiped. Edward flailed with his arms to steady himself, while screaming, "Hell! I am going to kill you tomorrow!" He stood staring as the horseman disappeared.

Walking to Edward, Maria Ignacia tried to calm him. She reached to touch his forearm, and he jerked it from her and brushed her hands away, while spitting out his words. "I am not staying here with a wife who makes love with other men." He strode off and soon was riding his horse south towards Yount's ranch.

Julia came beside Maria Ignacia who was shouting to Edward to come back. "Edward, Edward, you need to know something about Salvador. Come back!"

The two women fell together into each other's arms. Julia suggested, "I think you should rest inside awhile. I want to wash the cut on your cheek."

Maria Ignacia's face expressed surprise as she touched the cut and said, "Oh, Julia, they had never met until today. So many years have passed, and I could never get Salvador and Edward in the same place to meet each other. What is worse is that Edward does not understand. Salvador is an expert swordsman. He has won honors for his sword fighting. With this challenge, Salvador has the right to kill Edward. Oh, Julia, what am I to do?"

"Nothing. You can do nothing. If I understand it, no one can stop a duel.

You know that." Julia led her into the house. "Are you sure you are not hurt anywhere else?" After seeing a nod, Julia insisted, "Come and rest."

Mia did not understand the situation, did not know about duels, and did not want Dr. Bale to be hurt or killed. She wiped the tears forming in her eyes. "I'll help with the little ones. I'll stay all night to help."

In the darkness before dawn, people started arriving to witness the duel. Captain Salvador Vallejo had a large following with the native troops under his command, and a multitude of them were there. Salvador and Edward were both tall, handsome, and close in age, but their similarities ended there. Salvador, the young Mexican, was well trained and accustomed to confrontations in and out of battles. Edward, the Englishman, lacked any military training.

The sun lightened the sky in the moments before the swords were drawn. With the first clash of steel, cheers rose from the spectators. Within the next minute, Salvador lunged to make a superficial cut in the shoulder of Edward, and it was obvious to everyone that he could have sunk the sword through Edward's chest instead. Salvador countered all of Edward's moves with ease, but after a few more clanks of the blades, the situation changed. Bale stepped back a few steps and stumbled, falling to his knees. When he leaned forward to rise, Salvador took the flat of the blade and spanked Edward with several swats.

The crowd roared and laughed at the spanking.

Infuriated, Edward stood, dropped his sword, pulled his hidden pepper-box from his waist, and fired two shots.

Both missed.

Edward turned and ran to his horse.

At the surprise of a gun being drawn and fired, everyone was caught off guard, and Edward got away. Foolishly, he rode to Fort Sonoma, galloped to the medical offices where he worked, and hid in a storage room.

The native troops, under Salvador's command, followed. Minutes later, they found and arrested him. Dr. Edward Bale occupied a jail cell for attempted murder again.

Not until the sun was high in the sky and the fort was bustling with the daily military practice, did General Mariano Vallejo hear the news. He was in his

Casa Grande on the north corner of the central plaza of the fort in Sonoma. It was an impressive one hundred ten-foot-long building with two stories. In the west wall stood a four-story tower, from which one hundred square miles of territory could be seen. Vallejo's home was a small fortress and demonstrated how he wanted Sonoma to appear—imposing to any enemies. However, the news about Dr. Bale that was brought to his door this day diminished any feeling of power or pride.

"Maldito! Bring Captain Salvador Vallejo and Governor Juan B. Alvarado to me immediately. Maldito!" He stomped his foot. "Bale has done it again." He began to pace and complain aloud. "An Englishman! Why did my niece marry an Englishman! An Englishman who is a thorn in my side."

When the two men arrived, they sat down to a meeting and argued.

Mariano reminded them of the situation. "If I do not protect him and England learns about Bale, the fifty million pesos we owe England from loans will have to be repaid. We have no money to pay the debt and would have to pay with land. Oh, more than anything, I do not want England to own any of Alta California. This is such a dilemma."

Salvador was adamant and said as much, "He tried to kill me, and you want me to let him walk away with no punishment? You saved him when he shot at Larkin." He stood and raised his voice to emphasize his point. "I will not allow him to go unpunished again."

Finally, they came to an agreement.

A flier was posted stating:

PUBLIC FLOGGING

of
Dr. Edward Bale

Saturday, March 16, 1844
in
the Plaza of Sonoma
and afterwards
Dr. Bale to be in the stocks overnight
for
All to view.

Ordered by Captain Salvador Vallejo

On the designated Saturday, the order was executed to the cheers of the townspeople and others who had traveled from far to witness the comeuppance of the notorious Dr. Bale.

Sunday evening, Edward returned home. After describing what had happened, he asked, "Please forgive me for everything. Especially forgive me for striking you as well as the words I said to you. I was not sober because I had been drinking at Yount's ranch."

She said nothing.

"Mari, please, I promise not to swallow a drop of liquor again. Please forgive me."

She stepped away from him and said, "Forgive you? Not now. Maybe never. Possibly, with time, I may forgive you. After I see you sober day after day, week after week, and longer. After years, maybe I will be able to forgive you."

He hung his head in his hands and wept.

She reminded him, "Your son is not yet three months old. You sleep upstairs in the spare bed. Good night. I am exhausted from hearing of all your failings, and I need to sleep before little Edward needs to nurse again."

Months passed with Edward not leaving *Rancho Carne Humana*. He had no source of liquor and remained sober; but, in silence he nursed his grudges. One against General Vallejo, another against Thomas Larkin for requesting his arrest warrant, and now he nursed a third grudge against Salvador. His disgrace in the community and the coldness from his wife, made him be more involved in his ranch: Working his land, organizing his papers, planning to build a sawmill, and interacting with his workers, the Wappos and Miwoks. Yet, each day he worked on the grudges, as well.

A few months after Edward's disgrace and flogging, Lita and Mari's father came for a visit. They were staying at General Vallejo's *Casa Grande* for a week and came to visit the Bales for the day.

Lita explained, "We wanted to meet your son before he grew to manhood. Who knows when you would have come back to see us in Monterey."

"Oh, Lita, please don't exaggerate. I will come for the year-end holidays. It is the summer; I have much to do here. Please hold little Eduardo while I get the tortillas." They were just sitting down to begin the afternoon meal. When she returned to the table with a platter full of tortillas, Dr. Bale walked in from the fields.

"Welcome to *Rancho Carne Humana*," Dr. Bale said, greeting his guests. Then he walked toward the other room. "Excuse me while I wash. I will be only a few minutes." When he returned, he wore a fresh white shirt and his hair had been combed. He stood trying to make amends with his in-laws by saying, "I am glad you both came. Maria Ignacia misses her family, and we feared that my disgraceful conduct might have caused a permanent separation. Again, I thank you for being here." He sat, and Mari passed him a plate already served with food.

Lita responded to his apology and said, "We are family and must support each other. If Mariano can find reasons to pardon you, we shall forgive you as well."

Mari's father chuckled and added his insight. "Well, Mariano fears problems with England. Edward, you should be grateful you are an Englishman. If Mexico did not owe fifty million pesos to England, you would still be behind bars or hanging from a rope." He took a bite of food and chuckled again.

Stunned at hearing those facts, Edward hesitated with his fork midway to his mouth—though only for an instant. Not wanting to appear, in front of his in-laws, that he was ignorant of the debt, he leaned into his fork, grabbed the food, and began to chew.

Maria Ignacia had not known about the fifty-million-peso debt either and saw Edward's surprise, so she distracted everyone by calling to Julia, "Bring Lolita in here when she is finished eating. She can sit next to her grandmother and practice talking." She continued her distraction because she feared her husband's anger would surface, by turning to Lita and saying, "Lolita is talking a lot, but I have a concern. We speak in English all day in the house so the children will know two languages, and I want her to speak well in Spanish, too. Lita, will you speak with her?"

"Of course, I would be delighted."

At that moment, a group of Wappos walked past the window. All were naked.

Lita gasped, "Holy Mary, Mother of God! Look, they have no clothes."

Maria Ignacia had thought this might happen, and she bit her lip.

Edward commented, "Yes, they live naturally here. I will not tell them to be Mexicans and dress like us. I want them to be free to live their lives as they have for thousands of years . . . well, until they were forced to change when Junipero Serra came."

Lita felt aghast and stated firmly, "My goodness, Maria Ignacia, surely you do not approve. You have two little girls playing outside every day. At least they could wear a loin cloth, as they did at the missions."

"Lita," Maria Ignacia said with compassion, "what my girls see is natural. I do not want to hide what is natural. I cannot hide the genitals of our dog, the teats of the cow, two birds mating, or anything relating to procreation." She stopped and inhaled deeply. "Please honor our wishes and do not speak about this nakedness. I do not want my children to hear such discussions. I have nothing more to say because this is natural, and these native people are our friends. Besides, we decided that we will not treat them in the same way the people at the missions did and force them to wear loin cloths."

"Humph. Well, they are not my friends, and I do not want to be outside with them walking about like that."

Edward spoke up again, "We will honor your feelings and hope you will honor ours. I will ask the Miwoks and Wappos to give us privacy when you visit."

"You need not worry," Lita said with disgust, "I may not visit again."

Julia brought in Lolita and Caroline, and Lita opened her arms to her granddaughters.

At that moment, Maria Ignacia's father stood and walked toward the door to the terrace. On the way he caught his daughter's eye and signaled for her to follow him. He walked outside.

Lita and the children were busy chatting and laughing. Maria Ignacia picked up dishes from the table and went to the kitchen a few seconds later. Soon she was outside with her father. She asked, "Father, what is it?"

"Oh, I need to tell you something that I do not want your Lita to know, just yet. She's your grandmother and my mother-in-law. As a mother-in-law I think she may not approve, even though her daughter, your mother, died fourteen years ago." He went quiet and shuffled his feet. "Well, you may not approve either." He stopped speaking again, before blurting a sentence that made Maria Ignacia collapse into a chair. He said, "I am getting married next week and moving to my *Rancho Los Ojitos* with my new wife."

"Oh, my! Do I know her?"

"I think you know of her, though you may not have met."

"Well, Father, are you going to tell me her name?"

He shuffled his feet again then said, "Raimunda Castillo."

Maria Ignacia's mouth opened, "But, Father, she is Juan B's mistress!" Her fist flew to cover her mouth, but too late to stop herself from saying *mistress*.

"I am sorry. I will not say that word again. Oh, Father, I do like her. I know her and hope your marriage will be wonderful. What happened to Juan B and her? They were together so many years and have children together."

Her father's eyes gleamed as he said, "Juan B proposed but she refused because she knew it would be impossible to live with a drunk." His hand went up to cover his mouth. "I am sorry that I said that word. Maria Ignacia, like you, I will not say that again."

"Father, that's fine. Edward no longer drinks, and he says he never will again. I believe him." She had another thought and said, "Years ago when I said Julia was getting married, you and Uncle Mariano thought she was too old."

"Yes, I remember commenting," he took out his handkerchief and wiped his brow before finishing, "and I remember what you said. You told me that one is never too old to be in love. I agree with you. I am fifty years old and in love."

The two of them hugged, laughed, and re-entered the adobe.

With extreme effort Edward remained calm and was civil to his in-laws the whole day. When they left, he exploded. "Did you hear what your father said about the fifty million pesos owed by Mexico to England?" Knowing she heard, he did not wait for her reply. "As I have told you, Mari, your uncle Mariano is deceitful. He spoke with me about how he wanted to help me overcome my drinking, and he said that being in jail would serve no purpose for my recovery. He NEVER mentioned the debt to England that is hanging over his head. He fears that debt will be called due if an Englishman is imprisoned. How deceitful. I should have known he had an ulterior motive."

All through the next week, he went on with his rant while a scheme was forming within him. Knowing about the fifty-million-peso debt gave Edward power over the Vallejos. He told Mari, "Don't you let your loving uncles and cousins know that I know about the fifty-million-peso debt." He grabbed her shoulders and squeezed a bit too hard while continuing to say, "And remember that you promised to never tell them of my reason for fleeing England. If they knew that I killed that important lord on the operating table, I . . . " He left his sentence unfinished.

"Edward, you're hurting me. Let go! You know I understand all of that. You know I love you, and now I will say that I forgive you for shooting at Salvador. I am so pleased with our life since you have stopped drinking." He released his hold, and she wrapped her arms around him.

But, unknown to her, he was drinking again, and that may have been the reason that her forgiveness did not calm his growing hatred. Or was the problem that his grudges had become obsessions over the years? Giving Mariano the Spanish fly medicine had been his way to retaliate against the lie about the Nicasio natives, but recently, he had begun to work on his grudge against Salvador, though an exact plan had not been finalized. Before walking back outside to work, a scheme started to form around the edge of his mind. When Mari could no longer see his face, he smirked.

During the next few days, Edward went to Yount's ranch often to develop his plan for confronting Salvador during a coming holiday. His plan involved the Americans at *Rancho Caymus*. Over drinks, he shared his ideas with every one of them, except George Yount.

Bale could not share his plan with George because George was a close friend of General Vallejo and might tell.

On a voting holiday in July of 1844 and as he had planned, Edward met a few of the Americans to have drinks before heading out on horseback. Outside of Sonoma, the whole group gathered before heading into town. Bale had found fourteen Americans who agreed that Salvador Vallejo had treated him with disrespect by spanking him with a sword and allowing his flogging on the plaza. They agreed that Salvador needed to pay for disgracing him. The group was well suited to the plan at hand:

> Benjamin Kelsey and his brothers had a bone to pick with Salvador for their personal reasons;
> Granville P. Swift was said to be the fastest load-and-shoot man in California and would enjoy the opportunity to show his skills;
> Ezekiel (Zeke) Merritt was Edward's best drinking friend who had experienced a sword spanking from Salvador just as Edward had;
> and
> the others were eager to shoot up any Mexican for any reason.

Edward thought that the timing could not have favored him more. As he rode with the fourteen men into Sonoma, he saw Salvador strolling in the plaza with his friend Cayetano Juárez. Instantly, Edward's anger rose until it felt like a hot poker stabbing at his chest. He hastened closer to his target and when in point-blank range—so close it was impossible to miss—Edward pulled out his pepper-box pistol.

But with so many people walking on the streets and in the square of the plaza, only a fool would have thought the timing favorable.

Such a fool was Edward Bale, as he fired twice.

He was not only a fool but also a poor shot. He missed his mark with both shots. One bullet grazed Salvador's chest through his uniform and, as often happened with such firearms, the burning wadding from the second shot flew one way and the bullet another. The wadding burned the jaw of Cayetano Juárez, and the second bullet hit nothing.

Edward slipped from his horse and ran, as he had before, but not very far. He ran to the house of his friend Jacob P. Leese, who lived across from the plaza. He rushed through the door, followed by two of the Americans, and shouted, "Help me! Bar the doors and windows. They're coming for me."

"What did you do now, Bale?" Leese inquired.

"I tried to kill Salvador and missed. He is still standing. Damn it all!"

They could hear loud voices shouting and people banging at the door, "Open this door! Bale, you coward, give yourself up."

The crowd grew, the noise increased, and chaos prevailed out around the plaza. Minutes passed, with people ramming the doors and shuttered windows. The wood held for the moment.

Soon a deep and powerful voice could be heard through the door. "Chief Solano here. Bale, I have fifty men with me, and we will tear down these doors. You should come out and take your punishment."

Bale cringed against an inner wall and asked Leese, "Is there any way out of here where they can't see me?"

"Hell, I can't help you. I am mayor of this town, and the Vallejos are my in-laws. Have you forgotten that I married Rosalia Vallejo, their sister?"

The door seemed to explode as wood splintered and fell into the house. Chief Solano ducked through the doorway, entered, and grabbed Bale by an arm, dragging him outside across the ground. As Bale twisted and flailed in the dirt, the mob threw rocks at him from the street. Salvador was well-liked by the townspeople, and most of them had enjoyed seeing the flogging. Dr. Bale provided excitement to their lives.

On the plaza stood an oak tree with a looped and knotted rope permanently attached. Chief Solano headed for the lynching tree, called *encina del castigo*.

Improbable as it seems, luck was with Edward Bale again.

General Mariano Vallejo had been meeting in *Casa Grande* with several of his men, and heard the ruckus. He stepped from his front door and heard from the crowd that Dr. Bale was the cause of the trouble. "*Maldito!* Again?" he screamed, throwing his arms to the sky. Calling into his house, he demanded all his men come with him. They pushed through the mob.

The six-foot-seven-inches-tall Chief Solano was easy to see from a distance, and Vallejo knew Bale's life was in danger with the Chief standing at the hanging tree.

Rushing to stop the hanging, Vallejo's men shot into the sky to get the attention of the mob before pushing their way up to the oak. "Buenos Dias, Sam-Yeto, my friend," Vallejo began. "Ah, what has Dr. Bale done now?"

Bale stood with the noose resting on his shoulders and connected to the rope looped over the tree, ready to be pulled.

General Vallejo appeared to be in no hurry and asked to hear in detail what had happened. After he heard, he looked at Bale and shook his head, saying, "Bale, what a scoundrel you are. And quite a fool never to learn how to hit anything with the pepper-box I gave you. Let me think; how many times have you missed your mark?" Not waiting for an answer, Vallejo placed his hands behind his back and turned to Sam-Yeto. "Will you walk a minute with me?"

The tall, muscular Chief Solano strolled away with his pudgy, short friend, General Vallejo. They laughed at something one said and turned to look back at Bale and laughed again at another remark. Finally, minutes later, they changed direction and started back toward the oak.

Vallejo said, "I am sure that Bale is guilty and should be hanged. However, I must honor the laws of Mexico. Chief, you know that I am in charge here and could be in big trouble if I do not honor the law."

Chief Solano nodded.

Vallejo stopped a step from Bale. "You will not go free this time. But a court must decide how to punish you. So," gesturing to his soldiers, "take him and these two Americans to the jailhouse."

Bale was fitted with leg irons, and the guards on duty were doubled to prevent any of Bale's other American friends, who had ridden away, from returning to storm the jail.

Unlike with his previous arrests, being in jail was different this time for two agonizing reasons: He would remain in the jail cell for months, and Maria Ignacia would not visit him even once.

At *Rancho Carne Humana*, Maria Ignacia was in agony. It was a quiet day with the heat of summer reaching its zenith; everyone found shade and sat while droplets rolled from their foreheads, backs, and underarms. Adobes usually remain cool, but after many days of extreme heat, the house had become an oven. Mari told Julia, "Ever since I saw Edward that day on the beach, I have loved him more than I thought I could love anyone; nevertheless, now he has ripped a hole in me, and it festers. I hurt in my heart, yet I cannot cry." She dabbed her dripping face—no tears, only sweat.

The two women sat in the shadow of the adobe, leaning their backs against the cool walls. Pepe sat whittling on a piece of wood under the oak tree, not far away; he liked to make wooden furniture but today he was making toys. The children seemed oblivious to the heat. Lolita played by running to Pepe and back to her sister who could not yet run fast.

Maria Ignacia rambled on, "We could have such a fulfilling life here at our ranchero, if only he could control his drinking, but now he has left me with a painful emptiness." She looked at Julia and her face contorted with her next thought. "He struck me and wanted to hit me more." In a whisper and a voice that caught in her throat, she asked, "How c . . . could he d . . . do that? And why did I forgive him?"

Julia patted her hands and pondered the question before saying, "I do not think there is an answer to heal your hurt. He has told you he is a devil when he drinks. Every time he drank, he was that devil, not Dr. Bale."

A month passed.

And another month passed.

Soon a third month was ending.

The trial was not held until September. An endless parade of witnesses, who had seen Bale take the shots at Salvador, arrived. The verdict of "guilty" was inevitable; therefore, no one was surprised when the judge stated, "Guilty!"

However, the judgment had to be confirmed by the highest authority in the supreme government, Governor Micheltorena in the capital of Mexico City.

The powerful Micheltorena never forgot the debt of fifty million pesos, which weighed on his shoulders every day while he was the authority in Mexico. He sent a message that ordered, "drop the case immediately."

General Vallejo read those words, slammed the papers onto his desk, and shouted aloud to his empty office. "Maldito! I am tired of seeing Bale never have to pay the price for his murderous behavior!" He paced the room before he decided to write to Micheltorena. He knew he should not defy Governor Micheltorena, yet he needed Bale to pay for his sins. In his letter he stated that Dr. Edward Bale had established his Mexican citizenship years earlier and, at that time, had renounced his British citizenship.

Only a day passed before Governor Micheltorena shot back his angry reply with words exploding on the page:

> *September 1844*
>   *Direct Order:*
>   *RELEASE DOCTOR EDWARD TURNER BALE*
> *IMMEDIATELY!*
>
> *Signed,*
> *Your Superior,*
> *Governor Micheltorena*

The courier who brought the message stood at attention and did not flinch when General Vallejo cursed under his breath, "Maldito!" The general's eyes narrowed, his mouth contorted into a grimace, as he bellowed, "Get out of my office!"

As the soldier reached the door, the General shouted, "Stop. Have my man at the desk send for Captain Salvador Vallejo," and he collapsed into his chair to wait for Salvador while his mind festered with anger at Bale. He clenched the arms of his chair and gritted his teeth. His frustration seemed unbearable.

Within minutes, a rapping at the door interrupted his suffering and he shouted, "Come in!" When Salvador strode into the room, the general didn't move from his chair and continued to shout. "No, don't sit. And I want no comments from you when you hear my orders. Salvador, you are to escort Dr. Bale from the jail, from my city, from my sight, and out of my mind." Now General Vallejo stood and leaned with his hands against his desk. "He is free. I cannot believe this myself. Governor Micheltorena has freed him." He showed

Salvador the order and slammed his fist on his desk. "Maldito! Why did my precious niece marry this thorn in my side?" He began to pace back and forth in his office and abruptly stopped. "Well, Salvador, go! You, **do** understand those orders, do you not?"

Salvador arrived at the jail and found Dr. Edward Bale almost unrecognizable with matted hair, a beard, and clothes that hung on his wasted body. As Bale shuffled from the cell, his stench preceded him. Salvador placed a handkerchief to his nose, headed for the outer room, and, without explaining to Bale what was happening, ordered the jailer to remove the leg irons.

Bale said nothing, asked nothing, was mute. When freed of the leg irons, his legs were seen to be crusty, callused, and covered in bloodied cracks where the heavy iron had rubbed for months. His skin had split, bled, and scabs had formed. Bale squatted to massage his exposed ankles and decayed debris crumbled off.

Impatient to go outside for fresh air, Salvador said, "Stop that and come with me."

As Edward rose to leave, the jailer handed him a random pair of shoes without laces.

Salvador blurted out, "Don't look for your pepper-box! I took that to Maria Ignacia months ago."

Other than the shoes, he walked outside in the same clothes in which he had arrived, but filthy. Bale, still silent, shivered and buttoned his shirt up to his chin as he stepped out into a gray, gloomy day.

They crossed the wide avenue in front of the plaza, heading for the stables. Finally, Salvador stopped to wait for Bale and began to speak. "I find you to be worthless and the lowest form of life; but I have my orders, and you have been freed by the highest man in the land, Governor Micheltorena."

Bale turned his head with a jerk to look at Salvador, as if doubting what his ears had heard. For three months he had accepted his pending fate of hanging, yet with a single sentence he experienced freedom again. He opened his cracked lips, which had not spoken for so long, but his throat was dry, and he coughed trying to speak.

Salvador frowned in disgust and emphasized, "No one here will agree with Micheltorena's decision. In fact, Mariano and I are furious that you can go free. Hurry up, let's go."

Though Salvador and Edward were nearly the same height, Bale was too weak to stride in his normal manner. They continued at a slow pace across the grass until Salvador stopped again and turned to say in an irritated tone, "Twice you have shot at me. Both times you intended to kill me." He put his hands to his hips, holding the hilt of his sword with one hand. "And I want you to know that I plan to get even—some way and someday. I will let you wonder and worry about how and when." Salvador stood unmoving, glaring at Bale, who was unsteady on his feet and swaying.

At long last, Salvador let more of his thoughts spill forth. With his voice full of deep hate and his face contorted in revulsion, he said, "From the first day we met at your adobe, you've puzzled me. I don't understand how your mind works. **I do not understand what my beautiful niece sees in you.** When I come to kill you, I will make you suffer pain and a slow death, I promise."

They stood face to face; yet, in a blink of the eye, Bale was on his knees in front of Salvador, wrapping his arms around the legs of this enemy and whispering, "Forgive me."

They were in the center of Sonoma with many people watching and aware of whom they were. Salvador and Dr. Bale had stopped in the grass on the edge of the plaza.

Bale's voice sounded hollow as he spoke. He repeated, "Forgive me," and peered up at Salvador, dressed in his elegant uniform. "I was wrong to do . . ." but he choked and started coughing.

Passersby stood and watched. A little girl in a white dress had been running in the plaza and, seeing a man on his knees in front of the uniformed Captain whom she knew, she stopped a few feet from them to try to understand this unusual behavior. Others waited and watched, curious about what was happening with Dr. Bale.

His coughing stopped and, after clearing his throat, he spoke in a hoarse voice. "Humph. Please, I beg for your forgiveness." Bale's vacant and hollowed eyes peered at Salvador. "I know I can't expect forgiveness for what I did. I should not have tried to kill you. I was a fool, and I am so sorry."

"Let go of my legs! Get up, Bale! You're pathetic."

The crowd was growing.

Salvador turned to them, flung his arms out to shoo them away, and said, "Go! All of you. Go home." When the people didn't move fast enough, Salvador shouted, "I said to get out of here. Now!" All the people scattered except the little girl in the white dress. She stepped behind a tree near them and peered around the trunk to watch.

Bale was still on his knees, struggling to rise.

Salvador grabbed him by the arm and jerked him upright, saying, "Edward, let's walk to the stables." As Bale stumbled along, it was apparent how weak he was. Salvador called to the little girl, "Come here and help us." He pulled a coin from his jacket. "Go buy some bread and cheese. We will wait on that bench." They made their way to the edge of the grass and sat.

Bale pleaded, "If you cannot forgive me, how will Mari?"

Salvador's normally passive face looked puzzled. He blinked and shook his head. "Bale, you are so pitiful." Finally, in a calm and forceful voice, said, "I loathe to admit you are family. I will never understand you but, I may as well try to forgive you. I believe my niece will eventually forgive you, and I do not want to cause her more distress."

Bale nodded and a glimmer of a grin appeared.

"And, though I said I will forgive you, you must change to have my respect."

The little girl returned with the food. Salvador tore off a hunk of the bread and handed it to Bale who crammed it into his mouth.

Salvador opened the paper wrapping around the cheese and cut a slice. Passing it to Bale, he said, "Eat slower. Take this bite of this cheese and save the rest for your ride."

They sat while Bale finished chewing.

Once at the stables, Salvador handed over the paper-wrapped food and said, with a devilish smirk, "Besides this bread and cheese, I am sending you to your home with hugs and kisses for your wife. Do you understand, I am sending kisses to Maria Ignacia? Kisses from me, and you must deliver them."

The message's meaning was not lost on Bale. He pursed his lips and bobbed his head while muttering one word. "*Touché.*"

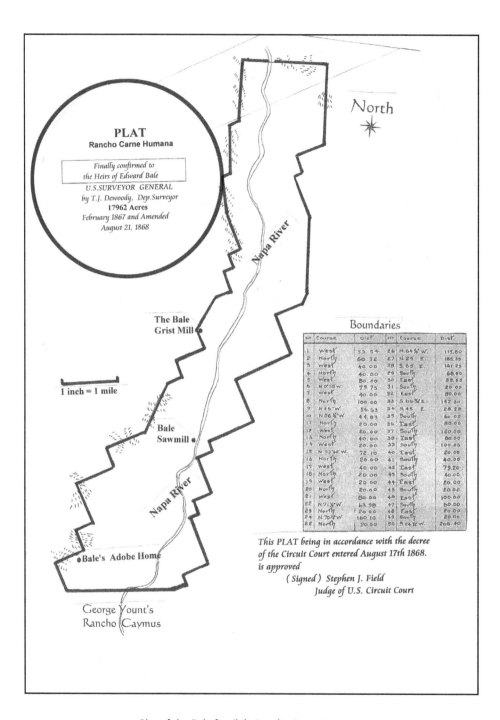

Plat of the Bale family's *Rancho Carne Humana*

CHAPTER EIGHT

REBUILDING LOVE

END OF 1844-1846

Dr. Edward Turner Bale rode from Sonoma toward his home at a slow pace with many doubts filling his mind. *Will my family welcome me?* He allowed the horse to mosey along and stop to munch on grass, because he could think of no reason to rush. *Surely, Mari doesn't want me. I must have destroyed any love she had for me.* At a stream, he removed the shoes that had belonged to an unknown man whose feet were a smaller size. He washed his tortured feet, soaked his aching ankles, and let his thoughts continue with the excruciating memories of his past mistakes.

As he ate more of the bread and cheese, his mind became clearer, and the significance of his release began to have more meaning. For the last three months, he had assumed he would never be with his wife again. *I was sure they would hang me.* His chest filled with worries and his stomach churned. *After shooting at Larkin and twice attempting to kill Salvador, would she, or could she, still love me and want to live with me?* Unlike during his first time in jail, this time she had not gone to visit nor sent letters. He had often wondered if it was too painful for her to go and see him in jail this second time or if she never wanted to see him again. While languishing in jail, he had never resolved which was the reason.

As he sat on the side of the stream, the water garbled in the stream and emitted sounds that he heard as words:

Love forgives and never stops flowing. Once you love, it continues like the ripples over the hard stones of sins and mistakes.

For too long, he had had no one with whom to speak, and for too long, he had been alone in his own mind. He knew his thoughts were not lucid. *But I think the months in jail changed me. I feel I'm a different man.*

He removed all his rank clothing and, standing in skin and bones, watched each piece float away. *If only my mistakes could float away as easily.* With nothing except sand to rub against his crusty, rank skin, he immersed himself in the stream and washed. Floating in the cold water, he gazed up at an overhanging limb and watched two nuthatches pecking at the trunk of the tree. He began to speak aloud to them. "How do you live day after day with only small grubs and worms to eat? What gives you meaning for life? Do you sin and make mistakes like me? No, you live and do what you know you must. I will be as you, little birds. No more jealousy, no more hate, no more . . . liquor."

Gentle rain started to fall. Before mounting his horse, he picked a bunch of wildflowers that grew next to the stream. Riding away, he glanced at the shoes left on the bank and said, "Shoes, I leave you, and I leave my jealousy and hate and desire for drink, too." He tucked the flowers under an edge of the saddle blanket. Grasping the reins tightly and going at a slow trot, he headed toward his *Rancho Carne Humana* with his own human flesh exposed.

Mari looked out the window, but she did not recognize the bearded man riding toward the adobe. His ribs protruded and his long-matted hair flew in the wind. She saw Pepe run to the man when he dismounted at the shed. He was naked. She stared with eyes stretched wide, not able to look away, and as she stared, she thought it strange that Pepe hugged the man and grabbed a poncho to cover him. In a moment of surprise, the hair prickled on the back of her neck; she saw a gesture that identified the naked man to her.

Screaming, she ran from the house, "Edward, Edward, Edward!"

"He came home," Pepe called.

As she hugged Edward with her arms slipped beneath the poncho, shock rippled through her body. "Edward, you are skin and bones. Pepe, please start the cooking fire pit. We need to celebrate tonight with meat to put flesh back on his bones."

"Oh," Edward reached toward the saddle while Pepe still held the reins of his horse. "I brought you some . . . " His voice faded as the flowers had. His manner showed confusion. "They were pretty when I picked them for you."

Mari saw the toll his body had paid while in jail, and it was obvious that his mind had been weakened, too. His eyes seemed glassy and unfocused. Edward did not look at her. She took the bunch of drooping flowers. "I thank you for your thoughts. For now, let's go inside; tomorrow we can walk our ranch and you can pick more for me." She led him inside to rest.

Within the coming days, Edward's health improved yet Mari saw he was different. She saw simple, but unusual, actions. Once, when Mari walked in the garden one morning, she saw Edward in the distance on the side of the wheat field. He was on the ground with six Wappos playing a native game with little rocks from the stream. They were laughing. He had never done that before. She enjoyed seeing this.

As the weeks rolled away into months, she saw that their life was fulfilling him. The planning for the land, the work with the crops, the interactions with his family, and all aspects of his life seemed to have a day-by-day importance. He showed no inclination to imbibe in spirits again and did not visit George Yount's place. Over and over, he told Mari he would make the ranch profitable for their family. She believed him. Their life settled into a daily routine.

Elsewhere, unrest grew in Alta California, but the Bales chose to ignore it. Edward told Mari, "I see conflicts increasing from two opposite factions—the Californios and the Americans. We should not take sides."

She asked, "What are you saying?"

They had just come down the wooden stairs from the second floor after putting the children to bed. "Let's talk while we get ready for bed," he said. A successful ranch required owners who worked sunup to sundown; Edward and Mari ended their days tired from hard work.

Their adobe was an unusual design. Most were built with only one floor because mud bricks crumble under extra weight. Therefore, their home had thicker adobe bricks on the first floor to support the upstairs, and they had constructed a wooden stairway on the outside of the house to put less strain on the mud bricks. The upstairs had four rooms. Julia had her bed upstairs in the same room as Lolita and Caroline. Pepe had a room next to them, and there were two rooms for future children and guests.

Once downstairs in their bedroom, they prepared for sleep and Edward explained, "The Californios are fighting against their own and are too involved in that to see any threat from the Americans. But the threat is there. I don't think the Californios understand the significance of Larkin's new assignment." Edward's mistrust of Larkin remained still, and his skin cringed just saying the name, yet he was trying to forgive Larkin for signing the warrant for his arrest. "Mari, I think what is happening is like a chess game in the making. Many American players are arriving to fill the chessboard. I think the game will begin soon. Thomas Larkin has been moved to an important position by the United States; he's the American Consul. He is a key player for the Americans." Edward took her hands and pulled her close. "You know I don't mean a real game, don't you? But I mean a real war." She nodded, and he finished stating his concerns. "What's occurring seems to be unknown to the Californios."

"Yes, I agree," she said and kissed the freckle on his eyelid. "Enough talk of politics for tonight. You know that I told you about the freckle on your eyelid in a poem. Remember? Did you know it was there?"

He kissed her lips before saying, "What are you talking about?"

"You have a freckle on your left eyelid. I saw it on the beach when you were almost dead. The freckle is one of the reasons I fell in love with you."

"Hmm, obviously you are bored with talk of politics," he kissed her and finished his sentence, "and I am bored with talk of eyelids. Come here." Side by side in bed they snuggled under covers. He caressed her face while brushing strands of her hair away. Though she had braided her hair for bedtime, stray hairs slipped from the twists. "I love your hair. I love your eyes, your mouth, your skin, and everything about you. Have I ever told you?"

She kissed his eyelid again and said, "Yes, you have and please never stop."

"I will not and cannot." He turned and blew out the candle next to their bed. With the vanishing light, night activities began. An owl hooted and his mate echoed back; a male cricket hummed his tune, and a female joined him; the coyote pair howled before their nightly hunt; and the humans made love with soft, throaty sounds.

The Bales rarely left their ranch and would have been oblivious to the developing two conflicts about which Edward had spoken, if it were not for visitors who stopped at *Rancho Carne Humana* from time to time. The Vallejo family members often came to visit, as well as some of his American friends.

Toward the end of 1844, Salvador and his wife became regulars at the Bale dinner table. To the amazement of Maria Ignacia, a friendship had developed since the apology of Edward on his knees.

They sat at the dinner table, savoring a roasted young pig in honor of Edward's birthday. Mari said to her guests, "I am so grateful for the gift of our sow from the family. She had ten piglets a few months ago and now we have this luxury. My, oh my, this pork melts in my mouth."

With a full mouth, Salvador could only nod in agreement.

Edward asked Salvador, "I heard about the raids by Micheltorena's troops. Do we need to fear them attacking us?"

Salvador swallowed and answered, "They are not in this area. They are stationed south of here. When Mexico City sent Micheltorena up here to make Mexico more secure from any takeover, they created more problems and insulted us. He ranks above all of us, even Mariano. And Mariano and I don't agree with what he is doing. You expressed a fear of attack and rightly so. Many Californios not only fear them but also hate Micheltorena's troops."

Maria Ignacia asked, "Why is that? We don't get all the details when we hear the news."

Salvador asked. "You don't know about Micheltorena?" He saw them shake their heads and answered, "He's the Brigadier General sent north from Mexico City with troops who are convicts assigned to military duty. Brigadier General Manual Micheltorena is to be feared. He wants power. Those convict-troops have been raiding food supplies in warehouses, assaulting people, and disobeying laws without punishment. The problem is that no one is above Micheltorena, so we can't prosecute them."

This same topic was being discussed miles away at *Casa Grande*. Juan B. Alvarado had arrived to discuss a plan with his cousin, General Vallejo. He was emphatic in his plea. "We need to take power from Micheltorena. The people's complaints are not being addressed, and they're angry. I am planning a takeover. The people are sick and tired of the abuses from his convict-troops. We should disband them and send them back to Mexico City." To emphasize his comment, he slammed his fist on the table. "You must join us. It will succeed. I have many followers, but I need your troops from Sonoma and, of course, your support."

Calmly, Vallejo sipped his hot tea and said, "No, no. Juan B, you always want to overthrow whoever is in power. You succeeded once back in thirty-six, but now this is different. I cannot and will not support you in this endeavor." Vallejo's stern face and firm voice conveyed he was adamant about not taking part in any plan for a revolt.

In fact, within the next few days, he had secretly warned Micheltorena of Juan B's intentions.

Upon hearing that no support was coming from General Vallejo, Juan B. Alvarado's followers took the whole affair into their own hands and, in the night, stole all Micheltorena's horses. Solders without their mounts were useless.

Juan B went back and begged General Vallejo for help. "Look, he is without an army because they have no horses. With you and your Sonoma troops we could overthrow him."

General Vallejo was no fool. He wanted no part in Juan B's plan and knew it was inevitable that Micheltorena, who was his superior, would order him to fight the rebels to defend the government of Mexico.

Vallejo found it unthinkable to fight his family but knew he could not disobey a superior. He was caught in the middle. So, he devised his own plan, using his admiration of Roman strategies.

Without a word to anyone, General Vallejo dismissed his whole regimen and sent this message to Micheltorena:

> *November 28, 1844*
> *My dear and esteemed*
> *Brigadier General Manual Micheltorena,*
>
> *With great regret I am informing you that I recently had a crop failure that reduced my resources and prevents me from supporting a regimen of two hundred men.*
>
> *Therefore, I have had to dismiss all the troops from Sonoma. As you know I have outfitted and fed all of them, often at my own expense, for over a decade in order to have protection for the area of Alta California surrounding Sonoma.*
>
> *I gave my men each a horse and the freedom to go live anywhere—north or south.*
>
> *I remain, your loyal supporter,*
> *General Mariano Guadalupe Vallejo*

Juan B was infuriated by his cousin Mariano's maneuver and went to tell him. "Maybe Micheltorena believes your lie, but I know better. You are a rich man. I estimate that you have an annual income close to $100,000 per year, just from your hides and tallow." He paced in front of his cousin's desk, only stopping his rant when a servant brought a tray of tea. After the worker left, Juan B began again, but with a quieter voice. "I hope he didn't hear our conversation.

It's best no one knows what you're worth. However, I sat down and did the calculations. I know you are rich. You get commissions from wheat growers and fees from sales to Hudson's Bay Company. I know there's more, but I became bored looking into the sources of your wealth. I have more important work to do." They moved to a sitting area in the *Casa Grande* to drink their tea. "With you or not, I am not giving up on my plan. Tomorrow, I head south to confront Micheltorena."

Mariano nodded, "You always do what you want. Go! Just remember you do not have my support."

To Juan B's delight, dozens of the unemployed soldiers from Sonoma drifted south to join him and his men in San Jose where Juan B's rebels had bivouacked, making his forces two hundred and twenty strong.

By December 1844, Juan B. Alvarado had shown his strength without a battle. Through lengthy arbitration, he won the signature of Micheltorena on the Treaty of Santa Teresa, an agreement that stated that the convict-army was to be sent back to Mexico.

Without troops in Fort Sonoma, Salvador had little to do. His visits to the Bales became more frequent.

Edward suggested, "Ride with me to see how my sawmill is progressing. It's on the Napa River a few miles north of our house."

While they rode along the rich fields of *Rancho Carne Humana*, they talked. Salvador asked, "I hear you are having another grist mill built. Why a second one? And what made you want to construct a sawmill?"

Edward looked to him with a puzzled face and commented, "The Napa River runs through the middle of my ranch. I want to use the power of that water in any way I can to make money to support my family. Also, more and more ranches are planting wheat. My small mill works with oxen or mule power and will not be able to handle all the wheat. The new mill will be water-powered. I would think my reasons are obvious."

"Nothing about having a ranch is obvious to me," Salvador said, "I have been in the military all my life. In fact, I can't stop thinking as a military man. Because Mariano disbanded all his troops, he has left Sonoma without protection. How could he do that? He is my all-powerful and all-knowing brother. This was not like him. What was he thinking? I believe, while Juan B and Micheltorena are in this power struggle, more and more Americans will continue to move to Alta California. I fear they will attempt a takeover. It could become a war."

Edward frowned, "Power struggle! I thought Micheltorena signed a treaty, and it was over."

"No, no, Micheltorena reneged on that treaty. Nothing is settled, and the convict-troops are still here."

Edward looked concerned and asked, "Should I fear for my family with those convicts still running around?"

"I think not. They are still down south in the San Jose area. Besides, you have hundreds of natives living near your home. They have no guns, but they could overpower any robbers that came in the night. Have a group sleep near your house, but only if you hear that the convicts are getting closer."

Keekeekeekeekeekeekuk kuk!

Loud screeching of a wild creature interrupted the topic of conversation and Edward pointed to a downed tree in the woods.

Keekeekeekeekeekuk kuk!

With a look of excitement, he told the amazed Salvador, "It's this huge bird. See! Over there, on that dead trunk, a woodpecker the size of a crow. I always see him when I come here. When I first heard his screech, he scared the life from me. I was with a Miwok friend who laughed and told me about this bird who makes a square hole in the trees when he looks for ants to eat." Edward laughed again and asked, "Can you see the big red crest on his head?"

Keekeekeekeekeekuk kuk!

Salvador jumped again. "I do. What a bird!"

Edward said, "We are approaching the site of my sawmill, and the mill makes even louder noise than this bird." Buzzing intensified with their approach and prevented more discussion. While several men were feeding logs into the saws, Bale went to speak with the man in charge. After a short while, he mounted his horse and waved to Salvador to follow him. Once far enough away from the drone of the saws, he said, "Now I want to see the progress on my new grist mill. It's just a couple of miles to the north."

"How can you afford to construct all these new projects? They must be expensive."

Bale rubbed his chin. "Before I built anything, I was land-rich. Had over seventeen thousand acres of land. It didn't benefit me because I could not work it all. I decided to pay for the mills with land. The man who did the ironwork on this new grist mill was paid with six hundred acres and I paid others with land, too." They were riding in a wooded area and soon heard hammers banging. "We are almost there."

In the distance was a beautiful structure with a twenty-foot wheel. It had wooden cogs that would catch the water once it was running. "Get off your horse this time and come with me to see the making of a grist mill. It has an overshot system where the water enters above the wheel. We had to divert the water source to make it flow over here. We dug a ditch to make the sluice and have a wooden flume system." Bale turned with pride to say, "I helped dig that ditch."

Salvador nodded, yet his expression showed that he did not delight in the idea of digging a ditch. He said nothing. Later, he followed Bale around without much interest as he watched him inspect all the parts of the mill.

On their ride back to the adobe, Salvador commented, "You are to be commended. I could not do what you are doing."

"Oh, you could if you had to. I have a family and must provide for them in any way I can. When I tried to make money with my medical practice, it was not enough. I still do a little doctoring, but not too much."

They had arrived at *Rancho Carne Humana* and went to sit outside under the grape arbor with Maria Ignacia and the children. Edward greeted his wife with a kiss on the lips. Salvador gave Edward a sly grin and said, "Will you shoot me if I give my niece a kiss, too?"

"Not anymore. That jealous husband is gone."

She looked at Salvador and asked, "How did you like the trip around our ranch? Tell me about it." She was mending one of Edward's shirts, and the two little girls were playing with cloth dolls.

"It was exhausting." He smiled mischievously. "Seeing all the work that Edward does exhausts me. However, I am impressed with your ranch."

"Thank you, Salvador. I love it here." Maria Ignacia pointed. "See the rose bushes I planted last year around the house? They should have buds on them this spring."

"I look forward to seeing your roses." Salvador turned to Edward and asked, "With all the work on the ranch, Edward, how do you still see patients?"

"My medical practice is limited to people here on the ranch and our friends. I do not practice medicine with any others."

They were speaking English and Salvador said, "I enjoy coming to visit here and practicing English, but I find it to be a strange language in so many ways. The pronunciations are unbelievable as are the uses of some words. I just said that I like to practice my English, and you used that word in another way. Why do doctors refer to their medical profession as a medical practice?" He grinned at Bale and said, "Surely your patients do not want you to practice on them."

Without a hesitation, Bale answered, "The Latin root is *practicare* which means *to do or perform* and often with reference to a profession. I hope my patients do not think as deeply as you about the meaning of the word."

They all laughed.

"Edward, I am constantly impressed with your knowledge, and I have heard you are an excellent doctor."

Maria Ignacia asked, "who told you about Edward's ability as a doctor? Someone from the military?"

Salvador shook his head and said, "I was thinking about his famous operation in London. I understand all of England knows of his abilities."

Maria Ignacia dropped her mending. Edward's head jerked towards Salvador. Neither of them moved. Only the voices of Lolita and Caroline filled the air until the little girls noticed the silence, too. "What's wrong, Mamá?"

Salvador became aware that something was amiss and in the next second he understood, saying, "*Madre de Dios!* Mariano never told you?"

Edward slid to the edge of his chair and leaned closer to Salvador, "Never told us what?"

Maria Ignacia was more to the point and asked, "How do you know anything about Edward's medical practice in England?"

Immediately, Salvador related the conversation of Sir George Simpson, Mariano, and himself. He spared no detail about the successful operation to remove the infected appendix of Lord Willington. He talked for many minutes before saying, "I was rarely around you and Mari. I assumed that Mariano had told Edward. It was long, long ago."

"How long ago?" Edward's voice was demanding.

Salvador shook his head and ran his fingers through his hair before saying, "Oh, let me think."

Mari spoke up. "I know when it was. I went to the celebration in Sonoma for George Simpson. Edward, you had recently been released from jail after shooting at Thomas Larkin and were avoiding people. It was after the Christmas holidays, in January of forty-one."

Edward exploded, "Almost four years ago!"

Salvador defended himself. "I had never met you, Edward, until forty-four when we had that duel. I cannot remember if I saw Maria Ignacia during those years. I may not have seen her at all. I never gave it any thought, that Mariano would not have told you. Please do not blame me."

Mari stood and wrapped her arms around Edward before saying, "We don't blame you. Isn't that correct, Edward? Of course, Salvador would have assumed that Mariano had told us."

Edward swallowed and turned to Salvador. "Yes, I do not blame you. In fact, I'm just grateful that you told me now. Thank you!" He shook his head and said, "My, how I have changed." A chortle came from deep in his throat, "Ho, ho, yes, leg irons changed me. I am not angry. I have no anger inside me. You cannot imagine how I feel, knowing that I did not kill Lord Willington. I was not sober when I operated. I have been ashamed for so many years."

Mari added a thought. "Just think, Edward, your parents have known the truth all these years. You have been upset at the shame you brought to them. Now we know they have had no reason to feel shame, in fact, they have to feel pride that you were successful at that operation."

"Yes." Edward repeated. "Salvador, thank you." He stepped closer to Salvador and hugged him. The two men exchanged grins.

Mari had a thought and said, "Oh, Edward, you need to write to your parents and let them know where you are. Let them know about your family." She picked up her mending and sat back down. "If you don't write to them, I want to."

Edward stared out at nothing.

She was sure he had heard her, though he appeared to be lost in his thoughts.

He would write a letter to his parents and, in the coming year, that letter would travel its long journey on a ship across two oceans—south in the Pacific Ocean around Cape Horn and north through the Atlantic Ocean—to England.

Later, Mari and Edward discussed the matter in their bedroom. "Now, do you believe me when I tell you that I do not trust your Uncle Mariano? I don't know what he hoped to gain by not sharing the conversation he had with Simpson. But I know he must have had a reason. Oh, he is so cunning. On second thought, he may have been waiting for the moment when it was to his advantage to tell me." He shook his head and slapped his thigh. "I do not trust him."

Mari remained silent.

Edward made a small laugh, "Thinking again, I say that he may have had no reason."

Edward took his wife's hands in his and brought them to his chest. "But, Mari, I am not angry with your Uncle Mariano. In fact, I pity him. Oh, Mari, I am ecstatic with the news that I did not kill Lord Willington."

"Edward, of course you are. What a surprise! This news removes the pain you have had for years. And I am proud to have such a husband as you."

"Now, Mari, this does not mean that I trust your Uncle Mariano. I am saying that I am not angry with him." Edward snickered. "It means that I am not going to pull my pepper-box and shoot at him. Not once nor twice." He looked directly at her to say, "Not three times either. Did you know that little gun can shoot three shots without reloading?"

Through the whole year of 1845, the Bales worked hard and prospered.

One day, Bale's old friend Nathan Spear from Yerba Buena arrived in a wooden wagon drawn by two horses. Nathan, who in the past had had an ample roll of skin under his chin, as well as a round belly, was skin and bones.

Edward approached the wagon and was startled at the sight of him. "Nathan, my friend, how good to see y . . . " Without ending the sentence, Edward caught Nathan as he fell from the seat. His friend was burning with fever.

Nathan mumbled something impossible to understand.

Edward said, "Don't try to talk. We're going to get you comfortable." He called to a couple of Miwoks who were nearby, working in the vegetable garden, "Xavier and Tzum, come give me a hand with my friend." They placed him on the couch in the living room.

Mari came from the kitchen and was also startled. "Oh, Edward, I can see Nathan has been sick awhile. He's lost so much weight. Let's put a bed here in the living room; in that way we can give him constant care. Besides, he cannot possibly have the energy to climb the stairs to the guest room."

The two Miwoks brought the bed downstairs from the guest room to a corner of the living room.

Pepe came in to see who had arrived in the wagon and said, "One of his wheels has broken spokes. He's lucky to have made it here without the whole wheel breaking."

Edward nodded and suggested, "Pepe, why don't you start to make replacement spokes. Don't replace the spokes without me, I want to help and learn. For now, I need to examine Nathan." He noticed that his two girls had come inside to see. "Girls, help me carry all his belongings out of the wagon into the house. Yes, Lolita, you can help. I saw a case that looks as if it has a fiddle in it. If you are careful, you can carry it. Pepe, I saw a rifle; don't let the girls take that. It probably is loaded and ready to use."

Mari came with a bowl of cooked vegetables and gravy from last night's dinner and, after Nathan was propped up with pillows, she spoon-fed him a few bites until his head dropped to one side and he slept. Walking back to the kitchen with the bowl, she said to Julia, "He ate only five spoonfuls. I imagine he needs sleep as much as food." She stopped and tilted her head in his direction, "Listen, he is snoring now." She rinsed the bowl and spoon in the soapy dishwater they kept ready to use. "He may have an illness that could make us sick. So, we should not use his dishes. I will put this bowl and spoon on the windowsill."

Julia commented, "You look tired."

"I am and don't know why. I haven't accomplished much of anything today. I think I will go rest on my bed." Once stretched out with her forearm draped over her forehead, Mari took a deep breath and felt the tenderness of her nipples against her bodice. She touched her breasts and began thinking. *Of course! I'm with child again. We've been so busy that I didn't notice not bleeding this month. My, maybe it's been two months. I'm always tired and not hungry in the morning.*

This is wonderful. Hmm, we were married six years ago this March, and soon we will have four children. She glanced out the window to where a pear tree stood and talked to it in her mind. *Hello tree, you had blossoms for the first time this year. You are going to bear fruit like me. It is wonderful to bring little ones into the world.* She giggled and thought, *what am I doing, talking to a tree?*

After several weeks of observing and searching his medical books for a solution, Edward could not find a specific diagnosis for Nathan Spear. "He seems to have heart trouble. His fever makes me think he has malaria. However, he's improving. Mari, I think you are curing him with food faster than anything I can do."

After months of convalescing, Edward suggested, "Nathan, I think you're well enough for a wagon ride. Not a horse ride, yet. Pepe and I mended one of your wheels, so your wagon can be used. I want to show you my new grist mill. We call it the Bale Grist Mill because it deserves a name—it is big and beautiful. You will find it different than the one you built for me. I'm excited to show you."

The six-mile trip went quickly, yet the jostling of the ride exhausted Nathan.

When approaching the wooded area around the mill, Edward said, "I want you to lie in the wagon bed for a while before we go inside. Remember, the mill is not ready to use because . . . " He stopped mid-sentence and pointed, "Wait, there's Ralph Kilburn getting on a horse. He's the man in charge, and I want to talk with him." Edward passed the reins to Nathan and jumped down from the wagon.

Kilburn dismounted and spoke with Edward briefly before mounting his horse again and riding away. Edward was shaking his head and his jaw was clenched when he walked back to the wagon and said, "He quit. He said it never would work for lack of a sufficient sluice. He thinks there will never be enough water to run this huge wheel. Damn! Look at it. Everything looks ready. How is it that he only discovered this problem now?"

Nathan wanted to help. "I know nothing about this type of mill, Edward, but do not despair. I know several men who might be interested in helping."

But months passed without progress on that new grist mill.

Meanwhile, George Yount told Edward about a ship heading for the place where the Napa River pours into San Pablo Bay. "They's wantin' ta load up on tallow and hides 'fore headin' back. Ya got any cattle ta slaughter?"

"I bloody well do."

Yount said, "My problem is that I ain't got any way to git all the hides and tallow down to the ship. Do you?"

"Hell, George, let those cows walk there. I have enough Miwoks to help me skin them and store the tallow right on the banks of the river. Let's go together."

In a few days, they headed south at dawn, following the Napa River with two hundred head of cattle from the two ranches. They figured the trip to be fewer than twenty miles. After traveling for a few hours, Edward rode closer to George and shouted over the bawling animals. "What an excellent idea, George. My herd was growing too big. We should be there by nightfall. We need a few days to slaughter all these cows, but we can do it, I know. I plan to pull out my knife and help."

"Why, sure. Every pair o' hands is needed. Will this be ya first time to skin a cow?"

After a hearty laugh, Edward said, "It's my first time to skin anything except a cadaver."

"A ca ... cad ... what?"

Now Edward bellowed louder, "Haw, haw, I said a cadaver. That's a dead person."

George scratched his head. "Well, whatta ya know."

That night the waters at the mouth of the Napa River and Suisun Bay turned red. The tide came up and the men continued tossing the cattle carcasses into the water. They worked all the next day and night. Men took naps whenever needed and awoke to start cutting again. Everything except the hides and fat for tallow was considered waste. A small group kept a fire going for warmth and for cooking pieces of the choicest steaks for the workers to eat. When the ship arrived, more meat was shared among the sailors. For decades, ships had come here to buy hides and tallow; the sailors knew how to cure and process these products on board during the journey.

The ship took much of the meat for their journey, but all the remaining meat was discarded into the water or left on the shore for vultures or any hungry animal.

On the ride back north without the bawling cattle, Bale and Yount talked with ease.

"Look at these hills, covered in blackened trunks of trees from the fires this past season. We were lucky that the fire did not spread up to our ranches."

Yount shook his head, "Yeah, ya woulda lost a lot of trees for yer sawmill and a lot of profit, I guess."

"Yes, that's correct. I'm building a business with that sawmill and thank you for telling me about this endeavor with the cattle. I will have a tidy profit even after I pay all the natives." Bale was on his way to having an exceptionally successful year.

The Bales and Nathan were relaxing around the table after finishing their dinner one evening while the children played in the living room. Suddenly Edward lamented, "I guess I should be pleased that we got the wheat ground from our fields and for a few of our neighbors; still, we lost a lot of money not having the new mill ready. I hated turning people away. Damn it all!"

Nathan nodded and said, "If one of the mules hadn't gone lame, we could have gotten a lot more ground at the little grist mill."

Mari commented, "I know the oxen are slower, but you hitched them back onto the grinding stones and kept going." She got up to take dishes to the kitchen. Julia followed with others, and Nathan reached for the water pitcher. He asked, "Anyone need more water? The meal was delicious, but I must drink a lot. I am still not accustomed to all the garlic and hot peppers."

Julia and Mari exchanged glances. Mari returned to the table and said to Nathan, "I tested Edward on my family's cooking before I married him. I had to have a man who could take the spicy food."

Julia came back with a glass of milk. "Nathan, water does not help; only milk will take the burn out of your mouth."

Everyone laughed while Nathan guzzled the milk.

"You were correct. It worked."

Feeling unusually talkative, Edward continued, "I don't mean to say that we didn't have a profitable year. We did. I wanted to emphasize that when we have that new mill running, we will earn a lot more. Oh, Mari, I need to tell you that Nathan and I have found a man to complete our Bale Grist Mill. His name is Thomas Kittleman. He assured me he could finish it by next year. He suggested that I order new grinding stones of superior quality from France, and I agreed. We are going to have the best mill in the valley."

Nathan added, "And your sawmill is doing well."

"Yes, that's so." Edward agreed, and his face brightened as he remembered something. "Oh, Mari, I forgot to tell you that I saw Thomas Larkin in Sonoma at your Uncle Mariano's house when I stopped yesterday. Remember, I told you I was going to take your uncle a sack of flour from our mill." Edward took a drink of water and wiped his mouth with a napkin. "Larkin and I talked a lot and traded stories as we had done years ago. I enjoyed seeing him. I brought up the coincidence that we each had daughters a couple of years ago and named them Carolina." Edward made a grimace and shook his head. "Seems Rachel is still angry with you and me. The point I'm making is that Thomas is not angry with me anymore.

"Oh, I just remembered that Larkin had a list of the articles available from a ship that is sitting in Monterey Bay right now. He gave the list to your Uncle Mariano's wife—I can never remember her name—but she wrote a copy for you. Let me go get it." Edward rushed to his desk, found the paper, and handed it to Mari, saying, "If you see something you want, let me know."

The ship from England lists the following cargo:
Bolts of:
Good stout velveteen (blue and black),
Cotton prints of handsome colors,
Flannel in red and white,
Muslin, and
Brown and white cotton for sheets and shirts.
Silk stockings
Gold and silver lace
Cashmere shawls
Needles
Thread of cotton and linen
Brass/silver thimbles
Scotch griddles
Glassware
Tea Trays
Carpets
Furniture of fine wood
Iron pots
Kettles
Candlesticks

After she read the list, Mari looked up and said, "I want two bolts of cotton prints for dresses, and I may want something more after I check my sewing basket."

"Oh, Mari, I'm forgetting the most important part and you will not believe this. Larkin ordered forty thousand pieces of cut clapboards from our sawmill!"

Mari put her hands to her cheeks and exclaimed, "My, oh my, forty thousand. Can you fill an order that large?"

"We will cut until we have ten thousand clapboards and deliver those. This is one of the reasons this year has been a profitable one." He stopped for the drama and grinned. "He already paid me for the forty thousand boards. I have four dated bank notes."

In the Bale household, Nathan Spear had become part of their family in the same manner as Julia and Pepe. For any holiday get-together, the Bales also invited George Yount, his wife Eliza, and Mia. So, on the last Sunday in December 1845, they all sat outside the Bale adobe to celebrate Christmas and the New Year.

Christmas had passed three days before and the New Year was coming in four days. "We're not going to church to hear a sermon, so the exact day doesn't matter," Edward said. "Living here in the middle of nowhere, we decide what we want to do each day. No one is going to tell us when to celebrate. I love my life."

"Here, here," said Nathan, "let us toast to our wonderful life." They all raised their glasses of juice, tea, or water.

Edward continued, "Look at this sunny warm December day. We're fortunate to have such enjoyable weather."

They had carried their large table out under the grape arbor and had eaten baked pig, beefsteaks, and all the fixings. When finished eating, they sat and talked while their food digested.

The women and Mia, who had grown to be a beautiful young lady, sat at one end of the table and the men at the other. The children played not far away.

Mia said, "I'm to be married soon."

Silence greeted her announcement.

Maria Ignacia broke the silence. "How is it we have not met this lucky young man?"

Mia explained, "I am sixteen. It's an age to marry but I wanted to marry a man from my people, so I went back to where my father found me and talked to the natives living there. One agreed to marry me."

Mari went and hugged Mia.

Edward spoke out, "Please bring him to our home. We want to meet and know him."

Yount said, "That ain't goin' ta happen. He ain't wantin' ta even meet me, her father. He won't come ta *Rancho Caymus* ta meet me. I don't like that but...." He stopped talking with a sad face and shook his head. "Mia insists she wants ta marry him an' leave me." He went quiet again, put his elbows onto the table, and leaned closer to say, "Mia leavin' me makes me so sad, but there ain't nothin' to say or do." He rubbed his face with his hands as if to wipe away his pain.

From the expressions on everyone's faces, silence was the most acceptable action at the moment.

George looked up and said, "Oh, I got more news to tell ya. I don' know if it bad or good news." He took a long drink before saying, "I heared that the U.S. President, Mr. Polk, sent a man called John C. Frémont on an expedition ta survey the Great Basin here in Alta California. He got ta Sutter's Fort 'bout two weeks ago. I met 'im. I ain't sure what it means fer us."

Everyone heard what Yount said but were still thinking about Mia's marriage, when they began to puzzle over that next news. No one commented.

That is, everyone was quiet except the three little children. Lolita and Caroline were chattering and giggling near the trunk of the large oak tree, not far from the gathering. Little Eduardo was crawling as fast as he could to get closer to his sisters. Because the conversation had stopped and the children could be heard, all eyes turned toward them at the oak tree.

Julia jumped up and screamed, "Aiiee!"

Mari, now large with child, struggled to her feet.

In a quick movement, Mia grabbed Mari's arm and pulled her close. "Don't move," she said while preventing Mari from going to her little ones.

Edward's eyes went wide as he stood. His face flushed with panic as he tried to decide how to save his children. He was unable to move.

Only George Yount knew what to do, as the two little girls moved toward a small grizzly that had come to eat acorns under the oak tree. Baby Edward increased the speed of his crawl, upon seeing the bear.

Sounds of delight—laughter and words of pleasure—came from the two little girls. "Hee-hee. He so cute."

George reached down under the table for his rifle and said in a forceful, but quiet, voice, "Don' none of ya move. Mama bear gotta be close by."

Mari gasped, "No!"

Now the two Bale girls were next to the baby bear and touching it. "He's soft. Oh, I like him." The little bear seemed as delighted as the girls and wiggled his rear end.

Mari started toward her children, and Mia pulled her back, saying, "No, you cannot go. Stay here."

Dr. Bale tentatively started to walk to the oak tree when a sudden, loud roar stopped him.

"AGHH!" The mother bear came from nowhere, loping toward her baby and growling, "Grrr! Hmph, hmph, GRRR!"

Unnoticed, Nathan had rushed into the adobe and returned with his rifle. He was leaning against one of the posts of the grape arbor to steady his aim at the charging mother grizzly.

George repeated in a shout, "Don' none of ya move! I'm gonna shoot and don' wanna to hit ya."

BAM!

George's rifle exploded, and the mother grizzly jerked at the impact and stopped, but she did not fall.

The children screamed in fear. The baby bear bolted up the tree trunk.

George went down on his knee to reload.

Mari could not stand back any longer. Her motherly instinct pulled her from Mia's grasp. She headed to her children. She reached her hysterical son, who sat crying. When she grabbed him, he was ten feet away from the tree and his sisters. Mari stopped long enough to assess the situation.

With their backs to their mother, her little girls seemed dazed and were quietly standing and holding hands. When they saw the huge mother bear coming at them, they screamed and turned. Seeing their mother, they shouted, "Mamá, Mamá," and started toward her.

The large grizzly ran for her cub just as Mari was going for her two girls. Mari reached the girls and went down on her knees as she wrapped her arms around all three of her children. Her belly was so large that she could not lift them, so she covered them with her body.

The mother grizzly arrived at her cub, clinging to the trunk of the tree. She was between the little bear and the humans.

Regretfully, the progress toward their young put the two groups closer to each other.

The mother bear turned and stood on her hind legs, fewer than ten feet from Mari and roared, "AGGHHH!"

BAM! Nathan took his shot and hit the mother bear between the eyes.

The large grizzly fell.

Mari clutched her children and saw the cub coming down to be with its mother. Mari screamed, "Don't hurt the baby bear!"

Bam!

She had shouted too late. Yount had reloaded and killed the little bear.

Regrettably, the excitement of the bears obliterated any prior conversations.

Yount's mention of John C. Frémont arriving at Sutter's Fort in December of 1845 was forgotten and would not be remembered for months. Mia's upcoming marriage was not mentioned again that day either. After Mia departed to be married in the next week, she was never seen again by any of them.

The Miwoks working nearby came running with the gunfire. Edward asked them to take care of the bears. "I understand you enjoy bear meat. The two bears are yours. Please take them away so my children will be calm."

"The mother bear is too big to move. We will skin and collect the fat and meat where she fell under the oak tree. Later, when she is in pieces, we can haul her away from the house."

"I see," Edward said, "so I shall move my celebration to the other side of the house."

Five-year-old Lolita and three-year-old Caroline would not stop crying. Edward carried the two in his arms while others helped move the table and chairs from the arbor. Once on the far side of the house, Mari and Edward still could not quiet their girls. It seemed impossible to return to their celebration.

Pepe approached and said, "I have Christmas gifts for you girls. I was going to give them to you later. I think now is a better time." Blinking, the little girls looked to him with teary eyes, and he continued talking. "I thought to make these gifts when the two of you were wanting to play with your mother's ivory animal. They are my Christmas gifts to you both." He turned to Mari and asked, "What is the name of your tall thin animal from another country far away?"

"Oh, you mean my giraffe—my mother's ivory giraffe."

"Yes, yes, the giraffe." Pepe had the attention of the children and squatted down to them to say, "I saw that you both wanted to play with the giraffe, and your mother was afraid you would break it. Besides, there is only one giraffe and you each could not hold it at the same time. So, I had an idea for your Christmas gifts. Remember I carve wood. Can you guess what I did?"

The crying was over, and they shook their heads.

"Come upstairs with me to my room. I will show you what I made for you."

Relieved, Mari waited at the bottom step until the girls returned, bounding down the stairs in excitement.

"Look, Mamá, Pepe made me my own giraffe, and he made one for Caroline."

Pepe came down the stairs after them and said, "One giraffe is bigger than the other, just like you girls. A big sister giraffe and a little sister one. I made with wood that is not delicate like your mother's ivory one." After the two ran off to play, Pepe looked dubious, shook his head, and told Mari, "I wanted to make a toy for little Edward and started making a bear." He pursed his lips before saying, "After today, I'm thinking that maybe a bear is not the best idea."

"Oh, Pepe, a bear is perfect. A bear will remind us of this day, and we can talk about it with little Edward as he grows. Thank you so much for the gifts for my children."

Everyone was seated again around the table. Nathan had gone for his fiddle and began to sing:

"Came to a river and couldn't get across,
Paid five dollars for a blind old hoss'
Wouldn't go ahead, nor wouldn't stand still,
So, he went up and down like an old sawmill.

Turkey in the straw, turkey in the hay,
Roll 'em up and twist 'em up a high tuckahaw,
And twist 'em up a tune called Turkey in the Straw."

Nathan called out, "Everybody join me for the chorus again,

Turkey in the straw, turkey in the hay,
Roll 'em up and twist 'em up a high tuckahaw,
And twist 'em up a tune called Turkey in the Straw."

With music filling the air, they ended a memorable day and celebrated the close of the year, 1845.

Original Flag of Bear Flag Revolt and the Proclamation

To all persons, citizens of Sonoma, requesting them to remain at peace, and to follow their rightful occupations without fear of molestation.

The Commander in Chief of the Troops assembled at the Fortress of Sonoma gives his inviolable pledge to all persons in California not found under arms that they shall not be disturbed in their persons, their property, or social relations one to another by men under his command.

He also solemnly declares his object to be First, to defend himself and companions in arms who were invited to this country by a promise of Lands on which to settle themselves and families who were also promised a "republican government," who, when having arrived in California were denied even the privilege of buying or renting Lands of their friends, who instead of being allowed to participate in or being protected by a "Republican Government" were oppressed by a "Military Despotism," who were even threatened, by "Proclamation" from the Chief Officer of the aforesaid Despotism, with extermination if they would not depart out of the Country, leaving all of their property, their arms and beasts of burden, and thus deprived of the means of flight or defense. We were to be driven through deserts, inhabited by hostile Indians to certain destruction. To overthrow a Government which has seized upon the property of the Missions for its individual aggrandizement; which has ruined and shamefully oppressed the laboring people of California, by their enormous exactions on goods imported into this country; is the determined purpose of the brave men who are associated under his command.

He also solemnly declares his object in the Second place to be to invite all peaceable and good Citizens of California who are friendly to the maintenance of good order and equal rights (and I do hereby invite them to repair to my camp at Sonoma without delay) to assist us in establishing and perpetuating a "Republican Government" which shall secure to all civil and religious liberty; which shall detect and punish crime; which shall encourage industry, virtue and literature; which shall leave unshackled by Fetters, Commerce, Agriculture, and Mechanism.

He further declares that he relies upon the rectitude of our intentions; the favor of Heaven and the bravery of those who are bound to and associated with him, by the principle of self-preservation; by the love of truth; and by the hatred of tyranny for his hopes of success.

He further declares that he believes that a Government to be prosperous and happyfying [sic] in its tendency must originate with its people who are friendly to its existence. That its Citizens are its Guardians, its officers are its Servants, and its Glory their reward.

— *William B. Ide, Head Quarters Sonoma, June 15, 1846*

Chapter Nine

War

1846

The next year arrived with storms that never abated throughout the winter. The rain was incessant. The creeks filled and overflowed, the rivers rose, the mountains carried water in endless rivulets, the meadows became marshes, and the yard outside the Bale's adobe had inches of mud, as soil washed from the hills surrounding their house. The bedcovers, all clothing, horse blankets, leather saddles, and the rugs at the door were continually damp. Nothing would dry unless hung in front of the fireplaces in the kitchen or the living room. What was worse, the grain in the grist mill began to mold, and the winter wheat in their fields was driven into to the ground, ruined.

"What a loss. At least we can run the sawmill," Edward told Mari at dawn. "I am working on the Larkin order. Today, we plan to move thousands of the clapboards on wagons. A barque is coming, and I want to load all we can onto that ship. So, I will be working at the sawmill all day to make sure it all goes well. Don't expect me home until late."

A lighter rain fell in the morning when Edward left for work. The water ran off his wide-brimmed hat and dripped onto the flanks of his horse. He wore a poncho of wool, covering him down to his boot tops, and he marveled at how well it kept him dry. He patted his horse and told the animal, "They should use ponchos in rainy London. What an ingenious design."

Once at the sawmill, he was elated to learn that they had created a large increase in the number of clapboards by working through the night. Men were loading wagons under the overhang of the roof, built for loading in the rain. The manager told him, "We will cover the wood with a paulin; that's a tarred canvas just like what they use on ships. If the rain can drain off, the wood should stay dry. If the clapboards do get a little wet, they'll dry out later and be fine."

Owning a wagon gave many settlers an income when they offered it for service to others. The caravan of wagons started out at midday, heading down the same route Edward and Yount had taken with the cattle the previous year. Edward recalled it had been an easy trip. He expected no problems because he was remembering the trip, taking the cattle last year. But it had not been raining.

An hour after the wagons left, the rain increased to a downpour. Edward had stayed to look over the books and talk with the manager. Before long, one of the workers in charge of the saw came to them about a problem.

They went to the cutting room and found that an inch of water had accumulated on the floor. The Napa River was rising.

"It's high tide down in the bay. That affects our water up here. It can't drain as fast as usual. And with all this rain coming down the hills, there's water seeping through the floor and under the base of the walls."

Within an hour, they could no longer work the saw, and the workmen were sent home. "No need to come back until after the rain stops. It ain't going to get better till all this water drains."

Edward arrived home to hear the crying of a newborn. Rushing to his bedroom, he found Mari nursing their new daughter. He said, "Oh, I wanted to be here."

To assuage his guilt, Mari said, "She was an easy birth. Don't be concerned. But I'm glad you are home to help me choose a name for her. You pick the first name, and I'll pick the second."

Without hesitating, he said, "Let's call her Ana."

Mari loved the idea and said, "Oh, yes, Ana Guadalupe Bale, and we can call her Anita for short."

Edward retorted, "Our son is Edward Guadalupe Bale. Why name her the same?"

"Oh, Edward, Guadalupe is a strong family name. You know that people of Spanish descent do this. You know that Guadalupe is one of my names, and my Uncle Mariano's middle name. Please do not object."

He did not.

Mari told of the name she had been considering. "Oh, I had been thinking about a different name. If our next child is a girl, I want her to be called Juana. Our son is named after you, Edward, and I want a girl with another one of my names. We will have an Anita and a Juanita. I think that's a delightful idea!"

Julia was removing all the soiled bedding and laughed. "Maybe this is not the time to plan for a Juanita to go with Anita."

Edward agreed. He was hanging over the bed looking at his newest daughter and complained to her. "Mari, what are you doing? How can you already be thinking of another child—and another daughter?"

Mari grinned mischievously, never guessing it possible that, before the year ended, they would become parents again to another new daughter—Juana

Maria Bale. Two children born in the same year.

Likewise, Edward and Mari never guessed it possible that, before the year ended, they were to be on the road to becoming members of another nation—The United States of America.

However, at this moment in January of 1846, the Bales would find that just as this day contained both a joyful birth and a disheartening disaster at the sawmill, the rest of the year would be full of the same—a mix of good and bad events coming at them—starting that night.

Bang, bang, bang. Someone beat on the door and called, "Dr. Bale, Dr. Bale."

Jumping from his bed, Bale rushed to the door and learned that the wagons with the clapboards had been caught in mudslides.

"I was the last wagon in the caravan and turned back when I saw other wagons disappearing under all this mud, rumbling down the hills. It was an unbelievable sight! And unbelievable sound like thunder! Now, I don't know if any men got stuck under the mud or not. I pulled out one with my ropes. He was the man in front of me. It was hard to do. That mud seemed alive. But I couldn't go farther into that mud to help any others."

Bale responded, "Let me slip my breeches on, and we'll go see if someone needs help. I bet I know where it happened." While dressing, he said, "Last year, I saw naked hills where the fires burned away all the brush and blackened the trees. I imagine the mudslides happened there."

No man was lost because of the drivers working for hours. They made sure they pulled everyone out of the muck. Most of the wagons and clapboards could not be saved.

One man suggested, "After this damn rain stops and everything dries, we can come back to try and dig those wagons free."

Dr. Bale agreed. "I'll help do that. Let me know when you decide to go."

Within the next month, Bale took a trip to Monterey to give Larkin the unfortunate news about the clapboards. With his sawmill unable to function, he told Larkin that he could not fill the order. "I know you paid me, and here are the bank notes that I did not use. However, I did cash two. Could you agree to let me pay you back with monthly payments? I already calculated that I could pay two hundred seventy-five pesos within five months."

Larkin agreed and wrote a promissory note for Bale to sign. That settled, Larkin talked about John C. Frémont's expedition to map the west coast. "I am sure you could make extra money being on-call as a physician for his men. He's going to be heading to Oregon in a couple of weeks. You could talk with him when he returns to Sutter's Fort."

"Sutter's fort is a sixty-mile-trip from my home, just one-way. I would rather not make that trip."

Larkin had an idea. "I could get someone to send word to Frémont about you." After this discussion, Dr. Bale was listed as a volunteer surgeon for Frémont.

The actual reason for Frémont's presence was a national secret. Only Larkin, being the U.S. Consul, knew why John C. Frémont had come. Frémont was biding his time while players moved into position: He was accumulating American followers, and ships from the United States were to arrive in Monterey and Yerba Buena. Larkin had requested the *Portsmouth* to come to Monterey and a second ship called the *Savannah* was to arrive. In March, Larkin sent a message to Frémont not to oppose or confront the Mexican army, stating that it was not the right time.

In the meantime, Frémont traveled to Oregon, learning the lay of the land and killing natives as he traveled.

Word got back to Bale and Yount about Frémont's slaughter of Native Americans wherever Frémont found them. Yount said, "I hear'd, in April, near Redding, that they kilt hundreds of Injuns. In May, in Oregon near Klamath Lake, Injuns attacked them, and the chief was shot dead. So, the next couple o' days, they attacked a Klamath village and kilt dozens."

Bale added what he had heard. "Some American friends stopped at my ranch yesterday and mentioned that Frémont is camped about sixty miles north of Sutter's Fort right now and has killed many natives in that area. They've killed so many natives that people started calling it The Massacre at Sutter's Butte."

Bale frowned and commented to Yount, "It's obvious that Frémont didn't come here just to map the western coastal area."

The Mexican army was arriving at the same conclusions about Frémont and began to amass as large an army as possible to be prepared for a fight. The problem with getting more men was that Mexico City had sent a five-thousand-man army northward to Texas, where the United States had troops on the Rio Grande River. Of course, they knew that fact, but they did not know one important detail: The United States had declared war on Mexico on May 13, 1846.

The news of that declaration of war would not reach California until August.

Meanwhile, Frémont created a notice filled with lies:

> ### ATTENTION TO ALL IN ALTA CALIFORNIA!
>
> *Be aware that more than 200 armed Spaniards on horseback in the Sacramento Valley have been seen destroying crops, taking cattle, and burning homes. Come to the Buttes to join Captain Frémont at his camp to put a stop to this!*

All lies, but Frémont wanted to agitate the populace. He succeeded.

After people read that notice, additional rumors started running rampant among the American settlers in Alta California. Many were ready to join any group to take control from the Mexicans. A few men from one place and then another man would hear the rumors and join them. Soon, about ten volunteers met up with four of Frémont's men and rode out to rustle a herd of one hundred seventy horses away from the Mexican military.

Their success at stealing those horses began an open rebellion. They drove the horses to Frémont's Butte Camp, where more men joined them.

The number of American rebels grew to twenty men, ready to rile up more. Someone suggested, "Let's show them Mexicans that we can take the town of Sonoma. They ain't got a garrison there to stop us. Did you hear that General Vallejo let all his soldiers go?"

"Yeah, let's head out there. Oh, they got something else," one of the rebel-rousers exclaimed, "they got important people living there. We could take hostages."

The group set out from Sutter's Fort without Frémont and without a designated leader among them. They left in the afternoon of the eleventh of June, knowing they had three mountain ranges to cross. At Cache Creek they stopped to rest and were joined by more rebels. At a home in Pope Valley, they had dinner, and more disgruntled settlers came along as they pushed on through the night.

It was not an easy trip. Though exhausted, they reached the Napa Valley near *Rancho Carne Humano* and came to a home where a neighbor of the Bales lived.

Someone suggested, "Hey, I know who lives here—name's Ralph Kilburn. Hell, this is good, because I know Kilburn is with us. Let's ask him if there's somewhere we can rest, without letting people know our plan to attack Fort Sonoma."

Unknown to Dr. Bale, Kilburn suggested, "You could rest at the Bale Grist Mill. It's still under construction. No one's there now, and there's plenty of room for all you men."

They settled in the empty mill for the night and sent messengers up and down the valley to gather more recruits.

One of those messengers stopped at the Bale's adobe. He knew a Doctor Bale lived there, though they had not met. It was late and the house was dark, so he shouted, "Anybody home?"

Dr. Bale rolled out of bed and went outside to ask, "What can I do for you?"

The messenger had been told to be vague when asking for volunteers and not to alert anyone who supported the Mexicans. So, he said, "I'm wanting to get men together against the Mexicans. Do you want to join?"

A short and terse reply came from Dr. Bale. "No, I do not. You'd best be on your way."

While the messengers had been instructed to knock on doors to find followers, they had been warned to leave if someone had no interest. "Leave quick. More importantly, be careful not to let anyone know where we are, how many we are, and what our plans are. If they aren't wanting to be with us, then they's probably against us."

Therefore, the messenger left quickly, and Dr. Bale returned to bed.

The Bale Grist mill was six miles to the north of the Bale's adobe, so the Bale family was unaware of what took place that night. Possibly, if the wind had been blowing in their direction, the Bales might have heard the noise, since the rowdy bunch made the loudest ruckus. During that night of June 13th, spirited harangues excited the already eager agitators, as more settlers arrived and joined them.

A week would pass before the Bale family learned the details about the use of their unfinished grist mill. When the Bales became aware of the incident, Mari put it succinctly, by saying, "Edward, we can do nothing about that meeting at our grist mill because we have no idea who was there, and it's done and over."

Another week would pass before they learned that the group that night included Bale's first miller, as well as the man who made Bale's first millstone, and a worker from Bale's sawmill.

Dr. Bale felt betrayed.

However, it would be many more weeks before the Bales learned what the group did after they rode away from the mill that night.

That group of thirty-four men left the Bale Grist Mill, rode to Sonoma, arrived at dawn on June 14th, 1846, and headed directly to Vallejo's *Casa Grande*.

After prancing on horseback down the wide street in front of the plaza, they came to Fort Sonoma. The building appeared to be a small fortress with the four-story tower rising from a barrier at the base and with gun slits in it for defense; it was General Mariano Vallejo's *Casa Grande*. They saw no one defending any structures. The deserted army barracks stood next to the house, with an empty flagpole and a heap of dry cattle bones in front.

A man who had taken the lead asked another beside him, "How'll we do this? There ain't no army ta fight."

"We need to take prisoners, don't we? Let's go to General Vallejo's house."

They dismounted and walked to the door. The others followed.

"Now what?"

"Just knock and see what happens." They raised the metal knocker and tapped it several times. "Maybe nobody's awake yet."

Mariano heard the knock, looked from his upstairs bedroom window, and went down to open the door.

General Mariano Vallejo stood in his slippers and a dressing gown held closed with a sash over his nightclothes and said, "Good Morning. how may I help you gentlemen?" He peered around the front two men and saw dozens more.

Two of them started talking together and made little sense.

Vallejo suggested by pointing to one man. "You talk, and no one else. I cannot understand when you speak at the same time."

"We came from Frémont's camp to take over California."

"No, no," the other one said, "you need to say, we rode all through the night and came to take California away from those Mexicans."

The one man pushed the other and said, "Ah, shut up!"

General Vallejo had heard the reference to Frémont and assumed they had come on Frémont's orders. After all, he thought, Frémont was a man sent here on President Polk's orders.

Mariano tightened the sash around his middle and said, as he took a step back, "Please come in. We can talk and discuss what is happening. Well, not all of you can fit inside." He stopped the parade of men after ten passed. "The rest of you can wait out here and look around to amuse yourselves."

As Vallejo closed the door, he indicated that they should enter the living room. "I do not have seating for everyone, so make yourself comfortable on the floor or anywhere. I was going to order my breakfast, and I invite you to join me." Vallejo clapped his hands, and a woman came from the kitchen. "Please prepare food for all of these guests. First, bring portions of last night's leftover meat and tortillas for us to start eating. Afterwards, prepare eggs and fry up vegetables. I am sure they are hungry after their long ride through the night."

From the men came various contradictory comments and questions:

"I'm real hungry. It sounds delicious."

"What's he tryin' ta do?"

"That's mighty nice."

"Did he signal someone to go for help?"

"That meat sounds delicious."

"I never liked those Mexican tortillas."

To Vallejo, their comments showed how disorganized they were.

The General addressed one of the questions he had heard and said, "No, I have not called for help. We agreed you were coming inside to talk. May I suggest that we draw up surrender documents and sign them?"

They stopped their chatter and looked dumbfounded, but some of the men nodded.

Vallejo continued taking charge, "Shall we begin talking about the terms of surrender while waiting for the food?" He stood and went to his desk.

Two men jumped up and followed him with their guns drawn.

Once seated at his desk, Vallejo said, "I have no gun here. I came to my desk to get paper from this drawer. You can open it and look."

After a few minutes, he realized he needed an interpreter. The Americans, having come from many different areas of the states, did not speak the King's English. Their accents and colloquialisms were often impossible for Vallejo to understand. He suggested, "Across the street is my brother-in-law, a Mr. Jacob P. Leese. He is an American and could help me understand your suggestions for this paper. Please send someone to get him. I will go get dressed while we wait."

"Not so fast, General. I'm sending two of my men with you."

"Of course."

When Vallejo returned in full uniform, the food was being devoured, and Jacob Leese had arrived. Jacob stood bewildered and asked, "What's happening, Mariano?"

"I need to write an agreement and cannot understand the American English. I need your help."

One of the Americans stood to declare, "You ain't goin' to write nothing without one of us seeing what's on that there paper." He turned to the others, "Okay, who's a good writer?" They chose a man named William Ide and declared him to be their Commander. He would lead in decisions on the proclamation to be written.

Hours passed without reaching an agreement on the wording. While they argued, Vallejo offered brandy and wine to those inside his home.

The group outside had confiscated a neighbor's barrel of *aguardiente* and had been drinking the homemade brew all day. Some were bored, others impatient, and many were getting unruly and fighting among themselves, when a rider approached. The horse carried Salvador, arriving for a scheduled meeting with his brother.

The Americans stopped all their activity and watched him ride up to the house.

Salvador dismounted among all the horses and men outside *Casa Grande* and started toward the door.

Two Americans blocked his way. "Whoa, there! Where you think you're going?

Another said, "Who are you?"

More of them gathered around,

Salvador, surrounded by men smelling of drink, said, "I'm going to meet with my brother, General Vallejo. He's expecting me."

An extra-drunk man pushed Salvador.

"No," someone shouted, "don't hassle him. Open the door and ask our Commander Ide what we should do."

They were instructed to remove all his weapons and allow him inside.

Salvador exclaimed upon entering the house filled with arguing men, "Mariano, what is all this?"

"No, no, no!" William Ide lost his temper. "You don't interrupt us with your questions. Just shut up."

Vallejo stood, "Please, may I introduce my brother, Jose Manual Salvador Vallejo."

"Oh, your brother! Oh, this is perfect." Commander Ide said snidely before turning and screaming, "No more talk. Everyone shut up. I like what we have on paper. No more changes to this agreement." He pivoted around and pointed to General Vallejo. "You, your brother, and your brother-in-law are my hostages. My men and I are going with you three to see Frémont."

Several men started to comment, and William Ide shouted again, "I said, NO MORE TALK. Get them on horses. Everyone in this room goes with me and the hostages, except you," he said pointing to one man. "You go outside and quiet them, and I'll explain to everyone what's happening." He pointed to someone else, "Take this chair outside so I can stand on it to talk."

The group shuffled out the door, and Ide climbed on the chair. He noticed that many of the townspeople were out and watching. He raised both arms, and all became quiet. "We are going to take these three men as hostages to John Frémont." Cheers exploded from his drunk crowd. Ide raised his arms again. They quieted again. "Yes, we are going to take over California and claim it as part of The United States of America." More cheers erupted, but this time Ide let them holler longer. Finally, he signaled for quiet and said, "Men, make room for the Mexicans, who are watching, to get closer to hear me. Now, I am going to read our proclamation:

All persons and the citizens of Sonoma are requested to remain at peace, and to follow their rightful occupations without fear of molestation.
I, the Commander in Chief of the Troops assembled at the Fortress

of Sonoma, gives his inviolable pledge to all persons in California not found under arms that they shall not be disturbed in their persons, their property, or social relations one to another by men under his command.

I also solemnly declares my object to be First, to defend himself and companions in arms who were invited to this country by a promise of Lands on which to settle themselves and families who were also promised a "republican government," who, when having arrived in California were denied even the privilege of buying or renting Lands of their friends, who instead of being allowed to participate in or being protected by a "Republican Government" were oppressed by a "Military Despotism," who were even threatened, by "Proclamation" from the Chief Officer of the aforesaid Despotism, with extermination if they would not depart out of the Country, leaving all of their property, their arms and beasts of burden, and thus deprived of the means of flight or defense.

To overthrow a Government which has seized upon the property of the Missions for its individual aggrandizement; which has ruined and shamefully oppressed the laboring people of California, by their enormous exactions on goods imported into this country; is the determined purpose of the brave men who are associated under his command.

We further declare that we believe that a government to be prosperous must originate with its people who are friendly to its existence. We declare the Citizens are its Guardians, its officers are its Servants, and its Glory their reward.

Signed by *William B. Ide, Head Quarters Sonoma, June 15, 1846*

The Americans threw hats in the air and cheered again.

Finally, Ide finished his talk, "Many of my men are to stay here. Any of my men who can write are to make copies of our proclamation and distribute it everywhere to everyone. That way, we can prove we took this fort and the barracks. As you know, because we stole those horses, some folks might call us robbers." He raised his arms again and shouted, "Remember, choose ye this day what you will be. Are we robbers or are we conquerors?"

They shouted, "Conquerors!"

The three hostages were led to horses. General Vallejo said to Jacob Leese and Salvador, "Do not worry. Frémont is my friend, and when he sees us, we will be released."

Just then, the secretary to General Vallejo rode up, He had arrived for work.

William Ide laughed, "He is already on a horse and ready to go. Bring him with us as our fourth hostage."

The Americans who remained in Sonoma, besides making copies of the proclamation to distribute, decided to make a flag, while they were in the barracks for three days. They put a large star on the upper left corner and a bear, which looked more like a pig, in the upper center with the words "California Republic" across the middle. Their flag was raised on the flagpole at the Sonoma Plaza.

Word spread across Alta California about that flag; the Californios started calling the whole incident, The Bear Flag Revolt. Those Americans who took General Vallejo hostage were called *Los Osos*, The Bears, in reference to the bear on the flag. If they had raised the flag of the United States government, the incident would have been more acceptable since many people wanted the United States in charge. The Bear Flag sent a different message, in that it represented an unknown group who had stolen one hundred and seventy horses and taken hostage their Mexican leaders. This did not sit well with the Californios.

Nor with Frémont.

After traveling more than eighty miles, they arrived at Frémont's campsite the next day with the hostages. William Ide and a few of his men entered Frémont's tent.

Frémont was furious. "Who in hell decided to steal those horses and take these men hostage?"

One man spoke up, "I heard you gave the order to steal the horses."

Frémont yelled, "Like hell I did!" The four hostages stood outside the tent with their hands tied and could hear. "And I did not give any order to raid Fort Sonoma. Whose idea was that?"

Someone muttered, "We thought you'd want it."

"Well, you all thought wrong." Frémont opened the tent flap and, with a jerk of his head, indicated he wanted the prisoners to enter. "And untie them."

He went to a trunk and ordered two men, "Lift those bags out." Now, he turned to the hostages and huffed, "General Vallejo, we have no campstools. Sit on the trunk and those bags."

They sat and heard, coming from the bags, the tinkle of silver coins.

Frémont explained about the sound of the contents, "Coins to pay my men," and stopped talking.

Silence, except the shuffle of feet, which lasted a lengthy minute in the tent, as Frémont pondered what to do.

Finally, General Vallejo said, "I wish you would tell us what you propose doing with us and . . . "

Frémont exploded. "No one said for you to speak. Speak only when I ask you to speak."

Silence filled the tent again, until Frémont began rambling about the situation and talking to no one in particular. "I had given no orders to take hostages and now I must decide what to do with all of you. I am angry that I have been put in this position and . . . " Unable to clarify a plan after talking for several minutes, he paced in the small space.

Loud and angry voices outside the tent demanded actions:

"We should hang them all."

"Nah, let's shoot them. Less trouble."

Finally, in frustration, Frémont decided to rid himself of having to decide any course of action. "I have nothing more to say." He addressed his men. "We must get these four Mexicans out of my camp." Of course, Leese was no Mexican, but that seemed irrelevant or unknown to Frémont. However, he did realize that he must stay with the hostages because his men might harm them. He had no orders from Washington and would be in profound trouble if any harm came to them. "Get my horse ready and we'll escort them to Sutter's Fort. I'm not keeping them here."

As John Frémont walked from the tent, General Vallejo started a sentence, "John, give me a minute . . . " and was ignored.

Once the hostages were delivered to Sutter's Fort, Frémont returned to his camp.

Before the week ended, Frémont took advantage of what had inadvertently occurred: The Bear Flag Manifesto had been written and seventy more Americans had joined the Bear Flag Republic. He decided to start signing his correspondence as *Military Commander of the U.S. Forces in California.* He was in command.

The Mexican forces started taking prisoners and positioning troops at various locations, and Americans were killed. Yet no major battles occurred until June 24th at Olompali, near the mouth of the Petaluma River when the Americans happened upon fifty uniformed Californios and a corral of horses. The Americans opened fire and killed a few men. This Battle of Olompali became the only official fight by the Bear Flag Republic.

For weeks, the hostages at Sutter's Fort were locked in a dark chamber without beds or blankets but were allowed outside to relieve themselves and take some exercise.

One day Frémont arrived at Sutter's Fort for the first time since the hostages had been delivered there. He screamed, "These men are prisoners. They are to have no special privileges. Prisoners are not to walk around freely. Who decided this?"

One of the guards mumbled to another under his breath, "Not you! Cuz ya ain't told us what ta do. We ain't got no orders."

Just as his men noticed, little by little it was becoming known by more important people that Frémont was fighting an unorganized war without orders from Washington. Frémont lacked a decisive plan of action, and his maneuvers often became a comedy of errors.

Meanwhile, the United States had sent the frigate *USS Savanah* with written instructions "to seize California while preserving friendly relations." The Americans were to conquer and befriend the Mexicans, but the fiasco of the Bear Flaggers had angered them and made it impossible. The Governor of Alto California declared that the Americans had started a rebellion and taken hostages; he decided that the Americans wanted a war.

And war began.

In the meantime, the Bales learned about the four hostages and the Bear Flag Revolt from George Yount who rode to *Rancho Carne Humana* to tell them.

When he walked into their adobe, he found Maria Ignacia alone in the kitchen. In his excitement and without taking time for a greeting, he blurted, "Mrs. Bale, your uncle . . . I mean, General Vallejo is mighty sick over at Sutter's Fort."

The pleasure that had come to her upon seeing George, vanished. Her expression changed to a puzzled look while she wiped her hands on her apron. She asked, "George, what you are saying? I don't understand."

Edward and Nathan had seen Yount arrive and overheard him as they followed him into the house. Edward exclaimed, "My word, why is Mariano at Sutter's Fort? What's going on?"

The whole story spilled from Yount. "Now, I ain't wantin' ta take sides. I's just saying that these Bear Flaggers—called *Los Osos* by the Californios—went on their own to the General's home and took him hostage. They got your Uncle Salvador, Jacob Leese, and General Vallejo's secretary as hostages, too."

Maria Ignacia gasped, "No!"

She went to Edward and, holding back tears, buried her head on his shoulder before looking up at her husband to say, "We must help my uncles."

George commented. "They's running crazy, those *Osos*. Don't got no plan, it seems, though Frémont's tryin' ta run everything. I hear'd that Frémont's men came upon a Mexican messenger and learned that the Mexicans were goin' ta attack the Bear Flaggers in Sonoma cuz they took over the fort and your uncles' houses. So, Frémont rushed there with his forces and discovered it were a trick. The Mexicans never came, and Frémont's own men started shootin' at him when he got there.

"Another time jus' south of Yerba Buena, Frémont and his men took hours pluggin' the touch-holes on ten Mexican cannons. They were crazy ta bother wit' that. Those were rusty cannons that ain't been used in years and probably weren't workin' anyway."

Edward asked, "When did all this start? No, I want to know when they took them hostage?"

George explained, "From what I hear'd, it were mid-June. He weren't sick back then, but I think General Vallejo has malaria now."

Now Mari was crying. "Edward we must help Mariano. It's mid-July. They have been prisoners for more than a month. Mariano must need medicine. You have quinine, don't you?"

Edward nodded, put his arms around her, and said, "Let me think." He turned to George and asked, "Is there more I need to know?"

"Yeah, there is," George sat down at the kitchen table and everyone sat down with him. "These Bear Flaggers made this ugly flag. It's got a silly bear that looks like a pig. Well, they riled up lots of people in Sonoma when they raised it at the fort. But now, they took it down and now the American flag of the United States flies there.

"But what I think ya need to know is 'bout the American ships in Monterey harbor and Yerba Buena."

"I do know about them," Dr. Bale said, "because I visited Larkin not long ago and they were there."

"Well," George said, "those two commanders on the ships, heck I don't know their names, but they thought Frémont were acting on orders from United States and that's why those two commanders demanded a surrender. They raised the American Flag in Monterey and made a 21-gun salute before they realized no Mexican army was in the fort."

Dr. Bale stood. "What? George, this is serious."

"Yeah, and later, the Mexican leaders wouldn't agree ta any surrender, and the two commanders learned they made a mistake and apologized ta all the Mexicans."

"George, what are you talking about?"

"I guess I'm gettin' to what's most important, Edward. Last week, I think it was the 19th of July, the commander on one of those American ships demanded the release of General Vallejo and the other hostages, cuz Frémont ain't workin' on orders from President Polk."

Mari grimaced and said, "Oh, George, you should have told us that at first."

"Guess I didn't say this story right cuz they's still prisoners tonight. Frémont decided not ta release them."

With George's last words, the group went quiet. The evening had turned dark and cool. Edward closed the kitchen door, returned to the table, and lit some candles. "Mari, please make a pot of coffee. I brought two pounds home a few weeks ago."

She stood and went to the pantry, returning with a small sack. "I'll make a big pot for us."

After a few hours, they had a plan. Dr. Bale would ride the fifty miles east to Sutter's Fort to see General Vallejo's condition and administer medicine, if necessary. "See, I have this paper saying I am the official volunteer surgeon for Frémont. They must allow me to do anything that's related to Frémont. I should be able to get in and help Mariano."

While Bale rode east to Sutter's Fort, George Yount rode fifty miles west to Yerba Buena to meet with the commander on the American ship called *USS Savannah*.

Two days passed before George was granted a meeting with Commodore Robert Field Stockton who, in mid-July, had been made commander-in-chief of all land forces in California.

Yount shook hands, "Glad ta meet ya, sir. I ain't nobody official or nothin', but General Mariano Vallejo is my friend, so I had ta come. Now, I ain't for either side in this conflict. I just want to be a messenger, cuz I'm worried about my friend."

Unaware of the recent events, Commodore Stockton asked, "What's the problem with General Vallejo?"

Yount told the whole story of the Bear Flaggers and of Frémont taking the prisoners to Sutter's Fort and said, "General Vallejo is still a prisoner and very sick."

Commodore Stockton sat pensive for a few moments at his desk before speaking. "Hmmm, I find your information interesting. I thank you for coming. I am going to tell you what has unfolded since I arrived on July fifteenth, so you can return to the valley and spread the word. I am pleased to know you are on neither side because that assures me that you will tell the facts to those for and those against in an unbiased manner.

"Now, Frémont is here on the Pacific coast. I mustered him and his men into the military for the United States, and then I sent them south. The American flag will be raised as he progresses down the coast. At a designated place, he will board a ship for San Diego and work his way north, claiming more land for America."

Yount's eyes widened, "Well, I'll be darned. That thar is a good plan." He swallowed and leaned forward in his chair to say, "But ya ain't said nothin' 'bout my friend Mariano Vallejo. He's sick and needs to go home ta git well."

"Yes, yes, I will help him and the other hostages. You can rest assured."

After the meeting, orders for the hostages' release were written by Commodore Stockton. George Yount rode with the messenger to Sutter's Fort to ensure its arrival.

Once at Sutter's Fort, Yount sat with Mariano, waiting for the orders to be completed. Never one to mince words, and never one to refrain from telling his opinion, he said, "Damn, Mariano, until I hear'd your voice I didn't recognize ya. Ya lost your belly. You're skin and bones. An' I ne'er thought I'd see ya wit' no sideburns." General Vallejo weighed ninety-five pounds—half his usual weight.

Salvador and Leese were still prisoners and sat with them. Salvador said, "He's been so sick. Thank heavens, Dr. Bale came and administered medications. Another doctor had come but Mariano didn't get better. After Dr. Bale left, he improved."

"Well, I ain't leavin' till they free Mariano. Then I'll take him to his family." George scratched his chin and frowned before continuing. "Listen, I need to tell ya 'bout your homes. I don't want ya ta die from a heart attack when ya see what those Bear Flaggers did ta everything."

The General's family was still in *Casa Grande*, but Salvador's family and Leese's had been pushed out of their homes and were living in *Casa Grande*.

Yount told Salvador, "What those rebels didn't haul away from your home just disappeared ta the wind. They kicked your wife and children out. Salvador, ya ain't got nothing left." Yount turned to Leese and pursed his lips, before he said, "The Bear Flaggers took over your house and made it their headquarters." Yount turned to Mariano's secretary and said, "I don't know nothin' 'bout your place."

On the first of August, General Vallejo was with Yount heading home but without Salvador or the other two hostages. George had apologized to them, "I didn't think to insist the ship commander write a release for the rest of you." George left with Mariano to assure his safe journey.

A week later, the other three hostages were released.

By mid-August in 1846, a proclamation announced that California was a part of the United States of America, even though fighting was still raging in the south.

In San Diego, Frémont and the Bears arrived by ship and occupied the city without firing a shot.

In Los Angeles, the Mexican's three hundred men were no match for Commodore Stockton's two thousand sailors and Marines, who were due to arrive at any moment, so the Mexicans sent a delegation to the Americans proposing a cease-fire. Commodore Stockton replied that he was there to take the country and refused their request but, he wrote, "If you agree to hoist the American flag in California, I will stop my forces and negotiate a treaty."

The Mexican general responded, "Never, never, never!" Retreat was the only option that the Mexicans saw as honorable. They withdrew out of Alta California into Mexico, leaving the fifteen hundred Angelenos to their fate.

Those Angelenos organized. On September twenty-third, a four-day siege ended with the Americans surrounded and taken to a merchant vessel, to be sent to sea.

Commodore Stockton headed south with a flotilla and ordered Frémont north to take down the rancheros and vaqueros of Los Angeles.

Months before, President Polk had ordered an army to go west and occupy the land. They had taken Santa Fe and were heading to California. When about thirty miles northeast of San Diego, they challenged a force of mounted Californios. The Americans were mauled; twenty-two dragoons were killed, a quarter of the Americans. The survivors traveled on to join Commodore Stockton.

At the end of December, the Americans had regrouped and, in two final battles outside of Los Angeles, took possession of the pueblo. But fighting continued in many areas for weeks.

Meanwhile, farther north at Chahuenga Pass on January thirteenth in 1847, and without the involvement of his superiors, Frémont succeeded in negotiating a treaty. Commodore Stockton was shocked at the liberal terms and the audacity of his junior officer but, having no other choice, he endorsed the agreement. Most bloodshed stopped. Frémont felt this was his finest hour.

At the end of 1846, the whole household of *Rancho Carne Humano* took a trip to Sonoma to see how the Vallejos were faring and to show their new baby to everyone.

During the first day of their visit, the Bales came downstairs and found Mariano in his living room with a blanket covering his legs. He said, "Without my extra bulk, I get cold easily, but I'm getting well. It's still hard to walk from one room to another without someone helping me; however, I am not complaining. I left Sutter's Fort half dead, yet I am alive."

Maria Ignacia asked, "They took so much from you. Aren't you angry?"

Vallejo screwed up his mouth and said, "You are correct that I lost more than one thousand horned cattle, and they took about six hundred tamed horses. And I no longer have most of the items of value from my house, except my wife and nine children. But I have assurances that the United States will speed the development of California as no other government can. This gives me contentment."

Edward commented, "Mariano, you always have favored the Americans. I cannot understand how you can still feel that way, though I see you do." He turned to Mariano's brother. "Salvador, you lost everything except your family. The military took over your house just as they did for Leese's. Can you be as accepting as your brother toward the Americans?"

"No, I plan to harass them until they compensate me."

Finally, everyone moved to the table for the meal. This was the first time the Vallejo family had gathered since the ordeal with the Bear Flag Revolt. Outside, frost sat on all the shrubs. The oaks, which usually do not lose leaves, were naked. Sonoma was experiencing exceptionally cold weather. The hills behind *Casa Grande* were whitish gray, with dead plants and ice, matching the clouded and gray sky. The bleak weather did not hinder the warmth of the family gathering and all were content until an incident towards the end of the meal.

Mariano's wife, Francisca, was not present at the dinner table because one daughter was ill. Servants had taken soup upstairs for them.

The conversational din from the dozen diners mixed with laughter from one end of the table to the other. From the corner of her eye, Maria Ignacia saw a servant rush to her uncle. Though she could not hear what was said, she heard an exclamation, "Oh, no!" escape her uncle's lips.

Maria Ignacia glanced at Mariano. The look on his face confirmed a problem. He took his cane and the arm of the servant for help to the stairs.

Maria Ignacia followed behind him saying, "Mariano, may I help with something?"

Besides being stiff in his older years, he still was recovering from his illness; he stopped in his ascent to turn his whole body to see who had asked the question. "Oh, Maria Ignacia, yes, come with me."

Upon opening a bedroom door, they saw Francisca, looking frantic. She rushed to Mariano's side and clutched his forearm, "Oh, Mariano, they tried to kill me."

He gasped and said, "What?" Releasing himself from the servant and reaching for his wife, he clutched his wife's shoulders and walked toward the bed to sit on the edge. Unable to speak from exhaustion, he patted the bed to indicate to his wife to sit next to him. Finally, he looked at his daughter,

Guadalupe, whose eyes were closed.

Maria Ignacia went to the girl and touched her forehead. Looking at the parents, she mouthed the word, "Hot!"

Guadalupe's eyes popped open.

"Hello, Guadalupita," Maria Ignacia said in a soft voice, "I am happy to see you. Wish you were not sick."

The girl made a slight turn of her head to see who spoke, before closing her eyes again without a word.

Maria Ignacia pursed her lips. She brushed some damp ringlets away from the girl's forehead and left her hand resting on the soft curls, while her eyes puddled with tears.

Francisca, still agitated, whispered something to her husband which made him jerk upright from the bed and hobble to the table where two bowls full of soup sat. He took a spoon as if to sample the soup, but the spoon made a grating sound when he scraped the bottom of the bowl. He raised the spoon to look closer and put a finger cautiously to the liquid in the spoon, before exclaiming, "*Dios Mios!*"

Maria Ignacia came to his side and gasped. "Is that a shard of glass I see?"

"Yes, I'm afraid so."

Francisca started to cry quietly. Droplets fell from her cheek as she choked on the words, "Who? Why?"

The sick little girl, burning with fever, heard nothing.

Mariano turned to his wife, "Did you or Guadalupita swallow any glass?"

"No, no. To make sure it was not too hot for her, I took a sip and got a few pieces of broken glass and spit everything back into the bowl."

A mournful groan escaped from deep inside of Mariano, and he reached to pull his wife into his arms.

"I'm going downstairs to get Edward," Maria Ignacia said. "He brought his doctor bag and may be able to help Guadalupe." She opened the door to leave.

"Wait, I'll go with you." Mariano patted his wife's hand and clenched his jaw. "I must go find who did this." He stopped and turned to his wife, "My dear, I will ask Edward to bring food for you."

Before the guests had gone to bed that night, Mariano had found the culprit. He learned that a servant named Canulo had put the broken glass in Francisca's soup. Other servants had seen him pounding a bottle to pieces earlier in the evening.

Mariano confronted him.

Canulo admitted it and told his employer, "Your wife lost one of my shirts and did not offer me a new one. I wanted to kill her."

Mariano surmised that the man was deranged and sent for the constable. Canulo was charged and taken to jail.

Guadalupita died later that evening from malaria. She was the sixth child of Mariano and Francisca to die. They had eight remaining children—four boys and four girls.

On the wagon trip back to *Rancho Carne Humano* with all their children nestled in the back, the Bales counted their blessings. "We have not lost a child."

Edward nodded, "We have Lolita, Caroline, Edward, Anita, and now Juanita—all healthy children. Oh, I have not entered Juanita on the list in our bible. I will do that tomorrow when we are home. Mari, I was so pleased when you gave little Juanita the middle name of Maria instead of Guadalupe."

"I am glad you like the names."

"Please explain why your family uses the name Guadalupe so frequently. Tonight, I was amazed; I hadn't known the middle names of many of the people in your family until this visit. Your Uncle Mariano has given three of his children the name of Guadalupe.

She sighed before explaining. "We are Catholics and believe in miracles. A marvelous miracle called Our Lady of Guadalupe happened a couple of hundred years ago in Mexico. The Mother Mary appeared to a peasant and imprinted her image on his robe and that garment was saved in Mexico City for all to see. We call that image: Our Lady of Guadalupe. Many in my family have traveled there to see it and we are honoring my relatives who have seen it and honoring our faith when we use that name."

The sunset burst with fuchsia and pinks. Mari looked with pleasure and hugged baby Juana closer as she nursed.

The next day, Edward did record his newest child, little Juana, onto the designated page in the family bible.

In three years, he would add one more child to the list and would shake his head while writing the middle name of his last child.

The Bale Children

1840-1908 Maria Isadora Bale (Lolita)
1842-1891 Carolina Bale (Caroline)
1844-1906 Eduardo Guadalupe Bale (Edward Jr.)
1846-1868 Ana Guadalupe Bale (Anita)
1846-1876 Juana Maria Bale (Juanita)
1849-1905 Mariano Guadalupe Bale

As the years passed, Mari recorded the death dates in their Bible for three of her adult children. Ironically, Lolita, the oldest child, would outlive everyone else in the Bale family and be the one to record all additional deaths except, of course, her own.

Like the months that must pass to create a child, a war in the eighteen-hundreds needed time to create an outcome. With the American president on one side of the country, hearing about the success of battles three thousand miles away, decisions took time. Not until February of 1848 was a complete treaty signed to finalize the end of the Mexican conflict and to claim American ownership of California.

Decisions take time. What John C. Frémont claimed as his finest hour turned, with time, into his demise. He was court-martialed, convicted, and given a dishonorable exit from the military.

Dr. Edward Turner Bale on his pinto horse

Chapter Ten

Keeping Their Secrets

1847-1849

George Yount always heard the latest news before the Bales. And, more often than not, he would ride over and share it with them, especially if he thought the news to be important. With many Americans camping at George's ranch and those Americans always roaming all over California, it was logical that they heard news and told George. According to George, if someone died or a baby was born, even if a wedding was announced or visitors from afar had come, none of that was important news. But what he heard, in early February of 1847, was reason for a trip to the Bales. George headed there with a once-in-a-lifetime kind of news.

In the past, Mia always had ridden with him, but not anymore.

Yount had not seen her since she left to get married, not that he didn't try. Twice, he had ridden to the village where he knew she lived. The natives would not let him go to her, and he wondered if she knew he had come. On his second trip, after being denied again, he had camped a mile away, planning to go back the next day. He had hoped someone in the village would have pity on an old man who wanted to see his daughter.

During that night in his campground, someone did.

An old woman sneaked to his campsite and told him about Mia. "She has a child, and another is on the way. She cannot talk with you because her husband said she can't." The old women's next comment made George decide never to return to that village again. She said, "He beats her most days. Both times, when you came, he beat her more. Yesterday when you were there, he beat her so hard she could not walk. Her belly is big; I hope the baby is not hurt."

The news George wanted to tell the Bales had nothing to do with Mia, and he had already told them about his attempts to see his daughter. Notwithstanding, as George rode, Mia filled his thoughts. In fact, he relived the rides he had taken with his daughter. This trip took only a short time because their ranches were not even ten miles apart. During his ride and in his thoughts, he heard his past conversations with Mia, felt the laughter they had shared, and saw the same landscape they had always passed. The ride meant a lot to him, since he had nothing left of her, except his memories.

Approaching *Rancho Carne Humana*, George often pondered what the name of the Bale's ranch meant. Sometimes he made a guess, but not today. Chills ran along his spine because he saw a relationship between the name *Carne Humana* and the news he would soon share.

At the adobe, George dismounted at the shed and walked toward the house while observing construction work. Coming around the corner, he said, "Mrs. Bale and Julia, good day. I must say that addition on your house looks mighty fine. What made ya decide ta build it?"

Maria Ignacia and Julia were taking the dry laundry off a clothesline. "Hello, George," they chimed together.

Mari responded to his question. "We needed rooms for growing children and visitors. That's why we made a one-story addition for bedrooms at the end of the living room."

Dr. Bale came from the other side of the house, "Hello, George, I saw you coming. We're going to eat soon; please join us."

Mari said, "After I drop these clothes on my bed, we will eat right away."

Julia left with the comment, "I'm going to gather the children. You men sit down at the table under the overhang of the arbor. No reason to eat inside on a beautiful day like today."

"I agree," said George as he sat, "and what luck to have this weather in February."

The Bales had stopped asking George about Mia many months ago. They could see it was too painful. They surmised that talking about the weather was a safer subject.

Not today.

The weather was part of the news, and George waited until they finished eating before he began. He put down his fork and leaned his elbows on the table. "They's people trapped in the mountain passes ta the east of us. Winter storms and snow caught 'em, and they got stuck. A few of 'em made it to a Miwok village and, after the Miwoks fed 'em, they led them to the Johnson Ranch, since it's the first homestead west of the Sierras. I hear'd that the ones left back in the snow are . . . " He stopped to choose his words. "Well, they's really bad off."

Mari asked, "How many? Do you know what happened?"

George shook his head. "I don' know much. A rescue party of men went in and should be comin' out soon. At least, I hope they will. I came here ta ask.

Could some of the children stay here when they bring 'em out?"

Dr. Bale insisted, "Of course. We have this new addition and a lot of room. We will be glad to help."

During the following months and little by little, the details of the Donner Party's ordeal seemed to arrive with the wind carrying the words that no one wanted to speak. The wind whispered, "People ate the frozen bodies of their loved ones."

George came again at the end of March. Julia, Pepe, several of the Miwoks, and the Bales gathered to sit under the large oak tree to listen to him. Recently, Pepe had taken to making benches and a table for the family to have a place in the shade for the summertime. For now, those who had no bench sat on the ground and leaned against the big oak.

By this time, everybody in the valley had heard about the Donner Party and was anxious to learn the story. Those who lived at *Rancho Carne Humana* were no exception. They wanted to understand how the ordeal happened.

George told them all he knew. "Here's what I hear'd. Thar were 'bout eighty people trapped by winter storms up by Truckee Lake in the mountains. We all know how cold a winter this year was. Up thar it was worse. After a couple of months, they knew they was all goin' ta die unless they got help. So, a group of fifteen called themselves the Forlorn Hope Group and left on snowshoes; seven of 'em made it out. It took 'em over thirty days ta go 'bout ten miles. Of the fifteen, the eight who died were ate." He pursed his lips, frowned, and shook his head. "Sorry, I say that bad. Hmm, eight were ate."

Maria Ignacia squeezed George's arm, resting on the table next to her. "Heavens! What horrors they must have endured! Is there more you can tell us about the survivors?"

"Thar is." He ran his fingers through his hair. "I went up ta Sutter's Fort ta see for myself what was happenin', and tents are everywhere outside the walls for the forty or so people who were saved. They's all skin and bones. It was hard for me to see that."

George continued talking and the March sun could not warm the listeners who shivered with the facts. He said that once the Forlorn Hope Group had arrived in the valley, three rescue parties were sent in, one per month in January, February, and March. "That last group of rescuers ain't back yet.

"Anyways, when I was at Sutter's Fort, I borrowed a wagon and took a group of orphans down ta my place. They's the Grave family. The Ma and Pa died up in the snow. I was wonderin', since we live so close, could you take the littlest ones? They's all crowded at my place, and they need more personal care. But if you take some, then they'd all be near to the others in thar family."

Maria Ignacia jumped to her feet and said, "Oh my, yes, George, of course." She walked over to her husband, dragging her chair, and took his hands into hers. "Isn't that right, Edward?"

"Yes, of course." He asked, "Do any need medical attention?"

George shook his head, "Mostly, they need food." He went quiet a moment. Everyone waited. By the look of anguish on George's face, they knew he had something difficult to say. "One little girl gots a problem. Her name is Nancy. I thought you and Mrs. Bale might take her and her sisters cuz little Nancy ain't talkin' cuz, ya see, she know'd that both her Ma and her Pa was cut into food ta eat. So, she don' want ta talk at all." George's fingers went into his hair, and then he rubbed his hands over his face, before he added, "Nancy's little five-year-old brother got ate, too."

Maria Ignacia sat back down and took her handkerchief to her eyes.

George corrected himself, "I think Nancy gonna need more than food. A lot of love, too." He listed the ages of the nine children, ranging from the oldest daughter, Sarah, in her twenties to a one-year-old girl named Elizabeth. The six others who still lived were Mary Ann (19), William C. (17), Eleanor (14), Lovina (12), Nancy (9), and Jonathan (7). Little five-year-old Franklin was the one who was eaten.

The Bales looked at each other and agreed without speaking. Dr. Bale said, "Pepe, help me get the wagon ready with a couple of horses. George, can we go to your ranch now?"

"Sure can."

Maria Ignacia told Julia, "We can add more carrots and potatoes to the stew to feed a few more. We made a large potful, anyway."

Julia agreed, "Yes, and we have tamales from last night. I'll warm them. Children usually like to eat tamales. Oh, if you bring the one-year-old here," Julia said, "I know a Miwok mother who is nursing her own. We can ask her to come and nurse her child and this one. A mother's milk is always best for little ones."

Over the coming months, the Bales and George allowed the Grave siblings to take a wagon whenever they wanted to go visit the others. Since *Rancho Caymus* and *Rancho Carne Humana* were side by side, there were daily trips. Slowly, as their bodies put on weight, their minds began to cope with the painful memories. They started to heal. Occasionally, they shared stories of their ordeal, but only one on one.

One day, Julia was talking with Sarah, the oldest.

Julia said, "My husband died. It was horrible. When I think about how he died, I have so much pain but cannot stop remembering. Maybe you have the same kind of pain I have."

Sarah took Julia's hand as they sat on the bench under the oak tree and said, "My husband, Jay, died in the mountains. One morning, I learned of another couple in our Forlorn Hope Group with a dying husband. I took the wife's hands in mine and picked up a knife. We walked back to Jay. I asked her to help me. She and I prepared cuts of his flesh, so her husband could live."

Silent tears rolled from Sarah's eyes and dripped off her chin to her lap. "I was the first woman to cut meat from a human." Sarah began to sob uncontrollably and leaned into Julia's shoulder and arms. "But I refused to eat my husband."

Julia rocked her as they huddled on the bench. Stroking her hair, Julia whispered, "You did what was needed to save others. You were brave."

Sarah sat up and wiped her face on her skirt. "The others ate my husband, my Jay. They had not eaten anything since we ate our moccasins four days before. Yes, my Jay saved their lives." She took her handkerchief and blew her nose. "My sister Mary had shot a deer, so I had food. In addition to all the deer meat, we shared the deer's head, feet, hide, the entrails, just everything."

Another day, Mary Ann was changing the cotton drawers of her baby sister while sitting on the grass next to the slough, and Dr. Bale walked down to be with her. They struck up a conversation, and she mentioned Dr. Bale's English accent. "I guess you are from England. Are your parents still living?"

He told her, "Yes, I believe so. I thought I had done something disgraceful to shame them before I left England. I thought I would never see them again. Well, this sounds so vague. I will tell the whole story." And he did, ending with the comment, "So, Mari and I wrote to my parents. It has been more than a year since I sent my letter. I hope a ship will come soon with a letter from them. I miss them."

Mary Ann was svelte and graceful, a beautiful girl with dark, bright expressive eyes that were sad now. She smoothed back her long, thick, dark, and wavy hair from her cheek and said, "I am happy for you. I shall never see my parents again." Her voice gave out, and she had to clear her throat. A strained look appeared on her face as she said, "My father was such a big, strong man and he knew about everything. He made the snowshoes that allowed us to walk out of the mountain. He had been raised in Vermont, in the Green Mountains, and knew all about surviving in mountains and snow." She began to cry, and Dr. Bale gave her his clean handkerchief. "When he was dying, he knew it and talked to Sarah and me. He named all the others in our family whom we left back in the cold and snow while we went for help. He told us that we must do everything to save our families. He told me that we were the last hope and must use his body to be able to live." Mary Ann sobbed after speaking.

Dr. Bale patted her hands and said, "I am sorry. So very sorry."

The three youngest girls of the Grave family slept at the Bale's adobe. After a few weeks, Lovina found comfort with Mari, who often hugged her and told stories to make her laugh. Baby Elizabeth was getting pudgy, as a one-year-old should be, and was always cheerful now that she had enough food and the Miwok's breast milk. Nevertheless, Nancy still had not spoken; she often sat alone and stared out in the distance.

One day, Mari showed Lovina where the embroidery thread was kept, and the girl started making designs on a square of cotton to be a scarf. They could see Nancy sitting outside and looking off into space. Lovina said, "Nancy was with my mother and little brother Franklin in the second rescue group. I was in the first. She saw . . . " The girl stopped mid-sentence and put down the embroidery. Blinking to fight back the tears filling her eyes, she swallowed and sat awhile, trying to contain her emotions.

Mari moved to sit next to her on the sofa, put her arm around the girl's shoulders, and said, "Cry, let yourself cry. Crying is best sometimes. If you can open that deep well of tears and let them fall, sadness flows out with them, and you feel better."

After a few minutes of Lovina's sobbing, Mari went for a clean cloth. Lovina took it, nodded her head in appreciation, and wiped her face. "I think I do feel better. Thank you." She looked up at Mari and tried to smile. "Thank you for everything." She cleared her throat. "I wanted to tell you about Nancy. Nancy's problem is difficult to talk about. But I want you to understand." She blew her nose and said, "Nancy saw our mother and brother die. But, what's worse . . ."

Again, the twelve-year-old girl began to cry, talking through her tears, needing to tell it once and for all. "She accidentally walked up and saw people cutting Mama to make food." Lovina fell into Mari's lap and bawled.

Mari caressed the girl's head, gently smoothing her hair while tears streamed down Mari's face, too, knowing they had more painful, horrible memories they would never tell.

In May of 1847, Mary Ann Graves married a man named Edward Pile, and the couple returned a few months later with a wagon to take her four little sisters to live with them. Dr. Bale commented, as they watched the little girls depart. "At least most of them look healthy, only little Nancy still looks so peaked."

Not much time passed before Sarah Graves remarried as well. Since few white women were available to become wives in Alta California, she had had many suitors. She and her husband took her two brothers with them.

As the Bales stood waving and watching the last of the Graves family ride away to live somewhere else in California, Mari said, "Oh, Edward, I hope they never learn Spanish and think about what *Rancho Carne Humana* means. I'm afraid, if they had asked me, I would have divulged our secret to explain that we were referring to our naked natives, nothing else."

"Mari, our ranch was named long before the Donner Party started out in their wagon trains. I have our dated Plat Map with the name from long ago. You could just show it. You have no reason to tell the secret of how we named *Rancho Carne Humana*. You promised never to divulge our secrets."

Mari and Edward still stood in the yard, watching the wagon with the Graves children grow smaller in the distance. Lolita and Caroline giggled as they ran around the large oak tree, being chased by their brother, who shouted, "Whoopee, my horse going to catch you. Whee!" Unlike the time when the mother bear and her cub were under that tree, Edward Jr. was old enough not only to keep up with his sisters but to run faster. Julia was sitting in the grass feeding the two smaller girls and talking sweetly to them. Nathan sat under the grape arbor tuning his fiddle. Pepe was in the shed hammering. The pings, giggles, soft words, off-key notes, and whoops of her son sounded like music to Mari.

Mari wrapped her arms around Edward's still-slim waist, leaned her head against his chest, and said, "Thank you, Edward, for giving me such a wonderful life. I love you." They kissed as if alone. When their lips parted, their eyes clung.

He bobbed his head in agreement and said, "Meeting the Graves family has made me know how fortunate we are to have this life. I could have ruined all this if I had kept drinking. Mari, mixed with my fears of losing what we have was my confidence that I could get better because you were always there for me. I know of no couple who has a love like ours."

This time, they kissed with only a brush of their lips, ready to get back to their tasks at hand. Again, their eyes met, and their hearts burst with love. Glances between lovers speak without words.

Two months later, Edward rode up to their adobe, saw Mari hanging clothes outside, stopped his horse next to her, and began his exciting news before his boots touched the ground. "Mari, do you realize that our days of living in Mexico are coming to an end? We will soon be a part of the United States of America." He had returned from a visit to George Yount and had learned about the significance of July Fourth. "I was talking to a bunch of my American friends over at George's and heard about this holiday that they celebrate. I decided on the spot that I am going to renounce my Mexican citizenship and," he grinned from ear to ear as he finished his sentence, "I said we would join the July Fourth party down at Rector Cañon. I hope Nathan will come with us and bring his fiddle." He wrapped an arm around her waist and did a little jig.

A mammoth oak tree provided them with shade for the hot July party in 1847. The singing stopped only when Nathan's fiddle stopped to let the fiddler get a drink. At one point, he put his fiddle to his chin and said, "Everyone sing *Yankee Doodle* with me and if you know any verses, start them up after I finish the ones I know."

> *Yankee Doodle went to town*
> *A-riding on a pony,*
> *Stuck a feather in his cap*
> *And called it macaroni.*

Yankee Doodle keep it up,
Yankee Doodle dandy.
Mind the music and the step,
And with the girls be handy.

Father and I went down to camp,
Along with Captain Gooding.
And there we saw the men and boys,
As thick as hasting pudding.

The Bale children delighted in singing the chorus of *Yankee Doodle*. George Yount grabbed the hands of two little ones to show how to march and sing at the same time. Everyone—the families of Rector, York, Hudson, Vines, Grigsby, Yount, and Bale—formed a long line and circled the oak tree over and over while pulling knees high and swinging arms left and right as they marched.

Yankee Doodle keep it up,
Yankee Doodle dandy.
Mind the music and the step,
And with the girls be handy.

Later that evening and after singing many songs, Mari had been delighted to hear her husband singing the *Star-Spangled Banner* louder than anyone else.

On the wagon ride home, Mari, wanting to feel more American, said, "My seven-word name is so Mexican. I am ready to change it."

Edward, sitting on the wagon bench next to her with the tuckered-out children asleep in the back, asked, "What do you mean?" He put his left arm around her while holding the reins in his right hand. "And, you never have explained why you have all those names."

She sighed, "Can you even say them? All seven names?"

"Of course, I can. You are Maria Antonia Juana Ignacia Guadalupe Soberanes Vallejo."

She leaned onto his shoulder and began to explain about each name. "Even I am not sure about one of my names. I will take them in order:

- Maria Antonia, my first two names come from my maternal grandmother. You know, from Lita.
- Juana was added during my childhood, after my Confirmation into the Catholic Church, and is the one name I am not sure where it came from. I think Juana was the best friend of my mother.
- Ignacia is the feminine form of my maternal grandfather who was Ignacio.
- Guadalupe, as I have told you, is the religious name used by many in my family because of the Miracle of Our Lady of Guadalupe.
- Soberanes, of course, is my father's surname, and
- Vallejo is my mother's surname.

"But now, after falling in love with you and marrying, I no longer am a woman with seven names. As far as I am concerned, I have one name. I am Mrs. Bale." With the end of the explanation, they stopped talking and enjoyed the quiet of the night.

Nathan and Pepe were riding horses and had gone ahead to the adobe. Julia, snuggled in the bed of the wagon, slept with all the children. Edward and Mari rode on the wagon bench with the night cradling them in their own private world. She put her hand on her husband's thigh when they could see their home. Even carrying all the children up the stairs to their beds did not diminish the desire that her touch to his thigh had started. Fireworks exploded in their bed on the night of the Fourth of July.

Debts grew during the rest of the year. Dr. Bale had many more expenditures than incoming payments for the mills and sales of animals. The new grist mill did not have the needed waterpower to grind all the wheat quickly, and they lost customers. Edward complained, "And those wooden cogs make such a racket that I cannot bear to be there while the mill grinds."

Most days, Mari saw Edward's distress in his stance and movements. His body drooped, and he moved more slowly than usual. He did not share all the financial aspects of their ranch with her though he knew she had learned accounting from Cooper and Larkin's accountant when she was young. He reasoned, "You have all the household worries and the care of the children on your shoulders. I carry the burdens of our financial situation. I think it's better not to have both of us worrying about money. Even if you knew the details of our financial situation, you have no way to improve it." She planned to look at their accounting books when he was not around.

The year ended with the Bale's account books in the red, Edward's mood black, and Mari feeling blue. Yet, by the end of January in 1848, those colors changed.

If a color was associated with hope, it was the color of bright yellow because, on Monday the twenty-fourth of January, a carpenter working for John A. Sutter discovered gold in Coloma, not far from Sutter's Fort.

In the first months of 1848, few knew of the discovery, and those few did not believe it. There was no proof. People brushed off the news as rumor, gossip, or hearsay until March when it was confirmed. Then, everyone who heard the news wanted their share of that gold.

One of those people was Edward, who had hopes of eliminating his debt by finding gold. Yet, he realized that he had no money to buy equipment for gold mining. More importantly, he did not have enough money to sustain his family. He knew, if he went to the gold fields right away, his family would not have sufficient money on which to live. He sat down at his desk to list ways to raise money and within the week began to execute his plan.

Before he left for gold mining, he needed to plant the crops for the coming season and slaughtered many of his cattle to sell the tallow and hides. To make more money, he went out and found people who needed cut wood; after he pocketed the money for that cut wood, he sold the sawmill. He sold sheep and pigs, leaving enough animals for the family. Finally, when he was finished with his list, and without knowing what he was doing, he planted one more item—a son into Mari.

At the end of May in 1848, he was ready to head to Sutter's creek where the gold had been found.

Long before dawn lighted the sky, Edward and Mari sat in the kitchen alone.

He said, "Do you remember when I was leaving on my first trip to see California with your Uncle Mariano? I talked about how wonderful we would feel when I returned, and we saw each other again."

"Of course, I remember. Today, just like that time, I brought you a handkerchief to carry in the pocket over your heart." She reached out and slipped it into his shirt pocket. "I had said to carry this close to your heart and think of me, because I shall miss you so."

Edward nodded. "And I had responded, 'Our separation will be good for us because we will yearn for the other and our love will grow.'"

Mari nodded. "But you said a bit more. Something about our love becoming greater than we ever thought. And I told you I hoped you were correct." They still sat at the table with the breakfast dishes dirty in front of them. Mari took his hands, "You were right. I never thought I could love you as I do today."

Edward confided, "I think I mentioned something about our first meeting on the beach. I have loved you since my first sight of you."

"Yes, you did say that, too. We feel the same about that day on the beach." She closed her eyes and took a deep breath. "I wish you would not go. Do we need gold when we have this love that no one seems to have?"

He didn't answer and, after he rode away, she felt empty and walked around the house touching his things. She opened drawers and caressed the belt he had not taken. From the chifforobe, she pulled up a shirt to cover her face as she inhaled his essence. Walking to his desk, she saw a medical book left open; the title of the section made her gasp. She sat down and read for many painful minutes about cancer of the colon.

The months passed and Mari's belly grew. It was incongruous to her that she was with child, and Edward did not know. Once or twice a week, she sat outdoors and rested beneath the wooden trellis filled with the leafless grape vines and thought she smelled the essence of Edward. She imagined that the wind passed him miles away, captured his smell, and brought it to assuage her longing.

Christmas came and went without Edward. The New Year followed without celebrations with her family because her pregnancy prevented travel. Maria Ignacia, Julia, and Pepe managed with dwindling funds and without any word from Edward.

Then in February, a letter arrived at the Vallejo's home in Sonoma, and Mariano sent it on to *Rancho Carne Humana*:

> *To Don Mariano G. Vallejo*
> *January 17, 1849*
>   *Dear Sir:*
>   *Do me the favor to inform Mrs. Bale that I have some chance of recovering and as soon as I feel able, I will visit Sonoma and by your permission I will take refuge at your house for a few days.*
>   *I have no news.*
>   *Please give my respects to Mrs. Bale and my children.*
>   *p.s. I send, for the use of Mrs. Bale, $80, by Francis Clark, the bearer of this letter.*

Not long after the letter, Edward arrived back home. His family was in the living room when he staggered through the door, tossing his saddlebag into the corner by his desk and saying, "Greetings to all. I missed Christmas, holidays and birthdays and I have no presents for any of you. I'm sorry, but so happy to be home."

The children rushed to him. Mari was big with child and struggled to her feet.

"No, no, Papá, you are our present," Lolita said and grabbed him around his middle. His other children danced around him.

"You have grown, Lolita. Look at you, getting as tall as me."

Being sick with a fever did not stop Edward from dropping to the floor to hug all his children in an armful. When he released his little ones, he reached for a chair to assist himself getting up. Mari waited for her embrace.

"Heavens, Edward, you are burning with fever."

"And you, my wife, are bulging with child."

"Yes, you left me a surprise present."

With an arm still wrapped around her, he caressed her baby mound and asked, "When are we to expect him to present himself?"

"Or herself. You tell me. If you remember when you departed, add nine months to that date." She took a step backwards to rest against the arm of the couch. "All I know is that this baby will be here soon. I think any day."

Collapsing onto the couch, he told Mari, "I am so tired and need you to feed me just as you did Nathan when he arrived so sick. I think it was you who made him well. I expect the same."

Later, in their bedroom, he sat on the edge of their bed. Mari helped him remove all his clothes, and she saw blood inside his breeches. It would be days before her mind flashed with the memory of the open medical book that she read on his desk just after he left. For now, she asked, "Edward, what happened to make this blood?" She lifted the blankets, and he slipped into bed.

Sprawled under the covers, his flushed face looked to her. "You undressed me. Surely you saw the gash on my hip." He pulled the covers aside to show her.

As she said, "Oh, my, it's infected."

Still holding the edge of the covers, he began to shiver. "It bled a lot." Pulling the quilt up, he rolled onto his side and whispered, "Please clean it for me."

She tucked the blankets around him, kissed his fevered forehead, and murmured into his ear, "Stay covered while I bring soap and water. You need to be cleaned everywhere."

After the bed bath, Mari sat and continued placing a cool, wet cloth on his face. A knock came at the door, and Julia passed her a hot bowl of soup. She managed to give him a few spoonfuls and asked, "Feeling better now?"

He made a slight nod without opening his eyes and, in seconds, succumbed to a deep sleep that lasted two days.

Happiness filled the Bale household even with Edward convalescing in bed. He was weak, but in agreeable spirits. His fever would subside and return, off and on, during the next week.

By February, Edward felt somewhat invigorated. Mari had given birth, so possibly his new son gave him some of that vigor. He began to walk around the house and, though he was still weak, he felt well enough to take his meals with the family.

One evening, as the meal was ending, five-year-old Edward asked his father, "Papa, can I have the pinto horse? I want that horse for me."

Dr. Bale was filled with a deep pleasure, as he thought, *this is one of the joys of being a father.* He allowed a serious expression to appear on his face. "Edward, that's my horse. You want to take my horse from me?"

The little boy didn't hesitate in his reply. "You can get another one for you. I want the pinto."

They were seated at a new, larger dining room table, that Pepe had made from an oak tree felled on their land and cut at their sawmill. Julia stood by to remove dirty dishes and turned her face to hide her amusement at the little boy's request. She worried that any hint of humor might interrupt this serious discussion between a father and son.

Dr. Bale was seated at the head of the table, with his son to his right. They stared at each other for a moment with stoic faces. Finally, the father said, "But I had an image made of me on my pinto." He pointed to the daguerreotype picture sitting on a side table. "Remember that man from the East, who came with all his equipment to make pictures of us? He made that for me, and now he has gone back to the East. How could I give that horse to you? I am sitting on the pinto and can never get another picture made on a different horse. That man is gone."

When everyone had first seen the daguerreotype, Dr. Bale had shown his happiness by exclaiming, "Look, it even shows my brand—a reversed *E* next to a *B*." They had mailed a copy of Bale on the pinto to his parents in England and with another daguerreotype taken of the whole family in front of the adobe.

Dr. Bale was certain that his son remembered.

The little boy looked forlorn and sat thinking. It was obvious that he could think of nothing to counter his father's reasoning, and he repeated his demand. "But I want the pinto."

Dr. Bale stood with a bright looking face and commented, "Edward, I have an idea, and I think you will like it. I need my ink box and a sheet of paper. I will return to the table; please remain seated. I will need all of you to help me."

Curiosity appeared on the faces around the table. Even three-year-old Anita understood that her brother was challenging their father for the pinto.

For Mari, this became a special moment, though she could not guess how her husband would find a solution to his son's demands. Everyone waited in silence. Julia was as curious as all the others and came from the kitchen to take her seat again.

When Edward returned, he placed the dark wooden box on the table and sat again. Lifting the hinged cover of the ink box exposed several compartments of stored writing paraphernalia and he removed an inkbottle from one. The cork squeaked as he twisted it off. The smell of ink wafted in the air. With care, he set the bottle with its black liquid on the table, saying, "This adobe house and all the land belongs to me, as do the cattle whether bovines, horses, sheep . . . " He stopped, looked up as he reached into the ink box for a quill, and asked, "What other animals do I own?"

First, Lolita answered, in a hesitant and quiet voice, "We have pigs."

"You mean **I** . . . I have pigs. What else?"

Intelligent Caroline understood her father's claim and stated clearly, "**You** have chickens, goats, and lots of geese. You're holding a goose quill from one of **your** geese."

Pepe had been quiet through the evening, as usual, however he made a response about what is important to him. "You have oxen."

"Thank you, Pepe. I thank all of you for indicating what I own. Hmm, now I need a sheet of paper." The ink box had a slim drawer below the compartments where the inkbottle and the quills had been stored. Dr. Bale opened the drawer and slipped a piece of paper from it. He spread the white sheet on the table and, for drama, smoothed it with his hands.

Mari looked puzzled. It was unlike him to claim blatantly that everything was only his. Since they had become a family, she had always felt that they shared everything, even though she knew legally the man of the house owned all of it. In her thoughts, she knew that he was up to something with his wry humor.

A loving and congenial smile spread across Dr. Bale's face. He said, "As you children may or may not know, I have a right to say to whom I want to give each of my possessions. When a person decides this, he writes a document called *A Last Testament and Will*. So, I am going to write now."

Dr. Bale dipped his quill into the ink then to the paper and wrote: *For my son, Edward Bale, I give the Pinto horse—a stallion—and* . . . He stopped to read what he had written and to ask, "hmmm, what else? Oh, I want to give you two hundred head of my cattle and five hundred of my sheep. How does that sound?"

No one spoke. Little mouths dropped open. They did not understand. The children were not old enough to know about *A Last Testament and Will*.

Little Edward frowned with a confused face.

Mari understood what her husband was doing and said, "Oh, Eduardo, your father just gave his pinto to you. This Will is a legal document, and it states that the Pinto is yours." Mari looked to her husband and asked, "What are you giving to Lolita?"

With a dramatic flair, he raised the quill and dipped it into the ink bottle before saying, as he wrote, "For my daughter Lolita . . . " " He looked up to emphasize a legal aspect. "I must use your real name on this document, so I will write Isadora." He dipped the quill into the ink again and finished the sentence, " . . . the flour mill and all the land, which is half a league, more or less."

All the children were leaning on the table with their eyes on their father.

The room remained quiet until Lolita asked, "What's a league? Why do I get only half of it?"

Stifling a laugh, Mari spoke again to explain, "A league is a word for the size of the land. Tomorrow we could walk outside to show you how big half a league is. I don't know but, hmm, I think, it might take us an hour to walk half a league. Would you like to do that?"

Meekly, the girl nodded.

In the same fashion, Dr. Bale and Mari worked down the list of their children with some humor. He gave *tame* cattle and *wild* cattle away with jovial comments. He said, "Juanita, you will have to tame your two hundred wild cows, if you want to have any milk to drink. Of course, you could ask your sister Anita for milk from her tame cows, until you can milk yours.

"Oh, we are to the last child. Hmm, what shall I give to the baby Mariano? Oh, Edward, you like horses, and he is a boy, too. Do you think he would want a horse?"

Little Edward stood, knocking over his chair, "He can't have my pinto!"

"Right, the pinto is yours. Oh, I will give him the bay stallion with four white feet. Your pinto has four white feet, too. That's good. The two brothers can ride their horses with white feet together. Sounds enjoyable, doesn't it?"

Still standing next to his overturned chair, little Edward put his hands on his hips and said, "He's too little and can't ride."

"Edward, I mean for you to ride with Mariano when he is bigger. He was born not long ago but he will grow fast and be a big boy soon. Now, I am not finished because I want to give something to your mother. Do all of you agree that I should give something to your mother?"

Most heads nodded except little Edward who was adamant and repeated, "She can't have my pinto!"

"That is correct, not your pinto. Now, I am going to write your mother's gifts quietly while all of you get ready for bed. Mari can read later what I write. The rest of you need to learn to read to see if I gave you what I said."

Lolita spoke. "I can read, Papá. Show me my flour mill on the paper."

He turned the paper around and pointed to her line.

She read, grinned, and hugged him around the neck. "Thank you, Papá."

Mari returned later and sat next to him to read her inheritance. She punched him in the ribs and complained, "I knew it! I get all the debts."

He said, "Oh, I have one more line to write. I want to leave something for Pepe."

> *Sunday, February 11, 1849*
>
> *Written by order and solicitation of Doctor Edward T. Bale,*
>
> ### His Last Testament and Will
>
> *For my son Edward Bale, the Pinto horse (stallion), 200 head of cattle and 500 sheep.*
>
> *For my daughter Lolita (Isadora) the flour mill and all the land etc., which pertains to said mill, a half league, more or less.*
>
> *For my daughter Carolina, the sawmill at the end of the existing contract with Mr. Kilburn and some 400 acres of land, more or less.*
>
> *For my daughter Ana, all the tame cattle of the ranch.*
>
> *For my daughter Juana, 200 head of wild cattle.*
>
> *For my son Mariano, the manada (herd) of the bay stallion with four white feet.*
>
> *For my wife Maria Ignacia, the house and all the land which remains after the partition before mentioned of the children, likewise all the cattle which remains, et supra, she remaining responsible for all the debts against me and to receive all the credits.*
>
> *For Thomas Knight, 2 yoke of oxen and 25 young cows.*

Mari stared at her husband. The whole evening of playful fun and games with her children about his *Last Testament and Will* no longer appeared to be fun or a game. It was a strange document with him giving more to some of his children, almost nothing to others. She decided to ask about all her concerns when they were alone. She was glad he thought of Pepe and used his legal name of Thomas Knight, but she asked herself, *Why did he do that and not include Julia?* But she didn't ask him because it was getting late.

For now, she walked to his side as he pressed the blotter over the last line and blew on the paper. Waiting, she rubbed his back, kissed the top of his head, and said, "I'll put the ink box away for you. Let's go to bed. You are not yet well and still need a lot of rest."

"Thank you," he replied, as he folded the document.

She went to the desk and, as she slipped the ink box into the drawer, she saw a letter she had put there months ago. "Edward, oh my goodness, I forgot to give you this letter. I didn't open it because they addressed it only to you. It came months ago when you were mining for gold and with your illness and the holidays and the baby being born, I forgot about it." She passed it to him.

His eyes beamed as he reached for his letter opener to slit the envelope with the names of John and Anna Turner Bale, his parents, on the back. Reading it, his pleasure grew until it glowed on his face. Finally, he extended the letter toward Mari. "Your turn to read."

While she absorbed every word, he stared at nothing, lamenting that he would never make a trip to England to see them, but declared, "Without fail, I must write my parents another letter tomorrow."

He dropped his folded *Last Testament and Will* onto the desktop. At that moment, he remembered, "Oh my goodness, I forgot to show you something, as well." He reached around into the back corner next to his desk and pulled out his saddlebag. "I have all the same excuses you gave to me. You know, my being ill, holidays, and our new baby. I forgot all about this. How absurd of me, but I was sick with high fever when I came home."

They walked a few steps to the dining room table, where he dropped the saddlebag. Before opening it, Edward noticed the wooden giraffe that Lolita had left behind. He lifted the giraffe off the table and then bent to retrieve the wooden bear on the floor next to Edward's overturned chair. Holding each in a fist, he said, "Frequently, when bedded beside the stream where I searched for gold, I thought about these toys." Still clutching Pepe's carvings, he shared his thoughts. "A giraffe and a bear. I knew you loved the ivory giraffe, and I felt it represented me—a tall, thin foreigner whom you loved." He raised the bear and shook it. "This bear is like me, too. I remember thinking that, like a grizzly I have been despised, unpredictable, and possessed with power to destroy our family, but you tamed me. Our love tamed me."

He placed the two animals on the table and pulled Mari into his arms. Moments passed before he eased back from his hold to peer at her. "Do you remember the last question you asked me before I left for the gold fields?"

Mari shook her head.

He reached into his saddlebag and pulled three small drawstring bags from it. "You had asked me, 'Do we need gold when we have this love that no one seems to have?' and I never answered you." He took hold of her hands and, cupping them in one of his palms, he dropped the three bags onto hers. When he removed his supporting hand, her hand and the three bags slipped to the table from the weight.

He chuckled, "I answer you now. We can have both."

And so, with bags of gold and lots of love, this story ends.

Or does it?

Some people believe if someone's name is said aloud, the owner of that name lives on and on. So, until no one exists who will say Maria Ignacia and Edward Bale, their story continues.

Bale Grist Mill in St. Helena, California

Wikimedia Commons
[This is an image of the building that is listed on the National Register of Historic Places in the United States of America. Its reference number is 72000240.]

Epilogue

<u>1848</u>: Mary Ann Graves of the Donner Party, who had married Edward Pile, became a widow when her husband was murdered a year after their marriage. Three to four years later, she remarried J.T. Clarke.

<u>1849</u>: In the fall, Dr. Edward Turner Bale sold much of his ranch to Ralph L. Kilburn, who had built his sawmill, and, that October at the age of thirty-eight, Bale died, probably of colon or rectal cancer.

<u>1850</u>: Mrs. Bale converted/expanded The Bale Grist Mill and made it profitable. It still functions today as a museum in St. Helena, California.

In the 1850s:
- Salvador Vallejo had a partial settlement from the United States to compensate for his losses from the Bear Flag Revolt. He was given $11,700 of the $53,100 he requested.
- The bull/bear fights ended because most Americans were repulsed by those spectacles.

<u>1855</u>: The Native American and adopted daughter of George Yount (named Mia by this author) was murdered by her husband.

Bibliography

Richard Henry Dana, Jr., *Two Years Before the Mast* (1840): Reader's Digest Association, Inc., Pleasantville, New York, and Montreal.

Richard H. Dillon, *Napa Valley Heyday* (2004): The Book Club of California, 312 Sutter Street, San Francisco, California, 94108.

John Mack Faragher, *California: An American History* (2022): Yale University Press, New Haven and London.

Augusta Fink, *Monterey-The Presence of the Past* (1972): Chronicle Books, San Francisco, California.

Virginia Hanrahan, *Historical Napa Valley*.

Malcolm Margolin, *The Ohlone Way: Indian Life in the San Francisco-Monterey Bay Area* (1978): Heyday Books, Berkeley, California 94709.

C.F. McGlashan, *History of the Donner Party: A Tragedy of the Sierra* (1880): Stanford University Press, Stanford, California.

Arthur Quinn, *Broken Shore: The Marin Peninsula, A Perspective on History* (1981): Peregrine Smith, Inc. Salt Lake City.

Alan Rosenus, *General M.G. Vallejo and the Advent of the Americans* (1995): Heyday Books, Berkeley, California 94709.

Tracy I. Storer and Lloyd P. Tevis, Jr., *California Grizzly* (1955): University of California Press, Ltd.

Jennie and Denzil Verardo, *Gleanings; Volume 2, Number 3, June 1979: Dr. Edward Turner Bale and his Grist Mill*; Napa County Historical Society.

Jennie and Denzil Verardo, *The Bale Grist Mill* (2nd Printing, 1997): California State Parks Foundation.

Elizabeth Cyrus Wright, *Early Upper Napa Valley* (1979): Napa County Historical Society.

Books by women, in the 1830's, referenced in story:

Elizabeth Margaret Chandler, *Essays, Philanthropic and Moral*: Philadelphia: L. Howell, 1836 (related to the abolishment of slavery in America),

Eliza Ware Rorch Farrer, *The Children's Robinson Crusoe or The Remarkable Adventures of an Englishman* (1830): Boston: Hillard, Gray, Little, and Wilkins,

Angelina Emily Weld Grimké, *Appeal to the Christian Women of the South* (1836).

Acknowledgements

The Bale Grist Mill State Historic Park in St. Helena, California, allowed me to visit, though it was closed because of the Covid-19 Pandemic. They host Old Mill Days, an annual festival in October, depicting events from the eighteen hundreds.

Milling demonstrations and the sale of the ground flour are available on scheduled weekends. For more information, contact: California Department of Parks and Recreation: http://www.parks.ca.gov/

My thanks to Mariam Handson, of the St. Helena Historical Society (https://shstory.org), who gave her time and knowledge. She referred me to many books which led to the development of the story of the Bales; her help and encouragement were invaluable.

I am grateful to Joy Fargo, Kristi Negri, and Dinah Stroe who read the first drafts, found inconsistencies, and suggested improvements, like limiting the numerous Spanish names I used from the early history of California.

Every book needs to have a final copy editor who finds all the grammatical errors, refines the words, and sentences; Sarah Hyman DeWitt was my proofreader who took on this task and has worked on some of my other books.

And finally, I want to say how much I appreciate my partner, Todd Silverstein. Without his support I would have no stories to tell.

Printed in the USA
CPSIA information can be obtained
at www.ICGtesting.com
LVHW041510260923
758851LV00002B/37